MERCENARY'S PERFECT MISSION

BY
CARLA CASSIDY

Carla Cassidy is an award-winning author who ha[s] written more than one hundred books. In 1998 she also won a Career Achievement Award for Best Innovative Series from *RT Book Reviews*.

Carla believes the only thing better than curling up with a good book to read is sitting down at the computer with a good story to write. She's looking forward to writing many more books and bringing hours of pleasure to readers.

Chapter 1

The Wyoming woods atop the tall mountains that cradled the town of Cold Plains were just beginning to take on a fall cast of color. This worked perfectly with the camouflage long-sleeved T-shirt and pants that Micah Grayson wore as he made his way through the thick brush and trees.

Although a gun holster rode his shoulder, he held his gun tight in his hand. Despite the fact that he had only been hiding out in the mountainous woods for two days and nights, he'd quickly learned that danger could come in the blink of an eye, a danger that might require the quick tic of his index finger on the trigger.

Twilight had long ago fallen but a near-full moon overhead worked as an additional enemy when it came to using the shield of darkness for cover.

As an ex-mercenary, Micah knew how to learn the terrain and use the weather to his advantage. He knew how to keep the reflection of the moonlight off his skin so as not to alert anyone to his presence. He could move through a bed of dry leaves and not make a sound. He could be wearing a black suit in a snowstorm and still figure out a way to become invisible.

The first twenty-four hours that he'd been in the woods he'd learned natural landmarks, studied pitfalls and figured out places he thought would make good hidey-holes if needed. He'd also come face-to-face with a moose, heard the distant call of a wolf and seen several elk and deer.

He now moved with the stealth of a big cat toward the rocky cliff he'd discovered the night before. As he crept low and light on his feet, he kept alert, his ears open for any alien sound that might not belong to the forest.

Despite the relative coolness of the night, a trickle of sweat trekked down the center of his back. During his thirty-eight years of life, Micah had faced a thousand life-threatening situations, the latest of which had been a bullet to his head that had sent him into a coma for months.

When he finally reached the rocky bluff he looked down at the lights dotting the little valley, the lights of the small town of Cold Plains, Wyoming. His brother Samuel's town. Micah reached up and touched the scar, now barely discernible through his thick dark hair on the left side of his head, the place where Samuel's henchman, Dax Roberts, had shot him while Micah had sat in his car. Dax had left him for dead.

Fortunately for Micah he hadn't died, but had come out of a three-month coma with the fierce, driving need for revenge against the fraternal twin he'd always somehow known was a dangerous, narcissistic sociopath.

Unfortunately, Samuel was also charming and slick and powerful, making him a natural leader that people wanted to follow.

Five months ago Micah had been sitting in a small-town Kansas coffee shop where he'd landed after his last mission for a little downtime when he'd seen a face almost identical to his own flash across the television mounted to the wall.

Stunned, he'd watched a news story unfold that told him his brother Samuel was being questioned by the FBI and local police in connection with the murders of five women found all across Wyoming. All the women had one thing in common: Cold Plains, the town where his wealthy, motivational-speaker brother wielded unbelievable influence and power.

Micah had immediately contacted the FBI and been put in touch with an agent named Hawk Bledsoe. The two had made arrangements to meet the next day but, before Micah could make that meeting, he'd caught the bullet to his head.

He'd been in the coma for ninety-three long days and it had taken him another two months to feel up to the task he knew he had to do—take out Samuel before he could destroy any more people and lives.

Which was why he'd spent these last two days and nights in the woods adjacent to Cold Plains.

Minutes before he'd made his way to the bluff, he'd met with his FBI contact, Hawk. Hawk had grown up in Cold Plains and after years of being away from his hometown had returned to discover that the rough-around-the-edges place where he'd grown up as son of the town drunk had transformed into something eerily perfect. A town run by a group of people who others referred to under their breaths as the Devotees and their leader, the movie-star handsome, but frightening and dangerous Samuel Grayson.

For the past two nights Micah and Hawk had met at dusk in the woods so Hawk could keep Micah apprised of what was going on in town and how the FBI investigation into Samuel's misdeeds was progressing.

As he thought about everything Hawk had shared with him over the last two days, a dull throb began at the scar in the side of his head. He drew in several deep, long breaths, attempting to will away one of the killer migraines that the bullet had left behind.

He turned and started off the bluff, deciding to make his way down the mountain, closer to town. The only time he dared to do a little reconnaissance of the layout of the town was at night. He knew that if anyone caught sight of him it would be reported back to Samuel, and the last thing Micah wanted Samuel to know was that he was not only still alive but he was also here and working with the FBI to bring him down.

As always, he moved silently, knowing that the woods held many secrets. Just the night before, he'd stumbled upon two women amid the brush and trees. Darcy Craven had fainted at the sight of him, assuming he was his brother, but the woman with her, June Farrow, had recognized that he wasn't Samuel and had taken him to the safe house located in an area called Hidden Valley.

The safe house and surrounding land, only accessible by hiking or helicopter, had become an important haven for those trying to escape Samuel and his minions. The woods weren't just filled with those trying to escape the small town, but also dangerous hunters tracking them down.

Samuel had to be stopped. The words had reverberated in his head the moment he'd awakened from his coma and that thought was the driving force that got him up each morning, his final thought before falling asleep at night.

He froze as he thought he heard a sound someplace to his left. It sounded like a baby's cry; there for just a moment and then gone as if stolen from the gentle night breeze. He remained still, his index finger ready to fire the gun gripped tight in his hand if necessary.

Micah wasn't given to flights of fantasy. He knew he'd heard something. It was possible that it had been some sort of animal, but there was no way he intended to leave this area until he found the source of the sound.

There were hunters in the woods, but Micah was one, too, and if he managed to get to one of the men who worked for Samuel, he'd turn them over to the FBI to help them build a case against the man, hopefully a case that would avenge the deaths of the five women Micah knew in his heart his brother was responsible for killing.

The noise came again…a quick cry that was just as quickly gone. The darkness of the night seemed to press in around him as he targeted in on the area where he thought the sound had originated.

The moon slivered through the tree branches here and there, filtering down enough illumination to be both a little bit helpful and definitely dangerous. Micah kept to the dark shadows as he made his way toward the noise.

Somebody was in the woods, of that he was certain. He wouldn't put it past Samuel to arrange for one of his minions to make the noises he'd heard, hoping to draw somebody out of the safe house, hoping that somebody could be taken into custody and then be forced to give up the location of the place of safety.

His heart took on the slow, steady beat of a trained soldier as he advanced forward. He'd just stepped around a tree when he saw her. Despite the fact that she was backed into the brush, her white-blond hair served as a beacon calling to the moonlight.

In an instant, he took in everything. Small and petite, her jeans and blouse appeared dirty and her hair was tangled with bits of leaves and brush caught in the curly length. She held a baby in a sling across her chest and a sharp, pointed stick raised in her hand.

If she thought that puny stick might be used as a weapon against him, she was sadly mistaken. Micah could have that stick out of her hand and broken in half before she ever saw him coming.

As he stepped close enough for her to see him, she looked up and gasped, her green eyes widening in abject terror.

"I won't tell," she exclaimed fervently. "Please don't hurt me. I swear I won't tell anyone what I saw. Just let me have my other son and we'll go far away from here. I'll never speak your name again." Her voice cracked as she focused on his gun and he realized she believed he was Samuel.

Certainly it was dark enough that anyone could mistake him for his brother. When the brothers were together it was easy to see the subtle differences between them. Micah's face was slightly thinner, his features more chiseled than those of his brother.

At the moment, Micah knew Samuel kept his hair cut neat and tidy while Micah's long hair was tied back. He reached up and pulled the rawhide strip, allowing his hair to fall from its binds.

The woman gasped once again. "You aren't him… but you look like him. Who are you?" Her voice still held fear as she dropped the stick and protectively clutched the baby closer to her chest.

"Who are *you?*" he countered. He wasn't about to be taken in by a pale-haired angel with big green eyes in this evil place where angels probably couldn't exist.

"I'm Olivia Conner, and this is my son Sam." Tears filled her eyes. "I have another son, but he's still in town. I couldn't get to him before I ran away. I've heard rumors that there was a safe house somewhere, but I've been in the woods for two days and I can't find it." The tears spilled a little faster. "I need to get someplace safe, where Sam can get something to eat and I can go back into town and get my other son."

Micah was unmoved by her tears and by her story. He knew how devious his brother could be and Micah would do everything possible to protect the location of the safe house. There was only one way to know for sure if she was one of Samuel's "Devotees."

"I need to see your right hip," he said.

Once again her eyes opened wide, but it was obvious she knew why he'd made the demand. The people closest to Samuel, the people who were a part of his "cult" were all tattooed on their right hip with a letter *D*. Before he took her anywhere, he needed to see that she wasn't wearing Samuel's mark.

She pulled the sling over her neck and placed the baby on the ground where he sat up and gazed at Micah with a drooling grin. Olivia stood, dwarfed by Micah's six feet two and as she looked up at him, he saw the fear that still simmered in the depths of her eyes.

Her slender fingers trembled as they unfastened her jeans and slipped them down low enough to expose one pale hip. Micah pulled a flashlight from his pocket and shone it on the area, wanting to be absolutely sure that he didn't miss any tattoo that would mark her as one of Samuel's closest followers.

Confident that there was nothing there, he motioned her to refasten her jeans. "You never told me who you are," she said as she fastened the jeans and then pulled on the sling and the child back against her chest.

"And you never told me exactly how you came to be in the middle of the woods in the dead of the night with only one of your two children," he countered.

In the light of the moon he saw her eyes darken and fear once again shine from the depths. She hesitated, as if unsure what to tell him, then finally released a weary sigh. "I was on my way to the child care center to pick up my three-year-old son Ethan when I saw something that shocked me…something that frightened me so badly I just ran. Please, I need help. We're hungry. My baby is hungry."

Micah knew he was a good judge of character and more than once that quality had saved his life. There was a genuine desperation in her eyes, and that, coupled with the absence of the telltale tattoo, allowed him to put away any misgivings about her credibility.

"What was it that you saw that scared you so bad you ran?" he asked.

She lifted her chin a notch and although her lips trembled slightly there was defiance in her stance as she straightened her shoulders and squared off to him. "I'm not saying anything more until I know who you are and what you intend to do with me."

"I'm Micah Grayson, Samuel's brother. I'm here to take him down, but right now I'm going to take you to the safe house. Stay close, move fast and keep quiet." With these words he turned his back to her and began to move.

Samuel's brother.

Those words were enough to shoot complete terror through Olivia's heart. She had no idea if she could trust him or not, but she knew with certainty that she and her baby boy couldn't survive much more time in the woods all alone without food or water. She hadn't slept for two days and nights, afraid of each and every sound the forest made as she'd tried to find the safe house and stay hidden from danger at the same time.

At the moment she felt as if she had no other choice but to trust him and so she hurried after him, her heart pounding a million miles a minute.

The only thing that gave her comfort was that he was leading her in a direction deeper into the woods rather than back toward the little town she'd recently escaped.

She cuddled Sam to her chest, hoping he'd fall asleep. He'd been fussy off and on throughout the evening and she knew he was hungry and tired of the sling. She'd managed to stave off some of his hunger pangs over the last couple days with the snacks she always kept stored in her backpack, but earlier that evening she'd given him the last of the crackers and the last sip of juice.

Nights on the mountain weren't kind at this time of year. Although a September day could be warm and pleasant, the nights turned cold and she hadn't been prepared or equipped with the supplies or the survival skills she'd needed.

She had to trust Micah because she had no other choice. He was a daunting man, tall and with shoulders the size of a small county. In the moonlight his green eyes had looked icy cold—deadly—but she had run out of options.

He kept up a fast pace, moving through the woods like a shadow as she hurried to keep up with him. As he led her to a narrow crevice in the side of the mountain, she realized that if this really was the way to the safe house she would have never been able to find it on her own.

It felt like they had walked for miles in the narrow crevice where only the faint beam of his flashlight lit the way. He paused as they appeared to be at a dead end and once again her heart banged frantically. Had he brought her here to kill her? Was he really working for his brother or had he told the truth and was working against him?

Despite the appearance of a dead end, he twisted his body into a seemingly invisible space and as she followed, she realized they'd entered a cave tunnel. She could feel a faint breeze on her face and knew the end wasn't far.

He paused once again, this time to pull a radio from his pocket. "It's Micah. I'm coming in with two."

"Copy," a faint voice replied.

Micah dropped the radio back in his pocket and moved forward. Within moments they had left the cave and entered a small valley. The moonlight was brighter now and she could see a man standing in front of a rocky entrance of a half-hidden cave.

He was armed, but greeted Micah by name. "I told June you're coming in," he said.

"Thanks, Jesse." Micah grabbed her by the elbow, his big hand warm on her skin.

They went through another small narrow passage and that opened into a huge cave that had been transformed into living quarters.

Olivia felt her mouth drop open as she took in her surroundings. It was like entering an alien world with huge ceilings and furnished comfortably with wood, bone, animal skins and whatever else the forest could yield.

"Follow me," Micah said. "June will probably be in the kitchen area and we have questions for you."

She had plenty of questions for him, too. She'd expected the rumored safe house to be a little cabin in the woods where people were spirited in and out of the area in the middle of the night.

But, as she heard the sound of laughter coming from someplace in the distance and followed Micah through the huge main room where the scent of something cooking wafted in the air, this place felt more like a thriving community than a pit stop on the way to safety.

Micah led her into a kitchen where the focal point of the room was a huge rough-hewn wooden table above which hung a chandelier fashioned from antlers.

A woman stood at a stove stirring what smelled like some sort of stew. She turned at the sight of them and offered Olivia a tentative smile. "Got the news there were two incoming, didn't realize it was really one and a half."

Olivia looked down at Sam, who had fallen asleep against her chest and fought the tears that pressed hot against her eyes.

"She says she's been in the woods for two days," Micah said as he gestured Olivia into a chair at the table.

"And you must be starving," the tall, willowy, red-haired woman said as Olivia took off her backpack and sank into one of the chairs. Micah took the chair next to her and she was instantly aware of two things—he smelled like the forest, fresh, wild, yet clean and utterly male. And even though he looked amazingly like his brother, Samuel Grayson was really just a pale imitation of the handsome, hard-featured man seated to her right.

"I'm June Farrow," the woman said as she set a bowl of hot stew in front of Olivia. "And I'd be more than happy to hold that sleeping little boy so you can eat."

Olivia looked down at Sam and for a moment the last thing she wanted to do was relinquish possession of the one child she had with her. Once again as she thought of her missing three-year-old, her eyes welled up with tears that she desperately tried to control.

"What's his name?" June asked softly.

"Sam. His name is Sam." Olivia pulled the child from the front sling and handed him into June's awaiting arms. She had to trust these people, she had no choice and the scent of the food cramped her empty stomach. She'd had nothing to eat for the last two days, afraid that if she took a single bite of anything that had been in her backpack, it might mean Sam going hungry.

Micah sat silently as she ate. She tried not to shovel

the savory stew into her mouth like a wild animal. She had no idea what exactly was in the stew, but nothing had ever tasted so good.

When she was finished she looked at June. "Is there milk? I have a bottle for Sam in my backpack but he emptied it the first night we were in the woods."

The area where she sat was warmer than it had been outside and with her belly full, all she really wanted to do was sleep. She'd only had unanticipated fitful dozes while in the forest; she'd been too afraid to allow herself any real sleep. The forest had been filled with critters, both animal and human.

"How about I get a bottle ready for Sam and put him down in the nursery?" June asked.

Panic once again clawed up Olivia's throat. "Nursery? Where is that? What, exactly, is this place?"

"You're safe here and nobody will hurt you or your son," Micah finally spoke. "Why don't you and June get the boy settled in for the night and then the three of us will talk some more."

Olivia hesitated for a long moment, so many questions whirling around in her head, coupled with the crushing fear for the child she had left behind.

She finally got up from the table and rummaged in the now nearly empty backpack for the empty bottle. June handed Sam back to her and Olivia watched as the woman washed the bottle and then filled it with milk. "Come with me," she then said.

The cave was a maze of rooms, some small, some much larger, some with wooden doors and some without. The temperature was slightly cooler away from the kitchen area, but not unpleasantly so.

They finally came to a medium-sized room that held

several cribs and child-sized cots. "We have a couple three-year-olds, but they're sleeping with their mommy in another room, so right now he's the only little one we have here," June said as she motioned for Olivia to place Sam in one of the cribs.

Sam awakened and as always gave his mother a beatific smile and then when he saw the bottle June held, his fingers worked in a gimme fashion. "Bot," he exclaimed.

June smiled and gave him the bottle and as he began to drink it, his eyes drifted closed once again. The two women backed out of the nursery and June showed her the room next door. "We'll put you in here, that way you can hear if he needs anything throughout the night."

This area was small, with a door and a double bed covered with what appeared to be clean sheets and a lightweight blanket. A small rustic wooden table sat next to the bed with an oil lantern burning to light the room. "I'm afraid it isn't exactly the Ritz, but we all manage."

"It's fine," Olivia replied, still feeling as if she'd entered a surreal world she didn't quite understand.

"We'd better get back to Micah. He's probably chewing off his own arm waiting to ask you some questions."

When they headed to the kitchen, the scent of freshly brewed coffee filled the air. Micah was seated where he'd been when they had left, but three cups of coffee were on the table. "I wasn't sure how you drank yours," he said to Olivia.

"Black is fine." She curled her fingers around the warmth of the mug and then looked at June. "What is this place and what are all of you doing here?"

"The cave was built a long time ago by an architect

who went crazy and became an eccentric survivalist—decided to prepare for the end of the world. He was something of a genius when it came to using the natural resources accessible in the mountains. Rumor has it that he died when he'd finished construction and it was left to a distant relative of his. About five years ago, when we realized what was happening in Cold Plains, we knew we'd need a place of safety so we contacted the owner who told us to do whatever we wanted with it. We did a little refurbishing to make it once again livable and here we are," June explained.

Olivia was aware of Micah's dark gaze lingering on her, but she wasn't finished getting answers from June. "So, this is about an investigation of some sort? Are you a police officer of some kind?"

June smiled. "Heavens no. I'm just a widow who, years ago, lost my family to a cult and now I've made it my life's mission running safe houses for members who leave and need a place to hide and to be deprogrammed."

"A cult? But Cold Plains is just a beautiful small town, a wonderful place to raise children. It's a place of health and prosperity." She frowned, recognizing she was parroting Samuel's words.

She tried not to think about the fact that she'd planned on getting the *D* tattoo on her hip before she left Cold Plains and that she'd been completely devoted to Samuel Grayson—until that moment two nights ago when everything she'd believed about the man had exploded apart.

"It's definitely a cult and it's run by a very dangerous man," Micah said.

"Your brother."

He nodded and his green eyes transformed to a darker shade like the deepest forest shadows.

"You look a lot like him," she replied.

"An unfortunate accident of genes. We're fraternal twins. I'm here working with the FBI to bring down Samuel and all his cult enforcers."

Olivia stared first at June and then back at Micah, trying to wrap her mind around the fact that the perfect little town she'd called home was actually run by a group of evil "cult" members. "It's a beautiful town. Everything shines with prosperity and newness. They're even drawing in celebrities and big investors. I lived in a charming little house and had a great job. My children were happy and had the best health care available." Once again she was aware that she was saying what she'd been told, what had been almost a mantra of the townspeople who followed Samuel's teachings.

Still, she didn't need to be deprogrammed by anyone. Her break with anything to do with Samuel and his messages and his way of life had happened in a single heart-stopping instant.

"So, what are you doing here? Why were you hiding out in the woods looking for the safe house?" Micah asked.

Olivia's heart began to beat an unsteady rhythm as she remembered what had happened, what she'd seen two nights before. "I worked at the Community Center as a secretary. That day Sam had been fussy so I'd kept him with me at work. Samuel never minded if I needed to have him with me. As usual Ethan, my three-year-old, had gone to the Cold Plains Day Care."

She took a sip of her coffee, hoping the warmth would heat the icy chill that had suddenly gripped her heart. "I worked a little later than usual, so it was dark when I finally left the Community Center. The day care wasn't far away and I took off walking, knowing that Ethan would be eager to see me and his little brother after such a long day."

Emotion once again pressed tight in her chest, rising up the back of her throat, but she swallowed hard, needing to get through this before she allowed herself to completely fall apart.

She took another sip of the strong coffee as Micah and June waited patiently for her to continue. She set the cup back on the table, aware that her fingers were trembling.

"There was an alley adjacent to the street," she continued. "I saw Samuel and another man standing there talking and I didn't really think too much about it. They didn't look angry or upset, but as the man turned to leave, Samuel pulled a gun and shot him in the back of his head. There was no sound. He must have used a silencer, but as the man fell to the ground, I ran."

She had run like the wind, with panic stealing away all rational thought. Get away. Get away, that had been her only thought. She'd dashed away, praying that Samuel hadn't seen her, fearing not just for her own life but for Sam's life, too.

"Did Samuel see you?" Micah asked as he leaned forward.

A trembling began in the very center of her very soul. "I don't know. I didn't stick around to find out. I just ran, with no thought, with no particular plan in mind. I'd heard rumors that there was a safe house someplace up the mountain but I had no idea how difficult it might be to find. I went for Ethan, but the day care was dark, empty, and I didn't have time to locate him. I was afraid that if Samuel had seen me, I'd never make it to my son. And I'd be putting Sam in danger, as well."

"You need to give this information to Hawk," Micah said. "An eyewitness account to murder is just what we need to get Samuel into custody."

"Who is Hawk?" Olivia asked.

"Hawk Bledsoe. He's a native from Cold Plains but he's now an FBI agent working on the case."

"And what exactly is the case?" Confusion coupled with exhaustion made everything difficult to comprehend for her at the moment.

"The main investigation is into the killing of five women. We believe Samuel is responsible for their murders."

Olivia gasped and shot a hand to her head as an ache began to pound at her temples. She'd heard some vague rumors, but she hadn't believed any of them. Still, as terrible as it sounded, at the moment she didn't want to hear about murdered women. She didn't want to hear about cults and Samuel.

She dropped her hand back to the table and looked Micah in his cold, dark green eyes. She raised her chin, refusing to be intimidated by him and firm in the decision she'd just made. "I'm not talking to anyone until I get my son back."

And then to her horror she burst into tears.

Chapter 2

"Can we trust her?" Hawk asked Micah an hour after Micah had radioed for Hawk to see him. The two stood in their meeting place, a small rocky area next to the stream that eventually made its way into Cold Plains where it became Fog Creek. There was a tree nearby that had been scarred by a lightning strike at some point in the distant past.

Fog Creek was important to Samuel. His cohorts bottled the creek water and sold it to everyone who attended Samuel's many seminars. It was rumored to have magical healing properties, but Micah knew the only thing it really did was line his brother's pockets.

"She seems like the real deal," Micah said as he thought of the pretty blonde. Once June had led her away from the kitchen to show her the shower facility and to find some clean clothes for her to wear, he'd taken off to meet Hawk and let him know this latest development.

Hawk's brown eyes narrowed as he quickly raked a hand through his sandy-colored hair. "It would be just like him, you know—to use a woman and a child to try to find the whereabouts of the safe house."

"Believe me, that thought crossed my mind," Micah replied drily. "But her story had a ring of truth and she seemed genuinely traumatized." He quickly told Micah what Olivia had told them about seeing Samuel shoot the man in the alley. "She freaked and she ran and, in her terror, she had to leave behind one of her kids who was no longer at day care."

"A shot to the back of the man's head." Hawk leaned against the tree behind him. "Sound familiar?"

"Too damned familiar," Micah replied darkly. They both knew that Samuel's favorite form of murder was a bullet to the back of the head; clean, cold and efficient. Unfortunately, knowing it and proving it were two different things. And so far, Samuel had managed to evade all efforts to tie him personally to anything nefarious that was happening in the town.

"Is it possible Samuel kept one of her kids as leverage and then sent her out here to spy on us?" Hawk asked.

"You know with Samuel anything is possible," Micah replied, his stomach churning at the possibility.

"I'll check her out and if she is the real deal, then a statement from her would go a long way in helping us build our case against Samuel," Hawk said.

"She already told me she isn't talking to anyone official until she gets her other son back."

"Are you sure there really is another son?" Hawk's distrust was warranted. If there was one thing Micah had quickly learned in his brief time working with the

FBI, it was that nobody in the town of Cold Plains could be trusted.

"The only thing I'm sure of at the moment is that she won't be left alone until we're sure we can trust her. June or one of the others won't let her out of their sight," Micah replied.

"I'll do a little snooping around in town and see if I can definitely confirm her identity and her story," Hawk replied as he shoved himself off the tree where he'd been leaning. "It shouldn't be too hard to find out if the secretary for the Community Center has suddenly disappeared and left one of her kids behind, although it might be more difficult to identify who Samuel shot."

"And it's a sure bet that if Samuel didn't know she saw what he did, he'll definitely wonder what drove her away from town without Ethan and he'll be frantic to find her." Micah felt the muscles in his jaw tighten as he thought of his brother, who had grown more and more dangerous with each passing day, especially since feeling the pressure of the investigation.

If Olivia Conner was truly who and what she said she was, then if Samuel found her, she would probably wind up like the other five dead women…with a bullet in the back of her head.

Five murdered women and any number of other deaths, all attributed to Samuel and his cult henchmen. Devotees, that's what Samuel called the people who followed him and his teachings like blind sheep. Some of them were simply deluded, others desperate to belong to something bigger than themselves, but there were a handful of Samuel's closest followers who were simply evil at their very hearts and souls.

"I'll check in with you in the morning, let you know

what I've found out," Hawk said and a moment later he'd disappeared into the darkness.

Micah remained where he stood, the memory of one particular woman filling his head. He rarely allowed himself to go back in time to when he'd been in high school and ridiculously in love with Johanna Tate.

Even now after all these years he could still remember the vanilla scent of her straight black hair and the long lashes that fringed her pale brown eyes. He still remembered the sound of her laughter, a melodious sound that had melted his heart the first time he'd heard it.

He'd loved her with all the lust and passion that a teenage boy could own. At the time he'd thought her the woman he'd marry and build a family with, the one who would be at his side throughout his life.

Unfortunately, she'd only been his for a brief period of time before Samuel had seduced her away from him. Even after all these years Micah still felt the pain, the rage, of what his brother had done.

He'd seduced her, brought her to Cold Plains where she had been rumored to be Samuel's main girlfriend, and then she'd been killed with a bullet to the back of her head, her body found eighty miles away in Eden, Wyoming.

Despite the distance between Samuel and where her body had been found, Micah knew in his gut that his brother was responsible for her death.

He now headed back to the safe house, a burning in the pit of his stomach as he tried not to think about how many other lives his brother had destroyed.

As he drew closer to the house, his thoughts turned to another woman, one with eyes the color of the forest and hair like spun silk, a woman who had been prepared to attack him with a sharp stick as she'd huddled in the brush with her son.

Olivia Conner. Even with the dirt on her face and leaves in her hair, holding a baby in one arm and a makeshift weapon in the other, Micah had, on some base level, registered the fact that she was an extremely attractive woman. He was vaguely surprised that he'd even noticed. It had been a very long time since a woman had appeared on his radar in any fashion.

At the moment she was potentially an eyewitness to a murder that Samuel had committed. If he could convince her to talk to one of the FBI agents working the case, then her statement might prove invaluable in breaking everything wide open.

Samuel had always been so careful. It was rare for him to get his own hands dirty but, in Olivia Conner, he'd apparently unknowingly allowed an eyewitness to get away. Micah knew the more Samuel recognized a loss of control, the more dangerous he became.

The best thing for everyone was for Olivia to speak to the authorities and give them a statement, and then be spirited away from here and into some sort of protective custody far away from Cold Plains.

It was this thought that filled his head as he slipped back into the cave where June and two other women were seated at the rough-hewn table. Olivia wasn't one of them.

"She took a shower and then went to bed," June said before he could ask. "The poor thing was absolutely exhausted after being in the woods for two nights all alone with her baby."

Micah poured himself a cup of coffee and then joined them at the table. "Hawk is planning on checking out her story. We want to make sure she really is who she says she is."

"Her little boy is a doll. I peeked in on him when I heard they'd arrived," Darcy Craven said.

As always when Micah looked at Darcy with her beautiful long, dark hair and blue eyes, he felt a strange sense of familiarity. Her eyes were those of a woman he'd known a long time ago in his hometown, but then again he couldn't imagine what this young woman would have to do with anyone from his past.

He knew little about Darcy, only that she'd come to Cold Plains seeking news of a mother she'd never known and had developed a romance with Rafe Black, a new doctor in town.

Rafe had shown up in town because the fourth murder victim, Abby Michaels, an old girlfriend of his, had contacted him to tell him he was the father of her three-month-old baby boy. Abby's body had been found in a wooded area in Laramie, fifty miles away from Cold Plains Day Care Center, where she'd worked as a teacher's aide. The baby, now an almost nine-month-old named Devin, had been missing since her disappearance.

A month earlier a little boy had been found by police officer Ford McCall with a note stating that he was Devin Black and needed to be reunited with his father. According to what Micah had heard, Rafe believed he'd finally had a happy ending, not only with his son found but also with a romantic relationship with Darcy.

But, the happy ending had been short-lived. The baby boy had been kidnapped by a man claiming to be the real child's father. A birthmark on the boy had confirmed it. He had said he'd been forced by Samuel and Bo Fargo, the chief of police and Samuel's right-hand man, to give up the boy for the good of the community. He'd done what he'd been told, but couldn't live with his actions.

He'd stolen the baby back from Rafe, leaving the doctor to wonder about the whereabouts of his own son. The man had refused to make any official statements indicting either Samuel or Bo Fargo in the scheme and had disappeared from town soon after.

Even though he and Darcy were still very much in love, Rafe had insisted Darcy go to the safe house until his son could be found again.

There were so many players in this deadly game, and both June and Hawk had spent a lot of time trying to fill Micah in on everything that had been happening both in the town of Cold Plains and in his brother's life.

At night Micah's head spun as he tried to put names with people and figure out who was on their side and who was one of Samuel's Devotees. There were so many people in town that nobody knew exactly where they landed in the grand scheme of things—if they were Samuel's people or not.

In the brief time he'd been in the safe house, Micah had recognized that it was basically a clearinghouse where June helped deprogram those who needed it and the FBI aided in relocating victims to new lives. The people were in transition and most didn't stay too long, but rather were eager to get as far away from Samuel and Cold Plains, Wyoming, as quickly as possible.

He now leaned back in his chair and took a sip of his coffee, his thoughts on the newest members of the house. "If she'll talk to Hawk and some of the other FBI agents, then we could potentially get an arrest warrant for Samuel for the murder she witnessed," he said. "We'd have a reason to get inside his house, maybe find some real concrete evidence to put him away forever."

"I wouldn't push her too hard," June warned. "She seemed pretty fragile."

"This whole situation is fragile," Micah replied drily. "We have five murdered woman that were all tied in one way or another to Cold Plains and Samuel. We have enough additional dead bodies to fill an entire cemetery."

"And missing children and people with disabilities who seem to have vanished into midair," Darcy added, her hauntingly blue eyes darkening.

Micah frowned and took a sip of his coffee. Aside from the murdered women, this was one of the most disturbing things about this case. The streets were filled with only attractive, robust people seemingly not only physically fit but mentally well. There was no sickness, no imperfections of any kind and those who showed signs of either disappeared and were never seen again.

"There are rumors that those people are held in secret rooms or basements, prisoners for the good of the town. The worst part is the children," Darcy said. "I think we've all heard the rumors of children who are born with slight 'defects' or deemed unworthy in some way and are hidden away someplace in town and eventually adopted out."

Her face displayed a myriad of emotions and Micah suspected she was thinking of Rafe Black's missing son. Was he hidden in some secret location in town or had he already been adopted out by Samuel for a huge fee to a couple in another state, another country, desperate for a child?

"Of course, we don't have to worry about anything now that the FBI have arrested some of Samuel's henchmen and they've confessed to the murders of some of the women," June said sarcastically.

Micah snorted. "They might have confessed to being the ones who actually pulled the triggers, but they still refuse to give up Samuel as the brains. Until we can cut off the head of the snake, nobody is safe and we'll never know for sure who in town we can trust." He knew that a man and a woman had been arrested by the FBI and had confessed to some of the murders of the women, but they'd refused to name the man who had given them the orders to commit the crimes.

Once again his thoughts turned to the pretty blonde now sleeping in the depths of the large cave. She was the key. She had the kind of solid information that could put Samuel behind bars.

All he had to do was figure out a way to force her to do the right thing.

Olivia awakened slowly, her brain fuzzy with residual dreams of her childhood. It had not been a particularly good upbringing and the dreams hadn't been pleasant ones.

She'd grown up in a trailer park with her sickly mother who liked to drink. Olivia never knew if her mother was sick because she drank, or drank because she was sick. Her main memories of her youth were of too little food, too little heat and far too much responsibility.

Her mother died when she was twenty-two and Olivia had known two things: she wanted to get as far away from the trailer park as possible and she was desperate to build a different kind of life for herself.

Two children later, abandoned by her boyfriend on Main Street in Cold Plains, Olivia had embraced the town and thought she'd finally come home.

As she thought of that moment in the alley when she'd watched the man she'd believed was her salvation and mentor cold-bloodedly shoot the man in the alley, she had gasped and sat straight up, disoriented for a moment as she looked around.

The cave walls in this room were particularly smooth with a small outcropping of rock that made a natural stone bench against one wall. The small oil-burning lamp still flickered, creating a pool of illumination that allowed her to maneuver easily through the room.

Sam!

Thoughts of her youngest son shot her off the bed. She'd slept in the clothes June had graciously provided her, a pair of jeans, and a T-shirt that was a tad too small across her full breasts.

She knew her hair was probably in wild disarray, but the only thing that mattered at the moment was seeing Sam's smiling face, assuring herself that he was okay.

She couldn't even think about her three-year-old still someplace in Cold Plains. Ethan would probably be scared, needing his mommy and if she dwelled on that thought for too long she'd come completely undone. She had to keep it together, for Sam's sake…for Ethan's sake.

Racing into the room where she'd placed Sam in a crib the night before, she stopped short in the doorway as she saw that the crib was empty. She whirled around, running wildly down a corridor, wondering if perhaps she'd trusted the wrong people after all.

As she wound around corners and ran into blind passageways, her heart banged discordantly, making her half-breathless as she felt like Alice suddenly falling down a rabbit hole.

She whirled around one corner and slammed into a brick wall. The wall was Micah Grayson's hard, muscled chest. "Whoa," he said and grabbed her firmly by the shoulders.

"Where's my son? Where's Sam?" she asked.

He dropped his hands from her shoulders. "I just saw him in the kitchen eating some breakfast."

A shudder of relief swept through her. "Where's the kitchen? This place is like a maze."

He pointed down the nearest passageway. "Go straight and take the left turn. You'll be in the kitchen."

As her panic ebbed, she once again noticed that Micah Grayson wasn't just hard and dangerous looking, but also handsome and sexy in a way that might have affected her under different circumstances.

"Thanks," she said and started to move past him, but he reached out and grabbed her arm before she could scurry away.

"I'd like to speak with you later…after you get some breakfast and settle in." His hand was big…weighty on her forearm.

She frowned. She couldn't imagine what he might want to talk to her about and, if she were perfectly honest with herself, she would admit that something about him unsettled her more than a little bit. All she really wanted to do was make sure Sam was safe and then figure out some sort of plan to return to Cold Plains and retrieve Ethan.

She wasn't interested in whatever investigation they were conducting in the town. She just wanted to have her children safe and with her and then she'd go from there.

"Olivia?"

Her name sounded strange on his lips, reminding her that she knew nothing about this man, these people and the touch of his big hand on her arm felt too warm, oddly intimate.

She pulled away from him and took a step backward. "Obviously I'm not going anyplace but the kitchen for the time being. You can find me there after breakfast."

This time when she turned to walk away he didn't stop her although she imagined she could feel his piercing green eyes lingering on her back.

She breathed a sigh of relief as she entered the kitchen where June sat at the table with her coffee and Sam was locked into a high chair happily smooshing scrambled eggs into his mouth.

"Mama!" he exclaimed with a happy eggy grin as she entered the room.

"Sammy," she replied and planted a kiss on the top of his forehead. She offered a tentative smile to June. "I had a moment of panic when I woke up and didn't find him in his crib."

"I'm sorry. I didn't mean to frighten you. He woke up earlier and you were still sleeping so soundly, so I figured I'd get him up and change his diaper and see about a little breakfast for him." June smiled sympathetically. "I knew you were exhausted from your time hiding out so I hated to wake you when he got up."

"Thank you for taking care of him," Olivia said as she sank down at the table. She still felt as if she'd entered some strange subterranean world filled with people in crisis. She was in crisis. There was a simmering anxiety inside her that threatened to burst into full-blown panic, but she used every ounce of her ability in an attempt to hold herself together.

"Coffee?" June asked as she rose from the table.

"I can get it," Olivia replied. "You don't have to wait on me."

"Nonsense," June replied and waved Olivia back into the chair. "As an official member of the household, you get one day of acclimating yourself before we assign you any duties. Scrambled eggs?"

"If it's not too much trouble," she replied, feeling guilty, but yet oddly relieved that for the moment somebody else was in charge.

What she wanted more than anything was to eat breakfast, regain her strength and have a chance to formulate some sort of a plan to get Ethan out of Cold Plains. Unfortunately, part of the problem was she wasn't sure where he would be. The last time she'd seen him had been when she'd left him at the Cold Plains Day Care Center to go to work in the Community Center. But when she hadn't returned to get him after normal work hours that day, he was simply gone.

Her stomach cramped with anxiety but she forced a smile of gratitude as June set a cup of steaming coffee in front of her. "How many people are staying here?" she asked as she waited for the coffee to cool a little bit.

"We have between eight and ten people at any one time," June said as she broke a couple eggs into a small bowl. "The numbers are constantly in flux, but right now we have Darcy, sometimes here and sometimes at her new boyfriend's. And then there's Lacy Matthews and her three-year-old twins and, of course, Micah."

"I see," Olivia said.

"And also there's Jesse Grainger."

June's cheeks pinkened slightly as she poured the eggs into an awaiting skillet. "Jesse was beaten and left for dead in the woods a month ago. His brother is one of Samuel's followers and he's hoping to be able to get him out of town, but Jesse has to be careful because Samuel assumes he's dead." There was something in June's voice when she said Jesse's name that indicated to Olivia that he might just be more to her than a man she had rescued from death.

"I know Lacy," Olivia said. "She works at the Cold Plains Coffee Shop. I often went in there to get a cup of coffee on my way to work at the Community Center."

"She finally decided to take her girls and run. Samuel was pressing to make the coffee shop a place that wouldn't serve anyone who wasn't a Devotee and Lacy was determined that anyone who came in was welcome to buy a coffee whether they followed Samuel's teachings or not," June explained.

By this time June was finished making Olivia her eggs and toast and Sam was using his sippy cup to drink a glass of milk. They fell silent for a few minutes and Olivia once again found herself going back in time, terrified by how close she'd come to falling completely and irrevocably beneath Samuel's spell.

If she hadn't seen Samuel murder that man with her own eyes, then perhaps today would have been the day she got her official tattoo on her hip, proclaiming her a true believer in Samuel and the philosophies he espoused. She would have turned a deaf ear to all the whispers about unsavory things going on in the town, like so many of Samuel's other true believers.

All she'd ever wanted was a place where she felt like she belonged and she'd thought she'd found it in Cold Plains, but she'd been sucked into the vortex of an evil storm named Samuel. The only thing she could focus on now was the fact that she and Sam had escaped, but she'd been forced to leave behind her precious Ethan.

She wrapped her fingers around the warmth of the coffee mug in an effort to combat the icy chill that threatened to shiver through her as she thought of her son. Hopefully Samuel hadn't seen her. She had no idea what anyone in town would think about her sudden disappearance, but surely somebody was taking good care of Ethan.

She had to believe that to be true and she had to figure out a way to somehow get him back where he belonged, in the safety of her loving arms.

As she finished her breakfast, Darcy entered the kitchen and bid them all good morning. As Olivia got a good look at the young, pretty woman, she was startled to realize that Darcy had a lot of the same features as Micah and Samuel. Of course her bright blue eyes were in opposition to their green ones, but she had the same cast to her chin, the same strong, bold features.

Maybe Olivia was just imagining things, dreading whatever it was that Micah thought they had to talk about. She didn't want to think about the deep betrayal she felt where Samuel was concerned. She didn't want to discuss building a case against him. All she wanted was to get her son back and figure out where her life went from here.

When she had finished eating, she carried her dishes to the sink and washed them as June explained that most of their water came through a filtering system from the creek that ran nearby. Electricity was provided by either solar energy or a generator that they preferred not to run unless absolutely necessary. Throughout many of the rooms, they depended on oil lanterns and candles to conserve energy.

As Micah sauntered into the room, a spark of energy surged up inside her and she couldn't tell if it was positive or negative. There had been no man in her life since long before Sam's birth. Maybe it was only natural that she'd respond to a hot male who had brought her to safety.

She walked over to Sam, who raised his arms to be lifted from the high chair. As she pulled him out, he snuggled against her chest with a happy sigh.

"You want to take a walk with me?" Micah asked, his gaze enigmatic.

"Okay." She tried to ignore the pound of her heart as she followed him out of the kitchen. She reminded herself she had nothing to fear from him. He'd found her in the forest and brought her here to safety. He'd given her no real reason not to trust him…at least not yet.

Still her distrust of men in general ran deep. It had begun with her absent father, a man she had never known, and continued with Jeff Winfry, the man who had fathered Sam and Ethan. He'd promised to love her, to marry her and settle down as a family. She'd met him just after her mother's death and even though she'd known he wasn't Mr. Perfect, she'd believed herself in love.

There had been no settling down. Jeff had dragged

her and the children from one small town to another, working odd jobs that barely kept them fed and finally he'd dumped her and the kids just outside of Cold Plains, telling her his future just didn't include a family. Her father, Jeff and then Samuel. She was determined not to give her trust so easily again.

Micah Grayson was just as formidable from the back as he was from the front, she thought as she followed him. His shoulders were broad, his hips slim and she had to hurry to keep up with his long-legged gait.

She gasped in surprise as he opened a door and they stepped outside into the bright sunshine. They were in a small clearing filled with a babbling brook on one side and a healthy looking vegetable and herb garden on the other.

"What a beautiful place," she exclaimed.

He nodded and motioned her to a fallen tree trunk that had been fashioned into a bench. "According to June, they try to be as self-sustaining as possible here. So, she grows what she can and depends on some of us to provide the other necessities from neighboring towns."

She sat next to him on the bench and placed Sam on the grass at her feet where he immediately became enchanted with a leaf that had fallen from one of the nearby trees.

"Aren't you all afraid somebody might see this place?" she asked.

Micah shook his head, his dark hair gleaming in the sunshine. "We're sitting in a small valley between two mountains." He pointed to the jagged edge of the range that surrounded them. "The only way to get here is through the cave and you saw last night how difficult it was to find."

Although they sat several inches apart, despite the scent of the fresh herbs in the air, she could smell him, that woodsy, clean male scent that curled a ball of tension in her stomach.

"What was it you wanted to talk to me about?" she asked, eager to get this conversation over with and away from the man who seemed to both draw her and scare her just a little bit.

"I had your story checked out by a friend of mine, Hawk, the FBI agent. One of many trying to build a case against Samuel for the murders of those five women, among other things." He stretched his long legs out before him, appearing to be completely at ease.

"And what did he discover?" In contrast, she was a bundle of nerves and wanted to curl into herself to escape everything that had happened in the past two days.

"That you are what you say you are." His green eyes drifted downward, making her suddenly far too conscious of how tightly her borrowed T-shirt pulled across her breasts. She hunched her shoulders forward slightly.

His gaze lingered there for just a second and then snapped back up to meet her eyes. "You worked as a secretary in the Community Center, meaning you obviously worked closely with Samuel. You might have some valuable information that could help all of us."

"So, basically what you're saying is that you would like me to help you and your FBI friends." She held his gaze intently. "I'll do whatever I can to help you if you'll get my son out of Cold Plains and back safely here with me. But, until that happens, I have nothing more to say to you."

His stare grew harder, colder but she refused to look away. If he wanted to use her, then she had no qualms about using him first.

Samuel Grayson stood at the window in the large meeting room in the Community Center where an hour before he'd finished one of his nightly seminars. Although he'd given a rousing speech about love of community and building good lives here, the crowd had been smaller than usual and the sales of the healing tonic water after the meeting had been pathetic.

You're losing control, a little voice whispered inside his head. "No," he said aloud. It was just growing pains and the result of the investigation he knew was taking place. People were on edge because of the FBI presence in and around town, and that meant he'd just have to work harder to assure them that he had things under control.

Dammit, he'd thought he'd removed any danger to himself and his plans when he'd sent Dax Roberts, one of his most trusted men, to kill his brother. He'd known that if Micah had caught word of the investigations into the murders he wouldn't be able to keep his nose out of things. It had been easier to take him out before he became a problem.

Unfortunately, he knew he was under investigation for the murders of those women. He knew there were people in his own town working against him and it was getting more and more difficult to tell who could and couldn't be trusted.

His remaining henchmen—those not already in jail—had been working overtime, taking out the people who were overtly working against him, those who had taken a path in direct opposition of him.

He felt as if the walls of the town were slowly closing in on him and he didn't like it. He didn't like it one bit. He'd worked too hard and too long to be brought down by anyone. This was his town and he deserved all the power and money that had come along with it. He wasn't going to let anyone take it away from him.

He turned from the window, and as he walked out of the meeting room, he paused and stared at the desk where Olivia Conner usually sat.

Yet another mystery, he thought. She'd simply vanished into thin air, leaving behind one of her children. He had no idea what had happened to her, had no idea if she was dead or alive. He'd put the child with the other one, hidden away in a secured location until he could find out what had happened to Olivia.

He'd had a couple of his men check her house and they had reported back that nothing seemed to be missing—no clothes and no baby items. There had been a Crock-Pot plugged in with what appeared to be Swiss steak charred to a crisp. They'd unplugged the pot but had touched nothing else.

It was possible she'd been grabbed off the street by the FBI because of her position at the Community Center. The joke would be on them. She knew nothing except how to schedule therapy sessions for him with the locals or renting out the space in the basement that was used for weddings and celebrations.

They'd get nothing from her that could harm him. She'd been simply the office help, although he'd been close to turning her completely, and once that happened he wouldn't have minded a little intimate time with her. She'd been a hot little number despite her two brats.

Whatever had happened to her, it had appeared she'd had every intention of returning home the day that she had disappeared. If he didn't hear from her soon, he would make the appropriate plans for Ethan. He would fetch a lot of money, a handsome little boy in perfect health. Just this thought alone made him feel more in control.

He was going to be fine. The people against him would eventually drift away and he would continue his work here in Cold Plains. He wouldn't be satisfied until everyone in town sported the small *D* tattoo on their hip that marked them as his.

Chapter 3

By six o'clock that afternoon, Micah realized they didn't have enough diapers for Sam. "I feel terrible," Olivia said as several of them sat at the table. "I have a huge box at home, but I never got a chance to go back there and grab anything before I took off."

"Not a problem," Micah said. "I'll sneak into town tonight to your house and grab whatever it is you need."

June gasped. "Micah, you know you'll be shot on sight."

He smiled, a mirthless gesture that didn't lighten the dark green hue of his eyes. "They'd have to see me to shoot me."

"I don't want to put anyone in danger," Olivia protested.

He hadn't seen her since their discussion that morning. Most of the time in the afternoons, Micah went to one of the darkest, smallest rooms in the cave and slept so he'd be prepared to stay up through the night when he could use the cover of darkness to explore Cold Plains.

"I've been in town after dark several times before. It shouldn't be too great a challenge to get into your house, grab some things and then get out," Micah replied.

June looked at him dubiously. "You could always drive into Laramie and pick up whatever is needed."

"That's fifty miles away," Micah replied. "Besides, I intended to go in tonight anyway and see if I can find out where they might be keeping your son. I've already put out the word to FBI agents working the case that we're looking for the whereabouts of a three-year-old. All I really need from you is a list and a location and a house key if you have it. I'd rather go in through the door than break a window that might draw unwanted attention to your place."

"As important as the diapers are, I need you to find Ethan." Her eyes were simmering pools of emotion, pools that if he wasn't careful he felt like he might fall in.

He knew nothing personal about Olivia Conner. He had no idea what had brought her to Cold Plains, what had happened to the father of her children or who she was at her core. But, what he did know was that she drew him as a woman, not as somebody to be used to further his goals.

There was something about Olivia Conner that reminded him that he was more than just a mercenary, more than a hunter seeking the source of a deadly disease named Samuel in a small town.

Something about her softness, her aura of vulnerability reminded him that he was also a thirty-eight-year-old man who had basically been alone for all of his life.

"I just don't want to be responsible for anyone getting hurt on my account," she said.

"Trust me, I have no intention of getting hurt," he replied smoothly. "Just make me a list of things you want and as soon as it gets dark, I'll go in." He got up from the table, both uncomfortable with her nearness and knowing he needed to get some sleep before night.

He decided to check in with Hawk and used his radio to call the agent. Cell phone usage was impossible amid the mountains and beneath the cave. So, old-fashioned handheld radios were still the best form of communication between the agents hiding out in the area.

Minutes later, Micah left the cave entrance and made the long trek down the narrow passageway that would eventually lead him to the forest where he'd found Olivia and Sam.

He got to the meeting place first and stood watchful, as usual listening for sounds of anyone else nearby. An unexpected bullet to the head had not only left him with killer migraines and a burning need for revenge, but also a heightened awareness of his surroundings. Never would anyone sneak up on him again.

Normally he didn't hear Hawk's approach until he was almost on top of the meeting place, but this time he heard the snap of a dried twig and the faint whisper of feet against the forest floor.

He held his gun, alarmed by the unusual noise and then relaxed only slightly as the sandy-haired, brown-eyed FBI agent appeared. He wasn't alone. Beside him was a somber-looking dark-haired man with pain-filled brown eyes.

"It's okay," Hawk said, indicating that Micah could put down his gun. Micah pointed the barrel to the ground, but didn't holster it. "This is Dr. Rafe Black and he wanted to speak to you personally."

Micah knew that Rafe and Darcy were a couple and he also knew that Rafe was one of the good guys, helping to not only bring down Samuel, but also desperately seeking the child he'd never met but was certain existed. Rafe had his own practice in town and treated anyone who needed medical attention while walking a fine line between pretending to be part of the cult and actively working against them.

"I'm looking for my son," Rafe said without preamble. "I had a photo of him, but it has mysteriously vanished. In the picture he was about three months old and he has brown hair and brown eyes like me. He'd be about nine months old now."

"I heard from Darcy that you thought he'd been found," Micah said.

Rafe nodded. "They tried to fool me by giving me somebody else's child and pretending it was my Devin, but the real father came back and reclaimed his son."

"And you're sure Devin really exists?" Micah asked. Darcy had told him that Rafe had learned about his son when Abby had called him and that he'd sent money via Western Union for her and the child. Sounded like a potential scam to Micah.

Rafe's eyes darkened. "Definitely. Abby wasn't the kind of woman to lie. Besides, if Devin didn't exist, then why did somebody in Cold Plains go to so much trouble to force a man to give up his own son to replace mine?"

"Good point," Micah conceded.

Rafe shook his head. "Devin exists and he's being hidden someplace in town. I'll pay you whatever you want to find him. I know what you do. I know that you work for a fee. You just name your price and I'll see to it that you get it the minute that Devin is in my arms."

Micah held up his hand to stop Rafe's pleas. "I'm already on the hunt for one kid and it's possible they're both being held in the same place. All I can promise is that I'll look for Devin and there's no charge. Believe me, I'm doing all this for my own satisfaction." And of course to get Olivia to cooperate with the FBI, he reminded himself.

"You know there are rumors of secret rooms in basements where the elderly and the infirm are held until they either die or can be transported far away," Rafe said. "I've done what I can to find them, but I have to be careful because I'm still trying to win people's trust. There are also rumors about an adoption scheme and my biggest fear is that, if I don't find Devin soon, he'll be lost to me forever."

His concerns echoed those of Olivia and although Micah couldn't begin to identify with the gut-wrenching grief of a parent for a missing child, he did feel a deep worry for any child that was in his brother's clutches.

"We've been searching for these hidden rooms," Hawk said, "but so far no luck."

"If they're there, I'll find them," Micah said with grim determination. After another promise to Rafe to look for his son, the three men parted ways.

Micah headed back to the safe house, knowing that two hours later the sun would be down and darkness would begin to shroud the "perfect" little town of Cold Plains.

Once he got back, he met Olivia just inside the door,

a smiling Sam in her arms. Olivia wasn't smiling. In fact, he had yet to see her smile. Her eyes were filled with worry as she handed him a list of items she'd like retrieved from her home. Then she held out a small photo. "This is Ethan. It was taken a month ago."

He examined the photo of the handsome little boy. His blond hair was neatly cut and his features were those of his mother. He had a bright smile and green eyes that looked eager to explore whatever lay ahead.

He needed to be with his mother and his brother. It was obvious that Olivia was the kind of mother Micah hadn't had, a woman with the need to protect her children, and Ethan belonged here with her.

"I don't feel good about this," she said as she also handed him a note with her address written down and a key to the door.

Micah fought the impulse to reach out and smooth the tiny furrow that had appeared between her brows. "I'm not doing anything different than I have every night since I've been here. I'm getting to be an expert at skulking around houses, trying to catch snatches of conversations, identifying the people who are with Samuel and those who are secretly working against him."

"Just be safe," she said, the words both surprising and oddly touching to him.

At that moment Sam leaned forward in his mother's arm and with his chubby hand grabbed Micah's ear. "Ear," he pronounced proudly.

An unaccustomed smile stretched Micah's lips. "Yeah, buddy, that's my ear." He gently disengaged Sam's little fingers and stepped back. "And I'm hoping the next time I see you I'll still have both my ears."

"Don't even joke like that," Olivia protested.

Suddenly he wanted to see her smile. "If I can't manage to get him diapers then we'll figure out a way to fashion waterproof leaf covers that will make him look like a baby Tarzan."

He was rewarded by a smile that whispered an evocative warmth through him. "I'm not at all sure that I'm ready to raise a jungle boy."

Just as quickly as he'd wanted her smile, he now wanted to escape it, escape her and the little boy who cast him a wide, slightly drooling grin. He'd chosen to live his life alone, trusting nobody, caring for nobody and nothing was going to change that, especially now in the midst of his battle with his brother.

"I need to prep to get out of here." He moved past her, wanting to forget the beauty of her smile, the fact that just by looking into her soft green eyes, she got to him some way that made him both uncomfortable and just a little bit excited.

An hour later he stepped out into the deepening shadows of twilight. He had an empty rucksack on his back that could carry anything Olivia might need from her home.

As he made his way soundlessly through the woods, his mind focused only on the tasks at hand. His first was to get into Olivia's house, retrieve the items she needed and then leave as quickly as possible.

He'd hide the filled rucksack and then return to town to try to find the secret rooms that had been rumored to hide the people, including the children, not fit for Samuel's vision of perfection.

Micah knew tunnels had been found and some secret rooms discovered beneath the Community Center and under the hospital clinic, but there had been no sign in those places of the children or some of the other townspeople who had vanished.

He knew that none of the FBI agents working the area had been able to get close to Samuel's house. The stately home was guarded by armed men at all times. The general consensus was that Samuel would be a fool to have any evidence inside his private abode that tied him to anything, but Micah knew how perverse his brother could be and it would be just like him to be arrogant enough to hide evidence in plain sight.

Sooner or later he intended to get into Samuel's home. It wouldn't be tonight, it might not be tomorrow, but Micah would breach the security if for no other reason than to prove that he could.

As much as Micah would like to find Olivia and Rafe's children, he'd also like to get some concrete evidence that Samuel was behind the murders of the five women, one who had once owned Micah's heart.

He couldn't get sidetracked by Olivia's soft green eyes and need for her son. He couldn't afford to forget the reason he was here: to bring down Samuel and avenge the death of the only woman he'd ever loved.

He emptied his mind as he made his way down the mountain. The crisp night air surrounded him, adding to the adrenaline pump that had begun the moment he'd left the safe house.

By the time he'd reached the outskirts of town, complete darkness had fallen. When evening came and the nightly workshop that Samuel gave was over, most people vacated the streets of Cold Plains quickly, except the men on Samuel's payroll, men seeking those who worked against Samuel.

At this time of night, Main Street looked almost magical. Even in the bright light of day, there was sheen to the storefronts and they weren't the kind of stores you'd see in most average small Wyoming towns.

In most little towns, you'd expect to see a well-worn café with mismatched glasses and silverware, a general store where items were slightly dusty on the shelves and maybe a gas station where you could still get your windows washed by a friendly attendant.

Cold Plains was a different animal altogether, thanks to Samuel. There was a health club, a book store, a fancy vegetarian restaurant and the large Community Center. The facades were clean and colorful, breathing of a prosperity that was both inviting and insidiously seductive.

Micah knew that his brother used cult psychology not only to control those who were already under his influence, but also to recruit and bring in new members who could serve him.

He demanded a zealous commitment to his beliefs, dictated how these people should think and act, plus taught that his people in Cold Plains were the special ones, chosen to build something nobody had done before him—the perfect town with a healthy, happy community.

As he entered town he clung to the deep shadows near homes. According to the address Olivia had given him, her home was located a block off what had once been called Main Street. Samuel had renamed the streets to reflect his new society with ridiculous names like Prosperity and Tranquility.

He had no idea how long Olivia had been in Cold Plains or how she could afford to rent or take out a mortgage for her own house on a secretary's salary. He wished he'd asked her more questions about her time in Cold Plains and made a mental note of ones he would ask when he eventually got back to the safe house.

He approached her small, neat beige house from the rear. She'd told him the key worked in both the front and the rear doors. There was a nice shade tree in the center of the backyard and he stood behind it, watching the house for any signs of life.

The house was dark, but that didn't mean there wasn't somebody waiting inside. Surely Samuel was curious about her disappearance. Micah wouldn't be surprised if he'd stationed a man within to either await her return or see who else might enter the premises.

He remained behind the tree trunk for several long minutes. Nothing moved, there was no indication of anyone being inside. Finally deciding to take the chance, he darted for the back door.

The key slid in smoothly and with a faint click the knob turned easily in his hand. He opened the door slowly, his gun clutched firmly in his other hand, and waited—listening for any hint of movement, a whisper of breath that would indicate anyone was in the house.

The interior held the kind of dead silence that made him believe he was all alone. He closed the door and relocked it behind him and then pulled a small flashlight from his pocket.

He knew he was in the kitchen and smelled the odor of overcooked meat. The flashlight beam caught the white Crock-Pot on the counter and a lift of the lid let him know it was the source of the smell. Somebody had unplugged it which let him know that someone had been in the house since Olivia's disappearance.

He flashed the light around the kitchen, unsurprised to find the front of the refrigerator cluttered with displayed artwork that could only belong to a fanciful, happy three-year-old. There were landscapes with bright yellow suns and big green trees. A four-legged creature Micah suspected was a dog smiled in front of a bright red little house.

Not willing to spend more time than necessary inside, he quickly moved to the living room. It was a nice-sized room, with a beige sofa covered in multicolored throw pillows. A rug matching the colors of the pillows sat beneath a wooden coffee table and an entertainment center held a small television and an array of children's books and puzzles.

There were three bedrooms. The first one belonged to the missing Ethan. It was decorated in navy blue. Games, more puzzles and books were neatly stacked on a bookcase. Micah opened several drawers and pulled out underpants, jeans and a couple T-shirts then thrust them into his rucksack. If he managed to get the kid back, then Ethan would need some clothing besides whatever he might be wearing.

From there he moved to the next room, which was Sam's. He found the big box of diapers in the closet and jammed them all into his bag, along with a couple of tiny long-sleeved shirts and long pants.

Finally he went into Olivia's room. Although she had asked for nothing for herself, he knew she'd come to the safe house with only the clothes on her back. And there was a part of him that recognized if he had to see her in those too-tight borrowed T-shirts any longer he'd go mad.

Her room was distinctly female with a pale pink

bedspread and a vase full of fake flowers in light and dark pinks on one of the nightstands.

Inside one drawer he found a stack of multicolored bikini panties and he tossed a half-dozen pair into his rucksack, trying not to think of how they might fit across her slender hips and rounded butt. He then moved to her closet where he pulled T-shirts off hangers and grabbed an extra pair of jeans.

By this time the rucksack was full and he knew it was time to get out of the house before somebody inadvertently caught the shine of his flashlight and came to investigate.

At the last minute as he was about to walk out of her bedroom, he spied a bottle of perfume on the top of the dresser. He picked it up and sniffed it, recognizing it as the faint scent he'd noticed on her the night he'd found her. On impulse he threw it into his bag, not wanting to examine the reason for his action.

He left the house the way he'd entered, through the back door. With the weight of the rucksack tugging on his shoulders, he headed for the woods. He'd drop the baggage in a safe location to be retrieved later and then head again into town to see what he could find.

He picked a huge bush in the backyard of a house nearest his escape route into the mountains to hide the bag and then went to the streets.

He knew there was a long tunnel that ran beneath the Community Center and eventually led into a utility closet inside the building. The story was that the tunnel had been built over a hundred years ago to avoid Indian raids. Micah had wondered if perhaps this would be Samuel's escape route if he found himself boxed in.

As far as he knew Samuel didn't know that the

tunnel had been found by the agents, but he couldn't be sure what Samuel knew and didn't know.

But finding that tunnel had led Micah to wonder what else might lay underground—and all things seemed to start and stop at the Community Center, Samuel's magnificent building in honor of himself. Was it possible they had missed a second tunnel?

The building was a huge structure of concrete and marble with thick columns rising up and darkened windows that allowed people to see out but nobody to see inside.

An old church bell hung high above, rung to announce unexpected town meetings and the nightly workshops that Samuel insisted his people attend.

His people. Micah frowned as he clung to the shadows and worked his way around the back of the building. The Devotees got the tattoo on the hip to mark them as his own. But Micah also knew that Samuel had to know he could no longer trust his own tattoos, that some of the people who sported them had turned on Samuel, or were working undercover.

The Community Center was the true lair of the beast, the place where Samuel brainwashed people. This is where he brought the outcasts and made them feel a sense of belonging. This is where he preyed upon their weaknesses to make them his and he was good at taking the disenfranchised and giving them hope and a false sense of power.

Micah couldn't help but believe, if there were more secret rooms, then they existed in this place, in the very heart of Samuel's work.

There were no building plans on file anywhere in the town, no way to know exactly what secrets the building might contain. But, knowing his brother, Micah had a feeling that Samuel would take a perverse pleasure in holding meetings in the large room inside, throwing parties in the basement and having captive children and ill people in secret rooms right below.

Unfortunately, those working undercover in town and those working covertly on the fringes of town had been unable to find a way in or out that might hint of any other secret rooms.

Samuel's henchmen made sure that nobody wandered around in the building that was considered the very heart of the community.

If anyone would know anything about secret passageways or rooms, surely Olivia would have heard something considering the fact that she'd worked in the building five days a week as a secretary. He definitely needed to pick her brain when he got back to the cave. And maybe it would be easier if she was wearing one of her own T-shirts and hadn't sprayed on the fragrance that dizzied his senses just a bit.

If he listened closely, he could hear the sound of the bubbling creek that ran just beyond the Center. The creek was what had brought Samuel to Cold Plains, the creek with its rumored mysterious properties that healed all kinds of ailments. According to what he'd heard, Samuel had more than a cottage industry going in bottling and selling the water.

He'd begun by forcing his Devotees to buy the liquid at twenty-five dollars a pop and the latest rumors had it that Samuel was expanding the business and exporting the bottles to distributors out of town. Selling miracles from creek water, that's what Samuel did. He was like an illusionist who could take the ugly and make it magical.

Micah moved around the side of the building but stopped and froze, slamming his back against the cool concrete as he spied Chief of Police Bo Fargo and Dax Roberts talking beneath a nearby streetlamp.

Micah hated the tall, muscular, dark-haired man who had put a bullet through his head, but he also held a pure disgust for the balding, husky man who had taken an oath to protect the town and who had become one of the most dangerous men in the area. Hell had a special place for Chief of Police Bo Fargo.

Micah also knew that if either of them caught sight of him, they'd shoot to kill. Of course it might take Dax Roberts a minute to get over the fact that Micah wasn't a ghost, considering he believed he'd killed Micah months ago.

He wished he could get close enough to hear what they were saying, what plot they might be hatching on Samuel's behalf, but they were too far away for him to make out their actual words. But he was also afraid that any movement at all on his part might draw their attention to him.

As long as they remained where they were, Micah was trapped with his back against the building, hoping neither one of them happened to glance his way.

He should have looked before he moved around the corner but now he was helpless until they moved away. He wasn't arrogant enough to believe that he could take out both of them without being shot himself.

Minutes ticked by and still the two men lingered, occasionally laughing. The sound of Dax's laughter drove a stake through Micah's heart and his finger itched to kill the man who had tried and nearly succeeded in killing him.

But he couldn't take care of that particular piece of unfinished business right now. There were too many other things that needed to be done before he could pay back Dax for what he'd done and moving a single muscle now would be a deadly mistake. He had to sit tight and wait.

His tension increased and a sense of panic started to sweep over him as bright spots began to dance before his eyes. He closed his eyes in an attempt to banish them, but when he opened his eyes again they reappeared. Auras.

A bad sign.

A very bad sign.

Crap, not now. He closed his eyes once again, attempting to will away what he knew would follow. The migraines had been a curse left behind by the bullet to his head and the last thing he needed was for one to appear at this moment.

However, the flashing-light auras continued and always preceded a particularly bad one. He figured he had about thirty minutes before he'd be brought to his knees with the most excruciating pain he'd ever experienced.

Already he felt the side of his head starting to throb. If he didn't manage to get out of this situation soon there was no way they wouldn't know of his presence.

There was no way he wouldn't be dead.

Chapter 4

Olivia paced between her room and the kitchen as she waited for Micah to return. She'd put Sam down for the night hours ago and it had been that long since Micah had left to go into town. With each minute that passed, Olivia got more and more nervous, although June tried to allay her fears by reminding her that Micah was an intelligent man, a skilled mercenary who wouldn't take unnecessary risks with his life for a couple diapers.

Still, she would never forgive herself if something happened to Micah because of her. She didn't want to be responsible for his safety. She just wanted him to get back here safe and sound, with or without diapers.

Olivia had no idea what the dynamics were between Samuel and Micah but wondered how two brothers who were fraternal twins could be so different, could be at such odds. It was obvious that Micah's goal was to take down his brother and it was just as obvious that

Samuel needed to be taken down. How had two brothers become so different at the very core? What had the Grayson family dynamics been like that had produced the two men?

The place was quiet, the other women and children having gone to sleep and the men either in the woods on security duty near the entrance of the cave or out foraging in the woods to see what might lurk there, keeping danger away from the safe house.

Never had Olivia felt so alone, and in the silence, in the utter loneliness, her thoughts turned to Ethan and she felt as if her heart was being ripped from her chest.

She should have never left without him. Somehow she should have pulled it together, hidden out until Samuel had left and then searched for her missing son. If only she'd done that, then the three of them would all be here together.

Instead she'd panicked and left her precious boy behind and if something happened to him, if she never saw him alive and well again, she'd never, ever be able to forgive herself.

She'd had a sorry excuse for a mother and she'd always vowed that she would be the kind of mother she'd longed for when she had children of her own. Jeff had certainly been a mistake in her life, but Sam and Ethan had been like two little miracles she'd been gifted with to make up for a crummy youth.

She finally stopped her nervous walking and sank down on the edge of the mattress in the small room where she'd slept the night before.

The oil lamp flickered and created dancing shadows on the walls. Was somebody feeding Ethan? Did whoever had him know that he was afraid of the dark?

That she always kept a night-light burning in his bedroom? Was somebody kissing his forehead at night before he fell asleep, waylaying his fears and wishing him happy dreams?

The idea of him alone in a room, in the dark and scared shot an excruciating pain through the very center of her. She squeezed her eyes shut to staunch a flood of useless tears.

If only she knew for sure if Samuel had seen her when he'd killed that man. If he hadn't seen her, then she might take a chance and go back to town with some wild story to explain her absence. She'd get Ethan and then leave town forever.

But if he'd seen her and she returned, she knew not only would she be lost but both of her boys would be, as well. Samuel would never allow them to leave the town alive knowing that she had information that could potentially get him arrested.

She jumped off the bed with a gasp of surprise as Micah staggered into the room. He dropped the rucksack to the floor and leaned weakly against the wall, his face blanched of all color.

"Micah, are you all right?" she asked in alarm.

"Headache." His deep voice was faint as he reached up and placed a palm against the left side of his head. "Migraine."

She grabbed him by the arm and led him to the bed where he collapsed on his back, his eyes closed as he pressed both hands to each side of his head, as if trying to keep his skull together.

He said nothing and she stood next to the bed trying to think of something she could do to help him. She knew that making noise by talking to him would probably only make it worse.

He needed quiet and as much darkness as possible and he had both with just the faint flicker of the oil lamp lighting the space.

She left the room and hurried to the kitchen where she grabbed a clean dishcloth and ran it under cold water. Her mother used to have migraines, although they were usually after a night of too much booze. Even as a little girl, Olivia could remember ministering her mother in the mornings with a cool cloth on her head.

She hurried back to Micah and found him in the same position where she'd left him. He dwarfed the double mattress, but the pain that sharpened his features, that tightened all of his muscles, made her hurt for him.

She carefully lowered herself on the edge of the mattress next to his head. He squinted open one eye and winced in pain. "I have a cool cloth," she explained softly. "It might feel good across your forehead."

He closed his eye once again and dropped his arms to his side, allowing her to tend to him. She placed the cloth across his forehead and gently ran her fingers back and forth across the cool cotton.

Immediately his muscles began to relax and he released a deep sigh. After a few minutes had passed, she knew the cloth had warmed with the contact from his fevered brow and she flipped it over and once again moved her fingers slowly, smoothly over the cloth, hoping that the gentle massage might be helping.

She felt the tension ebbing out of him, his body relaxing into the mattress and before long she realized he'd fallen asleep.

She stopped her massaging and removed the cloth

and leaned back and stared at the man sprawled on her bed. How often did he get the migraines? Had something specific happened that had brought this one on? She felt responsible for his pain, that somehow by sending him into her home she'd given him too much stress.

As she sat there, a weary exhaustion played through her. It had to be at least two or three in the morning. She didn't want to disturb Micah, but she also couldn't stay up for the rest of the night and had no idea where else to go to sleep.

There was just enough room on the edge of the bed for her to stretch out without bothering the sleeping, wounded warrior who had carried in a rucksack of diapers for her son.

She placed the cloth on the table next to the oil lantern and then tentatively lay down next to him, not touching him in any way and closed her eyes. She could smell him. The wild scent of the night and the forest clung to him, a pleasant scent that filled her head with an odd comfort.

She must have fallen asleep for when she awakened again she found Micah spooned around her back, one of his arms flung around her as if to keep her trapped against his warm, firm body.

Her internal clock told her she hadn't been asleep for just a few minutes, but rather a couple hours. Still, it was early enough she heard no morning wake-up cry from Sam.

The cave was utterly timeless, with no sunlight to allow anyone to know if it was day or night. At least she had her wristwatch but at the moment it was on the nightstand and she wasn't inclined to move a single muscle.

She figured it was probably around four or five in the morning. She also knew she should roll away from Micah, somehow extract herself from their intimate position, but she didn't move. She scarcely breathed.

He felt warm and strong and utterly male and she felt herself responding in a way that was completely inappropriate and yet she remained in place, her heart beating way too fast.

For just this single moment in time, she felt more safe than she'd ever felt in her life…in the arms of a virtual stranger. How pathetic was that? How well that spoke of the choices she had made so far in her life, choices that had led her to a man who'd left her alone with one child and pregnant with the other, and then to another man who was a cold-blooded killer among other things.

She had no idea who Micah was beneath his skin. She didn't know what forces drove him or what demons he might be battling. She only knew that there was a solidness about him that called to all the insecurities inside her. There was a directness to his gaze that made her believe she could trust him despite all the reasons she might have not to.

But you're just a pawn to him, a tiny voice whispered inside her head. *You're simply a tool to help him bring down the brother he hates.* And she would do well to remember that fact.

"Are you awake?" His deep voice was a soft, heated whisper against her neck.

For a brief instant she thought about not responding, pretending to be still asleep so she wouldn't have to move away from him. But instead she whispered yes, a bit guilty that she hadn't moved the moment she'd first awakened. As he raised his arm from around her, she rolled over to face him. "How's your head?"

"Better, thanks." He made no move to get off the mattress and so she remained where she was, warmed by the heat that radiated outward from his firmly muscled body.

"Do you get migraines often?" she asked. She liked the way he looked in the faint glow of the lantern, his features relaxed in a way she hadn't seen them before, making him look not as daunting and less like his brother.

"I didn't start getting them until five months ago after my brother sent one of his hit men, Dax Roberts, to put a bullet in my head. Unfortunately, he succeeded."

Horror swept through her at his words. How could a man be evil enough to send anyone to try to kill his own brother? And Samuel was the man she'd believed was going to help her build the life she'd always dreamed about. She'd been so deluded.

"Fortunately, it didn't kill me," Micah continued. "But, it did put me in a coma for three months. Eventually I got back on my feet and the only lingering issue is the occasional migraine."

She eyed him curiously. "What happened to Samuel? I mean, what made him the way he is…so dangerous?" she asked.

He leaned up on one elbow and reached out to push away a strand of her hair from her face. The soft touch shot a flare of heat in the pit of her stomach. He dropped his hand between them and released a deep sigh.

"We could have a long discussion about nature versus nurture. Our father was a brutal man who beat both of us on a regular basis, that is, when he wasn't beating our mother. But, from the time we were young kids, I knew there was something off about Samuel."

A frown tugged across his forehead. "He was a quiet kid, always watching, observing people around him. When we were young kids, he had no friends and seemed quite content to be alone."

"The two of you were never close?" she asked.

Tension rolled off him. "No, never. I realized early on that he was an evil little boy. Anything that was important to me, he broke or stole. Any friendships I tried to have, he'd ruin in one way or another. He liked torturing stray animals. I'd wake up sometimes in the middle of the night and find him standing next to my bed just staring at me." He hesitated a moment and then added, "He scared me more than my father." He released a rusty laugh. "I've never admitted that to anyone before."

She wanted to reach out and touch him, to assure him that his secret was safe with her. She wanted to hold the child he had been and tell him he was safe and nobody, not his father or his brother, could ever harm him.

"My old man and his beatings were pretty predictable. I could tell by the sound of the weight of his footsteps on the wooden porch when he got home after work if it was going to be a night of beatings. I knew when he drank he was always a mean drunk. I learned fairly early how to recognize the danger signs when it came to my father and avoid him whenever possible."

"A child should never have to learn to recognize danger signs in their father," she replied. "What about your mother?" Olivia knew in her heart and soul that she would never be able to stay with any man if he raised a hand to her or her children. She'd rather be homeless and alone than allow any man to harm her babies.

"My mother was a timid woman who rarely spoke and seemed too weary for the world all my life. She died of heart failure when Samuel and I were seventeen. I think she willed herself to death because it was the only way she had the courage to leave my father."

"I'm so sorry," she whispered and this time followed through on her need to touch him in some way. She covered his hand on the mattress between them with one of her own. "So, you said that Samuel scared you more than your father did," she said, wanting to understand the dynamics that had created a Micah, the same dynamics that had also created a Samuel.

"Like I said, my dad's rages were predictable. But Samuel was a different kind of animal." His eyes narrowed slightly. "He was impossible to read, and even when he displayed appropriate emotions it felt forced to me, like he was mimicking how he'd seen others react in the same circumstances. As far as I'm concerned, he's a narcissist without a soul, a sociopath with illusions of grandeur and he really started coming into his own in high school."

"What do you mean?" Her heart lurched a bit as he turned his hand to encase hers. This all felt so intimate…the semidarkness, the early hour, his touch and the secret of his past that he was sharing with her.

"It was as if, when he got into high school, he'd honed all the skills he needed to manipulate and fool people. He recognized weaknesses in others and exploited them." His hand tightened on hers and his eyes seemed to transform from forest green to black with his memories.

"There was only one person I ever really cared about in my life. She was my high school sweetheart, Johanna Tate. She was pretty much everything to me, but on prom night I went to the bathroom and I came back to find that she was gone, along with my brother. He took her away from me that night and she never spoke to me again. She became his. She's one of the five women we believe Samuel has killed. She's one of the reasons I'm here now. I want to avenge her death and I want to make sure my brother never has a chance to create a Cold Plains again, to hurt anyone else ever again."

He withdrew his hand from hers and sat up. "Now, tell me how you came to be in Cold Plains and exactly how close you were to the devil before I found you in the woods."

There was a sudden hint of steel in his voice that made her realize he'd withdrawn into himself and she had now gone from a friendly face who'd heard his confessions to a suspect in the breadth of a heartbeat.

She sat up as well, both of them sitting Indian style and facing each other. She wanted to meet him eye-to-eye as she told him her story and she had no intention of mincing the truth. "I grew up in a trailer park in Oklahoma with a sickly, alcoholic mother. I had no friends and no place I felt I really belonged." She told him this not to gain any sympathy but merely as a statement of fact.

"My mother died when I was twenty-two and six months after that I met Jeff Winfry. He was basically a drifter, living out of a camper on the back of his pickup. He was handsome and charming and was making his way toward California with grand schemes for his future. I bought into him and his silly dreams and before I knew it, I'd sold my mother's trailer and hitched my star to Jeff."

She swallowed against the self-disgust that rose up in the back of her throat as she thought of the incredibly stupid choices she'd made so far in her life.

"Soon after that I got pregnant with Ethan." Her voice broke as she spoke the name of her missing child. "Jeff kept telling me we were going to get married and settle down someplace and like a stupid fool, I believed him as we went through small town after small town. In each place he'd work side jobs for cash and made me believe he was checking it out to see if the area was good enough to settle down with a family, but he rejected each town and we'd move on."

She frowned, remembering her feeling of helplessness, of hopelessness and the self-recriminations that had filled her with each day that passed.

"When I was six months pregnant with Sam, we hit Cold Plains. Jeff pulled up next to a bench along the sidewalk on Main Street and told me that he'd realized he really wasn't cut out to be a family man, that Ethan and I were cramping his style. He left us there with a suitcase full of clothes and a hundred dollar bill and then he drove away."

She could still remember the utter terror that had consumed her at that moment. She was six-months' pregnant and with a two-year-old, abandoned in a strange new town where she knew absolutely nobody.

"Did you love him?" Micah asked.

She didn't answer immediately, but instead took the time to really think about it, about Jeff. "I thought I was in love when I left Oklahoma with him, but I realize now that I was really in love with the idea of escaping the place that had been such an unhappy home, I loved the idea of an adventure with a man who I thought loved me. And then once I got pregnant with Ethan, I thought I loved him because he was the father of my baby and I wanted to build a family. But, now I recognize that it wasn't love that drove me, but rather need, the need to belong to something…to someone." She released a humorless laugh. "God, I sound so pathetic."

"No, you sound human," he countered with a gentle tone. "When I was eighteen, I joined the navy for the same reason. I needed a place where I felt like I belonged. I was a Navy SEAL for five years before I went out on my own. You've probably heard I'm a mercenary. I take money to get rid of problems that our government doesn't want to touch." He studied her, as if waiting for a negative reaction.

She was in no position to judge anyone for the choices they had made in their lives. Besides, she didn't care what he'd done in the past. All that mattered was that he was here now to take down his brother and hopefully help her get her son back.

"So, you were dumped in Cold Plains. What happened next?" he asked.

"I was still sitting on the bench crying when, a half an hour later, Samuel found me. He got me to tell him what had happened and he was so kind to me. He told me not to worry, that I'd landed in the right place where people would help me get on my feet and that he could teach me how to live a healthy, happy and productive life in a wonderful town."

She felt the burn of tears in her eyes as she thought of how easily she'd allowed herself to fall under Samuel's spell. "He was so soothing, so persuasive and he immediately took control of the situation. He led me to a small furnished house where he said we could stay for the time being. Several men brought in food and then Samuel told me about his workshops, that there was one that night and I should attend. I did and I almost immediately bought into everything he proselytized. He gave me my job and allowed me to remain in the house." She felt the warmth of heat in her cheeks. "I even named Sam after him."

"A perfect town where there's no crime, no illness, no drug or alcohol abuse. A perfect town where everyone is healthy and happy and a leader who is willing to work and see that come to fruition, of course you bought into it. You were all alone and afraid, a perfect victim for my brother."

"I was a fool," Olivia replied with a touch of anger. "I gave up my free will, took the job he offered me, lived where he told me to live and didn't even think about doing anything to break one of his many rules. I was ready to get a tattoo to show my devotion to him when I saw him shoot that poor man. In that single moment, it was like I woke up from a dream and realized I'd given up everything I had to him. I gave my mind, my heart, my very soul, to a cold-blooded murderer." She fought against a chilly shiver that threatened to run up her spine.

"And that's when you ran," Micah said.

She gave him a curt nod. "At first it was sheer panic. I needed to think. I needed to process what I'd just seen. I felt as if the world had suddenly shifted and I couldn't hold my balance. I ran for the woods and hid."

"Do you know the identity of the man he shot?"

She shook her head. "It was too dark for me to see who it was. There was just enough streetlight shining for me to see Samuel, but I couldn't make out who was with him."

"And you don't know if Samuel saw you or not when he killed that man?"

"If I knew for sure he hadn't seen me, then I would have gotten Ethan before I ran." She couldn't stop the emotion that welled up in her chest, pressing tight and making it nearly impossible for her to draw a breath.

Hot tears began to streak down her cheeks. "Once I'd run to the edge of town and into the woods, I was afraid to leave Ethan, but I was more afraid to go back into town. I figured if Samuel had seen me, then I'd put Sam at risk as well as Ethan if I went back."

She was unable to stop the tears as her emotions careened further out of control as she thought of her little boy. Like the migraine that had brought Micah to his knees, the pain inside her nearly incapacitated her.

Shoving a hand to her mouth in an attempt to staunch the cry of pain that thoughts of Ethan brought, she looked at Micah helplessly.

She knew she was falling apart from the inside out and he seemed to sense it, too. He knelt and pulled her up to her knees, then wrapped his arms around her as she began to shiver with the fear she'd scarcely allowed herself to feel when she thought of her absent son.

If not for his arms around her, she'd shatter. If not for his strong thighs against her own, she'd explode into a million pieces, so great was her sense of loss at that moment.

She almost believed she was going to be able to regain control, she almost had herself convinced that she was strong enough to step away from the dark abyss that called to her, and then he gently caressed her back.

"Let it go," he said softly in her ear. "Just let it all go."

As he gave her permission, the grief that had ripped at her very soul since the moment she'd left Ethan behind overwhelmed her. Weakly she leaned into him, allowing her tears to fall in earnest as deep, gulping sobs began to escape her.

Flashes of memories shot off in her head. Ethan gazing up at her proudly as he completed one of his puzzles. His blond hair shining in the sunlight; his laughter riding the breeze as he tried to catch a ladybug; he'd been her heart since the moment of his birth.

Each memory only made her cry harder. Micah didn't say another word, but he tightened his arms around her and continued to move his hand up and down her back in a soothing fashion.

He didn't seem uncomfortable with her display of emotion, at least she didn't sense any uneasiness. Instead there was simple acceptance and, in that acceptance, a comfort she knew she wouldn't find anywhere else.

Finally her tears slowed and then stopped and still she remained in Micah's embrace, slowly becoming aware of the faint scent of shaving cream that lingered on the underside of his jaw, the taut muscles of his shoulders beneath her fingertips and the slow, steady beat of his heart against her own fluttering heartbeat.

Within moments her heartbeat mirrored his, slow and steady as she felt the last of her sad emotion ebb away and a new one begin to take its place.

She couldn't ever remember feeling so good in a

man's arms and as he reached up and stroked the length of her hair, she felt the quickened beat of his heart.

Suddenly she felt less safe than she had moments before. A faint sense of danger simmered through her, a danger that wasn't all unpleasant, but rather whispered of delicious undertones.

She was leery of trusting anyone in her current situation and given her bad history, but Micah called to something inside her. But she couldn't allow herself to let down her guard in a moment of an emotional outburst.

She pulled back from him enough that their bodies no longer touched. "Sorry about that," she said as she swiped at her cheeks.

"No need to apologize," he replied, his eyes dark and glittering in the faint light. "Sorry about this."

She looked at him curiously just before he wrapped one of his hands around the back of her head and pulled her toward him. She had no time to process, no time to deny him as his mouth took possession of hers.

The kiss torched fire through her entire body and despite the fact that she hadn't been prepared for it, that didn't stop her from responding completely. She opened her mouth to welcome it, to welcome him, and his tongue tasted of hunger as it danced with hers.

When he finally released her, she stared at him, appalled that she wanted more, that something about Micah Grayson touched her like no man had ever before in her life.

"I'll find your son," he said, his eyes still glittering like a wild animal's trapped in the faint illumination. "No matter what it takes, no matter who I have to go through to get him, I promise I'll find your son for you and bring him home, no strings attached." His voice rang with a conviction that made her believe him.

His gaze softened and she thought he was going to kiss her again but, at that moment, Sam hollered from the room next door, his cry of Mama echoing through the cave.

"Thank you," Olivia said as she got off the bed, her head still reeling from the kiss they'd shared. As she left the room, she tried to prepare herself for another day in hiding, another day without her beloved Ethan and attempted not to think about what might have happened if Sam hadn't awakened at that very moment.

Chapter 5

Micah sat in the kitchen alone, half-irritated by his promise to Olivia. He didn't make promises—to anyone, ever—and yet he'd made one to a blond-haired, green-eyed woman who had somehow managed to get under his skin. Not just with the haunting sadness in her eyes, not just with the sobs she'd been unable to control, but also with the story she'd told him about who she was and where she'd come from.

She'd never had a chance in hell against a man like Samuel. She'd been a victim ripe for the picking, already kicked around by life. He was only surprised that Samuel hadn't tried to take things further with her, make her one of his very special girlfriends. Of course, that probably wouldn't have happened until Samuel personally tattooed the *D* on her hip, marking her as his forever.

Micah wrapped his hands around the coffee mug,

the thought of his brother touching Olivia making him half-sick. Thank God Olivia had gotten out when she had. It was just unfortunate that she'd had to run before grabbing her son.

It was midafternoon. Breakfast had come and gone and everyone in the house was busy with duties or whatever.

After Sam woke up, Micah had left Olivia's room and gone to his own quiet small space where all he'd been able to think about was the kiss he'd shared with Olivia. He was shocked to realize he somehow wanted to be the hero she'd never had in her life, the man she could depend on to get her son back, to make her world right.

If Sam hadn't awakened when he did, Micah had a feeling the sexual attraction between him and Olivia might have spiraled completely out of control. It had been a long time since he'd been with a woman, an even longer time that he'd been with a woman whose name he'd remembered after having meaningless sex with her. He wasn't proud of that, it was simply a part of his life he hadn't thought much about.

Once he'd lost Johanna to Samuel something had broken inside him, the part of his heart that allowed people in, the part that allowed him to trust. He'd decided at that time that he would live his life alone, and up until now he'd never regretted that decision.

His sole goal when he'd arrived here was to pay back his brother for the bullet to his head, for the migraines that sometimes brought him to his knees and for the death of the woman he'd believed he'd once loved.

Now he'd made a promise to a woman he couldn't seem to get out of his head, a woman whose kiss had fired a flame inside the pit of his stomach that still hadn't stopped burning.

Despite all the reasons he shouldn't, he trusted her. He believed her story and he also believed her new-found horror of Samuel. Samuel might have been able to "turn" her at one time, but Micah knew there was no way she could be corrupted by Samuel again.

She wanted her kid back and then they'd figure out a place for her to go where she could start a new life and this time learn to stand on her own two feet. He sensed a deep core of strength inside her. All she had to do was tap into it and she and her kids would be just fine.

He'd finally fallen asleep and had awakened just a few minutes before, long enough to pour himself a cup of coffee and sit at the table to think about options for finding Ethan and Rafe's little boy, Devin.

He looked up as Darcy Craven entered the kitchen. She paused at the sight of him, as if considering run-ning out of the room. Since the moment he'd met her, she seemed to be avoiding him and that, coupled with a strange sense of familiarity about her, intrigued him.

"Darcy, why don't you sit and have a cup of coffee with me?"

"Okay," she said with a faint touch of reluctance.

He watched as she got a cup and filled it with the brew. Darcy was young, probably no older than twenty-two or twenty-three, but she gave the aura of an older, more mature woman.

She sat across from him at the table and he noted her long, dark hair and bright blue eyes. Was it her eyes that made him feel the odd sense of familiarity? Or the shape of her face? She definitely reminded him of a woman he'd known years ago, but if he thought about it, she could remind him of lots of women he'd known through the years.

"I met your fiancé. He's asked me to look for his son," Micah said.

"He's frantic to find him." Her blue eyes flashed with the fire of anger. "It was wicked for somebody to give him a little boy and tell him the child was Devin and then have the baby ripped away from him by the true biological father."

Micah nodded. "So, what's your story? I'm still trying to figure out who is who and all the connections between Samuel, Cold Plains and everything else."

Darcy looked down into her coffee cup, as if considering how much or how little to share with him. "A few months ago I discovered that the woman who raised me, Louise Craven, wasn't my real mother. As Louise was dying, she told me that I'd been left with her by my biological mother who feared for my life. Louise told me she was haunted by my mother who seemed to vanish into thin air and now that I was an adult it was time I searched for her and become the family we were meant to be."

"No leads at all?" Micah asked, still studying her features intently.

"Ford McCall, he's one of the local cops and one of the good guys, showed me a picture of one of the dead women, one who is a Jane Doe. He seemed to think I looked like her, but really the only resemblance was that we both have blue eyes. I don't know if she's my mother or not."

"Do you have the picture?" Micah was aware that one of the five murder victims was listed as an unidentified Jane Doe, but he hadn't had any contact with

Ford McCall, one of the few law enforcement officers in town who was working on their side, or seen whatever picture the man might possess.

"No, but I can get a copy from him." She took a sip of her coffee. "I just want to find out who my mother is, whether she's alive or dead and why she left me with Louise when I was a baby. Louise told me my mother grew up as a foster child in a small town. I found out she was from the small town of Horn's Gulf and I went there and showed the photo around but nobody could tell me if she was the foster girl who lived in town for a short period of time."

"Horn's Gulf. That's where I'm from," Micah replied in surprise.

"I know." She frowned and in that gesture a rivulet of shock shot through Micah.

The shape of her face, the dark hair…the frowning gesture that he'd seen not only in his own mirror on occasion but also on his brother's face. Was he just imagining the resemblance?

"What about your father?" he asked with a forced nonchalance, although his heart suddenly beat an unsteady cadence.

Once again, Darcy looked down into her coffee mug, as if unwilling to meet his eyes. "What about him?" she countered in a faint whisper.

"He's Samuel. Samuel is your father, isn't he?" Micah felt as if his heart had stopped beating in his chest.

Darcy's blue eyes looked miserable as she met his gaze. "There was a note pinned to my pajamas the night my mother left me with Louise. It said 'keep my precious baby safe from Samuel. Never let her know the truth.' But, before she died Louise told me the truth, that my father was a dangerous man named Samuel Grayson who was running a cult in Cold Plains. That's what brought me here in search of my mother."

She paused to take a sip of her coffee and he noticed her hand tremble slightly as she set the cup back down on the table. "I came here and forced myself to go to some of Samuel's seminars. I made friends with some of the Devotees, all the while trying to find out any information about my mother that I could, but nobody was talking. I got a job working as a receptionist in Rafe's office and I finally told him the truth about my father. Rafe knows, and June knows, and now you know, too, and I hate it. I hate that he's my father," she said fervently.

"But that makes you my niece," Micah replied, the new information rolling around in his head.

A tentative smile curved her lips. "And I haven't decided yet if that's a good thing or a bad thing."

An unexpected burst of laughter left Micah's lips and he wasn't sure who was more surprised by the spontaneous response, he or she. "I hope given some time we'll both decide it's a good thing."

"Time will definitely tell," she said, meeting his gaze boldly now.

A sense of respect swept through him for the young woman…his niece. She'd come into the lion's den seeking answers about her mother, answers that so far hadn't been forthcoming.

She would be a fool to trust him completely, knowing him for only a couple days and knowing that he was Samuel's brother.

A surprising swell of emotion rose up in his chest.

He had no family except for Samuel. There had been no aunts and uncles, no cousins, only a nervous mother who had escaped a brutal man five years before he'd met his own death in a drunk-driving accident.

Micah had never thought much about having a family. He'd certainly never felt any family love or support when growing up on the small ranch in Horn's Gulf.

His mother had been distant, his father had inspired fear rather than love and he'd written off his sick brother when they'd been young kids.

When he'd arrived here at the safe house, he hadn't expected to find a niece, nor had he expected to find a woman like Olivia. He wasn't sure how to handle the whole thing.

He hated the fact that Olivia had seen him at his very weakest, so sick with his vicious headache the night before. When the two men standing beneath the streetlamp had finally parted, Micah's head had reached full pound mode.

He was both nauseous and weak as he'd made his way back to retrieve the rucksack and continued on to the safe house. He'd barely managed to make it to safety.

"Are you okay?" Darcy's voice pulled him from the moment of the night before when he had feared his headache would ultimately be the death of him.

"I'm fine, just trying to digest everything that I've learned in the week that I've been here."

"All you really have to remember is that when meeting people from Cold Plains, you can't trust anyone other than the people Hawk introduces you to or the ones June has vetted." She took another sip of her coffee and then carefully set the cup on the table. "I just want to find my mother."

Her blue eyes filled with emotion. "I'd hoped to find her alive, to be able to build a relationship with her, but I think she might be dead. I think she might be the Jane Doe that Ford has been trying to identify. Unfortunately, until he identifies her with her name, I won't know if she's my mother. Louise told me my mother's name was Catherine, but that's all I know."

Micah frowned. "Catherine George. That's who you reminded me of the night I first saw you in the woods. I think I called you that."

Darcy leaned forward. "That must have been after I fainted at the sight of you." When Micah had stumbled into Darcy and June in the forest the first time they'd met, Darcy had assumed he was Samuel and had dropped into a dead faint. "Catherine George? Was she in Horn's Gulf?"

"Yes, but there were several Catherines in our school. To be honest, I didn't pay much attention to the girls who flocked around Samuel, but the moment I saw you I thought of her." He shrugged. "And now I see myself and Samuel in your features, but your eyes still kind of remind me of Catherine George. Maybe it's just because they're so blue. I wouldn't take that name to the bank. It's possible Catherine George is alive and well and never had a daughter she gave up to protect. You get that picture from Ford and I'll take a look at it and maybe I can make a definite identification."

She flashed him a grateful smile and then stood. "Thanks." She paused for a moment. "You know, you might look a lot like Samuel, but you're really nothing like him."

"That's the best compliment you could give me," he replied. She nodded and left the kitchen, leaving Micah alone with his thoughts. There were times when he was haunted by the possibility that he was more like Samuel than he wanted to admit.

He'd worked as a mercenary, infiltrating for the sole reason of taking out a life. He'd fooled men and women, pretending to be something he wasn't, focused solely on what he'd been paid to do.

Did that make him like his brother? Were they both narcissistic power seekers who simply used different methods to achieve their goals?

Disturbed by his own thoughts, he got up from the table and carried his and Darcy's cups to the sink where he washed them out and set them on a drainer to dry, then went in search of Olivia—telling himself he needed to pick her brain about everything she knew about the Community Center—but in the depths of his heart he suspected he just wanted to see her beautiful, sweet smile to erase the doubts about himself he'd just entertained.

Olivia had learned soon upon arrival at the safe house that it was located in Hidden Valley, and her favorite place to spend time was in the secret garden where the sun shone down and Sam could play in the last of the late summer grass.

Besides, she felt like they needed the sunshine to keep their internal clocks set right. It would be easy in the cave to lose track of day and night and she wanted to know exactly how many days she'd been without her baby Ethan.

At the moment she was seated next to June, who

had been sharing with her the trauma of nearly dying a month before when two of Samuel's henchmen had managed to infiltrate the safe house. Nearby, Jesse Grainger, a rancher from the Wind Rivers foothills, walked the rows of vegetables, giving the two women a chance to talk alone.

Initially it had been June who had saved Jesse's life when she'd found him half-dead and suffering from amnesia in the forest. But on the night of the attack, it had been Jesse who had saved June's life and in the process he'd won her heart.

One of the infiltrators had been killed and the other had been taken away by the FBI, leaving the location of the safe house a secret.

Sam sat at their feet, his attention divided between the sippy cup of juice he clutched in his chubby hand and Eager, the black Lab that lay dozing at June's feet.

"Sooner or later Sam's going to make a grab for Eager," Olivia said as she watched her son sizing up the big dog.

"Eager is very tolerant of people and children as long as I don't have his work leash on him," June replied. Eager was a search and rescue dog who June often took with her to the woods to help hunt for people in trouble—or people trying to cause trouble.

The warmth of the mid-September sunshine on Olivia's face was welcoming and yet she couldn't help but wonder if Ethan was enjoying the sunshine. Was he someplace swinging or playing in a sandbox, enjoying the last of summer with other children his age? Or was he locked up in some room with an armed guard as a playmate?

"Micah promised me last night that he'd get my son out of Cold Plains," she said to June.

"He strikes me as a man who doesn't make promises easily," June replied with a touch of obvious surprise.

"I just hope Ethan is still in town." Olivia swallowed hard against the lump that had risen in her throat. "You know there have been those rumors of illegal adoption activity."

June nodded. "That's Rafe and Darcy's biggest fear for his son, that he's already been adopted out to somebody and they'll never be able to find him."

"If that happens to Ethan then I'll spend the rest of my life looking for him. Surely when Samuel is eventually brought down, the FBI will find paperwork or something that will name a baby broker, somebody who will be a lead to where the children went." She tried to tamp down the anxiety that threatened to take hold of her.

But a different kind of anxiety filled her as Micah stepped outside. Every nerve in her body hummed at the sight of him. Instead of wearing the camouflage clothing she'd been accustomed to seeing him in, he wore a pair of jeans that hugged his slim hips and a long-sleeved navy polo shirt that stretched across his broad shoulders and muscled chest. He was clean-shaven and the scent of minty soap clung to him.

He looked sexy and rugged and utterly capable of accomplishing anything he put his mind to. He smiled as he approached and her heart fluttered, the memory of those sensual lips pressed against her own heating her insides.

"Nice day to be out here," he said as June stood from the bench where she and Olivia had been seated.

"Unusually warm for this time of year," June replied. "Won't be long and it will be too cold to sit out here. I hate to think about the snow falling." She looked from Micah to Olivia and smiled. "I think I'll head inside and get started on something for dinner." As she moved toward the door, Jesse gave a nod to Micah and Olivia, and then, along with Eager, they all disappeared back inside.

"Mind if I sit?" he asked and gestured to the place next to her on the bench.

"Of course not," she replied, although she couldn't halt the rapid race of her heart at his nearness. "I want to thank you for all the things you got from my house." She'd been delighted when she'd opened the rucksack earlier and had discovered not only diapers, but also clothes for both her boys and for herself.

"I figured your life was in a big enough uproar that at least you should have some of your own things to make you feel better."

She rubbed her hands down the thighs of her wellworn, comfortable jeans. "I definitely feel better in my own clothes." The long-sleeved cotton red blouse she wore didn't tug across her breasts and made her less self-conscious than she had been in the borrowed things. And she couldn't believe he'd thought to throw in the bottle of her favorite perfume.

"I want to pick your brain about the Community Center," he said.

"What about it?" she asked in surprise.

"I believe that somewhere in that building are the secret rooms we're searching for, that it might be the place where Samuel is holding both Rafe's son and yours. It's just a gut feeling, but I want you to tell me about every room, every doorway you know of in the building."

"Why do you think there are any more secret rooms there?"

Micah's eyes narrowed slightly and, with the cast of the sun on his lean face, he looked more like his brother than ever before. "Because Samuel is a sadist and I think he'd get off on the idea of having his nightly seminars with all his people gathered in the auditorium and not knowing that some of their loved ones are locked up right beneath where they stand."

He shrugged. "I'm just trying to get into his head, to think the way he'd think."

"Try not to do too much of that," she said drily. "I think his head is a very dangerous place to be."

He smiled and in the warmth of that gesture all semblance of Samuel fell away. Samuel smiled often, pretending to be a loving father figure, a benevolent leader who wanted nothing but good for the town and its people. But she realized now that when Samuel smiled, no real warmth danced in the depths of his eyes.

"There really isn't a lot to the Community Center. Samuel has an office there, where he spends most of his time during the days and the evenings. I sat in the reception area. There are a couple small rooms that are used for more intimate counseling, and then there's the auditorium where he holds his town meetings and seminars."

"What about storage closets?"

"There are three that I know of," she replied thoughtfully. "But somebody told me they'd already found a tunnel beneath the Community Center that led out of one of the closets."

Micah nodded. "I can't help thinking if there's one tunnel then there could possibly be another one, leading to another place inside the building. I know the one that was found is thought to be an old settler tunnel used as a hiding place from marauding Indians, and I assume Samuel might intend to use that as an escape route if he ever needs to. It leads partway up the mountain, but he isn't the type to leave himself only one option for escape."

Sam reached out and grabbed Micah's knees and pulled himself up to his feet. Micah looked surprised as Sam gave him one of his most charming grins.

"Sorry," Olivia said and reached out to grab her son.

Micah lifted a hand to stop her. "He's fine."

Sam slapped him on the knee and laughed, as if agreeing with Micah that he was just fine. A small smile curved the corners of Micah's lips. "He doesn't seem to have many trust issues," he observed.

Olivia smiled ruefully. "He's never met a stranger he didn't like. Children are born pure and trusting. They have to be taught not to trust. Unfortunately they learn too early that people aren't always what they seem, that promises are rarely kept and that sweet unadulterated trust they're born with is broken."

She should have learned her lesson about trusting men when she'd been old enough to realize her father had abandoned her and her mother when she was just a baby.

"Have you ever been in Samuel's house?"

She blinked at the question that came out of nowhere. "A couple times, mostly just long enough to step into his foyer to deliver or pick up paperwork. But, last year he gave a big Christmas party there and invited all the people who work for him. Why?"

"According to what Hawk told me, they haven't been able to get anyone inside. They have no grounds for a warrant and it's guarded at all times. Not even any of the men who are working undercover have managed to get through the front door. What's it like on the inside?"

Sam sat back down on the ground, apparently bored by the adult conversation. He made no move to crawl away. Sam was pretty much content wherever he found himself. It was Ethan who had been her little explorer, always crawling or running with her chasing after him.

"Olivia?" Micah's voice pulled her back and she looked at him.

"Samuel's house is beautiful. I'm sure you already know it's in an area of town with huge houses and yards that abut the mountains. Inside, there's a large foyer with a grand staircase that leads to the next floor, although nobody went upstairs the night of the party. The party was held in the great room, and it is magnificent with a stone fireplace and a wet bar and a wall full of sliding doors that lead out to a balcony. The house is built on a rise, so when you walk in you're actually on a second floor."

"Selling tonic water must be lucrative," Micah said drily.

Olivia grinned ruefully at him. "Oh, Samuel gets money from much more than just the tonic water. We pay to attend his workshops. If he suggests private therapy then that's another expense. I imagine he probably gets a kickback from all the businesses in town."

"Yeah, that's what we figure, but according to Hawk they've been unable to gather enough evidence of anything to get Samuel behind bars. He's played things very safe and close to his vest. Even some of his devoted worker bees that we've managed to gather up won't turn on him."

Olivia leaned back thoughtfully and raised her face to the sun, needing the warmth to fill her soul as she went back to the night she'd seen Samuel kill a man.

She finally returned her gaze to Micah. "You know, even if I go to the FBI and tell them what I saw Samuel do, it's only my word against his and I'm sure he'll have half a dozen people who will alibi him for that time on that night. I honestly don't think my statement would move your investigation any further along and, at the moment, all it would do is put my son at greater risk."

Micah raked a hand down his lean, handsome features. "And we don't want that to happen." He released a deep sigh. "As much as I hate to admit it, I think you're right. If it comes down to your word against Samuel's, he'll be pulling alibi witnesses out of his ears."

"There's a lot of fear in that town. People are afraid to speak up against your brother," she said.

They fell silent, the only sound the song of a bird in a nearby tree and Sam patting the ground like it was a drum. For Olivia it was a tense silence as her mind refused to stop playing the kiss they'd shared through her head.

She couldn't stop thinking about the way it had felt to be held in his arms. She also couldn't help but worry about him. It was obvious he was determined to take down Samuel at all costs. Hopefully in the process he'd find her son and reunite her with him.

But, in the meantime, she knew the danger he faced each time he got near Cold Plains. She understood that those nights when he crept beneath the cover of darkness into the streets of Samuel's paradise, the risk of him losing his life was very real.

Definitely her trust in him grew by the minute, especially after he'd shared so much personal information with her. But she didn't want to care about him. She didn't want her heart to somehow get tangled up in his.

There was a battle brewing, a battle of epic proportions. What frightened her more than anything was the fact that there was no way of knowing which brother would remain standing when the war was won.

Chapter 6

As Micah and Hawk moved through the forest toward the small cabin where three FBI agents were hiding out, Micah couldn't get Olivia and her children out of his head. When Sam had pulled himself up using Micah's legs as support and given Micah that wide grin, something soft had risen up inside Micah, something he hadn't known he possessed.

The last thing he wanted at this moment was to embrace anything soft that might be hidden on the inside. He needed to be tough. He needed to be strong and single-minded for what lay ahead.

Get Ethan and Devin out of town and take down Samuel. Avenge Johanna's death and cut the evil cancer from the earth forever. It was like a constant mantra in his head as he moved behind Hawk toward the meeting place.

Still, it was hard to stay tough, and not to allow some

of the softness he'd discovered to seep to the surface whenever he was around Olivia.

It had been a week since he'd found her crouched in the bushes and had taken her to the safe house. In the last couple days, she had seamlessly fit into the group, offering to help whenever possible and building a special relationship with Darcy because of the two missing children.

He'd spent a lot of the last week with her, talking not just about the Cold Plains and Samuel, but also about her life with her alcoholic mother and her desire for something so much more, something so much better for her own children.

It was only after Sam had gone to bed, when the night was full upon them that he saw the despair creeping into her eyes, that he watched the slight tremble of her hands as she realized yet another night was about to pass with Ethan still gone from her arms.

When she finally went to her room, he fought the impulse to go with her, to hold her and comfort her, because he feared that comfort would lead to another kiss and a kiss would lead to something far more than either one of them needed in their lives at this time.

He was here with a single purpose and when that goal was accomplished he had no idea what the future held for him, but he was certain it wasn't a fragile blonde with two fatherless children.

They were in the very depth of the forest now and Micah knew Hawk was as tense as he was as utter darkness folded in around them. Scurrying noises indicated furry creatures shunning their human presence in the wild domain that should have belonged only to them.

Micah knew the difference between the natural

sounds of the forest and the alien sounds of hunters and he knew Hawk could discern the difference, as well.

Each man carried a penlight to shine on the faint, overgrown path they followed. Although they would prefer to move with no light at all, it was impossible as not even a sliver of moonlight penetrated the wildness that surrounded them.

Some of the tension that had ridden Micah's shoulders eased as he spied a faint light flicker in the distance. The cabin. Hawk had told him there were three FBI agents holed up there, coordinating the investigation, and Micah was anxious to talk to them, to kick around ideas for making some sort of forward progress.

He felt as if everything had stalled out, and each time he saw that sadness that shadowed Olivia's beautiful eyes, his need to do something to break the case wide open grew more intense.

Hawk halted abruptly and Micah nearly back-ended him. The agent took a radio from his pocket and warned the men in the cabin that he was coming in with one.

From the outside the cabin appeared to be an abandoned hunter's hideaway. The rough wood of the small place blended perfectly into the tall trees that huddled against it.

As the two men approached, a flash of light shone at a window, there a moment and then gone. It was only when the door opened that a light spilled onto the forest floor and then quickly disappeared as the door slammed shut behind Hawk and Micah.

In the first instant of being inside the cabin, Micah was eternally grateful that he wasn't one of the three men sharing the small space. Before the introductions between the men were made, Micah felt more than a faint touch of claustrophobia building up inside him.

Boyd Patterson, Stephen Jeffers and Lawrence Rosenbloom all had the wild eyes and vibrating energy of men cooped up in a small space for too long. They greeted Micah and Hawk with the friendliness of long-lost relatives, obviously eager for somebody's company besides their own.

They gathered around a wooden table that took up the center of the room. Three cots lined the walls and a small cookstove and sink took up what was left of the cabin.

"Pretty stark conditions," Micah said as he eased down across from Boyd.

"Hey, at least we have a bathroom with running water. Things could be worse," Lawrence said.

"You really do look like him," Stephen observed, his gaze intense on Micah.

Micah nodded and reached up to touch a length of his long hair. "The major difference is at the moment Samuel is working his movie star persona and I'm sporting more of a homeless look."

Stephen cast him a wry grin. "I hope that's not the real major difference between yourself and your brother. Still the resemblance is really remarkable."

Just that quickly the conversation turned serious as Micah began to tell the agents about the Samuel he'd known as a child, the Samuel who had appeared to come into his own during high school and the man who was now the charismatic leader of the "perfect" people in the "perfect" town of Cold Plains.

"I still don't know all the players," Micah said. "Hawk has been trying to fill me in, but there's a lot going on in town. I do know that two children are missing and one of my personal priorities is to find them and return them where they belong."

Boyd nodded. "Rafe Black's baby and Olivia Conner's son. We're aware of the situation and we have agents attempting to find the location of the children, but so far with no success."

"People are afraid to talk even if they aren't a part of Samuel's nonsense. Their fear of reprisal from him is too high," Lawrence said.

Stephen leaned forward. "What we were hoping you could give us is some idea of any weaknesses that your brother might possess, some quality that we can exploit to our advantage."

Micah frowned. "I've stayed up nights trying to figure out a weakness Samuel possesses that can be utilized. The only real weakness is his own arrogance, but he's also highly intelligent and apparently has made few, if any, mistakes." Micah shrugged. "I'm not sure anything I know about him can help you."

Micah didn't even consider mentioning to these men that Darcy Craven was his brother's daughter. There was absolutely no way Micah wanted her used somehow as leverage even if it meant losing the war. He would not allow his newly found niece to be collateral damage in the battle against Samuel.

"We've been keeping track of the traffic in and out of town and, if it's any relief at all, we believe the children have not been transported from the area," Boyd said.

"Has anyone managed to get inside Samuel's house?" Micah asked.

"None of our people, but we've spoken to some who have been inside. We've surveyed the area around the house and have found nothing suspicious. But without a warrant, our hands are pretty well tied. Why?" Boyd's gaze was as intense as the other three on Micah.

"We know about the secret passageway beneath the Community Center. I assume Samuel probably figures that's an escape route for him if anything goes down there and he needs to get out. I can't imagine him not having another from his home," Micah replied.

Stephen nodded. "We've thought the same thing, but the house is guarded 24-7 and we can't find a way to get inside legally, and of course officially we can't go in illegally."

"You can't, but I can," Micah countered. "I don't have to cut through red tape or follow anyone's rules. I don't work for the FBI."

"Yeah, but to get into that house, you've got to go through big burly men carrying big burly guns," Lawrence said.

Micah recalled what Olivia had told him about the wall of sliding glass doors that led out to a balcony. "Maybe…or maybe I can find a way around them."

Hawk's eyes narrowed. "What are you talking about?"

"Don't worry about it," Micah replied, deciding the fewer people who knew his plans the better. "Now, tell me exactly where we are in the investigations into the murders."

It was a little over an hour later when Hawk and Micah finally left the cabin. They moved silently through the forest until they reached the place where they normally met to speak to one another.

"Are you heading back to the safe house?" Hawk asked.

"No. I'm heading into town. It's relatively early and Samuel should be in the middle of one of his nightly brainwashing sessions," Micah replied.

He needed action. A restless adrenaline surged up inside him. He needed to do something to break this all wide open. For Olivia. For Darcy. And for every vulnerable person in Cold Plains and the entire state of Wyoming or wherever Samuel might decide to set up a new kingdom.

"Don't do anything stupid," Hawk said softly. "We still need you alive and working on our side of this thing. You're a vital piece of this operation."

"Trust me, I plan on being around until the bitter end. I'll check in with you tomorrow," Micah said as he turned and headed toward town.

He knew that almost every night at eight o'clock Samuel gave his seminars and demanded that most of the townspeople attended. If anyone was going to get inside Samuel's house and explore, the best time would be during the seminars when Samuel was busy "teaching" his flock.

Micah had no intention of trying to get inside tonight. He'd need the right equipment to play spider and get up to the balcony. He didn't have time to get the hook and rope he'd use from the safe house and then return to town and take care of business before Samuel ended his nightly meeting.

Tonight was strictly a reconnaissance mission, to see the lay of the land around his brother's house and find out how many guards were on the place.

Although he'd been in the area almost two weeks, he had stayed away from Samuel's home, instead focusing on checking out the Community Center and learning the positions and names of all the players in this deadly game.

It was difficult to be thrust into the middle of an operation where you couldn't be sure who to trust, where the enemy could come at you with a smiling face and a knife tucked behind his back.

He'd had months of catch-up to accomplish, thanks to the bullet to his head. But now he was ready to truly begin the hunt, both for the missing children and the key to bringing down Samuel's kingdom.

As he headed into Cold Plains, his thoughts went to the victims that they were certain had been killed by Samuel or at the very least at his bidding.

Shelby Jackson had been found five years ago in Gully, Wyoming, a mere five miles away from Cold Plains. She'd been twenty-nine, single and rumored to have been dating Samuel at the time of her disappearance. Hers had been a cold case until the other victims had begun showing up.

The second victim was the Jane Doe that Darcy suspected might be her long-lost mother. Her body had been found four years ago and she'd had a tiny temporary black *D* written with a Sharpie pen on her right hip. It was possible she'd been attempting to pull herself off as a Devotee without getting the actual tattoo, perhaps working undercover.

Victim number three had been Laurel Pierce, found three years ago. She'd been dating Jonathon Miller, a personal trainer at Cold Plains Fitness, which was owned by Samuel. Miller had been cleared of any connection with her death.

Abby Michaels had been a new teacher's aide at Cold Plains Day Care Center, the mother of the missing

Devin. Her body had been found in the Laramie area, fifty miles away from Cold Plains, a few days before the fifth body was found.

And finally there was Johanna Tate, found on April 2, almost six months ago. It had been the report of her body being found that he'd watched in that coffee shop in Kansas, along with a fresh-faced reporter indicating that her body was one of five all tied to the small town of Cold Plains and a man named Samuel Grayson.

In the moments immediately following the newscast, a myriad of emotions had crashed through Micah. A grief like he'd never known before, coupled with a killing rage directed at his brother, nearly brought him to his knees.

He'd paid for his coffee, stepped out of the coffee shop and had immediately put in a call to the FBI, deciding at that moment that he would join their fight to bring down the brother who he knew was evil at his very core.

It had taken only hours before Micah got a call from Hawk Bledsoe, the agent in charge of the investigation. They had planned a place and a time to meet the next day. And that night Micah had gotten into his car to drive to a café for some supper and before he could start his car engine, Dax had appeared at the side of his car.

"Your brother says hello," he'd said as he'd shot Micah through the head.

Micah stopped in his tracks, drawing a series of deep steadying breaths as he fought against the memories of the past. He'd had no idea how Samuel had found him in that small town. According to the doctors and nurses it had been nothing short of a miracle that he'd survived the gunshot at all, especially without any signs of brain damage.

There was nothing he could do now about the months he'd lost in the coma. There was also nothing that could be done to save Johanna. All he wanted now was to somehow save Olivia by finding her son and in the process get whatever information he could to see to it that Samuel was destroyed.

As usual when he entered the town, he moved through the backyards of houses, using trees and brush and whatever else was available to hide his presence.

When he got close enough to the Community Center, he moved closer to the street where he saw cars and trucks parked in front, attesting to the fact that Samuel's nightly gathering was still ongoing.

A slight nausea welled up inside him as he thought of Samuel preaching to his flock, filling their heads with the kind of cult programming that stole away the ability to think for oneself. If he listened carefully, it was possible he would hear chanting coming from the building, the chanting by rote that altered the way people viewed their surroundings, the entire world. Us against them, that was the message Samuel would deliver on a regular basis. Us against the rest of the world. He'd use those words to work on building paranoia and allegiance to his cause.

The still-in-progress meeting would definitely make it easier for Micah to check out his brother's house. Despite the guards he'd been told were always on duty around the mansion, he wanted to get as close as possible to survey the landscape around the structure, to see if getting onto the balcony and in through the sliding glass doors that Olivia had described was a viable option.

Samuel's neighborhood was one of the newer upscale areas that had appeared in the small town. Micah had heard the house next to Samuel's had been built by a successful actress who used the place as a vacation home when she wanted to escape the stress of Hollywood.

Micah wasn't sure who the other neighbor was, but it was a no-brainer that whoever it was was wealthy and influential and had bought into Samuel's fantasy of life in this particular small town.

Thankfully the houses were built on two-acre plots that were covered in trees, making it easy for Micah to keep his cover as he advanced closer to Samuel's place.

He stopped behind a large tree when he had the house in sight. Just as Olivia had said, it was an impressive structure and from his vantage point he could easily see the balcony that ran the length of the place, a balcony that could be reached with a simple grappling hook and rope.

He tensed as he saw a large man with a rifle slung over his shoulder walk around the back of the house. *One of the guards,* Micah thought. He wondered vaguely how Samuel justified armed guards on his home in a town where he professed there wasn't any crime.

The guard looked bored; he walked the perimeter at the rear of the residence without casting a single glance around the area, as if the last thing he expected was any kind of trouble.

Good. Complacent guards were far easier to take out or to get around. Still Micah remained where he was, knowing he needed to keep watch to see who else might make the rounds, see if he could get an exact number of men and how often they made the trek around the structure. He checked the illuminated dial on his watch to note the time.

As he waited, he couldn't help that his thoughts returned to Olivia. Her appearance made her seem fragile, but he knew there had to be a core of steel inside her and he found that as attractive as her aura of vulnerability.

And it wasn't just Olivia who was crawling under his skin, it was Sam, as well. The kid had definitely taken a shine to Micah and he had to admit he found the little boy both fascinating and charming.

He kept telling himself he needed to keep his distance from both her and the kid. He didn't know how to be a partner and he definitely didn't know how to be a father. He was the very last thing she needed in her life.

He was built to be alone and she needed a man who would know what normal was when he saw it. Micah had never known normal. His family had been the poster image for dysfunctional and he would never know if the parenting he and Samuel had endured was ultimately what had created a monster like his brother.

As a second man began to make the trek around the back of the house, Micah instantly recognized him as Dax Roberts. Micah glanced at his watch and realized fifteen minutes had passed since the previous guard had made the rounds.

He settled in to watch for another hour or so, wanting to make sure that the timing of the guards remained about the same. In fifteen minutes Micah could easily be up a rope and onto the balcony without anyone realizing his presence. But he had to be sure of the routine of the guards before he could chance a bold move like that.

The next hour ticked by slowly, but confirmed to Micah that the guards made the rounds every fifteen minutes or so. There appeared to be only two guards, as Dax and the other man alternated trips around the house.

After an hour had passed, Micah felt that he had the information he needed. He waited to leave until Dax had made his pass around the back of the house.

Dax was halfway around when he stopped suddenly and his head snapped in the direction of the trees where Micah hid. Micah froze, scarcely breathing. He knew he hadn't made a sound, but it was as if Dax sensed a presence…a presence that didn't belong.

Micah remained frozen, hoping he blended into the landscape perfectly. There was no way Dax had actually caught sight of him. Maybe he was just doing a general scan of the area, taking his job more seriously than the other guard had done.

Both men were frozen in time, Micah hidden and Dax hunting. Sweat trickled down Micah's back as Dax took a step toward the area where Micah was hidden.

The last thing Micah wanted was a showdown now and instinctively he took a step backward and the crisp snap of a twig beneath his foot cracked in the air.

"Who's there?" Dax's rifle was immediately ready to take aim as he began to run in the general direction of where Micah was standing.

Micah's gun was ready as well, but in an instant all kinds of scenarios flew through his head. The sound of a gunshot would bring more men and there was a possibility that Micah would never make it back to the mountain alive.

At one time he would have taken the chance, he would have shot Dax and to hell with the consequences, but he had the weight of a pair of beautiful green eyes and a promise he'd made to Olivia to consider.

If he died now, who would look for Ethan Conner and Devin Black? The FBI agents were focused on bringing down Samuel, and Micah feared that finding the kids was secondary to their ultimate goal.

Someplace in the very depths of his soul, Micah believed he was Ethan's only chance. It made no sense to feel that way, but he couldn't control what he felt in his heart. And with this thought in mind for the first time in his life, Micah ran from a fight.

He turned and didn't even bother to mask the sound of his escape. He just ran, dodging from tree to tree to avoid a bullet to his back. "Hey!" Dax shouted. "Halt."

Micah did no such thing. He crashed through the trees and then along the back of the houses, heading toward the mountain at the other end of town where he knew the terrain, where he knew he could get lost.

As he raced, he was vaguely aware of the sound of Dax chasing after him. Too much moonlight, Micah thought as he tried to keep himself from becoming a target for the shotgun.

As skilled as Micah was in subterfuge, Dax proved a worthy opponent when it came to hunting. Not only was Dax an issue, but the other guard had apparently joined the game, as well.

Micah breathed shallowly through his nose, his focus solely on getting to the mountain wilderness where hopefully he could lose both of his pursuers. Still, his heart pounded with adrenaline as he jigged and jagged through yards, around houses and behind sheds. He jumped fences and crashed through bushes, ignoring barking dogs and the flash of backyard lights blinking on.

He'd just managed to reach the woods when Dax's voice rang out from far too close behind him. "Stop or I'll shoot."

Micah felt the rifle pointed at his back and he knew Dax wouldn't have a problem pulling the trigger. The only thing he had going for him was an element of surprise. Hopefully he could use that to his advantage.

He stopped and slowly raised his hands above his head as if in surrender and then turned to face Dax. In the bright moonlight that spilled down, he saw Dax's face blanch of color and for just a moment the rifle in his hands dipped toward the ground.

Micah sprang sideways, throwing his body down to the ground and into the brush. He rolled as far as possible before rising back to his feet and running.

He'd only gained a few seconds' lead, but it was enough to momentarily lose Dax. He knew that if he ran to the left he'd be taking Dax in the general direction of the safe house. If he ran straight ahead he would eventually wind up on the cliff with no way to escape. The only choice he had was to veer right and hope he could somehow lose the man he knew would kill him if he got the opportunity.

He ran as fast as he could for several minutes given the darkness and the terrain and then stopped, slowed his breathing and listened.

He heard a faint crunch of leaves to the left of him and knew that a true cat-and-mouse game had begun.

He had two objectives. If he couldn't lose his hunters, then he could at least lead them far away from the direction of the safe house. His second objective was to find a hiding place so good, they'd eventually give up looking for him and head back to town to report to Samuel.

The moonlight created dancing shadows among the trees, and every nerve in Micah's body was on edge as he tried to move as silently as possible while keeping alert to any imminent danger.

He knew there were at least two of them and there was no way of knowing if they'd radioed for any backup. There was a strong possibility that, within minutes, the forest would be swarming with men all with one single goal in mind—to kill Micah.

And Micah didn't dare try to use his radio to summon backup. The crackle of the radio would alert anyone nearby to his whereabouts. He just couldn't take that chance. He was on his own.

He threw himself to the side, his heart skipping a beat as the rifle cracked and a piece of bark chipped off a tree nearby. His heart pumped as fast as his thoughts while his gaze darted first one direction and then the other, seeking escape.

Funny, he'd never thought much about self-survival before this moment. Throughout his years as a mercenary, he'd taken dangerous risks, aware that the outcome might ultimately be his death and that had never bothered him before.

But now he had Olivia and Sam to think about. He had two little children missing from their parents who needed him to find them. He had a niece he had just met, a young woman he already admired and would like to get to know better.

For the first time in his life he felt as if he had people depending on him, a reason for being and all he wanted to do was get out of this forest alive.

Chapter 7

Olivia awoke, her heart banging hard in her chest from the nightmare that had just jerked her from her sleep. In the dream Samuel had been chasing Ethan down the street as the little boy ran for the safety of her outstretched arms.

In the dream she'd been frozen in place, unable to do anything to help Ethan as he ran. Samuel streaked after him, his features twisted into the image of a horrendous monster.

"Run," she'd cried to her son, her heart crashing against her ribs as she fought to break the spell that held her motionless. "Run, Ethan, run to Mommy!"

She now drew a deep breath and released it slowly to calm the frantic beat of her heart. The worst part was that she'd awakened just before Ethan's little body had slammed into hers, just before she'd been able to wrap him in her arms and smell the scent of him, feel the sweet warmth of him.

Sliding her legs over the side of the bed, she decided going back to sleep would be impossible for a while. She still tasted the terror of Samuel on her tongue, still felt the weight of despair of not being able to grab Ethan away from him deep in her heart.

She threaded her fingers through her hair to smooth any sleep tangles as she made her way to the door. Maybe a cup of hot tea would soothe away the residual tang of terror, the overwhelming sense of loss that still lingered in her soul.

She opened the door, taking one step out into the hallway, and came face-to-face with Micah. It was obvious he'd just come in from the forest. Wildness was not only the scent he wore, but also what radiated from his eyes, the wildness of a man pumped up on sheer adrenaline.

"What happened?" she asked, tension instantly flooding through her.

"Nothing. Everything is fine." His words were clipped, his voice deeper than usual.

"You don't look fine. You look like you're about ready to jump out of your skin," she replied.

He stared at her for a long moment and then grabbed her by the wrist, pulled her back into her room and shut the door behind him with his foot.

She barely released a gasp as he backed her against the stone wall, leaned into her and took her mouth in a searing kiss that buckled her knees and sent her senses reeling.

The intimate contact against her let her know that he was erect and someplace in the back of her mind she knew she should push against him, halt the kiss and step away. This was dangerous.... He was dangerous, but it was a danger that called to her.

His mouth was hot and hungry against hers, as if he'd lost all control and although she had no idea what had happened to him outside tonight, his obvious need stoked a flame inside her that she allowed not just to burn slightly, but to completely explode.

She yielded to him, raising her arms and locking them around his neck as she pulled herself more tightly against him. She had no idea what had happened, could scarcely process what was happening at this very moment, but she knew whatever it was, she was going to encourage it to continue.

He finally tore his mouth from hers and leaned back, staring into her eyes as if seeking an answer to an unspoken question. The wildness was still there in the green depths of his eyes, but there was also a hint of desperate need and it was that emotion that drew her in.

She dropped her arms from around his neck and stepped back from him. His glittering eyes went flat, as if he knew he had overstepped boundaries and was now prepared for the consequences.

When she grabbed his wrist and tugged him toward the bed, his eyes glittered once again, this time with a flame that nearly stole her breath away.

Once they stood next to the bed she pulled her T-shirt over her head, just to make sure he understood her intentions. For a moment he appeared to be mesmerized by the sight of her in her plain white bra and jeans.

As he remained planted in place, she wondered if perhaps she'd misread the situation, taken it further than he'd intended for it to go. But as that thought fully formed in her mind, he pulled the long-sleeved black shirt he wore over the top of his head and tossed it to the floor.

If the kiss had simmered a flame inside her, the sight of his naked, hard-muscled chest shot desire like a wildfire through her veins. The flickering oil lamp played on the planes and contours of his bronze skin and with their gazes locked, he kicked off his shoes as his fingers went to the button of his black jeans.

This time she was the one who remained frozen in place as he took off his jeans, leaving him clad in a pair of briefs that did nothing to hide the extent of his arousal.

As he gazed at her, the wildness was still in his eyes and the energy that rolled off him filled the room, filled her. It was like being caged with a slightly dangerous animal, only she had no desire to escape, no desire to run from him.

Instead she took off her own shoes and then removed her jeans, leaving her in her bra and a pink pair of bikini panties he'd picked up for her when he'd gone into her house.

A tremble began deep inside her as he advanced toward her, his eyes gleaming with intent, with a hunger that felt as if he'd already touched every inch of her body.

When he reached her, he wrapped her in his arms and kissed her once again; she tasted his wildness in the kiss and she responded with an abandon of her own.

They fell on the bed, his mouth not leaving hers as he rolled so that she was beneath him. She knew this wasn't about lovemaking, but it didn't matter. It was about human connection, about the need to confirm that despite the chaos that surrounded them, they were both okay and still very much alive.

Still, when his lips finally left hers, he tenderly stroked her face as his eyes glittered down at her. "I want you." The words were stark, without any real emotion.

She had no idea what had happened to him tonight, but once again, despite the flatness of his tone, she sensed a need in him and it called to the same kind of emotion inside her. "You have me," she replied.

His eyes flared and he leaned to one side, allowing him to stroke down her neck, across her delicate collarbones and then capture one of her breasts through the material of her bra. Even through the cotton she could feel the heat of his touch and her nipple hardened in response.

She closed her eyes and gave herself to the sensations of his body next to hers and his hand touching her breast. It had been so long since she'd felt the quickening of her own breath with desire, the accelerated beat of her heart with sweet anticipation.

He reached behind her and unfastened her bra, then plucked it off her and tossed it to the floor at the side of the bed. His mouth replaced his hand, sucking in her bare, erect nipple and rolling it with his tongue.

A gasp of sheer pleasure escaped her lips as she grabbed hold of his hair in an effort to pull him closer... closer still. As he licked and teased first one nipple and then the other, his hands worked to remove her panties and when he got them partway down her thighs, she did the rest, removing them so that she was completely naked to him.

Within minutes he had taken off his briefs and their

touches, their caresses grew more intimate. As he moved his fingers against the center of her, she arched up to meet him as she felt the rising tension that begged to be released.

When the release came it washed over her in wave after wave, as she weakly clung to his shoulders and cried out his name.

He gave her no time to breathe, but instead took complete possession of her, sliding into her with a deep thrust. He took her hard and fast, as if exorcizing inner demons, but she didn't care. She met him thrust for thrust, releasing all her pent-up rage at Samuel, despair over Ethan and passion that Micah stirred inside her.

As the tension once again buoyed up inside her and he increased the speed of his strokes, she saw in the flickering light of the oil lamp the taut cords in his neck, the lack of control in his eyes. A second climax shuddered through her and at the same time he found his release, gasping hoarsely against her neck and then rolling from her and collapsing by her side.

For several long moments the only sound was the echo of their breathing as they waited for their heartbeats to return to normal, as they waited for their bodies to calm after the storm they'd just shared.

She finally turned over to face him, her body still tingling from his touch. "What happened to you tonight?" she asked, instinctively knowing that what had just occurred had been prompted by something.

"I just took you like a beast without any thought of birth control or anything else and you're wondering what happened to me tonight?" One of his dark brows raised as tension once again possessed his features.

"I'm on birth control shots and had my last one

less than a month ago. You don't have to worry about that. As far as you taking me like a beast, I was right there with you. No complaints from this very satisfied woman." She offered him a smile, hoping to erase some of the strain that showed on his handsome face.

He rolled over on his back and released a deep sigh. "I overplayed my hand tonight."

She leaned up on one elbow. "What do you mean?"

As he told her about scoping out Samuel's house, about being seen by Dax Roberts, fear for Micah shot through her, forcing her to recognize the growing feelings she had for him.

"I managed to lead Dax and one of the other henchmen toward the far side of the mountain and finally I lost them and came back here."

She knew there was a lot he wasn't telling her, that the chase through the forest hadn't been as easy as he'd related. She scooted closer to him as if by her close presence she could somehow protect him from the dangers outside of this room, outside of the cave.

He wrapped an arm around her and pulled her against his side. "The whole time I was running, all I could think about was that I'd made a promise to you and I had to stay alive in order to fulfill that promise," he said softly. "It's what kept me moving, what kept me from engaging into a fight."

Olivia's heart squeezed tight in her chest. "Then I'm grateful that you made me that promise," she replied, her voice thick with emotion.

"He nearly killed you before, Micah. I'm sure Dax Roberts would love to complete the job he thought he'd already done. Forget the promise you made to me. Don't go into town anymore. Leave it all to somebody else.

Hopefully the FBI working this case can find Ethan and bring him home to me."

He frowned. "I don't make promises often, but when I do, I never break them."

She reached up and stroked a hand across his furrowed forehead. "Then I release you from this one." As much as she wanted her son back, as much as she needed Ethan in her arms once again, she couldn't allow Micah to risk his own life to accomplish that feat. She moved her hand and placed it on his heart. The beat was steady and strong. "I'm afraid for you, Micah."

He covered her hand with his own. "There's no reason to be afraid. The only thing that's really changed is that now my brother knows I'm still alive."

And it was those very words that shot a shiver of fear straight through Olivia's heart.

"What is so damned important that you had to get me out of bed?" Samuel asked as he belted his silk robe more tightly around his waist. He stared at Dax Roberts who stood before him in Samuel's great room.

Dax Roberts wasn't a huge man, but he had the flat eyes of a cold-blooded snake and carried himself with an aura of suspended danger ready to break loose. Samuel knew just how dangerous Dax could be, but he'd never feared the man. Dax knew he belonged to Samuel and the man would be a fool to bite the hand that fed him, and fed him very well.

At the moment Dax's gaze refused to meet Samuel's and a hard pit of tension formed in Samuel's stomach. This could only be bad news, otherwise there was no way Dax would have awakened him in the middle of the night.

"What's happened? Spit it out, man." Impatience made the words snap from Samuel.

Finally Dax's black gaze rose to meet his. "We caught somebody skulking around the house while you were in the middle of your seminar."

"And?" The idea that somebody had been sneaking around the house didn't particularly bother Samuel. He knew the FBI were prowling around the whole town and it certainly wasn't a surprise that they would have agents slinking around his house. After all, he was their biggest target. Fortunately, they had no legal reason to get inside. That was the thing about law enforcement agencies…they had to play by the rules, but he didn't.

"And me and Larry chased him up into the mountain but we eventually lost him." Dax's eyes narrowed, as if affronted by his own failure to capture the intruder.

"And why is this important enough to wake me up?" Samuel asked, his irritation growing by the second. A threat that had vanished into the woods in the mountain was no threat now. "Couldn't this all have waited until morning?"

Dax's jaw muscles tightened. "I thought you'd want to know…. It was your brother."

Samuel stared at him, certain he must have misunderstood. "My brother? What are you talking about? My brother is dead. You killed him."

Dax frowned and his gaze shot to the floor at Samuel's feet. "Apparently he has nine lives."

The small pit of tension that had coiled in Samuel's stomach swelled outward, filling his chest with a barely contained rage. "Are you positive that's who it was?"

Dax gave a curt nod of his head. "It was him, there

was no question. I got a good look at him in the moon-light."

"So, it would seem you didn't do the job I sent you to do," Samuel said, his anger just barely controlled. Dax was lucky, for if Samuel had had his gun in his hand at the moment, Dax would be dead.

"I swear, I shot him almost point blank in the side of his head. He should be a dead man." Dax took a step backward, as if fearing the reprisal of the unsuccessful job.

Samuel balled his hands into fists at his side. "It appears you didn't complete your job. I don't like half-ass work, Dax. I expected better than that from you." Dax's eyes went flatter and the muscles in his jaw tightened. "Get out of here and don't talk to me again until the job is done correctly," Samuel said with disdain.

Dax wasted no time leaving the room. A moment later Samuel heard the sound of his front door opening and closing and it was only then Samuel allowed his rage to explode. He grabbed a nearby vase and hurled it at the fireplace, finding no relief in the splintering of glass.

Micah.

Micah was alive.

He stalked to the sliding glass doors and pulled one open, then stepped out onto the balcony and pulled his robe around him again against the cold night air. His gaze shot in the direction of the mountain looming high above in the night sky.

Someplace on that mountain the brother he thought was dead was not only breathing and alive, but was obviously actively working against him.

Samuel had spent years becoming the man he'd

become, building the skills necessary to take a small town and make it his own. He hadn't feared the fists of his father, he'd had only disgust for the woman who'd been his mother. But he'd hated the simple existence of Micah since he'd been a young boy.

He'd always felt like Micah saw through his carefully constructed facade, that somehow the fraternal twin that had shared their mother's womb with him was more like him than either of them wanted to admit.

Therefore he'd always seen Micah as a threat to all that Samuel wanted to accomplish, a potential obstacle that had to be removed.

He'd thought that had been accomplished. He'd thought Dax had taken care of the problem months ago. First thing in the morning he'd tell his men to be on the alert for Micah. He'd make sure they all knew there was a healthy bounty on Micah's head. And hopefully by this time tomorrow he'd have the body of his dead brother at his feet.

Chapter 8

Darcy awakened before dawn. She could tell it was early because there were no sounds echoing through the cave walls, no scent of early morning coffee to indicate that morning had arrived.

She leaned over to reach her wristwatch on the table by the bed and checked the time in the light from the flickering glow of the oil lamp. Just before five. June would be up within an hour or so. Most of the house came alive between six and seven.

She picked up the sheet of paper on the table and stared at the artist rendering of the victim still called Jane Doe. The woman's bright blue eyes stared back at her and long blond hair fell in soft waves down to her shoulders.

Jane Doe. Was this woman her mother? Darcy had gotten the copy of the picture from Deputy Ford McCall two days ago, but until now she'd been oddly reluctant to show it to Micah.

She desperately wanted an answer and yet was afraid of the answer she might get from him. She knew that if he recognized the woman from his hometown of Horn's Gulf, if he remembered her name had indeed been Catherine George, then that meant she was probably Darcy's birth mother and there would never be the reunion between the two that Darcy had hungered for.

She leaned back on the bed and stared at the dancing shadows on the ceiling. She didn't want her mother to be dead, killed by either Samuel Grayson or one of his henchmen. She squeezed her eyes tightly closed for a long minute, willing away the sudden press of tears.

She wanted the opportunity to embrace her mother, to ask questions that couldn't be answered by anyone else. She wanted to know all the reasons her mother had chosen to leave her behind. She needed to know if her mother had thought about her each and every day.

She wanted to see if her laughter mirrored that of her mother's, if they had the same slender fingers. She wanted to feel the connection to the woman who had given her life and then had left her in the care of another for safety's sake.

Louise Craven had been a kind and loving woman. She'd raised Darcy to have high morals and to be independent and strong. She wanted to have the opportunity to show her mother who she had become, that she was somebody to be proud of.

Darcy had become close to both Deputy Ford McCall and his fiancée, Gemma Johnson. Gemma had nearly been sucked into Samuel's control when she'd come to town after being beaten by her ex-husband, a brutal man who had eventually wound up murdered.

Like Olivia, Samuel had attempted to take the broken and wounded Gemma under his wing, but ultimately Gemma had fallen in love with Ford and been saved from Samuel and the cult.

Darcy knew how committed Ford was to finding out the identity of the Jane Doe, despite the fact that Chief of Police Bo Fargo had told him to lay off. The last thing Bo Fargo wanted was the identification of another woman definitely tied to his boss, Samuel. Still, Darcy had found solace both in Ford's undeterred commitment to give a dead woman a name and in Gemma's friendship.

She'd also found solace in Rafe's arms. It was hard for her to believe that in the evil town of Cold Plains she'd managed to find a good man with a good heart who loved her as deeply as she loved him. But Rafe would never be truly happy until he got his son Devin back. It was a missing piece of his heart that Darcy couldn't fill.

Darcy was reminded of Rafe's loss each time she saw Olivia, who feared for her own missing child. Darcy's heart ached for both of them, the man she loved and the woman she now called friend. She knew what it felt like to have a missing mother, but she couldn't imagine the torture of having a missing child.

Two weeks ago she'd been working as a receptionist in Rafe's doctor's office and spending her nights next to him in his bed. But Rafe had felt things beginning to unravel in town, had sensed that danger was getting greater and greater and in a burst of macho protectiveness had insisted she come and stay here in the safe house. But that didn't stop her from occasionally sneaking back into town to spend a couple hours in Rafe's arms.

His biggest fear had been that somehow Samuel would recognize her as his daughter and use the information in some negative way to hurt her. Samuel had already shown the fact that family meant nothing to him when he'd sent a man to kill his own brother. If what Darcy believed was true, it was possible Samuel had killed her mother. What would he do if he knew she was his daughter?

Rafe had said that he would explain her absence by telling people Darcy had left town. As far as anyone knew she had no ties to Cold Plains, had simply drifted into town months earlier. There was no reason for anyone to believe she might stick around.

She missed Rafe desperately during the time they were apart, needed his arms around her when she showed Micah the picture of Jane Doe. But he was on a hunt for his son and she knew by agreeing to spend most of her time here, she'd relieved his mind as far as her own safety was concerned.

Darcy got out of bed, recognizing that going back to sleep wasn't an option. She might as well hit the shower, dress and start the morning coffee.

As she left her room she wondered how this would all end? Would Rafe find the son he believed belonged to him? Would the FBI ever be able to get the evidence they needed to finally put Samuel behind bars?

Finally, was her mother alive and well or was she the Jane Doe in the picture? Killed by one of Samuel's men and buried a hundred miles away from Cold Plains?

Micah reluctantly escaped Olivia's bed at dawn and left the room, his head still dizzied with the scent of her, the warmth of her. He would have liked to stay and make love to her again, this time with tenderness and caring instead of the adrenaline-pumped possession of the night before.

He would have liked to linger in bed, watch her wake up and then show her that he could be a different kind of lover than he'd been previously.

But he had to meet with Hawk. He had to tell the man that Micah's presence here was no longer a secret to his brother. Leaving Olivia sleeping, he grabbed his clothes from the floor and went to the bathroom where he washed up and then went into the small room he called his own. He changed into a clean pair of camo pants and a long-sleeved matching shirt and then left the room. He saw nobody in the kitchen as he passed through but noticed that the coffee was already made. Somebody besides him had crawled out of bed unusually early.

Once outside the predawn air was cold, portending of the winter to come. Winter in the mountains would be harsh and make things a hundred times more difficult for the people in the safe house. Travel would be difficult and footprints were easily followed in the snow. He hoped to hell they would all be out of here by then.

Within minutes he didn't feel the cold as he hurried through the woods toward his meeting place with Hawk. He'd radioed Hawk a few minutes before to set up the encounter.

They occasionally met later in the morning to exchange any news that might be pertinent to the case. But Micah still felt the rush of the chase last night, the concern that now his brother had the knowledge that he'd survived the attack from months earlier.

When he reached the fallen tree where he and Hawk always met, he sat on the trunk, thinking about the night before. It had felt as if the chase through the woods had taken hours…days. Several times Dax and his partner had gotten close enough to fire shots, barely missing Micah as he led the two farther and farther away from the safe house location.

When he'd finally lost them and felt safe enough to double back to the safe house he'd still been pumped up, topped off with an adrenaline rush that had him half-wild. And what had he done? Grabbed Olivia, pulled her into her room and shoved her up against the wall like some crazed animal thinking only of his own needs.

And he'd needed to rid himself of the wildness, had needed to release the adrenaline. He frowned as he realized he'd also needed…he'd wanted Olivia. And she'd willingly accepted him, met him thrust for frantic thrust, as if the madness that had momentarily gripped him had been contagious.

The whole thing bothered him, but what bothered him more than anything was the question of when he'd come to a place where he needed anyone? When had it happened that he felt he needed Olivia?

After they'd made love, he'd stayed with her, pulling her tight against him as they both had fallen into an exhausted sleep. When he'd awakened this morning she'd still been sleeping and he'd spent far too long watching the play of the oil lantern glow on her features.

The scent of her had clung to his skin as he'd left her bed without awakening her. The scent, coupled with the memory of how she'd accepted him so easily into her bed, how she'd stroked his forehead as he'd told her about what had happened in Cold Plains, had made him feel for the first time in his life that he wasn't alone.

And for all of his life, Micah had been alone. He hadn't had a family to bond with, nor had he gotten close to any of the men he'd served with while he was a Navy SEAL. As a mercenary, being close to anyone, trusting anyone, was definitely a liability.

This thing with Olivia was like nothing he'd experienced before. He hadn't wanted to leave her this morning; already he looked forward to returning to the safe house just to see her face, watch that beautiful smile curve the lips that drove him half-mad with desire.

He even liked spending time with Sam, who made him laugh with his childish antics and obviously had taken a real shine to Micah, insisting that Micah pick him up whenever they were in the same room.

He frowned and shifted positions as he wondered what was taking Hawk so long. He didn't want to think about Olivia and Sam. Last night should have never happened. Making love to Olivia had definitely been a mistake. She and Sam were complications in the life he'd chosen for himself, people who had no idea that he had nothing real to offer them long-term.

As he heard a faint rustle of leaves, he jumped up, gun drawn and then relaxed as Hawk came into view. Hawk looked like he'd just climbed out of bed, but although his sandy blond hair was askew, his brown eyes were alert and curious.

"A little early for a meet. What's up?" he asked.

"I'm no longer the FBI's dirty little secret," Micah replied.

Even in the tiny beam from his flashlight, Micah saw the frown that creased Hawk's brow. "What are you talking about?"

"I was doing a little lurking around Samuel's house last night and I was seen by the two guards. They chased me up the mountain for probably an hour or so before I finally managed to lose them."

"What makes you think either of them recognized you? I mean, when you're all cleaned and spit polished you might look like your brother, but right now I'd think it would be hard for anyone to see a resemblance."

"Unfortunately, one of the men chasing me was the same one who put the bullet into my head almost six months ago," Micah replied.

"Dax Roberts?" Micah nodded while Hawk shook his head. "That one is a particularly nasty piece of work."

Micah fought the impulse to reach up and touch his scar. "Trust me, I know."

"Are you sure he recognized you?"

"Positive. He had a rifle pointed right at my chest and if it hadn't been for a moment of his stunned surprise at seeing me alive and well, he would have put a second bullet into my body. Thankfully I used his surprise to my advantage and dropped and rolled to avoid being shot. I figure within an hour of him losing me in the forest he informed Samuel that I'm still alive."

"I'd hate to be Dax right now," Hawk said drily. "I'll bet Samuel tore him a new one."

"Samuel doesn't accept failure well from those around him. It's possible Dax's body will turn up someplace far away from here and there will be a bullet in the back of his head."

"My recommendation to you is to lie low for the next couple days…maybe the next week. If Samuel knows you're alive, you'll be a number one priority to him and his henchmen. I'm sure he'll make his men understand that whoever brings you down will be well compensated." Hawk clapped Micah on his back. "You have now become a major liability, my friend, and you need to remove yourself."

"What about Olivia's son…Rafe's little boy? If I take myself out of this, who is going to hunt for them?"

"You know we're doing everything we can to find them," Hawk replied.

"It isn't good enough," Micah replied in frustration. "Each day that passes, the risk of those kids being whisked out of town increases and I'm afraid that once they leave Cold Plains, nobody will ever see them again." He thought of Olivia, who had been so strong through all of this.

"How's Carly?" he asked suddenly, an attempt to make Hawk think about family.

Immediately Hawk's features softened. "She's good. When this is all over and done, I'm hoping we can build a family here working her father's dairy farm."

Hawk and Carly had been romantically involved years before and then Hawk had left town and Carly had gone undercover to help save her sister who had become a cult member. In helping Carly save her sister Mia, he and Carly had rekindled their love for each other, resulting in the two of them having a small wedding with a deprogrammed Mia in attendance.

"We've just got to get this mission done," Micah said, his voice forceful with pent-up emotion. "Each moment that goes by, another person is put at risk, Samuel grows stronger instead of weaker. Somehow, some-way, we've got to figure out how to take him down."

"I know, we all know," Hawk replied. "And we're working to that end. But we're both aware of the fact that your brother has been very smart." Hawk took a step backward and turned off his flashlight. The morning sun was starting to rise, creating a faint dawn light. "The best thing you can do right now is stay out of the line of fire. Sit tight at the safe house and let us take care of things from here. Seriously, man, you're important to this mission and we can't afford to lose you."

Micah didn't reply. He had no idea why the FBI would think him so valuable to their mission. So far he felt like he'd been little help to the men who were attempting to build a case against Samuel.

"I'm serious, Micah, sit tight in the safe house and if things go bad there, the only place you'd be safe is the Pierce ranch," Hawk said.

"The Pierce ranch?" Micah looked at him in confusion. This was the first time he'd heard of the place.

"Nathan Pierce has a big spread on the outskirts of town. He lives there with his fiancée and a handful of people. It was Nathan's father, Evan, who sold Samuel Grayson the property where the creek is rumored to hold mystical healing powers, the place that ultimately became the cornerstone of Samuel's power."

"So why would I go there if things get bad?" Micah asked.

"Because none of them have bought into Samuel's teachings. The cult tried to kidnap Nathan's fiancée, Susannah, and the family fought back. They're solid in their hatred of the cult. They stay out of town as much as possible and mind their own business, but Nathan has made it clear that he can be trusted."

Micah stared at Hawk for several long moments. "You have some sort of information that the safe house location has been compromised?"

"No, nothing like that," Hawk replied quickly. "I'm just thinking that Samuel always saw you as a threat and wanted you taken out of the picture before you could hook up with the FBI. Now that he knows you're alive and here, he might push things. He might turn up the heat on finding the safe house. Let's hope if he gets frantic enough that he'll also get sloppy." Hawk shoved his hands in his pockets and reared back on his heels. "I just have a feeling that things are about to explode apart."

"They can't explode apart until we find those kids," Micah said firmly.

Hawk pulled his hands from his pocket. "Just stay put and leave that to us," he said, a hint of authority in his deep voice.

"I got it," Micah replied easily.

"Good, then I'll check in with you in the next day or so and let you know how things are going," Hawk replied. The two men said their goodbyes and Micah watched Hawk disappear the way he had come.

Micah returned to the fallen tree and once again sat, his thoughts racing. Hawk's "order" for him to stay at the safe house and out of the line of fire meant nothing to him. Micah didn't work for the FBI and he didn't take his orders from any of them.

He still didn't know why Hawk would be concerned about his safety. Sure, they had been working together as best they could, but Micah was no big piece to this puzzle. He probably knew less about his brother than the men holed up in the cabin, the agents who had probably studied every area of Samuel's life for the past five years.

Micah would lie low for a night or two, but he wasn't about to take himself out of the game. This wasn't just another job for Micah. This was a personal mission of retribution.

The moment he'd heard about Johanna's murder, he'd vowed vengeance and now it wasn't Johanna's light brown eyes that haunted him, but rather Olivia's sad green ones.

He couldn't take himself out of the game, not until he brought Ethan back to his mother's loving arms, not until he knew for sure that Samuel would never, ever hurt anyone else again.

With dawn fully breaking across the eastern sky, he headed back to the safe house, wondering what, if any, information Hawk had that he might not be sharing.

He'd said he felt as if things were about to explode apart, but, according to what Micah had heard, nothing had changed. The FBI had yet to be able to tie Samuel directly to the murdered women or any of the other dead and missing people from the small town.

They'd had almost six months to build a case. Micah had only been in the area three weeks and he already felt time slipping away too quickly.

How long would it take before the men working the case burned out, grew tired, got sloppy? How long before something bigger or more exciting drew attention and resources away from the little town of Cold Plains?

And although he knew it was crazy, he felt more than

a bit of responsibility for Samuel's sins. He'd known what Samuel was when they were young. He'd seen the cruelty, the signs of severe narcissism and sociopathic tendencies.

He should have told somebody. He should have warned someone that Samuel was capable of doing terrible things. But who would he have told? The father who beat them relentlessly? The mother who was afraid of her own shadow?

Besides, as a young kid he'd believed that if he told anyone and word got back to his father, then his father would beat Micah to death.

As he entered the safe house he carried with him the weight of both guilt and frustration. The first person he saw was Darcy, seated at the table with a cup of coffee before her.

"Good morning," he said. "You're up early."

"I woke up early and couldn't go back to sleep. I checked to see if you were in your room, but you were already gone."

He turned to look at her as he poured himself a cup of coffee. "You wanted to talk to me?" He moved to the table and sat across from her.

She looked unusually pale, her eyes filled with obvious anxiety as she nodded. "I have the picture of Jane Doe. I want to see if you recognize her." She pulled a folded piece of paper from her pocket, but seemed reluctant to push it across the table to him.

Micah knew the nervousness that had to be flooding through her. If he recognized the woman in the picture, then there was a strong possibility that it was Darcy's mother and she was dead. With a definite name, Ford

McCall could check out the background of the victim and determine for sure if she was Darcy's mother.

If he didn't recognize the woman, then she was left still wondering, still hoping for a reunion with a woman she didn't remember, but desperately needed in her life.

She finally laid the folded paper in the center of the table and he couldn't help but notice that her long, slender fingers trembled slightly.

He reached out and pulled it toward him, his heart hurting for the woman he now knew was his niece. Samuel was her father and that made it all the more important that she find out something good about her mother. She took a quick sip of her coffee as he unfolded the picture and stared down at it.

The blue eyes of the woman on the paper were definitely Darcy's eyes and Micah knew he'd seen the woman before, although it had been many years before.

He frowned, remembering who Darcy had reminded him of in the first moment of seeing her. "I remember her. She wasn't around town for long, but she was so pretty and I remember her being swept into Samuel's sphere." He looked at Darcy, hating the news he was about to deliver. "Catherine. That's definitely Catherine George."

He looked up from the picture to see tears welling up in Darcy's eyes. "She's my mother," she said as she tried to swipe at the tears that trekked down her cheeks. "He killed my mother and now I'll never have a chance to know her, to spend time with her. He stole her away from me and then he killed her."

"Maybe I'm mistaken," Micah offered, although he knew the odds of that were slim to none. "Maybe your mother is still alive and stashed someplace in Cold Plains."

Darcy shook her head and offered him a sad smile. "You don't really believe that, do you?"

Micah hesitated a moment and then shook his head. "No, but at least with her name, McCall will be able to determine if Catherine George is definitely your mother. Do you want me to contact him?"

She shook her head. "Thanks, but I'll take care of it." She rose from the table and carried her coffee cup to the sink. "I think I'm going to head back to my room and rest for a little while." With another achingly sad smile, she turned and left the kitchen.

Micah tightened his grip on his own cup, a deep ache in his chest. Jane Doe had now been identified, but would that move the investigation any farther along? He doubted it. He knew that Jane Doe's body had been found four years ago, nearly a hundred miles away from Cold Plains.

The only thing that had tied the woman to Cold Plains and Samuel was the small *D* on her right hip. It had not been tattooed on, but rather carefully drawn with a Sharpie pen. They would probably never know why she had worn a fake mark, but the odds were good she was working against the cult and Samuel and for that she had paid with her life.

And it was entirely possible that she'd given birth to Darcy and in a completely unselfish act of sacrifice had given her away so that Samuel would never know of her existence.

As he thought of Darcy's tears, a new burn started in the pit of his stomach. If the FBI thought he was just going to sit tight and hang around here for the remainder of the investigation, they were out of their mind.

He was tired of seeing Samuel's survivors and the pain that had been left behind. This had all gone on long enough and the longer it lasted the more victims there would be.

He'd lie low for tonight, but after that all bets were off. It was time he moved this game forward to some sort of conclusion, and if he didn't survive, at least he'd know he had died trying to destroy the scourge named Samuel.

Chapter 9

Olivia awakened alone in her bed, the scent of Micah lingering in the air, the warmth of him still deep in her heart. She'd slept without dreams, safe and secured by the weight of his arms around her, by the warmth of his bare legs against hers.

Micah.

Her body tingled with the sensations of their love-making. It had been wild and intense and had released some of the tension that had been knotted inside her since the moment she had fled Cold Plains.

But it hadn't been lovemaking, she reminded herself and she'd be a fool to think otherwise. It had been the release of sheer adrenaline, the rush of relief at being alive. It had been all kinds of things created by his wild dash for his life through the forest, but it hadn't been lovemaking.

Not hearing any noise from the nursery yet, she slid

out of the bed and threw on her clothes from the night before. She grabbed a pair of clean jeans and a T-shirt and headed for the bathroom, hoping to get in a quick shower before Sam awoke.

As she stood under the tepid, faint spray of water she tried not to think about the night before and she also tried not to think about her missing child. Both created different but very strong emotions inside her.

She finished her shower and got dressed. She spritzed her favorite perfume and thought of the man who had, in the midst of a covert operation, thought to grab the floral spray that reminded her she was a woman in this place of danger and intrigue.

By that time she heard Sam's good-morning cry coming from the nursery room. She greeted Sam with a forced happy smile as thoughts of Ethan slammed into her chest. As she changed Sam from his pajamas to his clothes for the day, her heart ached.

So many days and nights had now passed since she'd run terrified from the streets of Cold Plains. Did Ethan believe she'd abandoned him? Did he think his mommy had just given him away? Did he believe she'd forgotten all about him?

She shook her head as if to dispel the heartbreaking thoughts. She didn't want to display the piercing sadness inside her for Sam's sake. She didn't want to traumatize him anymore than she thought he already was.

With him in her arms, she mentally prepared herself not only to face another day without Ethan, but also to face Micah again.

The worst thing she could do was read too much into what had happened between them the night before, but she couldn't help that her heart had been touched by him in a way no other man had touched her. She couldn't help but wish for something more than a hot night of sex with him.

But falling in love with Micah Grayson would be just another mistake in a lifetime of bad judgment. He was a mercenary here on a job. Even though he had made a promise to her to help find Ethan, even though he'd come to her bed with fiery passion and need, that didn't mean he felt anything real and lasting for her.

He'd needed somebody last night and she'd just happened to step out of her room at the right time. She had a feeling any woman could have served the purpose he'd needed at that moment.

She was determined not to make another mistake where a man was concerned and she had a feeling loving Micah would be just that. Still, she couldn't help the way her heart jumped in her chest as she entered the kitchen and saw him seated at the table.

"Good morning," she said as she placed Sam in the high chair. "Where is everyone else?"

"Jesse and June are in the garden, Darcy went to her room a while ago and I haven't seen Lacy and her kids yet this morning. Why? Scared to be alone with me?"

She shot him a quick glance, relieved to see a teasing light in his eyes. "Not yet, but the day is still young," she replied with a light tone.

"The day might be young, but I've already met with Hawk and broken Darcy's heart."

She gave Sam a cracker to hold him over until she could make him some breakfast and looked at Micah in surprise. "What did you do to break Darcy's heart?"

She poured herself a cup of coffee and sat at the table

across from him as he told her what had transpired between him and Darcy earlier that morning.

As he told her about identifying the picture of Jane Doe and his suspicion that Catherine George was indeed Darcy's mother, Olivia's heart ached with the young woman's pain. She knew how much Darcy had hoped for some sort of happy reunion with her mother.

"She's contacting Ford to give him Catherine's name and hopefully before too long she will have a definitive answer."

"But you're sure Jane Doe is Darcy's mother."

He nodded, a weariness in his eyes. "I just feel it in my gut. I'm not sure why Catherine returned here after giving up Darcy, but I have a feeling she was either trying to save Samuel from himself or save the other people in town from Samuel."

"It's just so sad," Olivia said. She released a deep sigh. "I'm going to make some scrambled eggs and toast. You want some?" she asked.

"Are you eating?"

"Definitely. I seem to have worked up an appetite sometime during the night." She turned her back on him to grab some eggs and start breakfast, but she felt the heat of his gaze in the center of her back.

"About last night…"

She turned to face him, not wanting to hear any apologies or explanations, not wanting him to somehow take away from what had been a moment of passion in a place least expected.

"Please don't." She held up a hand to stop whatever he was about to say. "Let's not dissect, discuss or even talk about what's already done. And we don't have to get all touchy-feely about sharing emotions. Today is a new day with new challenges and we just need to get to them."

She turned back around and cracked the eggs into a bowl, hoping he took her advice. The truth of the matter was, she didn't want him to say anything that would take away the little bit of magic she'd found in his arms the night before.

Minutes later they sat at the table and laughed when Sam tried to share some of his toast with Micah, practically sticking it into his ear.

"Now that's a sound we don't hear often enough around here," June said as she and Jesse came into the kitchen. June carried a small basket of mixed vegetables and set the basket on the countertop. "That's about the last of the garden. It's getting too cold at night. If we want vegetables, we're going to have to depend on cans from now on."

"I don't want to even think about winter coming," Micah replied. "It would be nice if all of us were gone from here by the time the first snow falls."

Winter. Ethan loved wintertime. Last year during the first significant snowfall of the year, she'd bundled up the two boys in their snowsuits and they'd all gone outside to play. They'd built a snowman and she'd shown them how to make snow angels and then they'd gone back into the house with frozen fingers and toes to warm cocoa with marshmallows.

She could still remember Ethan telling her he was a snow bug as he'd rolled in a ball across the snowy yard. His laughter had accompanied each somersault and the memory caused a lump of emotion to rise up in Olivia's throat.

"What's new?" Jesse asked Micah as he poured himself a cup of coffee and joined them at the table.

As Micah told him about the flight through the forest the night before and the fact that Hawk had told him to stay out of things and let the FBI agents work the case, Olivia watched the play of emotions over Micah's face.

She could tell by the set of his jaw that he had no intention of obeying the FBI's order for him to sit tight. Even though she had no right to tell him what to do or what not to do, she wanted to tell him to listen to what the FBI had told him, to stay here, safe.

She desperately wanted her son back and she wanted Micah safe. Unfortunately, she wasn't at all sure the two were synonymous.

Most days Micah spent much of his time in his quiet little room, lying in the dark and either resting or strategizing for the night to come. But tonight he wasn't leaving the cave and there was no reason for him to isolate himself in his dark, lonely room.

Although there were plenty of people to talk to, to spend time with, he found himself drifting to wherever Olivia and Sam were located in the cave.

They were now seated in the living room area. Sam was on the floor playing with some toys that Jesse had picked up on his last trek into town for supplies.

Micah sat on the opposite end of the sofa from Olivia, but he could smell the floral scent of her perfume and liked the way her green T-shirt made her eyes appear as green as fresh spring grass.

She seemed at ease, but he knew the tumultuous emotions she had to be feeling and it frustrated him that he could do nothing about them.

"What are your plans when you leave here?" he asked, breaking the comfortable silence that had existed between them.

She tucked a strand of her pale blond hair behind her ear and looked at him. "It's hard to see a future right now. I'm just getting through minute by minute, trying not to completely freak out."

"I know." He was surprised by the small stab in his heart for her, for her pain. He'd spent most of his life trying to remain emotionless, but he couldn't succeed in that goal when it came to Olivia. "But eventually Samuel will fall, the children will be returned where they belong and life will go on. You need to be thinking about what happens when you get out of this cave."

She leaned back against the rawhide couch and frowned thoughtfully. "I love this place. The minute I saw the mountains they called to something inside me. I loved the house where we lived that had come to feel like home. Within six months of living in Cold Plains, I was certain it was going to be our home forever. The whole landscape called to something deep in my soul. I love the mountains and streams, the achingly blue skies and the wooded surroundings."

She shrugged. "But, I guess when this is over we'll move on. I have a little money saved up, enough for a two- or three-month start in a new town. I know I won't go back to Oklahoma. Maybe Colorado, where I'll have the mountains again and sparkling streams. I'll find a nice little town and start to rebuild."

"A little town where there's a local drunk and people gossip and bar fights happen on Friday nights?"

She laughed and the sound was like music. "Exactly. No more perfect towns for me. I want a place to live, blemishes and all." Her laughter died and her smile drifted off her lips. "It won't be easy. I'll be the single mother of two small boys with little training or education."

"You'll be fine. You're a strong woman, Olivia, and you're smart, smart enough to make choices that will give you a wonderful life with your sons. I see it in you and you shouldn't be afraid of whatever the future holds."

"The biggest fear I have right now is if I'm ever going to get out of this cave with both my sons," she replied drily. She snapped her mouth closed, as if she didn't want to say anything else.

He was surprised to realize that he thought he knew what she was thinking, that she desperately wanted her son back and she thought he was the man who could accomplish that, but she also didn't want him hurt or dead.

"You shouldn't worry about me," he said in a low voice.

"Why not?" Her gaze held his.

He frowned thoughtfully. "Because I'm not used to having anyone worry about me."

"Then get used to it," she countered. "Whether you like it or not, Micah, I've grown to care about you. You don't have to do anything about it. I don't expect anything in return. It's just there and that's that."

She said it all lightly, and yet the impact it had on his heart was sharp and poignant. So this was what it felt like to know that somebody cared about you? It was like a gift that he wanted to reciprocate, but he knew he shouldn't, he couldn't.

"What about you? What are your plans when this is all over?" she asked, pulling him from his thoughts.

"Are you going back to working for some covert government agency? Sneaking into foreign countries and doing mercenary kind of things?"

He started to answer flippantly, but halted himself and seriously considered her question. "To be perfectly honest, I don't know what comes after this, but I do know it's time to hang up my mercenary missions."

He leaned forward, aware that what he was about to tell her was something he'd scarcely acknowledged to himself. "The bullet in my head changed things for me. I can't trust myself anymore. I can't be truly effective anymore, never knowing if or when one of those migraines might strike."

"What have the doctors said about them?" She leaned forward as well, bringing with her the scent that had the capacity to heat the blood in his veins, make him want to carry her to his bed and claim her as his own one more time.

"They might get worse, they might get better, they could go away altogether." He shrugged. "None of the doctors are sure what will happen in the future. I've managed to put away enough funds that I can take as much time as I need to decide what comes next. Right now I just don't have any idea what that might be. Besides, I quit planning on a future when I was about eight years old and my father beat me so bad I had to miss school for a week."

He saw the jump of sympathy into her eyes and he held up a hand to halt whatever she was about to say. "I don't want your sympathy. I'm just telling you this because it made me the kind of man I am. I don't think too much about tomorrow and I don't think too much of other people."

It was a subtle warning to her not to care about him, not to give him her heart because he wouldn't have any idea what to do with it. His entire life had been about survival, nothing more, nothing less. And even when this was all over here in Cold Plains, unless they managed to round up every single one of Samuel's henchmen and fanatical Devotees, he had a feeling he'd be looking over his shoulder for a very long time to come.

They remained seated in the living room talking about everything and nothing until she got up to put Sam down for his nap.

Micah decided to head back into his own room and grab a nap, as well. The night had been too short and being around Olivia for too long of a time created a well of want inside him that he'd never felt before, that he didn't even want to acknowledge to himself.

It wasn't just desire to have her in his arms again, although that simmered inside him whenever she was near. Rather this was a wistfulness that he'd be able to listen to her laughter for a long time to come, that he'd see Sam grow up, that he'd not only save Ethan but also have the opportunity to get to know the child who had been separated from his mother for far too long.

Foolish thoughts, he told himself as he settled down on the cot in the quiet, dark room. He was born and bred to be alone and he'd only be doing Olivia a disservice if he forgot that fact for a single moment. He cared about her far too much to give her any false hope, to make her believe in any way that there was a future with him.

He fell asleep and awakened with the scent of dinner filling the air, letting him know he'd slept much longer than he'd intended.

The sound of laughter drifted from the kitchen as he

walked toward the room that was the very heart of the safe house. He could easily pick up the sound of Olivia's laughter among the others and he couldn't help the way it threatened to wrap around his heart and tie it captive. He consciously steeled himself against it, against her.

Laughter from any place in the cave was rare, but the moment he walked into the kitchen he saw the source of the merriment. Jesse was whistling an upbeat tune and Sam danced in the middle of the kitchen floor, his diapered butt beneath his little jeans shifting back and forth with each *Saturday Night Fever* move he made.

Olivia sat at the table, laughing so hard tears had sprung to her eyes and June stood at the stove, her face wreathed in a huge grin.

Jesse suddenly stopped his whistle and Sam froze in place, his gaze focused on Jesse. When Jesse began to whistle again Sam started dancing as if nothing had happened, a smile of bliss on his little face.

This caused the women to renew their laughter and Micah grinned at the small tyke who had brought even a little bit of joy to this place.

Sam toddled over to Micah and grabbed his hand, as if inviting him to join him in his dance. "Oh, no, little buddy," Micah replied and swung him up into his arms. "I'm not about to attempt dancing and let these people all laugh at me."

Sam studied him soberly and then threw his arms out, palms up as if to ask a question. "Eton?"

The laughter in the room halted abruptly and Olivia's eyes grew far too shiny with suppressed tears. Micah's heart dropped to his feet as he recognized what the little boy was asking.

"Ethan's not here right now, Sam. Ethan's gone for

now," he said, surprised at the lump that crawled up in the back of his throat as he looked into the little boy's bright eyes. "But he's going to be back very soon."

Sam stared at him for a long moment and then leaned forward and curled into him, placing his little head in the crook of Micah's neck, his breath a butterfly whisper against Micah's skin.

The sweet scent of little boy innocence, coupled with the utter trust Sam displayed as he snuggled tightly into Micah's arms, frightened Micah more than any other experience in his life.

Because he liked it. Because for just a single moment in time, he wanted this…a child who trusted him, a child who respected and loved him.

As Olivia got up and held out her arms to take her son, Micah found himself reluctant to relinquish him. Still, as he did, he made himself a new promise.

He'd abide by the wishes of Hawk and the rest of the FBI agents and lie low for tonight. He knew that Samuel's men would be pounding the pavement, turning over every rock and looking behind every tree for him in the next day or two.

But sooner or later Micah was going to ignore the advice the FBI had given him.

Sooner rather than later, he intended to head back into that town and somehow he would bring Ethan home.

Darcy raced through the dark woods, grateful that night had finally arrived. She'd spent the entire day in her room, needing to be alone, wanting the solitude to mourn the mother she knew in her heart was dead.

Twice June had come to check on her, to see if she

had wanted something to eat, if she needed some company, but each time Darcy had sent the woman away.

There was only one person Darcy wanted to see, needed to see and that was Rafe. And she'd had to wait for the cover of darkness before leaving the safe house to sneak into town.

Even though she still had to contact Ford McCall and let him do whatever he needed to do to confirm not only that Jane Doe was indeed Catherine George but also Darcy's birth mother. Even though she knew it might take a little time to confirm that the dead woman was her mother, Darcy didn't need the confirmation. She felt it in her soul that Catherine George had been the woman who had given her birth and was now dead because of Samuel Grayson.

Her father had killed her mother. How screwed up was that? As she stealthily made her way through the woods, always on the lookout for danger, she knew Rafe would be surprised to see her.

He never liked the idea of her slinking about in a town she'd supposedly left, but her need was far greater than any fear tonight.

As she reached the end of the woods, she surveyed the streets. Samuel would be in the middle of one of his nightly seminars, brainwashing his people, manipulating lives and perhaps plotting another woman's death.

She never forgot that half of her genes came from evil, but Rafe had made her realize she wasn't her father's daughter, that whatever genes of his resided inside her had nothing to do with the kind of woman she'd become.

She had no idea if Rafe would be at the 1930s converted bungalow he used as an office or if perhaps this early in the evening he'd be at the Urgent Care building where he volunteered time in an effort to network and find his missing son's location. Or he could already be home, in the small cottage at the edge of town.

It was in that direction she ran, along the perimeter of town toward the place they'd considered an asylum away from the craziness in Cold Plains.

The lights shining from the cottage were a welcomed sight as she went around to the back door and knocked. If he wasn't here, then she knew where he kept the spare key and she could let herself inside.

She knocked softly and when there was no reply she found the spare key where it was hidden behind one of the shingles and let herself inside.

The first thing she smelled when she walked through the door was the scent of Rafe's cologne, and it smelled like home. She curled up in the corner of the sofa to wait for him.

This is where she belonged, here with Rafe in this little house where they'd found such love for one another. When she'd taken the job as his receptionist, the last thing she'd had in mind was falling in love with her handsome boss, but she had and more amazing was the fact that he loved her back.

And she needed him now, with her grief a bitter taste in her mouth, with her heart broken by the shattering of the dream of a reunion with her mother.

She hadn't been there long when she heard his key in the front door. As he came into the door, his eyes widened at the sight of her. "Darcy, what are you doing here?" He quickly closed and locked the door behind him and then hurried toward her and pulled her up and into his arms.

"You shouldn't come here. You know it's dangerous," he said.

"I had to come. I needed you," she said into the front of his shirt.

He released his hold on her and instead framed her face with his palms so that she was looking at him. "What's wrong? What's happened?"

"Micah identified Jane Doe. Her name is Catherine George and I'm sure she was my mother." As the words left her lips she began to cry.

Rafe led her to the sofa and eased her down and held her until the torrent of tears had finally stopped. When the heartache was momentarily spent, she remained in his arms as he stroked the length of her hair.

"Sooner or later this will be over," he said softly. "We're going to find Devin and then we're all going to go far away from this godforsaken town. We'll find a wonderful place where we can build a life together. Devin and I will be your family and I swear you'll never feel alone again."

She clung tighter to him, hoping that his words would come true, praying that there was a happy ending not just for them but for every innocent victim of the man who was her father.

Chapter 10

Night had fallen, Sam was in bed and everyone else had disappeared into their rooms except Micah and Olivia who were once again seated on the sofa in the living room area. The room was lit with several oil lamps, creating a warm ambient glow that might feel romantic, if Micah had been a romantic kind of man.

"When I first arrived here, my only thought was getting Ethan back," Olivia said, her heartbreak shining in her eyes. "And even though that's still my first priority, now I also want Samuel gone forever and the town healed."

"We can take out Samuel, but I'm not so sure it's going to be easy to heal the town. We have no idea how deep the cancer runs in Cold Plains. Samuel isn't the only one who needs to be excised. Aside from Chief of Police Bo Fargo, who we know is crooked, there are people playing major roles in Samuel's game and we don't even know their names. They aren't even on our radar."

"What makes a town like Cold Plains?" she asked. "I mean, how does something like this happen? How does one man build such a powerful empire where so many people are simply puppets?"

It was getting late and Micah knew this was always the time of the evening when her thoughts turned to Ethan and he saw the whimpering panic beginning to simmer in her eyes. The best thing to do was to keep her talking until she grew too tired to think, too tired to grieve.

"Samuel certainly isn't the first charismatic leader to wreak havoc in people's lives. There have been lots of men before him, men like Jim Jones of the Peoples Temple and Marshall Applewhite, who got thirty-nine people to commit suicide along with him because they believed their bodies would be picked up by a passing UFO and taken to a new plane of existence beyond the human one."

"But those cults were based on religious ideas. Samuel hasn't advanced any religious ideology," she replied.

She looked so soft, so small curled into the corner of the sofa. There was nothing he wanted to do more than to reach out and pull her into his arms. Instead he focused on the conversation.

"Samuel made himself a kind of God here in town. The Community Center is his temple and his word is the law."

"But he's not even from Cold Plains. How did he gain so much power?"

Micah ran a hand through his thick dark hair and stared into the fireplace where no fire burned but logs were laid in wait for the colder months to come. The survivalist who had built the cave had vented the fireplace up through the mountain in two directions so that the smoke would be less visible if a fire burned.

"Samuel always had followers. I think before he arrived in Cold Plains he'd amassed quite a group of people who believed in him through his motivational speaking skills and charisma. Once he bought the land from old man Pierce here in town, he set about gathering those followers to this centralized location. As more new people moved in, the people who had lived here before found themselves faced with two choices, embrace the changes Samuel was making, embrace Samuel or work against him."

"And those who worked against him had unfortunate accidents, or went missing altogether," she added, her eyes dark.

He nodded. "I'm sure some of the townspeople were thrilled that somebody had come in and was making updates, cleaning everything up and taking them from a rough-and-rowdy town into something nicer and more upscale. Unfortunately, they didn't realize the price they paid was their soul to the devil."

He frowned thoughtfully, thinking of the way his brother had accomplished his goals. "There's definitely a group mentality at play. Samuel is good at fostering the 'you're with us or against us' kind of mentality. He creates an 'in' crowd and it's uncool not to belong. Peer pressure isn't just felt by teenagers and can be a terrible thing when it comes to situations like this."

She was silent for a long moment, her gaze troubled as she stared at the fireplace and then looked at him once again. "I've never heard any rumors about Samuel actually hurting children."

"I've never heard anything like that, either," he assured her, realizing that their discussion hadn't taken her mind off her missing son at all. "Samuel sees children like commodities to be sold. In Devin's case, he knew that Abby Michaels was dead so Devin became a candidate for an illegal adoption. With you missing and no father in the picture, that makes Ethan an adoptable commodity, as well. The absolute worst thing that could happen to Ethan and Devin is that they'll be sold out for adoption." She winced at his words. "But, the FBI have been checking vehicles leaving town and they feel certain the children are still there."

"But nobody knows where," she replied flatly. She rubbed a hand across her forehead, as if attempting to numb a headache. "Maybe I should go back to town. I could leave Sam here and make up some story about the FBI questioning me or something. I could tell everyone that I knew Wilma Lathrop would take care of Ethan in my absence." She dropped her hand back to her lap.

"Who is Wilma Lathrop?" he asked. It was a name he hadn't heard before.

"She's an older woman who works at the day care. She's sweet and very good with the kids. I'm hoping that she's taking care of Ethan in my absence."

"I'll tell you right now, you aren't going back into town," Micah said forcefully.

"But it might be the only way I can get information about where Ethan is being held," she protested.

"So, you're just going to waltz up to Samuel or one of his minions and ask where Ethan is after what you saw him do, not knowing if he saw you witness his crime that night? Olivia, if I have to hog-tie you to your bed, you aren't going back into that town."

"You wouldn't hog-tie me to the bed," she scoffed.

"Don't test me, Olivia," he warned.

She released a deep sigh. "If anyone needs to be tied up to keep them from going to town, it's you."

"I have no intention of going into town tonight."

She eyed him dubiously. "And what about tomorrow night or the night after that? The FBI have basically told you to stand down and stay out of sight. Are you going to listen to them?"

"I'm here, aren't I?" He didn't want her to know that he had every intention of returning to town. He'd made her a promise and even though she'd attempted to release him from it, he wouldn't be satisfied until she had her son back.

"You scare me, Micah."

He looked at her in surprise. "Scare you? Why?"

"I'm not scared of you hurting me or anything like that, but I'm afraid of you doing something to hurt yourself, taking chances you shouldn't take. I know I've been a neurotic crybaby where Ethan is concerned, but I don't want you to sacrifice yourself for him."

"You haven't been a crybaby. On the contrary, I think you've been amazingly strong through this whole thing," he replied. This time he couldn't fight the impulse that he'd been combating since the instant they had both sat down.

He leaned forward and touched her arm and she came willingly forward as if she'd just been waiting for the right moment. She leaned into him, her head resting on his chest, her body warm and softly feminine against his.

"I'm not sure how I could have handled all this without you here," she said.

He stroked the softness of her hair, the scent of her filling his nose, half-dizzying his brain. "You would have been fine without me here. You're going to be just fine when this is all over."

She was quiet for several minutes and then broke the silence. "Do you ever think about getting married... having a family?" She didn't raise her head to look at him.

About a million times since the moment he'd met her, he'd thought about what it would be like to come home to the same woman every night, to have a family to care for, to laugh with and to share a future with people he loved...with people who loved him. And each time he had imagined it, it was her he came home to and Sam and Ethan that greeted him at the door, that filled his life. But he didn't say this out loud.

"Never," he lied. "I don't want the burden. I've always traveled alone. That's what I'm used to, that's the way I like it." Funny that his words were in such a direct contrast to the fact that she was cuddled in his arms and he didn't want to let her go.

"That's too bad," she replied softly. "I have a feeling you would have made some lucky woman a wonderful husband, and seeing you with Sam makes me believe you would be a terrific father."

"I wouldn't have the first idea on how to be a father, given the role model I had," he replied.

"Being a parent is easy. All you have to do is love and allow yourself to receive love."

She raised her head to look at him, her green eyes warm and inviting. "And you are worthy of being loved,

Micah." It was at that moment he knew that if he allowed himself to, he could love this woman.

However he wouldn't allow it. Even though he'd decided that this would be his last mission, if he looked deep in his heart, deep in his very soul, he'd admit that he wasn't at all sure he was going to survive this, his final mission.

"There was definitely a chill in the air today," June said as she, Olivia and Darcy sat at the kitchen table eating dinner. Sam sat in his high chair, happily enjoying some of June's homemade applesauce and macaroni and cheese.

"Where are Lacy and her daughters?" Darcy asked.

"They were relocated last night," June replied. A touch of sadness darkened her eyes. "I'm going to miss those two little girls. They were such delights."

"It must be hard doing what you do," Olivia said. "Building relationships with people and then moving on to the next cult, the next victims." Her thoughts immediately went to Micah, who hadn't been seen all day. She tried telling herself that the building love she had for him was based on nothing more than the situation. Their enforced closeness had sent hormones into high drive, but she knew when this was all over she'd probably never see him again.

"That is the most difficult part of what I do," June replied. "It's hard not to build relationships in situations like this. But this is Eager's and my last job for a while." The black Lab lying on the floor nearby raised his head and looked at her.

"Doggie," Sam exclaimed and smiled at Olivia.

"That's right, doggie," Olivia agreed.

"You're going with Jesse to his ranch," Darcy said.

A smile swept over June's features, a smile of such love, of such happiness that it ached a little bit in Olivia's chest. "He says Eager will be kept busy chasing rabbits and I'm going to be busy chasing him."

They all laughed but Olivia felt a wistful envy raise its head inside her. Someday she wanted what June had found, the love of a good man who would be willing to step in and parent her sons, a man who would love her desperately, passionately until the end of time.

Each and every time she thought of such a man it was Micah who jumped into her head, but she knew that was just a ridiculous fantasy she had to get over.

Last night as they'd snuggled together on the sofa, he'd made it clear to her that he didn't want to be part of a family, that he wasn't a man looking for love or commitment.

But at the moment, with Ethan still a crushing pain in her heart and the uncertainty of ever seeing him again, the last thing on her mind was love. She just wanted her baby boy back and then she'd figure the rest of her life out from there.

She turned her attention to Darcy, who had been unusually quiet throughout the day. "Are you doing okay?" she asked.

Darcy nodded. "I saw Rafe last night and we called Ford McCall and told him that Micah had identified Jane Doe. He's going to do what he can to confirm that she's the woman who gave birth to me."

"Ford's a good man," June replied.

"It's amazing he's been able to work with that skunk, Chief of Police Fargo," Darcy said.

"Bo Fargo isn't just a skunk," June said with narrowed

eyes. "He's a dangerous man who has been given far too much power by Samuel. I wouldn't be surprised if he was the one who actually put the bullets in those poor women. Jesse believes that the good police chief is one of the men who beat him half to death and left him for dead in the woods."

For a moment they all fell silent. Olivia had no idea what the others were thinking but she was thinking about men like Bo Fargo holding her child captive someplace. She fought against the tears that burned behind her eyelids, refusing to allow them to fall here in the presence of her youngest son and the other women.

Jesse came in from the outside where he had been standing guard, indicating that somebody else had taken over for him. He wore a thick plaid jacket and brought with him the scent of the cold, fresh outdoor air.

"There's a thick layer of fog moving in," he said as he took off his jacket and slung it over the back of an empty chair at the table. "I have a feeling in another hour or so you won't be able to see your hand in front of your face."

"A good night for all God's children to stay inside and be safe," June said.

"Or a good night to create some mischief," Micah said as he came into the kitchen. He smiled at Olivia and she consciously willed her heart not to quicken.

"I hope you don't intend to make any mischief," she said.

"Not me, but I want to talk to Hawk and make sure that they're setting up traffic stops coming in and out of town," he replied as he sat across from her at the table.

He didn't have to say why he wanted to check on that. Olivia knew what he was thinking, that the cover of fog might provide a perfect opportunity to move two unwanted, highly adoptable children out of the area. If the FBI agents in the area weren't careful, tonight was the night she could potentially lose her child forever.

Once again the group fell silent as June busied herself fixing plates for both Jesse and Micah. After they'd been served, the conversation remained light and neutral, but Olivia's heart thundered with the idea of Ethan vanishing for good.

As she exchanged glances with Darcy, she knew the young woman shared the same concern about Rafe's son. Micah looked at her, his eyes slightly hard and filled with resolve. "We're not going to let those kids get away from us," he said, obviously reading her mind.

She nodded. Although she knew rationally it was impossible for a single man to control what was happening in and around an entire town, in her heart she desperately wanted to believe him.

After eating, as the women cleared the table, Micah left the safe house, she assumed for his meeting with Hawk or one of the other FBI agents working the case.

She knew she wouldn't breathe easily again until he returned. She lifted Sam from the high chair and carried him into the living room, followed by Darcy.

With Sam on one of the thick hide rugs with a pile of toys in front of him, the two women sat on the sofa. "I'm sorry about your mother," Olivia said.

Darcy gave her a bittersweet smile. "I think maybe I've always known deep in my heart that it wasn't going to be a happy ending for me, but I'd hoped..." She allowed her voice to trail off as her gaze lingered on Sam. "At least I have Rafe and hopefully before too long we'll have Devin and you'll have Ethan back."

"We can only hope," Olivia replied.

"You're in love with Micah, aren't you?"

Olivia looked at Darcy in shock and then was unable to control the nervous little laugh that escaped her. "Why on earth would you think such a thing?"

Darcy shot her a smug little smile. "Because you look at him the way I know I look at Rafe. Because I see the worry in your eyes each time he leaves this place."

"I worry about everyone when they leave here," Olivia countered.

Darcy smiled knowingly. "But you worry just a little bit more about Micah."

Olivia released a small sigh. "It doesn't matter what I feel toward him. This is just a crazy stop on our way to the rest of our separate lives. I mean, look around... We are sitting in a cave because a madman has taken possession of an entire town. Could it get more surreal?"

"It just goes to show that love can blossom in the strangest of places," Darcy replied.

"Trust me, Micah has made it very clear that love has no place in his life." A piercing sadness swept through Olivia for the man who had never known love as a child, for the man who had chosen to live his life alone. "Micah told me that you're his niece. I only hope that he'll allow you and Rafe and Devin to be the family he never had."

"I'd like that," Darcy agreed. She eyed Olivia soberly. "It doesn't bother you to know that Samuel is my biological father?"

Olivia smiled. "Darcy, I have no idea who my father is and my mother was a raging alcoholic who only got out of bed to get another bottle of booze. Unfortunately, we don't get to pick our parents. You are nothing like your father and in a million years nothing could make you like him."

Darcy reached over and grabbed Olivia's hand in hers. "I hope you find happiness when you leave here, Olivia. I hope you find a good man to love you and your two boys. We all deserve happiness after what we've been through."

"I definitely agree with that," Olivia replied.

At that moment Micah returned, his restless energy filling the entire living room. "Hawk has promised me that nothing is going to leave town tonight that we don't know about," he said. "The fog, along with the narrow roads that lead in and out of town, should make travel for anyone slow, and that works to our advantage."

He was amped up, much like he had been the night he'd come home after nearly being caught in the forest and had taken her to bed. The pump of adrenaline rolled off him in waves and his eyes had taken on the glittering of an animal on the prowl.

She knew in that moment that despite what he'd been told by the FBI to sit tight, that he was going out to do something dangerous, that he intended to use the fog cover for his own purposes.

"What are your plans?" she asked, unable to control the slight tremor in her voice.

"I'll just leave you two to talk," Darcy said as she jumped up from the sofa and hurried from the room, leaving Olivia and Micah alone.

"Nothing for you to worry about," he said as he started out of the room.

She followed behind him. "What does that mean?"

They passed the bedrooms and she stared at his back,

willing him to halt, to turn around and tell her he intended to spend the rest of the night in the safe house.

He didn't reply until they reached the tiny room where he slept. An oil lamp was lit, the illumination bouncing off the rocky walls. There was a single-sized cot and several canvas bags lined up against one wall.

He leaned over and picked up one of the canvas bags, then turned to face her. "With the fog it's a perfect night to check out a few places in town."

Olivia's heart pounded with anxiety as she stared at him with a horrible sense of dread. "I don't want you to go."

She took a step toward him, wondering if he could hear the thunder of her heart in the small space. "Stay here with me, Micah. You know it's too dangerous for you to go out there tonight."

He placed a warm palm against her cheek, his eyes holding both a softness and a distance that let her know he was already half-gone from her. "This is what I do, Olivia."

He dropped his hand from her face and left the room with her trailing behind him, trying to think of something, anything that would keep him here with her. He'd been told to stay out of things, to stay away from town. Why oh why wasn't he listening to the FBI...to her?

They reached the entrance to the cave and he turned to face her, his eyes already holding the wildness of the forest, of whatever mission he had in mind for the night.

He paused and dropped the duffel bag he carried to the floor and then wrapped her in his arms and pressed his mouth to hers in an intense kiss that tasted far too much like goodbye.

She clung to him, fighting tears as the kiss lingered.

He was breaking her heart. By leaving here, by kissing her the way he was, he was truly shattering her apart.

He finally released her and once again grabbed the duffel bag. With a curt nod of his head, he stepped out of the opening of the safe house and she desperately feared that she would never see him again.

Chapter 11

The fog had created a false sense of twilight as Micah stepped out into the woods. Although not as thick here as it would be in the lower valley that held the town of Cold Plains, the fog could definitely work for him or against him.

It would be more difficult for anyone to spot him, but it would also make it harder for him to see danger coming. Still, he felt no fear as he made his way down the mountain toward town.

In the distance a wolf howled, the sound mournful as it resonated deep in Micah's soul. Micah had always considered himself a lone wolf, but that was a mischaracterization of the wild animal. Even wolves lived in packs, with a mate and their offspring.

He shoved these thoughts away as he continued down the mountain. The farther down he went, the thicker the fog grew, enveloping him in a gray mist that stirred a faint anxiety inside him.

With each step he took, he stopped and listened, making sure there wasn't anyone else near him in the soupy fog. The dense mist seemed to amplify even the tiniest natural sound, making him more jumpy than usual.

One hand gripped the handle of the duffel bag and the other held tight to his gun. He finally reached the edge of Cold Plains and crouched behind a large tree trunk.

From this vantage point the only thing visible in the town was the barely discernible muted glow from the streetlamps. Micah set down the duffel bag and checked his watch. Five minutes until seven.

He'd sit tight for now and wait for the ring of the old church bell that would summon all the townspeople to Samuel's nightly seminar. Only when he knew his brother was busy shepherding his sheep would Micah make his bold move.

He'd spent most of yesterday working things around in his head, trying to think how his brother would when it came to safety and secrets.

He knew about the tunnel that ran underground beneath the Community Center. He also knew that hidden rooms had been found below the Urgent Care facility. But he couldn't imagine a man as crafty as Samuel sleeping in bed at night in a house that had no escape route but the front and back doors. It just didn't make "Samuel sense."

It was imperative that Micah got inside Samuel's house tonight and found out what secrets might be contained within its impressive walls. And this was the perfect night. While Samuel was leading his flock, Micah intended to check it out.

At precisely eight o'clock the church bell tolled, the sound muted and discordant as it traveled through the dense fog. Micah waited another ten minutes and then left the safety of his hiding place.

As usual he stuck to the backyards and what cover he could find, but the fog made it slow going as he could only see approximately a foot in front of him.

It took him much longer than he'd anticipated to finally reach the back of Samuel's house. Using the cover of the trees, he pulled the grappling hook and rope from the duffel bag and then watched to see if the guard presence had increased since the last time he'd been here.

Samuel's seminars generally lasted between an hour and an hour and a half. Micah couldn't wait too long to make his move or he wouldn't have the time he needed to explore the interior of the house.

He heard rather than saw somebody moving around the back of the house. As he watched with narrowed eyes, trying to pierce through the veil of fog, the man stopped and flicked a lighter to light a cigarette. The resulting glow from the lighter illuminated his features for just a moment and Micah identified him as the second guard who had chased him through the forest with Dax Roberts.

The man moved on and when Micah could no longer hear the whisper of his feet against the grass, he made his move. Although he couldn't see the balcony ledge above him, he made a calculated throw of the hook and fought against the triumphant cry he wanted to release as the hook didn't return to the ground.

Going up would be easy. Micah had climbed ropes a thousand times in his lifetime. Coming down could be more difficult because, in order to leave no trace of his presence, he'd have to remove the grappling hook and jump with it and the rope in his arms.

. He raced to the rope and tugged on it to make sure it was secure and then like a spider climbed. Once he was secure on the balcony, he pulled up the rope behind him and unfastened the hook from where it had grabbed on the wooden railing.

He left the hook and rope on the balcony and turned to the glass sliding doors. Holding his breath, he reached out and slid the door open.

Bingo. He knew Samuel would be arrogant enough to believe that the security he had in place was enough. Samuel would have never believed anyone would have the courage to breach his privacy even with an unlocked door.

The first thing Micah looked for was any indication that there was a security system in place, but he saw no panel blinking a warning, nothing that would make him believe that, electronically, somebody knew he was inside.

A shine of his flashlight let him know he was in the master bedroom. The room was palatial, the furnishings fit for a king. Micah's heart thundered a million beats a minute as he checked his watch. Too much time had passed, the fog had slowed him down. To be safe, he could only allow himself fifteen, twenty minutes tops, inside.

If there was any place in the house where there might be a secret escape route, Micah thought it would be here in the bedroom. There was no way Samuel would allow himself to be caught sleeping by an FBI raid or any other enemies that might make it into the house.

A stone fireplace took up the center of the wall opposite the bed. Above the mantel a huge television hung, and on either side of that, fine paintings surely bought and paid for by illegal means.

One entire wall was bookcases filled with not only tomes on self-motivation and achieving success, but also containing lovely vases and ornate sculptures arrayed in artful design. Samuel definitely enjoyed the finer things in life.

The other wall held an easy chair, a small table and a reading lamp. In front of the chair was an oversized oval Oriental rug in vibrant colors.

Micah had seen enough old movies to know that the best guess for some sort of secret passageway was behind one of the bookshelves. Would Samuel be so predictable?

Aware of the seconds quickly ticking off, Micah moved to the mahogany wooden cases and used his penlight to see if he could find some sort of mechanism that would move them in any way.

He realized at some point his main mission had changed. He still wanted to bring down Samuel, but more than that he wanted to return the missing Ethan to Olivia's arms. There would be others that would continue to work on getting Samuel to justice. He wasn't sure when, but at some point avenging Johanna's death had become second to healing Olivia's heart.

After a few minutes of searching, far too conscious of time constraints, he moved to the fireplace. There was no sign that a fire had ever burned in the ornate stone hearth and he climbed up into it, seeking a false back or something that would yield to a secret safe-room or passage.

Nothing. He checked his watch again and thought

about looking in other rooms, but the residence was massive and he was convinced that if there was an escape route anyplace in the house it would be here, in Samuel's bedroom.

He stood in the center of the room, seeking something, anything that might give him a clue. Something that didn't quite fit. Something that wasn't quite right with the room. Was he wrong? Was it possible that the rat didn't have a getaway hole from this space? Maybe there was an escape route in the bathroom, in the hallway. Hell, it could be anywhere in the house. He'd just thought the bedroom made the most sense.

He knew the odds of him having the opportunity to get back into this house again were minimal and he'd so wanted to go back to Olivia with some kind of news. Dammit, he'd wanted to be her hero.

Checking his watch once again, he flashed his penlight one last time around the room, the beam stopping on the Oriental rug. It felt just a little too big for the space. The settlers had used rugs to cover the entrance to root cellars where they could hide from marauding Indians. Was it possible?

He raced over to the rug and lifted it, his heart jumping in stunned surprise as beneath it he found a wooden door. *Score,* he thought as he pulled open the door and shone his light down a dark, narrow staircase.

Drawing a deep breath, praying that he had time enough to check it out and then get the hell out of here before his presence was discovered, he started down the stairs.

It felt as if he was heading into the very bowels of the earth before the staircase finally ended and he stepped into a narrow corridor lit by several dim light bulbs hanging from the ceiling.

Just ahead he saw a single doorway on the left side of the corridor that appeared to go on forever beyond the door. *You're running out of time,* an inner voice screamed in his head. He ignored it, moving closer to the closed door.

He froze as he heard a childish cry come from behind the door. The children. This had to be where Samuel was keeping Devin and Ethan.

"I want my mommy," the child cried. "I want my brother. I want Sammy."

His heart crashed in his chest, torn between the need to rush in and rescue and the intelligence to know that he'd never get out of this house alive with both children in tow.

As much as he didn't want to leave, he knew the smartest thing he could do right now was save himself so he could make plans with Hawk and the other men for an all-out assault that would assure the children's safety. As much as he wanted to, he couldn't act alone tonight.

He backed away, turned and raced up the stairs. Once he was again in the bedroom, he carefully closed the door and rearranged the rug the way it had been over the opening.

He wasn't home free yet. He still had to get out of the house and he knew that time was running out. Samuel rarely dawdled once his seminars were over and that bell calling the meeting to start had rung just over an hour ago.

Out on the balcony, he grabbed his hook and rope and then tried to peer down below. The fog was still so thick he couldn't see the ground. He had no idea where the guards might be or how soon one of them might round the side of the house.

If he jumped and landed wrong, he could break a leg or severely injure himself. That would put him in the hands of the guards, and he knew there would definitely be no mercy for him.

He crawled over the balcony edge and listened for the sound of anyone approaching. He heard nothing and he grabbed the lower part of the balcony railing, hung his body down as low as he could and then dropped.

The hard ground met him sooner than he'd expected, but he hit the earth with his knees bent and went straight into a roll to absorb some of the impact.

With his heart still crashing a mad rhythm, he darted in the direction of his duffel bag and then had to click on his flashlight to find it. He shoved the hook and rope inside the bag and then paused to draw several long, slow breaths.

Samuel's meeting would be breaking up by now, but Micah wasn't ready to return to the safe house yet. He'd found the entrance to the secret corridor inside the house but he didn't intend to go home until he'd found the exit and he knew that would probably be someplace in the wooded area behind the house.

Finding it was going to be a challenge, not only because Samuel was crafty, but also because of the fog that shrouded everything.

The good news was that he thought the exit was far enough away from the house that he wasn't too worried about encountering the guards. If he couldn't see them, then they couldn't see him, either.

He worked in a grid search fashion, methodically

checking every rock, every bush, every odd formation that the landscape had to offer.

He didn't expect to find anyone on guard at the exit point. Samuel wouldn't want to draw that kind of attention to it. If he was to guess, nobody, including Samuel's top men, knew about this particular escape route. He would have kept the information all to himself. Probably the only other person who did know about it was whoever was in charge of taking care of the children.

He found it just before dawn, hidden by a thick prickly bush that when pushed slightly aside revealed an earthen staircase going underground. He mentally marked the area using natural landmarks and then, realizing the sun was rising and slowly burning off the fog, he headed back to the safe house.

Happiness soared through him, a happiness he'd never known before. If all went right then by this time tomorrow Olivia would be reunited with her son. Her heart would be full and he couldn't wait to see the unadulterated joy light her beautiful eyes. He couldn't wait for the moment her family was whole once again.

Of course, his happiness was tempered by the fact that once she had Ethan back, it would be time for her to be relocated. The thought of not seeing her every day broke something inside him he hadn't been aware existed.

He loved her, but he had to let her go. She had a life to live far away from this town and Samuel Grayson. It was right that she move on. She deserved a man who knew more than Micah would ever know or be able to learn about love. She'd find some small town and a good man to love her and her children. He had to believe that.

It was the only way this would work. Once the kids

were back where they belonged, Micah still had work to do. He had to make sure his brother didn't manage to somehow weasel his way out of an arrest or escape altogether.

It had been an endless night and by the time dawn broke, Olivia fought against a hysteria she'd only felt once before. The night she'd run after seeing Samuel kill that man. The night she'd had to leave one of her precious sons behind.

Micah. Her heart had cried with each agonizing minute that passed, every hour that crept by. Where was he? Had he been taken captive by one of Samuel's men? Was he dead? Surely she would know if he'd been killed. Surely she would have felt his death at her very core.

When he walked through the door just after dawn, she threw herself into his arms, weeping at the very sight of him unharmed.

"Hey, hey," he exclaimed as he dropped the duffel bag to the floor and grabbed her to him. "What's all this?"

"I was afraid you were gone forever, that somebody had either caught you or killed you," she sobbed into the front of his jacket.

"Do you really think I'd let any of those bozos in town catch or kill me?" he replied lightly.

"Those bozos are dangerous." Her voice was half-muffled by both his jacket and her choked sobs.

"Come on, we don't want to wake up anyone else," he said. He led her to her room, where he pulled her inside and closed the door.

She burrowed into his chest and leaned into his body

seeking to warm the icy chill that had overtaken her as she'd awaited his return.

She looked up at him, tears still streaking down her cheeks. "I've been so afraid for you."

He used his thumbs to swipe away her tears. "Nobody has ever cried for me before," he said softly. "Besides, now isn't the time for crying. I think I found where the children are being held."

Her eyes widened as she stared up at him. "What… where? Oh, Micah, we need to go get them." She spun out of his arms and grabbed his hand, a warrior mother ready to go claim her missing child.

"Whoa, we can't do anything right now. It would be far too dangerous." He led her to the bed and pulled her down next to him and explained what he had done and what he'd discovered since he'd been gone.

Any weariness she might have felt from the night of worry dissipated as she listened to what he had found and the fact that he'd heard a child cry, a child who had cried for her and for his little brother. Had it been Ethan? Had her baby been crying for her? A piercing ache shot through her heart and she began to cry again, unable to control the emotions that tumbled inside her.

"Shhh." Micah pulled her back into his arms. "It's going to be okay, Olivia. I'll meet with Hawk sometime later this morning and make arrangements to get those kids out of there later tonight when Samuel is holding his evening meeting. You just need to stay strong for a little while longer."

"I can do that," she said, reluctant to move from the warmth and strength of his arms. But she knew what he needed more than anything at the moment. Sleep. If he was planning on some sort of attack in town tonight to retrieve her son, then he needed to rest. He'd been up all night long and so had she, worrying about him. She hoped to get an hour or two of rest before Sam awakened and the day officially began.

"Olivia, this will probably be our last time together," he said and she could feel the quickening of her heart against her own. "Once Ethan is back here, I'll make arrangements for you and your children to be immediately taken from this area. We'll see to it that you're relocated someplace where you can begin to build a new life."

She leaned back and looked at him, loving him with all her heart. "What about you? You know I'm in love with you."

His eyes darkened and he looked away from her. "I'm sorry that's happened." He drew a deep breath and then looked at her once again. "Olivia, you've made me feel things I've never felt before. You've been the sun in this godforsaken cave." His voice grew thick with emotion. "But I'm just another bad choice for you. I have a job to finish here and there's no room in my life for you and the boys."

She searched his features, wanting something different from him. She saw love for her in the depths of his eyes, felt it in his every touch. She was certain that he loved her, and yet she was absolutely powerless to stop him from turning his back on what could be.

The last thing she intended to do was beg for his love, for some sort of a commitment that when this nightmare was over they would find a way to be together.

He'd made her a promise that he would find her son and return him to her. Once that promise was done, he intended to walk away from her without a backward glance.

Knowing that these were the last moments they would ever have alone, she leaned up and pressed her lips against his, wanting to taste him, to feel him one remaining time.

"Then I want to make one final bad choice," she said. "Make love to me, Micah. Give me memories to carry with me when I leave here."

His eyes flared hot at her words. "That would be a sweet memory I would carry with me, too," he replied.

There was little talk after that. Within minutes they were both naked and in her bed and Olivia's mind emptied of everything but Micah. She drew in the scent of him, memorized the feel of his skin against hers, the sensations his every touch crashed through her.

This time the wildness was gone, replaced by a slow, sweet tenderness that was every bit as exciting as the first time they'd had sex.

This time she was truly making love to him and whether he admitted it or not, he was making love to her, as well. Their bodies moved together as if they'd been partners forever, as if they were made to fit together perfectly.

Joined together, his hands caressed down her back as his lips nibbled gently on her neck. He breathed her name and in the three syllables of the single word she felt more loved than ever before.

As he moved his body back and forth against hers, she placed her hands on the sides of his hips, loving the feel of his warm skin beneath her hands.

When he deepened his thrusts, pleasure swept through her, building to a point where every nerve in her body sang. As the sensations reached a crescendo, she held tight to him and cried out his name as she rode the waves of her orgasm. With a deep guttural moan, he stiffened against her as he found his own release.

When it was over, a bittersweet pain and pleasure filled her as she fell asleep, knowing that she would never experience the wonder of loving Micah again.

She awoke some time later, alone in the bed and feeling fully rested. A glance at her watch told her it was just after noon. She jumped out of bed, aware that somebody had been caring for Sam as she slept.

While the people here worked together as a family, helping each other out, she didn't like to burden anyone with the caretaking of her son. Still, she'd slept hard and now all her heart felt was the sweet anticipation of finally getting Ethan back.

She consciously didn't think about final goodbyes to Micah. She found everyone in the kitchen gathered around the table. Sam sat in his high chair and greeted her with a happy smile. She returned his smile absently and ruffled the fine hair on his head, her gaze focused on the three men seated at the table she didn't know.

"Olivia." Micah stood and gestured her toward an empty chair next to him. As she sat down, she noticed that he looked rested and alert and this was obviously a planning meeting for getting the children out of Cold Plains.

He gestured to a sandy-haired man. "This is Special Agent Hawk Bledsoe. He's going to be coordinating our movements this evening with the FBI. The two men with him are Agents Randy Avery and Lyle Kincaid. Both men have been working undercover in town."

"We've already determined that the best time to go

in for the children is during Samuel's nightly meeting. Most of the town will be at the Community Center and out of our way," Randy said.

"I'll go in through the exit hole I found and grab whatever kids are in that room down the corridor. You all wait and guard the entrance. If we're quiet, then not even the guards on Samuel's house will have any idea that something is happening. Once those kids are free, the most important thing is to get them out of town and back here to the safe house. After that's done, all bets are off for whatever you want to do as far as arresting Samuel and any of his minions."

"Oh, there're going to be arrests tonight," Hawk said, his eyes narrowing. "We're going to tear this town apart tonight and when we're finished, hopefully there won't be a bad guy left standing without wearing a pair of handcuffs."

"Finding those kids beneath Samuel's house was the break we've been waiting for," Lyle exclaimed. "We can get Samuel arrested for unlawful imprisonment, kidnapping and any number of other charges and once we have him, I have a feeling there's going to be a lot of singing going on from the others."

"Everyone arrested is going to want to make a deal to save themselves and that means they'll be pointing fingers at their leader and hopefully, when all is said and done, we'll have enough evidence to put Samuel away for the rest of his life," Randy replied.

They made it sound so easy, Olivia thought. Get in, grab the children, get out and make arrests. But nobody had mentioned that Samuel's men wouldn't go down without a fight, that Samuel himself would shoot to kill anyone he thought might be a threat.

The night was fraught with danger, their plan definitely not infallible. Olivia's heart banged hard against her chest as she realized some of the people sitting at this very table might not survive the mission.

Chapter 12

The plans were made. When the church bell tolled the hour of eight, the action would begin. At seven-fifteen Micah left his room in the cave and headed for the exit. His progress was halted by Olivia, who was clad in black pants, a long-sleeved black shirt and even had her shiny blond hair tucked into a black stocking cap.

"What are you doing?" he asked. "Playing ninja?"

She flashed him a look of annoyance. "I'm not playing at anything. I'm going with you." She raised her chin as if prepared to battle whatever protest he might throw her way.

He didn't disappoint her. "The hell you are. You're going to stay right here out of the range of danger." He motioned for her to step aside so he could continue, but she held her ground before him.

"I can either go with you or without you, but nobody, not even you, is keeping me here while you go after my son. You need me, Micah," she said desperately. "These are children and they'll be frightened by the sight of you storming in the room dressed all in black and grabbing them up. Besides, how can you use your gun if necessary if you have Devin in one arm and Ethan in the other?" She flushed, as if she were aware that she was talking too much, too fast, but he also saw the fierce determination shining from her eyes.

She reached out and placed her small hand in the center of his chest. "Please, Micah. I'm the one who left him behind and if I don't participate in trying to get him back, I'll go absolutely insane."

"What about Sam?" Surely she wouldn't want to leave Sam here without her.

"Darcy has agreed to stay here and watch him. She's good with him so I know he'll be fine." She pulled her hand away from him, but continued to hold his gaze intently.

Although the last thing he wanted to do was place her in any danger, part of what she said made sense. The plan required Micah to get into the tunnel, get the kids and then get out of there with as little noise as possible. If Ethan screamed and cried as he dragged him from the room, then it was possible all hell would break loose. And the last thing he wanted was any chaos in or around town until those kids were out safe and sound.

"Okay," he finally said. "You can come with me on one condition. You listen to every order I give you and you instantly obey. I don't want you putting yourself or anyone else in danger."

She nodded. "I can follow rules."

He hesitated another moment, but he could see in

her eyes that she hadn't been bluffing. With or without him, she intended to leave the safe house tonight.

"Okay, come on. We've got to get moving now." He turned and headed for the exit, hoping this all wasn't a mistake. As they stepped out into the night air, Micah was grateful that it was a night with thick clouds across the sky, obscuring not only the millions of stars that were normally visible, but also any sight of the nearly full moon.

As he began his trek down the mountain, he was pleased that Olivia moved quickly and lightly, making little noise as she followed directly behind him.

His muscles had tensed the moment they'd left the safe house, prepared for success…and afraid of failure. This was it. He knew they'd only get one chance at this and if they didn't get it done right, then the kids would disappear from Cold Plains forever.

He knew Olivia must feel the same way…the tensed muscles, the frantic beat of her heart, the knowledge that failure was a distinct possibility.

The plan was for Micah to get the kids to safety and then the FBI intended to move in and make arrests. There would be bedlam in the perfect little town tonight and it would take months for the FBI to clean up the mess, figure out who to charge with what and who to release or hold on charges.

Of course by that time, his hope was that Olivia and her two boys would be relocated someplace where they would be safe and happy and Micah…? He hadn't quite figured out what his next move would be. Once Samuel was behind bars, Micah would have time to figure out what he intended to do for the rest of his life.

He couldn't think about that now. He had to stay

focused on the next thirty to forty-five minutes when everything was at stake for the investigation…and for Olivia. This was the most important mission he would ever attempt and never had he wanted success as much as now.

Neither of them spoke as they continued through the forest. Micah knew that in all areas of the town, men were getting into position, awaiting word from him that the children had been saved and they could move in.

The closer they got to the exit of the tunnel that Micah had found, the harder his heart banged inside his chest. Olivia remained just behind him, stepping where he stepped, mirroring his movements in an effort to be completely silent.

Micah had given Hawk the coordinates to the exit and the FBI man was to meet Micah there, along with a couple other men.

For backup.

For unexpected trouble.

He stopped suddenly, Olivia bumping into his back as he caught the sound of something moving to the left of them. Whatever it was sounded big and didn't seem to attempt to hide the noise it was making.

With his finger firmly on his gun trigger, he flipped on his flashlight and caught sight of a moose in the distance. A small gasp escaped Olivia at the view of the magnificent creature. The animal shied away from the light and Micah and Olivia moved on.

That's what should be in these mountainous woods, elk and deer, moose and bear, not killers and survivors of the human kind, Micah thought.

They finally reached the bush behind which the tunnel existed, but nobody else was there yet. He pointed

Olivia toward a thick tree trunk and together they stepped behind it to hide and wait for Hawk and his men.

He wrapped an arm around Olivia, hugging her tight against his body, aware of the raging emotions that had to be rushing inside her. She had more to lose than anyone else in the town at the moment. In the next few minutes she would either have her son back or she would be forever broken by the loss of her little boy.

He also couldn't help but worry about Olivia's personal safety. If things went bad, there was a possibility she might catch a bullet as well as any of them.

She shivered slightly against him and he tightened his arm around her shoulder. It had been incredibly brave of her to leave the safe house, to leave behind the one child she had in her possession and come here. It was the kind of bravery that assured him that somehow, someway, no matter how this night turned out, she would survive. He'd have to make certain of that fact.

He tensed as he heard the faint whisper of footsteps approaching. "Micah?" His name was a mere whisper, but he recognized Hawk's voice.

He peeked out from behind the tree. "We're here," he whispered in return and motioned them to come closer. Hawk was with Agent Randy Avery. They had all agreed that the fewer people involved in this particular part of the operation the better.

The underground corridor that Micah had found had been empty and silent and he hoped to keep it that way. In and out, no trouble, no noise and definitely no drama. Get the kids to safety and then let the entire town explode apart as the FBI moved in to take over.

By the end of this operation, Olivia should have her

son back, Samuel should be in custody and the town could begin the healing process it desperately needed. It would take months, potentially years, before the town returned to some semblance of normal.

"We'll wait for the bell to ring," Micah said in a soft whisper. "And then I'll go in. The tunnel is long and the place where I saw the room and heard Ethan cry is about halfway between here and Samuel's house. It will take us a few minutes to reach the room."

"Us?" In the tiny glow of a penlight, Hawk looked from Micah to Olivia.

"I'm going in with him," she said, her soft voice holding a steely strength that brooked no argument. "He'll need help with the children."

Hawk hesitated a moment and then nodded, apparently finding it wise not to argue with a desperate mother.

"I'll radio you if we find anything or anyone unexpected," Micah said. "Hopefully we execute fully with nobody being the wiser."

"Everyone else is in place," Randy said. "We have men ready to move in the minute Hawk or you gives them the command."

"Just make sure that Samuel doesn't somehow slip this noose," Micah replied, his blood hot as he even considered the possibility of Samuel evading their snare.

The church bell ringing halted all conversation. A surge of adrenaline filled Micah as he looked at Olivia. It was time to go in.

He motioned to Olivia that he'd go in first. With his gun in one hand, he used his other hand to move the bush aside, revealing the earthen stairs that led down. Drawing a deep breath, praying that this went as planned, Micah began down the stairs.

Olivia followed Micah down the stairs, the scent of the earth pressing in all around her. This wasn't the lit corridor that Micah had told her about. This was a mole's tunnel, small and dark with just Micah's penlight to penetrate the darkness.

She imagined her heartbeat crashing in the silence, alerting anyone in the area that she was near. She drew deep breaths through her nose in an effort to calm her nerves, to slow the beating of her heart. She had to remain cool and collected. The last thing Ethan needed was a hysterical, out-of-control mommy riding to his rescue.

It seemed as if they walked forever amid the scent of dank earth when finally ahead Olivia saw a faint glow of light.

The corridor! Just like Micah had explained, and in that corridor was a room that he'd believed held the children. Ethan! Her heart cried out his name, her arms ached with her need to grab him to her, to feel him against her heart.

What if the children had been moved? What if they burst into the room and there was nobody there? No, she couldn't think that way. This had to be the place. She had to get her son back right now.

As they reached the wider corridor, Micah motioned ahead where she could see the door on their right. Despite her attempt to control her excitement, she couldn't halt a rush of adrenaline that filled her. She suddenly felt strong enough to break open a locked door, to face a giant and beat him down to get to Ethan.

Micah reached back and touched her arm, as if he felt the energy that rolled off her and needed to calm her. Step by step they approached the door.

There was no window, no way to tell who or what lay behind, but as they got close enough for Micah to touch the doorknob, Olivia heard the faint cry of a child.

The sound shot straight to her womb, the piercing ache of maternal need. She couldn't be sure that it was her son that she heard, but the mournful cry threatened to break her heart.

As Micah opened the door and entered the room in a crouched position, his gun held in both hands in front of him, Olivia moved right behind him, her brain working overtime to take in the scene before them.

The room was definitely a nursery, with a playpen, a crib and a small toddler bed along the walls. In the center of the room was a child-sized table with crayons and paper and a bowl of what appeared to be applesauce.

There was a dark-haired, dark-eyed little boy in the crib and next to him was a familiar woman who jumped to her feet at their entrance.

"Wilma," Olivia exclaimed in stunned surprise. She assumed the child in the crib was Devin Black, but there was no sight of any other child. Oh, God, where was Ethan?

"Are you alone?" Micah asked, his gun not wavering from the older woman.

She nodded, but her gaze slid to a second doorway in the room. Micah muttered a curse beneath his breath, advanced on the closed door and disappeared into the other room.

"Wilma, how could you?" Olivia asked the woman who had worked at the day care center, the woman she had trusted to take care of her children each day that Olivia went to work. "How could you be a part of this?"

Before Olivia could say another word, Wilma flew across the room, slammed her into the wall and wrapped her skinny fingers around Olivia's neck.

The shock of the old woman's action momentarily rendered Olivia helpless and, as the air was squeezed out of her lungs, her knees buckled beneath her.

Olivia couldn't make a noise as the surprisingly strong hands pressed tighter against her throat. "I'm getting paid a lot of money for my work," Wilma hissed as her fingernails bit into Olivia's flesh.

Black dots began to dance in front of Olivia's eyes and she realized if she didn't do something fast, she'd never get the chance to see Ethan again, to hold his little body close, to see his beautiful smile.

Tears blurred her vision as darkness began to creep in and suddenly Wilma was gone, plucked from her like a piece of unwanted lint by a silent, but raging Micah. He whirled the old woman away and she hit the wall and slumped down, obviously dazed.

In that instant a wave of despair swept over Olivia. Although she was happy that apparently they'd found Devin Black, where was her Ethan?

Suddenly his little blond head peeked around the corner of the room where Micah had gone. "Ethan!" Olivia gasped and crouched as he ran to her and slammed into her arms. She hugged him tight, weeping quietly with a combination of both joy and relief.

"Come on, we've got to get out of here," Micah said.

She nodded and stood and hurried to the crib where she lifted out Devin and then grabbed Ethan by the hand. "We have to be very quiet," she told the boys as Micah hurried them from the room in front of him.

Devin clung to her like a frightened little monkey as Ethan squeezed her fingers painfully tight. They raced toward the exit as fast as possible with the two kids in tow.

"Hey…hey, you! Stop or I'll shoot!" The deep voice came from just behind them.

They turned to see Chief of Police Bo Fargo racing toward them, his broad face bright red with rage. Olivia gasped as instead of running for the exit, Micah raced toward the chief of police.

"Micah!" she screamed just as Bo fired his gun. The shot went wild, missing Micah who kicked the gun out of Bo's hand. At the same time Bo threw himself on Micah and the two tumbled to the floor.

Olivia froze as she saw Micah's gun skitter out of his hand and along the corridor floor. Should she grab the gun? Run and get the children to safety? Love for Micah exploded inside her. She didn't just want her son back, she wanted Micah to be safe, as well.

At that moment Micah threw a flurry of punches that stunned Bo and left him inert on the floor. Micah grabbed Bo's handcuffs, rolled the big man on his stomach and cuffed his hands behind his back.

"Go," he said urgently to Olivia as he grabbed his gun and raced toward her. They left the corridor and raced toward the earthen womb that would eventually take them up to the surface, up to safety.

Devin cried softly, clinging to her in frantic desperation as Ethan scampered bravely next to her. She breathed a sigh of relief as they reached the stairs that led upward.

Hawk was there and immediately took Devin into his arms, while Olivia grabbed up Ethan and hugged him tight, tears streaming down her face.

"We heard a gunshot," Hawk said.

"Chief of Police Fargo is currently cuffed on the floor. He got off a shot that fortunately didn't connect," Micah said as he exited the hole in the ground. "Now, get them to the safe house. Keep them safe, Hawk."

Olivia looked at Micah in surprise. "Aren't you coming with us?"

"Not yet. I've got to be sure that Samuel doesn't get away," he said.

"Leave it for the other men," Olivia said, her fear for him all consuming.

"I can't. I've got to see this through." He looked at Hawk. "Take good care of them for me, Hawk. Hopefully I'll see you later."

Randy took Devin from Hawk and Hawk took Ethan from Olivia's arms. "Come on, we're going to be moving fast," Hawk said.

"Olivia." She turned to look at Micah, his face lit with Hawk's small penlight. His eyes shone with a softness she'd never seen before, a softness that was like a whisper inside her heart, a caress in her soul. "I'll never forget you," he said. And then he was gone.

Chapter 13

The minute Micah hit the town's main street, he knew the raid was in full progress. People ran wildly from the Community Center as men wearing jackets identifying them as FBI attempted to round up as many as possible.

Gunfire resounded in the air, along with frantic screams that created the kind of chaos everyone had hoped to avoid. Micah ran to one of the blue-jacketed agents who had a seemingly bewildered Mayor Rufus Kittridge under arrest. "Did they get Samuel?"

"Last I heard he went down his rabbit hole, but don't worry, we have a guy on the other end of the tunnel waiting for him to pop up."

Micah cursed, angry that Samuel had managed to slip through the initial raid and not trusting a single agent to be able to keep Samuel down in his hole.

With his adrenaline pumping, he took off running.

He'd fulfilled his promise to Olivia. She had Ethan back and Dr. Rafe Black and Darcy would get the happy ending they'd dreamed of if the other little boy proved to be Devin. And Micah couldn't imagine the child being anyone else.

Now it was time for Micah to take care of his final business and a reckless energy carried him along the mountain where he knew the tunnel from the Community Center came up behind a large rock structure.

He wanted to be there before Samuel came above ground and disappeared into the forest. He needed to be there to stop Samuel from somehow managing to escape.

As he ran, his mind tumbled with a million thoughts. Samuel had stolen the very soul of a town. He'd taken children from their parents, destroyed families and killed innocent people. If he wasn't caught he'd do it all again, in another state, in another small town and that couldn't be allowed to happen.

Personally, he'd stolen Micah's ability to love, his ability to feel love. When he'd taken Johanna away, he'd broken something vital in Micah.

Olivia. Her name sang through his soul even as he tripped over a hidden vine and nearly fell to the ground. Maybe in a different time, in a different place, he would have accepted what he felt in his heart for her—love.

But as he raced through the bramble bushes, tore through the brush and around trees, he carried with him the knowledge that he might not survive the night, that he had nothing to offer Olivia and her children. He knew that he loved her enough to let her go to find her future somewhere else, with somebody else.

The fact that he'd already let go of Olivia only shot his rage toward his brother even higher. Gasping and out of breath, he finally reached the rock structure behind which hid the tunnel egress from the Community Center.

His heart crashed to a halt as he saw the FBI agent dead on the ground near the exit. A knife protruded from his chest. Samuel had already come up. Micah knelt down beside the dead agent and felt his wrist. Still warm, and with the cold night air, that meant Samuel was surely only minutes ahead of Micah.

There was no way Samuel knew the forest like Micah did. Samuel was probably dressed in his fancy business suit and slick Italian loafers. Not exactly survivalist clothing.

Micah stopped and held his breath, straining his ears to hear any movement that might indicate his brother's presence. Straight ahead in the distance he heard the crash and crackle of something or somebody moving fast.

His heartbeat quickened as he hurried toward the noise. Samuel probably didn't know that he was running up the mountain toward the cliff that overlooked the town he had owned.

Micah prayed he didn't veer from his current direction. If he continued, he'd find himself stuck between a killer drop-off at a cliff and the brother he'd tried to have murdered. Dead end. Dead Samuel.

As Micah continued to track his brother's movements, he felt as if they were the only two people in the entire world. Cain and Abel. Micah didn't remember much about the biblical brothers, but he was pretty sure that Cain had nothing on Samuel when it came to wicked intent.

The clouds overhead parted and the shine of the moon filtered down, allowing Micah enough illumination to turn off his flashlight. He was in soldier mode now, calm and with his mind blank and his heartbeat slow and steady.

He didn't think about Samuel being his brother, rather the man he hunted. The man he chased was a faceless, nameless enemy. It was nothing personal, simply business that had to be taken care of and he couldn't allow the enemy to leave the mountain.

He had no idea if his enemy was armed. Micah had his gun, but despite everything that Samuel had done, Micah wasn't sure he could look his brother in his eyes and shoot him. That would be too easy.

Samuel would hate being locked up, put away in a prison where he had no power, where he had no flock to lead, no kingdom to rule. He would hate wearing a jumpsuit instead of his fancy silk shirts and sharing a communal shower with dozens of murderers and rapists.

Micah stopped once again, realizing he'd almost reached the cliff. He crouched and moved slowly, cautiously and in a shaft of moonlight he saw his brother there, at the edge of the cliff, looking down on the town he'd built, on the town he owned and the mayhem he'd thought he'd escaped.

As Micah stepped out of the woods and into the small clearing where Samuel stood, his brother whirled around to face him.

"Ah, and so it ends the way it began, with just the

two of us all alone," Samuel said with a charming smile. "Are you going to shoot me with that gun?"

"Only if you force me to," Micah replied. "The difference between you and me is that I'll do my own dirty work instead of sending a minion."

"I don't know what you're talking about," Samuel scoffed. "I don't have minions. I can't help it that people respect me and want to follow my teachings."

"It's just us now, Samuel. There's nobody else around so it's not necessary for you to put on your act."

Samuel's smile fell as he gazed at Micah in speculation. "How much money would it take for you to let me walk off this mountain?" he asked, his eyes narrowing as he stared down Micah.

A dry laugh escaped Micah. "You don't have that much money, but you can start by telling the truth. You killed those women, didn't you?"

"I don't know what you're talking about," Samuel said as he took a step backward, coming precariously close to the edge of the cliff.

"Cut the crap," Micah said impatiently. He needed closure. He needed to know what had happened to those women, what had happened to Johanna. It was the last piece of a puzzle that he wanted to know.

Samuel studied him as if he were a peculiar specimen beneath a microscope slide. "They were supposed to be my women. Their allegiance was supposed to be to me, but one by one they pulled away, they started to work against me." He said the words as if amazed that such a thing could happen. "Don't you understand? I had to get rid of them. They each threatened all that I had built here. They tried to undermine what I had worked so hard to control." He shrugged. "Sometimes sacrifices have to be made for the greater good."

"For your greater good," Micah replied, trying to control the rage of emotions that shook his insides.

"I'm not going to prison." Samuel took another step toward the cliff and it was at that moment, Micah knew his brother would rather jump to his own death than face a day in jail. And Micah was just as determined that Samuel wouldn't get his easy out.

He anticipated Samuel's move, dropped his gun and leaped forward on his stomach to the ground as Samuel stepped off the edge of the cliff. He managed to grab his brother's wrist as he hung over the abyss.

Micah's entire body began to tremble with the strain of hanging on and keeping Samuel alive and as he gazed into the cult leader's eyes, he saw the panic of a man who wanted to live, but was willing to die if he had to face the consequences of his crimes.

"Let me go," Samuel said.

"Not a chance," Micah said, sweat running into his eyes and down the sides of his face as he hunkered against the earth with Samuel's weight threatening to drag him forward. Micah wrapped a leg around a nearby young tree trunk and grabbed Samuel's wrist with both hands, determined not to let him fall.

"She was a virgin, you know," Samuel said, his voice a sly purr. "Johanna, she was a sweet virgin when I first took her and I used her every day until she was all worn out."

A red curtain of blind rage swept over Micah. There was nothing more he wanted to do than release his hold, allow Samuel to fall down the side of the mountain and die. Samuel laughed, as if he knew Micah's torment and reveled in it.

Drop him, a little voice whispered. Just let him go. It would be so easy. It would all be done. Samuel would be done.

With a roar and a burst of nearly inhuman strength, driven by a rage he'd never felt before, Micah pulled up Samuel over the lip of the cliff and then collapsed into a boneless heap.

"Good job," Hawk said as he stepped from the woods. He slammed his foot into Samuel's back and pulled out a pair of handcuffs.

Auras danced in front of Micah's eyes as he slowly sat up, watching dully as Hawk hauled Samuel to his feet and cuffed his hands behind him.

"He's responsible for all the murdered women," Micah said, fighting the building, nauseating pound in the side of his head. "He confessed to me."

"He's lying," Samuel replied indignantly. "I wouldn't confess to something I didn't do. He's crazy. He shoved me off the cliff and tried to kill me."

Randy and another FBI agent entered the clearing. Randy grabbed Samuel as Hawk gave him a smile of amusement. "It's a funny thing about working a case where you don't know exactly who you can trust. I learned early in my career that there was only one way to make sure there were never any misunderstandings."

He pulled a small tape recorder from his pocket. "It's running now as we speak and it was taping when you told your brother about having to get rid of those women." He turned to his men. "You know what to do, so take off."

Micah was vaguely aware of the two agents leaving with Samuel. Hawk crouched down next to Micah. "I thought you were going to let him go."

"I wanted to. God, I can't tell you how much I wanted to, but death is way too easy for him. It was what he wanted and this time he wasn't going to win." The speech left Micah depleted, sickened by his migraine, and as he lay back against the cool grass, he knew no more.

It was the middle of the night. Ethan was sleeping in the little bed next to his brother's crib after spending the last hour cradled in her arms.

"I tried really hard to be brave," he'd said to her earlier, before he'd dropped off to sleep. "I knew you wouldn't forget about me even though Mrs. Lathrop said I was going to go live with a new family."

"I would never, ever let that happen," Olivia had replied as she'd hugged him close. She'd sat with him until he'd fallen asleep and only then had she gone into the kitchen to see what the news was from town.

Unfortunately, there was no news. There was only June at the table. Darcy had gone into town to meet Rafe the minute Hawk had placed Devin into her arms.

Jesse was outside standing guard at the entrance to make sure that none of the Devotees escaping from town and up into the mountains found their way inside the safe house.

Now that Ethan was where he belonged, there was only one person that filled Olivia's head, that filled her heart. Micah. Where was he? Was he okay? A new ache of absence had taken up residence inside her.

I'll never forget you. That's what he'd said as she, Hawk and Randy had hurried away with the children. *I'll never forget you.* What exactly did that mean? Did it mean he loved her? Were those simple words supposed to last her a lifetime? It hadn't been enough.

With each hour of night that ticked by, her concern grew more intense. What was happening in the "perfect" town of Cold Plains? Had the FBI managed to arrest all of Samuel's minions? Was Samuel now in custody? Where was Micah? Why hadn't he returned to the safe house?

Breakfast came and went as did an uneasy lunch. Nobody had come in who had been in town the night before. Hawk hadn't checked in, Micah was still gone and Olivia felt as if she was slowly losing her mind.

After lunch, with both boys down for naps, Olivia was desperate to talk to somebody, to anybody who had been in town and could tell her what had happened. She needed to know what had happened to Micah.

"Once things settle down, they'll probably relocate you and the boys," June said. The two women were seated at the table and the cave rang with an unusual silence.

Olivia shook her head. "I'm not going anywhere until I get some answers."

"Jesse said he'd heard radio talk that the FBI have twenty people under arrest." She hesitated a minute and then continued, "But there's been no word about either Samuel or Micah. Nobody seems to know what happened to the two of them."

"So, they didn't arrest Samuel with the others?" Olivia's heart sank.

"Maybe by now they have," June replied hopefully. "Maybe that's what's taken Micah so long to get back here."

Olivia grasped onto the hope that at any minute Micah would walk through the door. Even though she had Ethan back, she couldn't move forward until she knew the fate of the man who had been responsible for his return. Even though she knew there was no future with Micah, she had to know what had happened to the man she loved.

Night had fallen and the boys were once again in bed when not Micah, but Hawk came into the safe house. He appeared weary beyond exhaustion as he sank down at the table with June, Jesse and Olivia.

"What's the news from town?" June asked anxiously.

"Is Samuel in jail?" Olivia asked.

Hawk shook his head, his jaw tense. "Samuel escaped into the mountains. We've arrested Wilma Lathrop and Bo Fargo, who have told us that they were behind the kidnapping and adoption scheme of the children. They insist that Samuel knew nothing about it."

"So, once again he's like the Teflon king and you all won't have any real charges to press against him when he eventually resurfaces," June said in disgust.

"We've cut off a lot of his tentacles. One of his main henchmen, Dax Roberts, the man who shot Micah months ago, is dead after a gun battle with an agent. Most of his other known men have been arrested. All the Devotees are going to be lost and questioning where to turn from here."

Olivia was glad Dax Roberts was dead. He'd tried

to kill Micah and now had paid the ultimate price for his allegiance with the devil.

Hawk leaned back in his chair and swept a hand through his sandy hair, his brown eyes holding a bone weariness. "We still don't know how deep the corruption ran. We can't know after this initial sweep if we got everyone who needed to be arrested. But it was a start, and if Samuel does return, he'll have his work cut out for him rebuilding what he once had."

Olivia felt as if she might explode. He was talking about people she didn't care about and hadn't once mentioned the name of the man she needed to know about most of all. She could stand it no longer.

"Micah." His name burst from her lips. "Where is Micah?"

Hawk's eyes darkened. "Actually, I came by here to see if I could borrow you for a while. There's someplace I need to take you."

Olivia stared at him, her heart in her throat. "Where? Where do you want to take me?"

He looked around at the others at the table. "Just come with me, Olivia. Don't ask questions. Trust me, this is something that has to be done."

Something that had to be done? Like saying goodbye to a dead man? Fear leaped into her throat, bitter and vile tasting.

"I'll keep an eye on the boys," June said gently. "There's no reason to pull them from their sleep."

Olivia stared at her blankly. Was Micah dead? Did Hawk want to take her to where his body was to give her final closure?

On wooden legs she rose as Hawk also stood. She

wanted to know now. She needed to know at this moment if Micah was dead or alive, but Hawk's eyes were dark and hooded, closed off to any more questions she might have.

June got up from the table and gave Olivia a hug. "Don't worry about the boys. They'll be fine here." As she released Olivia, her eyes held a sympathy Olivia didn't want to acknowledge.

She grabbed a jacket against the cold night air and followed Hawk as he left the safe house and down the mountain to a street on the outskirts of Cold Plains where a car awaited them.

Hawk got behind the wheel as she slid into the passenger seat, her heart thudding with a dread that made her feel nauseous. "Are you going to tell me where we're going?" she finally asked as he pulled away and headed out of town.

"Unfortunately I don't have the clearance to tell you anything. I'm just following orders."

Orders? Orders from whom? She loved Micah and if he was dead, he'd given his life all for nothing. Samuel was on the loose and there were still criminals walking the streets of Cold Plains.

Even though he'd told her he wasn't cut out to be a husband or father, there had been a part of her that had retained hope that somehow she could change his mind, that he would love her more than he feared a romantic commitment.

Now that hope was gone. But she reminded herself that his death hadn't all been in vain. Ethan was back where he belonged, as was Devin Black. If Micah was dead, then he'd died a hero.

This thought was little comfort as she fought against the tears that burned at her eyes. As she stared out into the darkness, she realized they were on the highway that would take them into the town of Laramie.

She frowned over at Hawk, who hadn't said a word for the last forty minutes. Was it possible that Micah wasn't dead but rather had been sent to the hospital here with grave wounds?

Was Hawk giving her a chance to tell Micah a final goodbye before he died? Her heart squeezed so tight at the thought she could barely draw her next breath.

When they reached the town, Hawk pulled up in front of a three-story hotel and stopped the engine. He turned to look at her, his eyes gleaming with a kindness that was nearly her undoing.

He pulled a room card key from his pocket and handed it to her. "Room 212. Everything will be explained. Now, go."

She got out of the car, unsure if she was walking into disaster or something else. Nerves jumped inside her stomach as she proceeded, unsteady on her feet, across the lobby floor and punched the elevator button for the second floor.

What was going on here? Why was she here? As the elevator doors whooshed opened, she stepped inside, heart pounding and nerves screaming just beneath the surface of her skin.

When she reached the second floor, she exited the elevator and walked down the hallway to 212. She paused outside the door, afraid to go inside, afraid not to. What or who was behind the door?

She slid the key through the slot and saw the green

light flicker to let her know she could open the door. With a deep breath, she pushed it open and realized the room was a compact suite. The space she entered was like a small living room and a man she'd never seen before jumped up from the sofa, a gun pointed at her.

She squeaked a surprise and he immediately lowered the gun. "Olivia Conner?" he asked.

She nodded and at that moment the door to the bedroom opened and Micah appeared. With a sharp gasp she ran toward him, slamming into his big, strong body as his arms wrapped tightly around her.

"I thought you were dead," she said and began to weep.

He pulled her into the bedroom and closed the door behind them with her still in the embrace of his arms.

"As far as you and the boys are concerned, I am dead. I just couldn't let you go without saying a final goodbye." His voice was a husky whisper in her hair.

She raised her head to look at him. "I don't want to say goodbye. I love you, Micah. I love you with all my heart and soul." The words spilled from her, unable to stay inside her another minute. "I know you love me, too. I see it when you look at me, I feel it with every part of me. Let it be, Micah, don't fight against it."

She saw his love now, shining from his eyes. "Go with us. Relocate with us and build a life," she continued. "Be the husband, the father that you were meant to be. You deserve to be loved, Micah, and you deserve happiness. We can give that to you. Let yourself accept it."

He disentangled from her and took a step backward, his eyes pools of tortured emotions. "There's more at play here than just you and me." He walked over to the edge of the bed and sat down, then patted the space next to him.

Olivia sank down, her head filled with the clean male scent of him, her heart aching with the wealth of love for him that felt too big for her chest.

"There's much to be done in Cold Plains," he said, as if that somehow explained everything. "We know we didn't get everyone who has dirty hands."

"What are you saying? That you're going to stay here and continue to work with the FBI?"

He hesitated a moment and then slowly nodded. "That's the plan."

"But you know Samuel will come back and if he knows you're here, he'll try to have you killed again," she protested.

Micah was silent for a long moment, his gaze holding hers intently. "What I'm about to tell you is top secret information. You can't share it with anyone. Soon enough June and Jesse will know along with a few key players in town, but that's it."

"Okay," she said slowly, her heart once again beating an unsteady rhythm.

"The official story is that Samuel escaped the FBI net and with Bo and Wilma proclaiming his innocence in the adoption scheme, there's nothing to arrest him for. As for me, I died on the mountain, shot by persons unknown."

"And the unofficial story?" she asked softly.

"Samuel is in custody," he replied. She listened as he told her of the battle that had taken place on the cliff, a chill shivering through her as she realized how close

Micah had come to death. While he'd been trying to keep Samuel alive, he could have been pulled over the cliff's edge and both brothers would have been killed.

"He confessed to me to being responsible for the death of all those women." He explained to her about the final moments of Samuel's freedom, how he'd proclaimed his innocence and Hawk's tape recorder that had caught the confession on tape.

"By the time Samuel was led away by a couple agents, I had passed out from a migraine." He frowned, as if hating the weakness that had been left behind when his brother had tried to have him killed.

"When I finally came to, Hawk was seated next to me. He told me that Samuel had been taken to a secret location and I was to come with him. And here I am."

"So, Samuel is gone. Why would you have to stick around here? You accomplished what you wanted," she said, trying to understand why he was here in this hotel, why the official word was that he was dead. And then she knew.

"I love you, Olivia. I want the best for you and your sons. I have another mission to accomplish and I battle migraines. I'm no good for you. I love you enough to let you go, even though it's killing me right now." His voice trembled with emotion and it was in the depth of emotion that she saw her future.

"I get cramps," she said. "Every once in a while I get stomach cramps and all I want to do is stay in bed with a heating pad. I have a mission to accomplish, too. I want my boys to know the love and guidance of a good man. I want a man who makes me feel strong and vibrant and passionate and that man is you. If you are planning on staying in Cold Plains, then so am I. I have a nice house waiting for my return. The Community Center will still need a secretary and you can't beat the scenery in town."

"Olivia…"

She placed a finger against his lips. "I know exactly what I'm getting into, Micah, and I'm all in. Don't throw us away. We need you, and I have a feeling you need us, too."

His eyes shimmered with a light that nearly stole her breath away. "I do need you, Olivia. I feel as if I've waited my entire life for you and those little boys to come along. I don't know much about being a husband and nothing about being a parent, but I do know that I love you and I'll do everything in my power to keep you and the boys safe and happy."

Tears of joy shimmered in her eyes. "That's all I need, Micah. We'll figure it out as we go. I think our two missions might work together very well."

He stood and pulled her off the bed and into his embrace. "I learned early in my life not to give my heart to anyone, but somehow you managed to get in under my defenses. You have my heart, Olivia."

She leaned into him and smiled. "And I'll take very good care of it."

He took her mouth with his in a searing kiss that spoke not only of tenderness and passion, of commitment and caring, but also of a future together that would contain all the things that made up dreams.

Olivia knew the next weeks and months might be difficult, but at the end of each day she'd find her comfort in Micah's arms and her sons would find the father they needed.

It didn't matter if Cold Plains was a "perfect" town or not. She'd found the perfect man to be her life partner and together they would build a life on the foundation of love.

Epilogue

It had been a week since the raid on the small town of Cold Plains, and in that week much had happened to forever change Darcy Craven's life.

Deputy Ford McCall had finally identified Jane Doe as not only being Catherine George, but also the woman who had given birth to Darcy.

Darcy now walked with Rafe through the cemetery where her mother had been buried the day before. Rafe pushed the stroller with Devin gurgling the nonsensical, but pleasant sounds of babyhood.

Darcy carried in her arms a bouquet of daisies. Daisies were Darcy's favorite flowers and somehow she believed her mother had loved them, too.

Although she was heartbroken that she'd never have the reunion she'd dreamed about with her mother, she was comforted by the fact that her mother had taken her to Louise to protect her, to save her from the evil man who was her father.

It had taken tremendous love and sacrifice for Catherine to leave Darcy behind and in many ways Darcy would be forever grateful to the mother she'd never had the opportunity to get to know.

As they drew closer to the grave site, Rafe stopped at a stone bench nearby. "Go ahead," he said to her. "Take a little time by yourself."

She nodded, grateful that he understood her need to just stand, to just be in the spiritual presence of her mother. She walked a few more steps and stopped in front of the headstone that read *Catherine George* with the years of her birth and death. Below that were the words *Beloved Mother*.

"Beloved mother," Darcy whispered softly as she leaned down and gently placed the flowers on the grave. "Thank you for being strong enough, for being brave enough, to save me." She straightened up, a piercing sadness in her heart, but also a sense of pride. There was no doubt in her mind that, along with her blue eyes, she'd gotten her inner strength from her mother.

She stood there for several minutes, allowing the pain of loss to peak and then slowly recede away. It was time to put the past behind her. She and Rafe had made the decision to stay on in Cold Plains. Rafe wanted to continue his medical practice and she would continue as his receptionist and watch Devin, who had gained her heart the moment he was placed in her arms. Rafe was a good man and Cold Plains was a town that desperately needed good men.

She turned now and gazed at the two men who held not only her heart, but also her future. Rafe smiled and suddenly she wanted away from this place. Yes, it was time to put the past behind her and focus on the future, her wonderful future with Rafe and Devin.

"All done," the man said as he took the cape off Micah's shoulders and brushed him down with a soft-bristled brush. When he was finished, Micah stood and straightened the collar of the white dress shirt he wore. The shirt cost more than any item of clothing Micah had ever owned, as did the suit coat he shrugged on. It was like donning another man's skin.

As the barber left him alone in the room, Micah closed his eyes and thought of Olivia and her boys. They had settled back in the house where she'd lived before her world had exploded apart and Micah couldn't wait for the time they could be together again and that was going to be soon…very soon.

He'd been told that while things were relatively calm in Cold Plains, everyone appeared to be uneasy, waiting to see what happened next. They were a flock without a shepherd, a group of bewildered people seeking leadership.

Micah knew what happened next.

He slowly turned around and gazed at his reflection in the dresser mirror. The barber had done a perfect job styling his new short haircut. The suit fit him as if tailored specifically for him.

The resemblance was now uncanny. The flock needed a shepherd and he was about to return.

Micah smiled at his reflection, aware that his new mission was about to begin. "Hello, Samuel," he said softly.

* * * * *

"You're afraid of me, Wyatt Ledger…

"Afraid you might fall hard for me and that I might interfere with your burning desire to settle a score for your mother no matter who it hurts."

"You're reading this all wrong, Kelly. I'm just following the lawman's code. A cop never gets personally involved with a woman he's protecting. It makes him lose his edge. Fear has nothing to do with this."

"Prove it."

She stepped right in front of him, so close he could feel her breath on his bare chest. "Kiss me right now and prove you're not afraid." She took his hand and pressed it to her breast.

He lost it then and he kissed her hard, ravaging her lips, exploding in a rush of desire he couldn't have stopped if he wanted to.

First published in Great Britain 2012
by Mills & Boon, an imprint of Harlequin (UK) Limited,
Eton House, 18-24 Paradise Road, Richmond, Surrey TW9 1SR

© Jo Ann Vest 2012

ISBN: 978 0 263 89557 5
ebook ISBN: 978 1 408 97247 2

46-0912

Harlequin (UK) policy is to use papers that are natural, renewable and recyclable products and made from wood grown in sustainable forests. The logging and manufacturing processes conform to the legal environmental regulations of the country of origin.

Printed and bound in Spain
by Blackprint CPI, Barcelona

COWBOY
CONSPIRACY

BY
JOANNA WAYNE

Joanna Wayne was born and raised in Shreveport, Louisiana, and received her undergraduate and graduate degrees from LSU-Shreveport. She moved to New Orleans in 1984, and it was there that she attended her first writing class and joined her first professional writing organization. Her debut novel, *Deep in the Bayou,* was published in 1994.

Now, dozens of published books later, Joanna has made a name for herself as being on the cutting edge of romantic suspense in both series and single-title novels. She has been on the Waldenbooks bestseller list for romance and has won many industry awards. She is also a popular speaker at writing organizations and local community functions and has taught creative writing at the University of New Orleans Metropolitan College.

Joanna currently resides in a small community forty miles north of Houston, Texas, with her husband. Though she still has many family and emotional ties to Louisiana, she loves living in the Lone Star State. You may write Joanna at PO Box 852, Montgomery, Texas 77356, USA.

Prologue

It was a country club neighborhood. Sprawling brick houses. Manicured lawns. A guard at the gate. The kind of community where people should be resting safely in their beds at 2:00 a.m. on a Sunday.

But in the Whiting home, one resident would never wake up to the smell of morning coffee—the latest Atlanta homicide to drop onto Wyatt Ledger's over-flowing plate.

Home murders were the worst, he lamented as he pulled up and stopped behind the two squad cars already parked in the driveway of a columned, two-story brick structure. A lone, bare tree stretched its creaking limbs toward the covered entry. Welcome to paradise gone brutal.

Not that murder was any more horrid or final here than in the backstreets and alleyways where so many of the city's gang and drug-related killings went down. But a home was a person's refuge, the haven from the outside world. Blood seemed so repulsively out of place splattered over pristine surfaces where violence had never struck before.

And home murders hit way too close to the nightmarish memories Wyatt could never lay to rest.

He turned at the squeal of brakes as a blue sedan joined the scene. A second later his partner rushed up the walk behind him, catching up just as he reached the door.

"Be nice if murders occurred during waking hours," Alyssa said as she twisted her skirt until it hung straight over her narrow hips. Even slightly disheveled, she looked good. In any other setting, no one would guess she was as tough and smart as any homicide detective in the city.

"Didn't you have a hot date tonight?" Wyatt asked, but his focus had already moved from Alyssa to the house's surroundings. Lots of trees and shrubs to offer cover for a perp. An alarm-system warning was planted in the front garden. He'd have to check and see if it had gone off.

"Kyle and I went out with friends and didn't get home until after midnight," Alyssa said. "I was sorely tempted to ignore the phone."

"You'd be yelling if you weren't invited to the party."

"Wrong. I hate crime scenes. I love arresting murdering bastards, so I forego sleep."

"I figure we may lose a lot of sleep over this one."

"Why?" Alyssa asked. "What do you know about the crime?"

"Probably the same as you know. Cops were summoned by a 911 call. Found a woman fatally shot. House belongs to Derrick and Kathleen Whiting."

Wyatt opened the unlocked door and stepped inside a high-ceilinged foyer. A multifaceted crystal chandelier dripped light over a marble floor and an antique cherry credenza. Cold air blasted from the air-conditioning unit, though it was already October and in the high sixties outside.

Low voices drifted down the hallway. Wyatt's gut tightened as he strode toward the conversation. He'd been in Homicide six years. This part of the routine never got easier.

He saw the blood first, streams of it flowing away from a body partially hidden by two uniformed officers. Wyatt knew both of the policemen—Carter and Bower. They'd worked night shifts for as long as he'd been with the Atlanta P.D.

"It's ugly," Carter said, stepping back for Wyatt and Alyssa to move in for a closer look. He added a few expletives to make his point.

The victim was lying facedown on the living room floor, wearing a pair of black pajamas. Her feet were bare. She'd been shot in the back of the head at close range. Two bullet entry points were clearly visible.

The wounds were enough to make most men puke. It worried Wyatt a little that he'd become so desensitized to the gore that he didn't pitch his dinner onto the sea of off-white carpet.

"The back door had been jimmied open," Carter said. "The TV is unplugged and pulled out from the wall. Looks as if the victim may have come downstairs and interrupted a burglary in progress."

"Or someone meant it to look that way," Wyatt said. "Did you check the rest of the house for other victims?"

"Yep. All clear. No one else is home. There are men's clothes in the closet in the master bedroom, but only one side of the bed appears to have been slept in. There's another bedroom. Looks as if it belongs to a teenage boy. Slew of baseball trophies on some cluttered shelves and a poster of the Atlanta Falcon cheerleaders on the wall. Dirty clothes piled on the floor. Bed hasn't been slept in."

A boy who'd come home soon to find his mother had been brutally murdered.

A surge of unwanted memories bombarded Wyatt. Events replayed in his mind in slow motion. Staring at his mother's brutally slain body, the pain inside him so intense he'd had to fight to breathe. The panic. The fear. The smell of burning peas. To this day he couldn't stomach the sight or smell of peas.

"Who called the police?" Alyssa asked.

"A neighbor. He said he heard what sounded like gunshots from the Whiting home, but that the alarm system hadn't gone off. When we got here we found the back door wide open, so we came in that way and then unlocked the front door for you guys."

"Have you talked to the neighbor?" Wyatt asked.

"We figured Homicide would want to be the first to do that," Bower said.

The front door banged shut. Either the wind had caught it or someone had joined them. Wyatt's hand instinctively flew to the butt of his weapon.

"Mother."

The voice coming from the foyer was youthful, male and shaky with panic.

Wyatt and Alyssa rushed to the hallway.

"What's wrong?" the boy asked. "Where's my mother?"

The boy looked to be twelve or thirteen, the same age Wyatt had been when his world had exploded. A man in a blue flannel robe stood beside him, his hand on the boy's shoulder. "Has something happened?"

Alyssa flashed her badge. "Alyssa Lancaster, Atlanta P.D. Are you Derrick Whiting?"

"No. My name's Culver. Andy Culver. I live across the street and a few doors down. Josh, here, was spending the night with my son Eric. He woke up and saw the squad cars in front of his house. Was there an accident?"

"There's a problem," Alyssa admitted. "Josh, do you know where your dad is?"

"He's out of town on business."

"Do you have any brothers or sisters?" Wyatt asked.

"No."

"Any other relatives who live nearby? Grandparents or maybe an aunt?"

"My grandparents live in Peachtree City. Why? What happened to my mother?" His voice had turned husky, as if he were fighting back tears.

"Why don't we step out on the porch while I explain the situation," Alyssa said.

Explain? As if they were talking about the boy's math homework instead of the end of life as he'd known it. Thankfully, Alyssa was better at talking to the family of a victim than Wyatt was, especially when they were kids.

Wyatt could handle the cold, hard facts of the crime, but he needed the sharp edges of personal boundaries to keep distracting emotions in check.

"Where's my mother?" Josh's voice had become almost a wail.

"I'm sorry, Josh." Alyssa stepped toward him.

Josh broke loose from the cluster and made a run for the living area where his mother's lifeless body lay drenched in blood. Wyatt grabbed for him as he scurried past, but Josh went in for the slide as if he were stealing home. By the time Wyatt reached him, the boy was standing over the body, his face a ghostly white.

Josh trembled, but he wasn't crying yet. That would come later. Now he was in a state of semishock, consumed by the nightmare and ghastly images his mind wouldn't let him accept.

"Mom's dead, isn't she?" His voice broke.

Alyssa slipped an arm around his shoulders as Wyatt took a position that hid the worst of the scene from the boy's line of vision. But nothing either of them could say or do could protect Josh from the horror or the agony that would follow. No one knew that better than Wyatt.

The best Wyatt could do was to apprehend the killer and see that justice was served for Josh's mother. That was a hell of a lot more than anyone had done for Helene Ledger.

Chapter One

Three months later

"The chief wants to see you in his office."

Wyatt looked up at the young clerk who had just stuck her head inside his cubicle. "Did he say why?"

"No, just that he wants to see you."

Wyatt shoved the letter he'd been sweating over into a folder and pushed his squeaky swivel chair back from a desk piled high with case files. He picked up the folder for the Whiting case. He hadn't even finished his written report yet, but he was sure last night's developments would be the topic of the chief's discussion.

He wouldn't be thrilled that Derrick Whiting would not be standing trial for the murder of his wife. But neither would he be walking the streets a free man, with insurance money in the bank and the sexy mistress in his bed.

Whiting had shot himself last night when Wyatt and Alyssa had shown up at his door, arrest warrant in hand. Fortunately, Josh was not there to witness the event. He'd moved in with his grandparents over a month ago.

Alyssa caught up with Wyatt just before he reached the chief's door. "So you were summoned, too."

"Yeah."

"Think Dixon's pissed that we couldn't stop the sick bastard from killing himself?" she asked.

"I'm sure he'd have preferred to have the guy stand trial, but it is what it is."

The door was open. Martin Dixon waved them both inside. He stood and moved away from his desk to welcome them. He wasn't exactly smiling. He never did. But his eyes and stance said it all. He was glad this was over.

"Hell of a job! Both of you. I wish we could have brought Whiting in to stand trial, but I can see why he took care of his own death sentence. And if he hadn't, the evidence you've collected would have guaranteed a conviction. No juror in his right mind would have let him off."

"It's the jurors not in their right minds I always worry about," Alyssa said. "But thanks for the kudos."

"The mayor called this morning," the chief continued. "Said to tell both of you how grateful he is for the way you handled the investigation. He wanted to congratulate you himself, but he's getting ready for a joint press conference he's giving with me in about an hour."

Wyatt grimaced. "You're not going to thank us by making us spoon-feed the details to the media sharks, are you?"

"No. The mayor and I will make statements. Louis will handle the questions about the case, but I need both of you to brief him."

"That, I can handle," Wyatt said.

Louis was in charge of APD public relations and he

had a way of feeding the media just enough to keep them happy without releasing any gratuitous details.

"Anyway, good work," the chief said again.

"Thanks," Wyatt said. "Just doing my job, and I'm certain the guy who ate the bullet was guilty as sin."

Wyatt and Alyssa had eaten and slept that case for three months. The murder had been carefully planned, and *almost* perfectly executed to make it look like a startled burglar had committed the crime. But Derrick had made a couple of fatal errors. Most murderers did.

Thankfully, Derrick Whiting was Josh's stepfather of just over two years and not his biological father. Josh admitted they'd never been close, though Derrick had painted a picture of perfect family harmony to his co-workers.

At least now Josh wouldn't have to live with the knowledge that his real father had killed his mother in cold blood. He wouldn't be forced to endure the cruel taunts of schoolmates for being a murderer's kid or have to wonder if the evil that possessed his father was buried deep in his own DNA.

"You're both up for a promotion," the chief said. "I've decided to skip a few bureaucracy hurdles and move that along."

"Now you're talking," Alyssa said.

The announcement caught Wyatt totally off guard. Great for Alyssa, but so much for the letter of resignation he'd been laboring over for the past hour.

"Is this a problem for you, Wyatt?" Dixon said, obviously picking up on Wyatt's discomfort.

"Not exactly a problem, but…" Might as well blurt this out. The decision was made. "I appreciate the promotion offer, but I'm turning in my resignation."

The chief looked stunned. Wyatt refrained from

making eye contact with Alyssa. He'd planned to tell her first. That was partner protocol, but news of the promotion took this out of his hands.

"When did you decide this?" Dixon asked.

"A couple of weeks ago, but I've been thinking about it for quite a while. I planned to see the Derrick Whiting case through before I talked to anyone about it."

"You should have come to me sooner. Whatever the problem is, I'm sure we can work it out."

"My leaving has nothing to do with department or the work," Wyatt added quickly. "Hell, this place is home. But I need a change. I've been with the APD ever since I dropped out of college and signed on as a rookie cop."

"What kind of change? If it's a move out of Homicide, we can—"

"I'm moving back to Texas," Wyatt said, hopefully ending the discussion.

Dixon looked skeptical. "To go into ranching with your family?"

"I doubt I'll live on the ranch," Wyatt explained, "but I've got unsettled business in Mustang Run and it's time I take care of it."

"Does this have to do with your mother's murder?"

"That's a big part of it," Wyatt admitted.

"Are you sure you've thought this through?"

"I'm sure," Wyatt assured him. He'd thought of not much else for most of his life. It was the reason he'd become a cop. He'd put it off as long as he could.

The chief shook his head, his expression making it clear he thought the move was a big mistake. "You said once that your brothers are all convinced of your father's innocence. I doubt they'll appreciate you stirring up trouble. And he's served seventeen years of a sentence. That's more than a lot of convicted perps serve when there isn't the slightest doubt that they're guilty."

"I'm not going after my father. I'm going after the man who killed my mother. If my father is innocent, I'll prove that beyond a doubt. If he's guilty, then I'll just have to deal with that. My brothers are grown men. They'll have to do the same."

"I hate to say it, but I can see where you're coming from, Wyatt. And I don't doubt for a second that you'll find the answers you're looking for."

"I hope that confidence is justified."

"Keep me posted. And as long as I'm heading up the force, there's always a place for you if you decide to come back."

"I appreciate that."

"When do you plan to leave?"

"My caseload is as caught up as it will ever be, so I'd like to clear out as soon as you replace me."

Dixon nodded. "The department will miss you."

"I'll miss being here."

Talk went back to the Whiting case, but the celebratory tone of the meeting had shifted. Wyatt, usually the first to make a wisecrack to alleviate the tension, could think of nothing to say. He loved his job, but he had to do this.

And he could use a change of scenery. His apartment walls were starting to close in around him. He needed a taste of wide-open spaces, hilly pastures and the quiet fishing spots Dylan, Sean and now Dakota were always talking about.

That didn't make going back to Mustang Run and Willow Creek Ranch any easier.

As soon as they stepped into the hallway, Alyssa

poked him in the ribs. "When exactly did you plan to hit me in the head with this?"

"At the last possible moment, so I wouldn't have to listen to you whine and lecture," he teased. "And don't poke me with those bony fingers."

She poked him again. "You'll go crazy in the Podunk town of Horse Run."

"*Mustang* Run. And I don't plan to be there forever."

"No, just long enough to cause trouble," Alyssa quipped.

"And I'm talented at stirring the pot, so that shouldn't take too long."

"Your dad's already spent seventeen years in prison before being released on a technicality. He's reunited with four of his five sons, even Tyler who's still on active duty in Afghanistan. He's a beloved grandfather. Have you ever considered just leaving well enough alone?"

"I'm not planning to go down there and string him up from the nearest tree. Troy claims he's looking for Mother's killer. I aim to help him."

"Oh, right, the good son. You can't even call him Dad."

Wyatt stopped walking and made eye contact. "Are you telling me you wouldn't feel the same if your mother had been murdered?"

"Okay, point made. But I'll miss you, partner. Worse, I'm selfish. Now I have to adjust to someone new. I'll probably get one who sweats profusely or passes gas in the car, or heaven forbid, treats me like a woman."

"He won't make that mistake but once."

She smiled as if that were the ultimate compliment. "Do me a favor while you're out there with those rattlesnakes and cow patties, Wyatt."

"Send you a snakeskin?"

"Don't even think about it. But if on the off chance you find a woman who can put up with you, don't push her away like she's been living with a family of skunks, the way you did everyone I tried to fix you up with."

"I'll keep that in mind."

"You know what's wrong with you?"

"I don't like skunks."

"You're afraid of falling. As soon you think you might like some woman, you make up excuses for why it won't work. She's too smart. She's not smart enough. She has cats. She has kids. She doesn't like cats or kids."

"You should get better friends to fix me up with."

"You may as well admit it. You're afraid of relationships."

"Shows how smart I am. Do you know the divorce rate among cops?"

"One day you'll meet a woman who'll knock you for such a loop you won't be able to walk away. I hear Texas is full of women like that."

"Could be." But a woman was the last thing he needed now. Texas and reuniting with Troy Ledger would be challenge enough. And now that the decision was made, he needed to move on. With luck, he'd be on the road by the middle of January.

He traveled light. That was just one of the advantages of never putting down any deep roots or acquiring things like mortgages or a wife.

He had no intention of changing that.

"It's the fuel pump, Mrs. Burger. It's going to have to be replaced."

Kelly groaned. She had another four hours to drive

and it was already after three. Plus, the weather forecast for tonight was a line of severe thunderstorms preceding a cold front moving in from the northwest.

The mechanic yanked a red rag from his back pocket and rubbed at a spot of grease on his arm that defied his removal efforts. "I can get to it first thing in the morning. And I'll be glad to give you a ride now to the nearest motel."

"I really need to get back on the road today. I'll pay extra if you can fix it this afternoon."

"I'm not sure how quickly I can get the part. I might be able to just run over to Mac's Garage and pick it up or I might have to have one shipped in."

Just her luck to have her car break down in a small town. "Can't you have someone drive to the nearest town with a Honda dealer and pick one up? I'll pay his overtime and buy his gas."

Jaci tugged on Kelly's skirt. "Can we go now, Momma?"

"Not yet, Jaci." She struggled to keep the frustration from her voice. She couldn't expect a five-year-old to understand why they were just standing around waiting instead of off on the adventure she'd been promised. Jaci had been such a trooper over the last twelve months when their lives had been in serious upheaval.

"Let me see what I can do," the young mechanic said.

He returned to the small waiting area ten minutes later, this time smiling.

"I found a fuel pump that I can have here in under an hour. If we don't run into problems, you can be on your way just after dark."

"Super." They'd arrive in Mustang Run too late to accomplish anything tonight, but at least she'd be at the new house when the moving van arrived in the morning. Not actually a new house—just new to her. Actually it was older than her grandmother who'd willed it to her. But it would offer Kelly a new start after her year from hell.

Not that she had a clue what shape the house would be in. It had stood empty for over a year now and the man who'd been managing the property was visiting his son in California.

All he'd told her over the phone was that the house would need an ample application of soap and elbow grease and paint. She'd decided to move in and fix it up one room at a time as she found the time and the money.

She had some savings but not enough for major repairs. Her husband's medical bills had taken most of it before he died three years ago. And last year, she hadn't earned a dime.

"I'm hungry, Momma," Jaci said, though Kelly suspected she was more bored than anything else.

"There's a McDonalds's out on the highway," the mechanic offered. "I can give you a lift over there if you'd like and pick you up when your car's ready. It's got a nice play area."

Jaci jumped around excitedly. "McDonald's. Please, Momma. Please."

Hours at a McDonald's surrounded by squealing kids and the odor of fries—or sitting here rereading for the twentieth time the two storybooks Jaci had brought with her in the car.

That was a no-brainer.

"That would be terrific," Kelly agreed. Jaci could play off some of her energy, have the chicken nuggets she loved and then she'd likely sleep all the way to the

Hill Country. They'd be back on track and hopefully to Mustang Run before the predicted thunderstorms set in.

Surely nothing else could go wrong today.

Chapter Two

Large drops of rain splattered the windshield as Wyatt pulled off the highway and next to one of the gas pumps at a 24-hour truck stop. Eighteen-wheelers lined the truck parking area off to the right, the drivers no doubt sleeping soundly in their fancy cabs.

He was the only gas customer and the parking lot in front of the café was empty except for a motorbike that looked as if it had seen its best days years ago, and a snazzy new Corvette.

Wyatt climbed from his brand-new double-cab pickup truck, his going-away present to himself for trading a job he loved for a reunion with his father.

All he owned was either tossed into the backseat or stored in the truck's bed beneath the aluminum cover. That included the fancy rod and reel the other homicide cops had presented him with as their going-away memento.

Stretching to relieve the kinks from his muscles, Wyatt massaged the stiff tendons in his neck. The beers he'd enjoyed with his buddies last night had left him with just enough headache pain to dull the fun of hitting the road.

The splatters became a pelting downpour as he filled

his gas tank. A gust of icy wind almost blew his black Stetson off his head. He tugged the hat lower with his free hand.

Just as he was returning the fuel handle to its cradle, a late model Honda Accord pulled up across from him and a woman stepped out.

The wind was blowing so hard now that the sheltering canopy above them did little to keep them dry. She pulled a denim jacket tight and glanced around nervously.

He tipped his hat. "Rough night for traveling."

"Yes. I was hoping the rain would hold off for another hour," she said, cautiously avoiding eye contact as she unscrewed her gas tank.

There was no one in the passenger seat, but he spotted a little girl in the backseat. Her face was pressed against the window as she peered at him. She opened the door for a better look.

"Don't get out of the car, Jaci. It's cold and you'll get wet." When the girl closed her door, the woman quickly locked it with the remote on her key.

"You're getting wet, too," Wyatt said. "Why don't you let me finish gassing up for you and you and the kid make a run for the café before it gets any worse?"

"We're not going in. And thanks for the offer, but I really don't need any help." Her tone and stare clearly told him to back off.

Smart woman. He was harmless, but plenty of men weren't. And a woman and a kid traveling alone would make an easy target for some of the perverts he'd dealt with.

If he was still carrying his APD identification, he could probably reassure her, but he was no longer a cop, at least not officially.

"I'd give the rain a few minutes to slack off before I hit the road again. Just a suggestion," he said, tipping his hat again.

He headed inside for a cup of coffee as the wind and rain picked up in intensity. He was less than thirty miles from Mustang Run but in no hurry to get there. He'd decided about forty miles back that he'd check in to one of the town's two motels for the night and then drive out to the ranch in the morning.

He needed a good night's sleep before he faced Troy.

Troy Ledger, convicted of murder, but still claiming his innocence. Wyatt hoped to God he was, but he'd read and reread the trial notes so many times he knew every last detail. If he'd been on that jury, he'd have come to the same conclusion they had. Guilty of murder in the first degree.

That was the Troy he'd be facing. But it was the other Troy he had been thinking about ever since he'd crossed the Texas line.

The father who'd chased monsters from his bedroom, taught him to ride a horse and a bike. Given him his first pony. The father who'd stayed with him all night when that pony had been so sick they thought they might have to put her down.

Wyatt stamped the water from his worn Western boots and made a stop at the men's room before entering the café proper.

"C'mon in," the waitress welcomed when he finally stepped into the main area of the café. She looked to be in her mid-thirties, blonde, with heavy, smudged eye makeup.

"You made it just in time," she said. "Sounds like a whopper of a storm kicking up out there."

"Is this your usual January weather?" he asked.

"No, but nothing about the weather's predictable in this part of Texas. One day you'll be in shorts, the next day you'll be wearing sweats. Where are you from?"

"Texas originally, but I've lived in Georgia for most of my life."

"Welcome back to the Lone Star State."

"Thanks." He shed his jacket and dropped it to one of the counter stools.

She handed him a plastic-coated menu. "You looking for dinner or just coffee and a warm, dry spot to wait out the storm?"

"Both." He checked out her name tag. "I'll start with a cup of black coffee, Edie."

"The cook's already gone for the night," she said as she poured the coffee and set it in front of him. "I can fix you a burger or a sandwich and fries. I can do most of the breakfast items, too. There was chicken tortilla soup, but a couple of truckers finished that off about thirty minutes ago."

"Whatever you're cooking now smells good."

"I'm making the guy in the back corner a grilled ham-and-cheese sandwich. I recommend it."

"Then I'll have that."

"You got it."

Wyatt glanced at the only other customer. He was bent over a road map that he'd spread across the narrow table. His hair was shaggy and looked like it hadn't been washed in days. His jeans were faded and frayed at the hem. Heavily tattooed muscles bunched beneath a wife-beater T-shirt, and there was a wicked scar at his collarbone.

He might be a perfect gentleman with a spotless record, but he was the kind of guy who always courted a cop's attention.

But Wyatt was no longer a cop. He turned his attention back to the front of the café. The rain slashed against the huge front windows now, and he thought of the woman in the Honda again. If she was trying to drive in this deluge, she was in for trouble. Visibility would be reduced to a few feet.

The bell above the front door tinkled. Wyatt looked up as the woman who'd said she wasn't coming in herded the kid inside and toward the restrooms on the right. Hopefully that meant she'd decided to sit out the storm here.

A loud clap of thunder rattled the doors and the lights blinked off and on.

Edie leaned over the counter in front of him. "I'm sure glad you stopped in. I get spooked if I'm alone or with only one customer when the power goes off. Normally if I yell, any number of truckers would come to my rescue, but they'd never hear me in this storm."

"Is the guy sitting in the back a regular?" Wyatt asked.

"Never seen him before." She leaned in closer. "Hope to never see him again. The way he looks at me gives me the willies. That's another reason I was glad to see you walk in. You look like a guy who can handle trouble."

"Only when trouble throws the first punch."

She smiled and stuck a paper napkin at his elbow. "Storms lure in lots of strangers, especially when the rain is falling so hard you can't see to drive."

Wyatt kept his gaze on the front of the café until the woman and kid came out of the restroom area. The woman looked around and met his gaze for one quick second before leading her daughter to a table at the front of the café.

The waitress sashayed over to them, starting up a new conversation about the storm.

"Just black coffee for me and a glass of milk for my daughter," he heard the woman say once they got around to the order.

"Sure thing. Are you traveling much farther tonight?"

"Just to Mustang Run. I thought I had enough gas to get there, but then the gauge dropped so low I was afraid to chance it."

"Good that you stopped and came in," Edie said. "One of my regulars ran his truck off the road last time we had a gully washer like this."

"We're moving to my great-grandmother's old house," the kid said excitedly. "It has a big yard."

"Lucky you. Is your daddy going to work in Mustang Run?"

"My daddy got sick and he's in heaven," the little girl said. "But I have a gramma Linda Ann in Plano. She's a schoolteacher. At a college."

So the woman was a widow, Wyatt considered. And she and her daughter were moving to the same small town as he was, on the same night.

Alyssa would claim it was serendipity and that he should go right over and introduce himself. But then Alyssa also believed that throwing pennies in the fountain in the courtyard of her favorite restaurant would help her meet the perfect man. If not, Facebook would.

"You're going to love Mustang Run," Edie said to the little girl. "I live about thirty minutes in the opposite direction, but I go into Mustang Run every year for the Bluebonnet Festival Dance. The locals are really friendly." She turned to the woman. "And the cowboys are *sooo* cute."

"I'm not looking for a cowboy."

Wyatt hooked the heels of his Western boots on the stool's rung. That ruled him out. Not that he worked with cows, but he was a cowboy in his soul.

"Where are you moving from?" Edie asked.

"East of here."

You couldn't get much more evasive that than, Wyatt thought. His cop instincts checked in and he wondered if she might be on the run—from the police or perhaps an unwanted lover.

"We're getting a cat," the little girl said.

"That will be nice," Edie said. "I had a cat when I was young. I named it Princess."

"I'm naming mine Belle. That's a princess name."

"It is. I like that."

"My name is Jaci."

"I like that, too. Now I better get back to my grill before I burn the ham."

The thunder was now a constant growl in the background and the pounding on the metal roof sounded like hailstones. The lights blinked again as Edie pulled sliced tomatoes, lettuce leaves and jalapeños from a small built-in refrigerator beneath the counter.

Wyatt shifted on the stool so that he had a better view of the woman at the front table without staring obviously. His mind automatically sized her up the way he would a suspect. The hair was strawberry blond, clean and shiny. It was cut short and in wavy layers that flipped about her chin. She had a cute nose that turned up ever so slightly on the end.

Nice breasts. Slender hips—he'd noticed those when she was pumping gas. Full lips. Great smile—when she smiled.

Okay, so maybe he was noticing her more like a

woman than a suspect. She did intrigue him, maybe because she was showing absolutely no interest in him.

She looked up, saw him watching her and shot him that same back-off stare she had aimed at him outside.

Once Edie put his sandwich in front of him, his concentration turned to the food. When he did look up, he caught the guy at the other end of the bar eyeing Jaci's mother. Wyatt couldn't fault him for noticing an attractive woman. He'd done the same.

But the way this guy was looking at her bothered Wyatt. He could see why the waitress felt uncomfortable around him.

Wyatt felt that copper's itch to find some reason to ask for the man's ID. He'd like to check him out and see if he had a record or an outstanding warrant for his arrest.

A few minutes later, the guy paid his tab, stood and swaggered toward the door. He stopped near the woman at the table and rested his right hand on his groin area, leering until the woman looked up. She glanced away quickly.

Wyatt's muscles clenched. Badge or not, he wasn't going to let the slimy weasel intimidate a woman while he was here to stop it.

But then the guy turned and strode out of the café and into the full fury of the storm.

By the time Wyatt had finished his sandwich and a second cup of coffee, the steady pelting against the roof had finally slacked off. The woman and kid were already pulling on their jackets. They left as Wyatt paid his tab.

He'd just shrugged into his own jacket when he heard the piercing wail. Adrenaline rushed his veins.

He shoved his way out the door, his instincts already kicking in and ready for whatever he might find.

Anything except this.

Chapter Three

The woman from the diner had shoved a motorbike to the pavement and was kicking the frame like she was attacking a hungry grizzly. Had it been a grizzly, the bear would likely be losing the battle.

"What's the problem?" he asked.

Her hands flew to her hips. "That hooligan stole my car."

Wyatt looked around. True enough, there was no sign of the Honda she'd been driving earlier.

"Don't just stand there," she demanded. "Do something."

"Looks like you have the bike subdued," he quipped.

"Not help with the bike. My purse is in that car. All my money's in it. He has my computer. A box of Jaci's favorite toys." She threw up her hands in frustration. "And half of our clothes!" She slammed the heel of her stylish boot into the bike's frame again.

The hooligan in question had a good half hour head start. With no idea which direction he'd gone in, chances were slim Wyatt could chase him down in his pickup truck.

"What in holy tarnation are you doing to my bike?"

This time it was the waitress's shrill voice that cut through the damp air.

The woman threw up her hands. "*Your* bike? I thought it belonged to the man who stole my car."

"That creep who was in the café stole your car?"

"Apparently."

"I knew he was up to no good the second he walked in. I figured he was just hanging around waiting for the power to go off so he could clean out the register."

Wyatt made the 911 call while the women righted the downed bike and the attacker apologized profusely for the damage her boot had inflicted.

The kid ran over to Wyatt. "Call the police and the game warden," she squealed. "That man stole my toys and my books."

Three near-hysterical females was downright scary. The light rain that was still falling did nothing to settle them down. At least the kid had sense enough to move to the cover of the aluminum canopy over the door after she put in her order for cops.

"Ladies," Wyatt announced when he'd finished the call. "A deputy is on the way. Let's go back inside and calm down."

"Easy for you to say," the woman snapped. "You have your truck."

No doubt because the thief didn't realize Wyatt had a couple of loaded pistols inside. Wyatt stopped at the Corvette parked in the lot as the three women marched inside.

If the guy hadn't been riding the motorbike, he must have been driving this. Ten to one it was stolen, as well. But there was nothing he could do about it until a deputy showed up.

Back in Atlanta, he'd have made a few calls and

had local cops and the state police already on the lookout for the stolen Honda. He'd have run a license-plate check on the Corvette. He'd have assumed control instead of waiting for a deputy.

Already he missed his life.

KELLY TOOK A DEEP BREATH and struggled to think rationally. Instead, she plunged into the frightening abyss of "what ifs." What if the creep had been the one pumping gas when she was? What if he'd knocked her to the pavement and stolen the car with Jaci inside it? What if she'd walked out while he was hot-wiring the ignition and he'd shot Jaci or her or both of them?

When she looked at it that way, the loss of her car and her belongings didn't seem nearly so horrific. But still, she was fed up with being criminals' prey. It was as if she wore a sign on her back that said *victim*.

"I'll start a fresh pot of coffee," Edie offered. "You never know how long we'll have to wait for a deputy in this weather."

Kelly and Jaci slid into one side of the narrow booth. Not unexpectedly, the cowboy slid in opposite them. Fortunately, he seemed to be taking command of the situation. Good that someone was, since she'd flown into a rage out there instead of thinking logically.

He was quite a hunk. Not that she hadn't noticed that earlier, but now she actually let her gaze linger on the rugged planes and angles of his face. He couldn't be many years older than she was, if any, but he had an edge about him and an aura of self-confidence.

She liked his hair—short but rumpled and dry— where hers was wet and dripping, thanks to the Western hat he'd just tossed to the booth behind them. His dark brown locks were streaked with coppery highlights, the artistic work of the sun.

But his eyes were the real draw. Mesmerizing. Piercing, but not threatening. The color of the coffee she could smell dripping through the pot.

"I think we should introduce ourselves," he said. "I'm Wyatt Ledger."

"Good to meet you, Wyatt, though I would have preferred to meet under better circumstances. I'm Kelly Burger."

It was a relief to finally use her real name again. Maybe one day she'd even be able to get past the fears she'd lived with for nearly twelve months. She extended her hand and when his wrapped around hers, the tingle of awareness danced through her. She pulled her hand away too quickly. Subtlety was not her strong suit.

She looked down at her daughter, thankful to break away from Wyatt's penetrating gaze. "This is Jaci."

The cowboy's lips split into a wide grin. "Hi, Jaci."

Attacked by one of her rare cases of shyness, Jaci twirled a finger in her hair and looked down at the table. It was well past her bedtime, and even though she'd slept some in the car, she was running out of steam.

Jaci pulled her short legs into the seat with her and finally looked at Wyatt. "Can you take us to our new house?"

"It's okay, Jaci," Kelly assured her. "The police will see that we get home tonight."

"Actually, I heard Jaci say earlier that you're going to Mustang Run," Wyatt said. "That's also where I'm heading, so I can give you a lift if you'd like."

The coincidence set off a warning bell in her head. For all she knew Wyatt could be as bad as the rotten thug who'd stolen her car. Boots and a cowboy hat didn't mean he was the real thing. "Do you own a ranch near Mustang Run?"

"My family does. I was a homicide detective with the Atlanta Police Department until yesterday. Now I guess I'm a freeloader."

"You're a cop?"

"*Was* a cop. Guess it doesn't say much for my detective intuition that I let the guy just walk out of here and steal your car. The fact that he left in the middle of a pouring rain should have tipped me off he might be up to no good, especially since I figured the motorbike was his, too."

"Why did you leave the force?"

"Personal reasons."

That she understood, the same way there were a lot of questions about her life she wouldn't want to go into with a stranger. Or with family for that matter. She hadn't even fully explained the year's disappearing act to her mother. There had been no reason to worry her. Kelly had been frightened enough for both of them.

"If you're a detective, you must know the routine. What happens when the deputy shows up?"

"He'll ask questions about the car. You'll answer the ones you can and then he'll fill out a police report."

"I know the license-plate number. Everything else, I'll have to get from my insurance agent. That may have to wait until morning. Hopefully, I'll have the car back before then."

"I wouldn't count on that."

"Why not?" Her frustration spiked again. "They will look for it, won't they? That's their job."

"That's *one* of their jobs. I don't know how they prioritize around here, but car thefts are not top priority in the big city unless they involve force, weapons or kidnapping."

Panic swelled again. "I need that car. It has my purse with my wallet in it."

"How did you pay your tab in the restaurant?"

"With the credit card I used for buying gas. After swiping it, I'd stuck it in the front pocket of my jeans."

"Did you leave your purse in the front seat? If so, that might have been the lure that made him choose your Honda over my new truck."

"I wasn't that stupid. I put it in the trunk, but there were personal items in the backseat and the sleeping bags Jaci and I were going to sleep on tonight."

"Where exactly were you planning to spread sleeping bags in a storm?"

"On the floor in my house. The moving van with my furniture won't arrive until tomorrow."

"If you have other credit cards, I'd suggest you cancel them at once."

"I don't." She wouldn't have this one had the FBI not obtained it for her. Her credit slate had been wiped clean a year ago and all accounts closed.

"Is there a key to your house in your purse or somewhere else in your car?"

"No, fortunately, I put the house keys on the ring with my car keys earlier today."

"What about your phone?" Wyatt asked.

"It's in the car. No… Wait. It's in my pocket. I forgot it was there. I could have called 911 myself. But my computer is in the trunk."

"What else is in the car?"

"There's a folder with information from the phone company, the electric power company, the natural gas company. The house I'm moving into has been empty for a year. I had to have all the utilities reconnected."

She blinked repeatedly, determined to hold back a surge of tears that was gathering behind her lids. This was no time to cry. She worked to revive the fury that would keep her from showing weakness.

Jaci's head drooped and came to rest against Kelly's shoulder. The darling had fallen asleep. At least she wouldn't see if salty tears started spilling from her mother's eyes.

"I can spread my jacket on that booth behind us if you want to lay her down," Wyatt offered.

"Thanks. I would appreciate that."

She lifted Jaci while he fashioned the makeshift bed. Jaci was so tired she barely stirred as Kelly leaned over and carefully laid her down. The masculine smell of leather and musky aftershave emanating from Wyatt's jacket was strangely reassuring. It had been a long time since she'd had a man help her put Jaci to bed.

Only this wasn't a bed. It was a faded and worn plastic booth in a truck stop. And Wyatt was a stranger who just happened to get caught up in her routinely disastrous life. A stranger who'd likely cut out and run as soon as the deputy arrived.

Who could blame him? Though to be fair, he had offered to drive her into Mustang Run.

Wyatt walked over to the counter where Edie was pouring steaming coffee into large white mugs. Kelly joined him. Before it had cooled enough to take her first sip, the door opened and two men in khaki uniforms with pistols strapped to their hips stepped inside. The law had arrived.

Still, she had the sinking sensation that her problems in moving to Mustang Run were just beginning.

WYATT SIZED UP the two officers. The older one was the sheriff. He looked to be in his midfifties, about the age of Wyatt's father. He was flabby around the middle with weathered skin from years of Texas sun and wind. His eyelids sported a drooping layer of baggy skin.

Yet he had an air about him that suggested he was in control and you'd best not put that to the test.

The second was a deputy. He was significantly younger, probably late twenties. The bottoms of his pants were caked in fresh mud, likely from working a vehicle accident during the storm.

The older man walked over to the counter. "What's this about a car being stolen from the parking lot, Edie?"

Obviously, they knew one another.

"Can you believe it? Some slimeball jerk who stopped in just before the storm hit left in the woman's car. And her with a kid. The gall of some creeps."

"You saw him drive off in the car?"

"No," Edie admitted. "But right smack in the middle of the worst of the storm, with the lights flickering and the power threatening to go at any second, the badass made a suggestive comment as I refilled his coffee cup."

"And you didn't dump the rest of the pot on him?" the younger deputy asked.

"I told him to go screw himself. He paid his tab, no tip, of course. Then he walked out without a word to anyone and drove off in this lady's car." She pointed toward Kelly and then propped her hands on her hips. "I should have at least spit in the slimy bastard's coffee."

"If you still have coffee, Brent and I could use a cup."

"No spit," Brent teased. "I'm armed."

"You'd deserve it, since you haven't stopped by in weeks." She smiled and cut her eyes flirtatiously.

The older man directed his attention to Kelly. "I'm Sheriff Glenn McGuire. Brent Cantrell, here, is my deputy. Sorry about the car, but we'll do what we can to get your vehicle back."

Sheriff Glenn McGuire. Wyatt recognized the name at once. The infamous sheriff had been the one who'd investigated the murder case against Wyatt's father and then made the arrest. He'd been a deputy back then. His arrest of Texas's infamous wife killer no doubt helped propel him to the position of sheriff. He'd held the position ever since.

Oddly, McGuire was practically part of the Ledger family now and apparently a capable sheriff. He'd helped out Wyatt's brothers on several occasions. Danger and mishaps had plagued the sons of Troy Ledger over the past year and a half since Troy had been released from prison.

Which meant that the good sheriff would know exactly who Wyatt was the second he gave his name. Then, in all probability, the entire Ledger clan would likely get word Wyatt was in town before morning.

"I really need to get my car back as soon as possible," Kelly said.

McGuire ran his fingers through his thinning hair. "Yes, ma'am. That's what we're here for. I'll need you to answer a few questions to get us started. It won't take long. If you live around here, you might want to go ahead and call your husband to come pick you up."

"I'm a widow, and I don't have any friends in the area that I can call. I'm in the process of moving to Mustang Run from another part of the country. The moving van is delivering my furniture in the morning."

"Mustang Run. Good place to live," the sheriff said. "Live there myself and have for most of my life. Believe me, you'll have plenty of friends soon. It's that kind of town." He nodded toward Wyatt. "So I take it you two aren't together."

"No," Wyatt said. "I was the only other customer when the car was stolen and I just stayed around to offer a little moral support. I can clear out now if I'm not needed." Before he ran smack into the legend of Troy Ledger. He'd as soon not face that tonight.

"How about hanging around a few more minutes?" the sheriff said. "Brent and I will want to ask you a few questions, as well."

That eliminated the easy escape. But on one level, he was relieved. He was curious about Kelly Burger. And a bit concerned that the thug who had looked at her like he was the wolf and she was the lamb now knew where she lived and had likely overheard Jaci's comment about her father being dead. He might figure she and Jaci would be alone tonight.

The bell over the door tinkled again and this time a burly guy accompanied by a petite blonde walked in. Edie greeted them by name. Judging from the comments, they were a truck-driving team who stopped by often. Edie scurried off to take care of them.

"Is that your Corvette out there?" the sheriff asked Wyatt.

"No. I'm driving the black pickup truck. I figure the guy who stole Ms. Burger's Honda drove up in that. It was the only car parked out front when I came in and he was the only customer."

"A Honda for a Corvette. Interesting trade. Brent, run the plates on the Corvette. My guess is it's hot."

Good assumption. Wyatt sipped his coffee while

the sheriff gathered the basic information from Kelly. His interest piqued when they got to the address where Kelly would be living.

"That's the old Callister place, isn't it?" McGuire asked. "Yellow cottage-style house, down from the old Baptist church."

"Yes. How did you know?"

"My daughter Collette rented the place for a while back when she was single. I was glad to see her move out."

"Why?" Kelly asked.

"I probably shouldn't even mention this," McGuire said, "but I'm sure you'll hear from someone else if not from me. My daughter's friend was brutally attacked in that house. She's fine now, but it was touch-and-go for a while. Turned out the guy was actually after my daughter. But don't worry. He's behind bars now."

"I hope your daughter is okay," Kelly said.

"She's fine now. Married and with a bun in the oven."

Wyatt was familiar with that part of the story. The sheriff's daughter was married to Wyatt's brother Dylan. This was becoming all too familial. All they needed was some fried chicken and banana pudding and it would be a family reunion.

How did people ever have any privacy in a town like Mustang Run?

"That house has been empty for over a year," McGuire continued. "Place needs a paint job and lots of work. Last time I drove by to check things out, I noticed an oak tree in front that needs to be cut down."

"I loved that tree. I remember climbing it when I was about Jaci's age and having tea parties with Grams under those huge spreading branches."

"Well, it's dead now. Lightning bolt last spring nailed it and it looks like the first good wind will lay it on the roof."

"I wasn't made aware of any of that."

"House was in perfect shape when Cordelia Callister was living. She'd probably roll over in her grave if she knew it was in such a state of disrepair."

"Surely it isn't that bad."

"It's bad enough that whoever rented it to you should have explained how much work it needs before they took your money. If you need help breaking the lease, call Judge Betty Smith. Number's in the book. She'll tell you what to do."

"Actually, I own that house," Kelly admitted. "I had no idea it was neglected. For years, I've been paying a man named Arnold Jenkins to manage the property."

McGuire rubbed his whiskered jaw. "So you own the old Callister home place? Did you buy it sight unseen?"

"I didn't buy it. I inherited it. Cordelia was my grandmother."

"Well, hell's bells. Then you must be Linda Ann's daughter. Why didn't you say so?"

"I didn't expect anyone around here to remember my mother."

"All the old-timers around here remember her. She grew up in Mustang Run and that was back when everybody knew everybody."

It appeared they still did.

McGuire hooked his thumbs in his belt loop and hitched up his pants. "Don't that beat all, you showing up back here after all these years? Linda Ann left Mustang Run right after she graduated from UT and that's pretty much the last we've seen of her. How's she doing?"

"Mother's doing well."

"I remember Cordelia talking about Linda Ann being a single mother after your father was killed. Car crash, wasn't it?"

Kelly nodded. "He died before I was born."

McGuire rubbed his jaw. "Did Linda Ann ever marry again?"

"Yes, six years ago. She married a physics professor that she worked with in Boston. He retired last year and surprisingly, they moved to Plano, Texas."

"Guess your grandmother figured Linda Ann wasn't ever going to move back to Mustang Run so she just left her property to you."

"Exactly. But apparently I should have checked on it personally before now. In my defense, I've been occupied with other matters and I trusted that Mr. Jenkins was taking care of repairs."

"I'm afraid Arnold's been snookering you for over a year. He's got the rheumatism so bad now he had to give up his membership in the local spit-and-whittle society. He's been at his son's house in California since before Thanksgiving."

"Spit and whittle?" Kelly questioned, confusion written on her face.

"The unofficial society for retired men," Wyatt explained. And now that he'd interrupted the dialogue, he might as well come clean and jump into the old-home-week party.

Wyatt stuck out a hand toward the sheriff. "I should introduce myself. I'm Wyatt Ledger."

The sheriff's eyebrows rose. He leaned back on his heels, studying Wyatt. "Yep, I see the family resemblance now. Dylan talks about you all the time, but he didn't say a word about his infamous Atlanta detective brother coming for a visit."

"No one in the family knows I'm here," Wyatt admitted.

"Planning to surprise 'em, uh? Believe me, they will be. Sure as shootin', Troy will kill the fatted calf. How long you here for?"

"I'm not sure."

"Well, I'd like to sit down and chew the fat with you while you're in town, see how the big-city way of doing things compares with our methods. The county is growing so fast, we're adding a specialized homicide division. I could use your input."

"I'd be glad to give it."

"Right now we'd better get to the business at hand."

Wyatt caught a whiff of Kelly's perfume as she and the sheriff stepped away. Add that to the sway of her hips and the effect was intoxicating.

A half hour later, it had all been said. As suspected, the Corvette had been stolen in Houston earlier that day, the keys taken from a woman in her own driveway as she was getting in the car.

While the sheriff had questioned Kelly, Brent had taken down a detailed description of the suspect from Wyatt and Edie. Jaci was still sleeping soundly.

McGuire took another call on his cell phone, the third since he'd arrived. Evidently the weather was playing havoc with driving. When the sheriff broke the connection, he gulped down the remains of his second cup of coffee and turned to Wyatt.

"I've got a truck that skidded off the road and into a ditch on Buchanan Road that I need to attend to. Seeing as how both you and Mrs. Burger are going to Mustang Run, how about you giving her a lift into town?"

An offer Wyatt had made earlier and had the proposal refused. But that was when he and Kelly were strangers. Now they shared a membership in the elite Mustang Run descendants club.

Now Wyatt was the one with concerns. "I'll be glad to drive Mrs. Burger into town, but I don't think it's a good idea for her to stay at her house tonight."

"The house needs work, but it's not going to cave in on her," McGuire argued. "It's been standing for more than a hundred years."

"The thief looked about as unsavory as they come," Wyatt said. "Even if he can't break into her computer files, there's information in the stolen car about where she lives. And I suspect he has a good hunch she'll be there alone."

"More likely, the thief is long gone from the area by now," McGuire said. "But the decision for where she stays is up to Mrs. Burger."

Kelly chewed her bottom lip nervously and turned toward Wyatt. "Do you really think Jaci and I might be in danger?"

"Probably not, but why chance it? Spend the night in a motel and give the guy plenty of time to move on. There are two in town."

"That's an option," the sheriff agreed, "but they might not have a vacancy tonight. They're small motels and there's a big gun show in town this weekend."

"It wouldn't hurt to check them out," Wyatt said.

The sheriff pulled a ring of keys from his pocket and rattled them as if he were eager to leave. "Tell you what, if you do stay at the house, I'll have one of the deputies do drive-bys every hour or so. If you get anxious or even think you hear someone trying to break in, call 911 and he can get there quicker than a snake can slither through a hollow log."

Kelly pushed her half bangs away from her face. "I'd appreciate that."

Wyatt still didn't like it, but it seemed he wasn't getting a vote. But as long as he was driving Kelly and Jaci into town, he still had time to talk Kelly into staying in a motel.

He was being overly cautious. But then, dealing with dead victims on a regular basis did that for a man.

McGuire got as far as the door and turned back. "Another option would be to drive Mrs. Burger and her daughter out to Willow Creek Ranch. I'm sure Troy would be glad to put them up for the night," McGuire said. "There's plenty of room in that rambling old house."

Wyatt nodded, but he wasn't keen on that idea.

"You two work it out and let me know what you decide. The deputy can be in the area if you need him, Mrs. Burger. But now that I think about it, staying out at the Ledger ranch is what I'd recommend."

"I'll go make room for a couple of extra passengers in my truck," Wyatt said, deciding to leave before he said too much. As far as he was concerned, the ranch was a last resort. Reuniting with Troy would be stressful enough without pulling a woman he barely knew into the sticky mix.

Fortunately, the rain had stopped, since making room for two passengers required moving his clothes from the backseat to the covered bed of the truck. When the truck was ready, he made one quick call to Alyssa and then went back for his two charges.

The intriguing and naively seductive Kelly Burger would be the first female passenger in his new truck.

This was where Alyssa's ridiculous raised-by-a-family-of-skunks analogy might actually come in handy.

Too bad that Kelly smelled so damn good.

Chapter Four

Miraculously, Jaci barely stirred when Kelly strapped her into the seat belt. Kelly made a support pillow of her lightweight jacket for her daughter.

"I'll turn on some heat," Wyatt said as she settled into the front passenger seat.

"Thanks. Neither Jaci nor I are dressed for this weather. I knew there was a cold front predicted for tonight, but I expected to be in Mustang Run long before now."

"What made you late?"

"Car trouble."

"Tough. That's the kind of luck I'd have wished on the thief."

They grew silent after that and she leaned back, closed her eyes and contemplated Wyatt and the idea of renting a motel room tonight. She'd counted on staying in the empty house, only now the pillows and sleeping bags she'd packed were speeding down the highway with a low-down thief.

The scenario that Wyatt had brought up was far worse. The thief with the stare that had made her skin crawl could be in Mustang Run, waiting for her and Jaci to arrive.

More than likely, he was miles away by now, just as the sheriff had theorized. But what if the sheriff was wrong? She shivered at the possibility.

"I think I will take your advice and stay at the motel tonight," she said. "Even if they catch the thief, it sounds as if there's little chance I'd get my car back right away. And without the sleeping bags, Jaci and I would be sleeping on the cold, hard floor."

"Good. That will save me having to sleep in my truck outside your house. Overnight stakeouts are the devil on a man's back."

"The sheriff offered protection."

"You know the old adage. A cop on the scene is worth two in a roaming patrol car."

"I thought it was a bird in the hand was worth two in the bush."

"Now who would want a bird in his hand?"

She smiled in spite of the tense situation. Wyatt Ledger was definitely nice to have around in a crunch.

"I hope there's somewhere I can rent a car early in the morning," she said.

"I kind of doubt there's a car rental location in Mustang Run, but if there's not, I can always drive you into Austin to pick one up."

"I couldn't ask you to do that. There must be some kind of taxi or car service to the Austin airport. I'm sure the motel will know how to contact them."

"My fares are a lot cheaper."

"I'm sure you have better things to do than chauffeur me around."

"Not particularly. I'm unemployed. I could use the entertainment."

"According to Sheriff McGuire, you'll be dining on a fatted calf."

"That's what I'm afraid of."

"Ah, now I get it. You're looking for an escape valve in case the pressure of family becomes overbearing."

"Darn. You figured me out." He slowed to maneuver around a low spot where water had collected on the road. "Seriously, you're having a run of bad luck, Kelly. It could happen to anyone, but I'd be a jerk not to offer my help and protection."

She'd like to believe that was the total truth and that all his intentions were good, but with what she'd been through the past year, it was hard to trust anyone.

Kelly shifted and stretched, fatigue settling into her shoulders and neck. "How long has it been since you've visited Mustang Run?"

"Nineteen years last September."

"You sound like my mother. She left Mustang Run and except for a few quick visits to check on my grandmother when she was ill, Mother never returned to her hometown."

"I'm sure she had her reasons," Wyatt said.

"If she did, she didn't talk about them other than to say that the town was too small."

"Obviously, you didn't agree with her since you're moving here."

"I'm not sure how long I'll stay. I'm in a regrouping phase of life." She leaned back and let her head drop to the padded rest. "How long has it been since you've seen your father?"

"Eighteen years, give or take a few months."

"There must be a story there."

"Yes, but it's not the kind you tell to impress a woman you've just met."

If he was trying to impress her, he was doing a

bang-up job of it. "Okay, let me guess," she said. "Your family is a notorious gang of bank robbers."

He faked a shocked expression. "You've met them."

"You're lying. Let me see… Second guess," she said, playing along. "Your brothers are secretly vampires in cowboy clothing."

He produced a lecherous smile. "Did anyone ever tell you that you have a lovely neck?"

"All the time," she said. "My earlobes get a lot of attention, too."

"I don't doubt it."

She closed her eyes as the knots in her stomach began to slowly unravel. She refused to let herself dwell on the idea of Wyatt's lips on her neck or any other part of her body, but his easy banter was definitely helping to put things in perspective.

Her car had been stolen. That was nothing compared to what she'd been through over the last twelve months. If she didn't get her car back, she'd collect the insurance and buy another one.

And the pervert who stole it was likely several counties away by now, using her cash to provide his next high.

They passed the Mustang Run city-limits sign, and Kelly turned so that she could check on Jaci, though the rhythmic sounds of her breathing were proof she was still asleep. The doll she carried everywhere was clutched to her chest.

"If I remember right, the house is only a few miles from here," Kelly said. "Could we stop by there on the way to the motel? After the sheriff's diatribe on the condition it's in, I'd just like a little advance warning of what I have to face in the morning."

"Sure. Where do I turn?"

"Wait. I have the address plugged into my phone's GPS system." She looked it up and fed him the directions. In less than five minutes, they turned off on a blacktop road. Two minutes more and they passed the old Baptist church she remembered from the few times she'd visited her grandmother.

"We should be just about there. You'll have to watch for the drive. The house may be hard to see in the dark."

Kelly's hands grew clammy as Wyatt pulled into the driveway. Before her car was stolen, she had been excited about moving into the house. She needed a place with continuity and history and a tie to the grandmother she'd loved but never really gotten to know.

Unlike her mother, Kelly found the idea of a small town appealing, especially at this point in her life. She wanted a quiet, safe town where she could take Jaci to the park and let her play in the yard.

Still, an unreasonable dread tightened her chest as beams of illumination from Wyatt's headlights disbanded the shadows. And then she spied the latest disaster.

Kelly jumped out of the truck the second it stopped and stamped to the steps for a closer look. A huge branch of the oak tree McGuire had mentioned had crashed through the roof of the house.

Chimney bricks and ripped shingles were scattered about the porch and the weed-filled flower bed. Turning away, she was lashed at by a gust of wind that whipped her hair into her eyes and mouth.

She kicked at a pile of shingles and then jumped back with a squeal when a giant tarantula crawled away from the debris.

"The spider's harmless," Wyatt said.

"That doesn't mean I have to like him."

Kelly clenched her teeth and tried to calm her wrath. She had little success, but she did lower her voice so that she wouldn't wake Jaci.

"I was prepared for a few loose shutters and peeling paint, not a hole in my roof that a helicopter could fly through."

That was a slight exaggeration, but nonetheless the house was totally unlivable. And she had a van full of furniture that had been in storage for a year arriving in the morning.

"How can anyone have the kind of luck I've had today?" Her words were clipped. Her insides were positively shaking.

"I'd say you've had at least one stroke of good luck."

"I must have blinked during that stroke."

"That car trouble that delayed you may have saved you and Jaci from serious injury when that tree fell."

She hadn't thought of that. It did little to ease her frustration.

"I can get my flashlight from the truck and check out the damage inside, but you won't be able to determine the full extent of the destruction until daylight."

"Don't bother with checking the damage. I've seen enough of the house and Mustang Run. I'd just get in my car and keep driving, except that I don't have a car."

Her voice broke and her eyes burned with salty tears. One escaped from the corner of her right eye and she brushed it away with the back of her hand. She'd lived though a year of hell, without once allowing herself to whimper or go berserk. She wouldn't break now. She was stronger than that.

Wyatt stepped closer and slipped an arm around her shoulder. "It's not the end of the world," he said. "It just seems like it."

"Don't be nice," she said. "I can't take nice." The tears started to flow and she couldn't stop them.

She didn't say a word. Neither did Wyatt. He just held her until her insides stopped shaking and the tears ran dry.

"I'm not usually like this," she said, finally pulling away.

"Good. I'd hate to have to wear a bib every time we were together to keep my shirts dry."

As usual, he kept the moment light. No doubt he didn't want her to read too much into his supplying broad shoulders for her to cry on. Kelly backed away from the mortally wounded house. "Let's get out of here. Just drop me off at the motel and you can escape before the black cloud over me sucks you into its vacuity too."

"Actually I won't be dropping you off. I'll be staying." She bristled and the air rushed from her lungs. If he thought holding her while she cried entitled him to—

"Not in your room," he said quickly, before she had the chance to make a fool of herself. "And before you get all bent out of shape, my decision to stay at the motel has nothing to do with you."

"Then what does it have to do with?"

"If I go barging in on my father unexpectedly this time of night, it's likely that neither he nor I will get any sleep."

"Okay, if you're sure. But don't stay on my account. I'm okay now. Really."

"I believe you. But since I'll be at the motel anyway, I may as well drive you wherever you need to go in the morning. Without strings, in case you're worried about that."

No wonder so many women loved cowboys.

Not that she had any intention of falling for Wyatt Ledger. He should be happy to hear that. It might save him from contracting the plague.

In fact, there was no real reason for her and Jaci to even stay in Mustang Run now. The anticipated roof over their heads had literally collapsed.

No vacancy.

The news was no better at the second motel they visited than it had been at the first. Considering the number of cars in the lot, Wyatt wasn't surprised.

"I wish we could help you out," the young clerk said, "but every room in the motel has been booked for months."

"You must have at least one no-show," Kelly insisted, a trace of desperation in her voice.

"Actually we had three last-minute cancellations, but we had a waiting list for the rooms."

"And all of this is for a gun show?" Wyatt asked.

The clerk nodded. "Happens every January. It's kind of a male-bonding ritual, like tailgating at the Longhorn games and drinking beer at fishing tournaments."

"There must be gun shows in Austin," Wyatt said. "What makes this one so special?"

"All the major manufacturers take part in it. And it's not just looking at the latest models. You get to handle the weapons and even shoot them for a small fee. There's shooting contests and they even have a wild-game cook-off tomorrow out in the parking lot of the town hall. Big prizes and good eating."

Jaci drowsily released her grip on her mother's waist and sat down on the floor.

Kelly stooped and picked her up, balancing the child on her right hip.

"Do you want me to hold her?" Wyatt asked.

Jaci tightened her grip around her mother's neck.

"Thanks, but she's not that heavy."

He breathed easier. Not that he minded the weight, but he hadn't been around kids much. He'd done all right with Jaci's crying mother, but no sense to push his luck.

The kid had woken just as they'd pulled into the parking lot, and Kelly had jumped at the chance for her and Jaci to come in with him. He figured she wasn't convinced he'd pleaded his case well enough at the motel across the highway.

"That significantly cuts down on our options," Wyatt said.

Kelly reached in her pocket and retrieved her phone as they left the motel and stepped back into the cold, damp air. "You have an option, Wyatt. You have family in town. I'm the one with the problem."

"So you're suggesting I just dump you and Jaci on the street and then go crawl into a warm bed?"

"I'm calling for a taxi to drive us to the nearest hotel, motel, B and B, dude ranch or any other establishment that actually has an available room for rent. I'm not too picky at this point."

"No telling what kind of dump you'd end up at."

"Fine by me, as long as it's a dump with a bed."

"Get in the truck, Kelly. You're tired. I'm tired. Jaci's exhausted. Willow Creek Ranch has plenty of beds and a roof."

He opened the door to the backseat so that she could buckle Jaci in.

"You've done more than enough—"

"Yeah, I know. I'm Mr. Wonderful."

"We should at least call your father and ask if he's okay with this," she said, obviously giving in.

"No need. He'll be thrilled. Troy's Mr. Wonderful, Senior. If you run into any of my brothers or sisters-in-law, they'll all assure you of that."

Kelly kissed Jaci on the top of her sleepy blond head and closed the back door. "You don't sound convinced of that fact."

"That's why I'm back in Mustang Run, so he can convince me. But don't worry. He's not an ogre. And unlike me, he's good with kids. He has two grandchildren. They love him and he practically worships them."

"I still think you should call him first."

"You heard the sheriff. The door to Troy Ledger's house is always open to family and friends."

Kelly didn't wince at the mention of Troy Ledger, which meant she had no idea who he was. But then according to the sheriff, Kelly's mother had moved out of Mustang Run before Kelly was born and that would have been well before the murder. Wyatt had been thirteen at the time, the oldest of all of Troy's sons.

"I guess I should call Sheriff McGuire and let him know I won't need his deputy to check on me tonight."

She made the call, filling McGuire in on the half of a tree that had crashed through her roof. After that, she leaned back and closed her eyes, leaving Wyatt to drive the rest of the way to the ranch with nothing but his own disturbing thoughts for entertainment.

There were times lately when he'd talked to Dylan, Sean or Dakota that he could almost believe that Troy was the same loving father he'd been when they were brats running wild and free around the ranch and not the hot-tempered, jealous monster his mother's family had brainwashed him to believe he was.

But Wyatt was a homicide detective. He knew how often the husband of the victim was painted in glowing terms by his kids before the perverted truth came out.

Wyatt hoped to God he'd find out his father was innocent—but either way, he had to know the truth.

Images flooded Wyatt's mind like the murky waters of a muddied bayou as he got out of the truck to open the gate to Willow Creek Ranch. His mother's body stretched across the floor, covered by a sheet someone had ripped from her bed. Blood pooled beneath her, smeared across her face, matted in her beautiful long, dark hair.

His mother. Always there when he needed her. Always smiling. She danced and sang around the house, was generous with hugs, but not a pushover for her sons' mischievous misadventures.

Helene Ledger. As steady as a sunrise. As comforting as moonbeams. She was the perfect mom.

But Troy had been his hero.

He'd lost them both that day.

He felt Kelly's eyes on him as he braked in front of the rambling ranch house.

"You look upset, Wyatt. What's wrong?"

"Nothing."

"Your mood has grown steadily darker ever since you drove through the gate. If you didn't want to bring me here, why did you?"

"My mood has nothing to do with you. But I admit there are unresolved issues between me and my father."

"What kind of issues, or is that none of my business?"

"You'll hear about my father sooner or later anyway, so I guess you may as well hear it from me. First, make sure Jaci is fast asleep. This is not a fit discussion for young ears."

Kelly shifted for a view of the backseat. "Out like a light. So what is it with you and your father?"

"Eighteen years ago he was convicted of murder one and sentenced to life."

"Oh, no."

"It gets worse. The victim was Helene Ledger, my mother."

"Oh, Wyatt. That's so sad. You must have been just a kid. But surely they found out that he was innocent or he'd still be in prison."

"He was released approximately a year and a half ago on a technicality."

"But Sheriff McGuire must believe he's innocent or he wouldn't have suggested you bring me and Jaci to the ranch."

"He may be convinced of Troy's innocence now, but Sheriff McGuire conducted the investigation that led to my father's arrest. But don't worry. I wouldn't have brought you and Jaci here if there was any chance that you'd be in danger. If Troy's guilty, Mom's murder was the only unprovoked violence ever attributed to him."

"Did he confess to the crime?"

"No, he's proclaimed his innocence since day one. And, according to my brothers, he spends every minute he's not working the ranch searching for my mother's killer or at least researching suspects."

As Wyatt turned off the ignition and switched off the high beams, the porch light flicked on and Troy Ledger stepped onto the porch.

Wyatt had waited eighteen years for this meeting. And yet as he climbed out of the truck, his legs felt like solid lead.

Chapter Five

Troy stared at the couple making their way up the short walkway from the driveway toward his house. The woman was holding a sleeping preschooler. The child was petite, but still you'd think the man would be carrying her since his hands were empty.

The woman stared at him, uncertainty in her step and plastered on her face, as if she wasn't sure they were at the right place.

He suspected they weren't. He wasn't expecting company, especially not at almost ten o'clock on a stormy night. The woman was attractive, but her shoulders drooped as if she were exhausted.

He turned his attention to the man. Tall. Nice Stetson. A swagger to his walk that suggested he knew exactly where he was. Recognition flickered and then rushed through Troy's veins like an injection of pure adrenaline.

His last son had come home.

Troy hurried down the steps to meet him, but once they were eye to eye, Troy's mouth went dry and he had to force the name from his mouth.

"Wyatt."

"Yep, it's me." Wyatt stuck out a hand in greeting.

Troy ignored it and flung an arm about his son's shoulder. He'd been through this with every other son, the painful silences and numerous obstacles to overcome while they were getting to know each other all over again.

But this was Wyatt, his firstborn. He still remembered his beautiful Helene laying Wyatt in his arms that first time. The responsibility of fatherhood had hung over Troy like a dead weight before that moment. But once he'd held Wyatt in his arms, he knew that he'd move heaven and earth to keep Helene and Wyatt happy and safe.

He'd failed them both.

"Why didn't you call and let me know you were coming?" Troy asked.

"I took my time driving over from Atlanta so I wasn't sure when I'd get here."

"You're here now. That's all that matters. Have you talked to your brothers?"

"Not lately. I figured I'd surprise them, too. I'll see Dylan and Dakota tomorrow since they're here at the ranch. I'll give Sean a call and try to catch up with him sometime this weekend."

"Good thinking. If you call them tonight, Dylan and Dakota will be here before you climb out of bed in the morning. It won't take Sean much longer."

Jaci squirmed and opened her eyes.

"I'm sorry," Troy said, turning to Kelly. "I was so excited over seeing Wyatt, I forgot my manners. I'm Troy Ledger."

"I'm Kelly Burger and this is my daughter, Jaci. I feel bad about intruding this way, but all the motels in town are full and Wyatt said you wouldn't mind putting us up for the night."

"Of course I don't mind. Any friend of Troy's is welcome anytime. Let's get you and Jaci out of the cold and then we'll do proper introductions."

"Good idea," Wyatt agreed.

"Wyatt, why don't you grab Kelly's bags out of the car while I show them inside, in case she wants to get Jaci settled in for the night."

"I don't have luggage," Kelly said, "but I'm sure Jaci will appreciate a bed."

Jaci balled her hands into fists and rubbed her eyes. "Are we home, Momma?"

"No, sweetheart, but we're going to stay with these nice people tonight."

Jaci looked around and then laid her head back on her mother's shoulder. "The bad man took our car."

"I'll explain it all inside," Wyatt said.

Troy led the way, pushing the door open and then standing back for Kelly to step inside.

"I hope we didn't wake you," she said.

"No, I just got back from the horse barn. A couple of the fillies get jittery during storms. If no one's there to calm them, they can get the other horses riled. Normally my daughter-in-law Collette would insist on being down there with them. But she's eight months pregnant now."

Jaci's eyes opened wider. "Where are the horses?"

Kelly brushed curly wisps of hair back from Jaci's face. "They're in the barn asleep."

"Why don't I go ahead and show you to your rooms?" Troy said. "Then you can get Jaci settled whenever you want."

Kelly switched Jaci to her other hip. "I'd appreciate that."

Wyatt didn't follow them down the hallway.

"There are several bedrooms, so you can spread out as much as you like," he offered, not sure exactly what kind of relationship Kelly and Wyatt shared.

"I'd prefer Jaci sleep in the room with me," Kelly answered quickly. "It's been a long, hard day for both of us and I think she'd feel more secure if I'm nearby."

"The guest room off the garden is the most roomy and comfortable choice. It has a queen-size bed but there's a room with two twins if you prefer."

"The garden room sounds perfect. I'm so tired tonight that I could probably sleep on the ground."

"Too cold for that tonight. They're forecasting freezing temperatures."

He pointed out the bathroom and the closet that held extra blankets and pillows if she needed them and then opened the door to the guest suite that Helene had created. She'd combed garage sales and auctions for over a year looking for affordable antiques. Then she'd spent hours refinishing them.

"It's a beautiful room," Kelly said.

"I hope it's comfortable for you."

"I'm sure it will be."

By the time he got back to the kitchen, Wyatt was on his cell phone, pacing the kitchen and doing more listening than talking.

Troy didn't intentionally eavesdrop as he pulled a couple of beers from the fridge, but there was no missing the troubled tone or the gist of what he overheard.

The discussion concerned Kelly Burger and Wyatt clearly didn't like what he was hearing.

Troy opened his beer and downed half of it while Wyatt finished the conversation.

"Care for a beer, or do you need something stronger?" he offered once Wyatt broke the connection.

Wyatt dropped into a chair at the kitchen table. "A beer would be great."

"Problems?" Troy asked as he sat down opposite Wyatt and pushed the longneck bottle across the table.

"Complications. Nothing I can't deal with."

"Is this strictly a friendly visit to Mustang Run or are you in the area on police business?"

"Strictly personal—at least at this point."

Troy wasn't sure what to make of that comment. "I'm glad you're here no matter the reason, Wyatt. Really glad."

"You already have four sons practically in your hip pocket."

Troy didn't miss the hint of sarcasm. He understood where it was coming from. "Your brothers had reservations when they first came back to the ranch, same as I'm sure you have. We worked through them—once they met me halfway."

Now Dylan and Dakota were living on the ranch with their wives. Sean and his wife and stepson, Joey, just lived over in Bandera. And Travis would return from Afghanistan in a matter of months.

Wyatt looked around the kitchen before making eye contact with Troy. "We have good reason for reservations."

"No one knows that better than me," Troy said. "I've made a lot of mistakes. I should have never accepted your grandparents' insistence that none of you wanted anything to do with me."

"Can't undo what's been done," Wyatt said.

"No, but we can move on from here. You're part of this family, a big part. Every one of your brothers has gone to you for advice at one time or another over the last year and a half."

"Doing what's right now doesn't make up for letting them down years ago."

"Are we still talking about you, because as far as I know, you never failed anyone."

"It doesn't matter. You're absolutely right, Troy. I'm here because I'm a Ledger."

Troy. As if Wyatt wasn't his son. It hurt, but he could understand his reluctance to call him dad.

"Hopefully you'll get to stay long enough that we can hash out the past and get to a better place," Troy said.

"That would be good."

"For all of us. And sometime while you're here, I'd like to pick your brain."

"About what?"

"My investigation into your mother's murder. I've spent hours trying to put my finger on a viable suspect, but every time I think I'm making progress, I run up against a brick wall. The clues are like a math problem where the numbers change before I can solve the equation."

Wyatt straightened in his chair and turned to stare out the kitchen window. "I promise that I'll make time to look at everything you've discovered."

The assurance sounded sincere, but Wyatt still seemed distracted. Troy had a good hunch that Kelly Burger and her stolen car had something to do with that.

"Kelly and her daughter seem nice," Troy baited. "Have you known her long?"

"About four hours." Wyatt took another sip of beer and then rocked the bottom of the bottle on the wooden table. "Kelly and I met earlier this evening at a truck stop café about forty miles from here. We'd both gone in to escape the worst of the storm."

"Smart move."

"It turned out to be an unfortunate move for Kelly."

"How's that?"

"There was just one other customer in the café," Wyatt continued. "He left in the middle of the storm. About a half hour later when the rain had almost stopped, Kelly went outside and discovered the bastard had stolen her car. The vehicle he left in its place was stolen, as well."

"You were right to bring them here," Troy said after Wyatt explained about the problems with Kelly's house and with finding a room. "They can stay as long as they like, unless you have a problem with their being here. They won't bother me and there's plenty of room."

"It works for me, but I'm not sure Kelly will take you up on the offer. She's spunky as hell and independent to a fault. But I figure I can at least help her get that tree off the house so that she can get an accurate estimate of the damage."

"Does she have insurance?" Troy asked.

"I'm assuming she does. We didn't talk about it." Wyatt finished his beer. "There's a lot we didn't discuss. But we will."

There was that edge again.

"Is there anything else about Kelly I should know?" Troy asked.

"You know as much about her as I do."

Troy suspected that wasn't quite the full truth. "She looked exhausted," Troy said. "I wouldn't be surprised if she's already asleep, but in case she isn't, there's a fully stocked basket of guest toiletries on the top shelf of the hall closet. And there's ham, cheese, bread and condiments if she wants a sandwich."

"I'll let her know."

"Are you hungry?"

"No. I had a burger earlier."

"Be sure and tell Kelly that there's milk for Jaci. Skim milk, however. That's all the doc lets me drink since my heart attack."

"Dylan tells me that you're back to doing almost everything on the ranch that you were doing before the attack."

"So far, so good."

"Good to hear." Wyatt pushed back from the table. "It's been a long day for me, too. We can talk more tomorrow, but I need to hit the sack now. Any bed will do."

"Kelly and Jaci are in the guest room that opens to the garden, but your old bedroom is available. There are clean sheets on the bed and fresh towels in all the bathrooms."

"Sounds as if you were expecting company."

"No, but Collette talked me into hiring a housekeeper. She was afraid that with all the work Dylan, Dakota and I have been putting in on the ranch, I'd let the house slide into a state of utter chaos."

Wyatt stood and looked around the spacious kitchen again. "Housekeeper must be working out. Things look good."

"Wait until you see the ranch."

"We'll make plans for the five-dollar tour after breakfast," Wyatt said. "What time is breakfast around here or is it every man for himself?"

"I'll be up with the sun. You'll smell the coffee and

hear the sizzle of turkey bacon shortly thereafter. But feel free to sleep as late as you like."

"Thanks. I probably won't be eating on the early-bird shift. I haven't had a lot of sleep the last couple of nights."

Wyatt stood, sauntered to the refrigerator and retrieved a second beer before walking away. Troy was tired himself but knew that sleep might be a long time in coming tonight.

Wyatt's homecoming was strained. That didn't surprise him. Too many years had passed, years when Troy had existed as the imprisoned killer whose blood ran through his sons' veins. Helene's parents had made sure that was all any of his sons knew of Troy, and he'd done nothing to convince them otherwise.

Troy spotted Wyatt standing near the hearth to the huge stone fireplace, staring at the spot where Helene's body had been found. His jaw was clenched. His face was stretched into hard, drawn lines.

Troy knew all too well the images that must be running roughshod through his mind.

For Troy, having to walk by that spot every day had been the most difficult part of returning to the ranch. Even now, the images were so real at times that Troy would break out in a cold sweat.

Troy ached to walk over and put an arm around Wyatt's shoulder, tell him that he knew his young heart had been brutally ripped apart the day she'd been killed. He'd like to apologize for failing Wyatt and all his brothers in the days and months following Helene's tragic death.

But words were meaningless. Like his four other sons, Wyatt would make peace with the past in his own way, in his own time. At least Troy prayed that he would.

That peace had never come for Troy. It wouldn't until he found the man who'd killed Helene and stolen all their lives.

THE GUEST ROOM WAS positively enchanting. Kelly felt as if she'd been dropped into the early nineteenth century, complete with the most charming bedside lamp she'd ever seen. The shade was handpainted with exquisite ruby-red roses. The frame was cast iron.

A similar lamp sat atop a carved mahogany antique dresser with a beveled mirror. The four-poster bed was in the same rich wood. Having spent countless hours scouring New Orleans antique shops before Jaci was born, Kelly could tell that the bed was an original antique that had been restored and meticulously extended in size.

Someone had spent many hours designing and furnishing this cozy sanctuary. She wondered if it had been Wyatt's mother. If so, Kelly would love to know more about her.

Had she been quiet and loving or filled with exuberance for life? Had she been happy here? Or had she longed to escape? Had she loved her husband? Had she feared him?

Had he killed her?

Coming home after nineteen years to the place where he'd known joy and such heartbreaking loss must be traumatic for Wyatt. And yet he'd kept that all inside, not showing the first signs of apprehension until he'd driven through the Willow Creek Ranch gate.

Yet with all that on his mind, he'd come to her rescue as if it were the most natural thing in the world to offer protection to a desperate woman and kid he'd never seen before.

He'd been calm and steady, keeping his own feelings locked away inside while she'd had a meltdown. No wonder he'd offered to bring her home with him. He probably thought her incapable of taking care of herself or Jaci.

Now she would be sleeping in the home of a man who'd been convicted of murdering his wife. She should be extremely wary. For some weird reason, she wasn't. Instead, Troy had made her feel at ease and welcome, almost like family.

Kelly considered the irony of that as she walked to the room's double glass doors. The curtains were already pushed back, letting in a glimmer of light through the fogged-over glass.

She released the latch and opened the door. A blast of icy wind slapped her in the face. She closed it quickly, and then used the palm of her hand to clear the condensation.

She was rewarded by an amazing view. A large courtyard garden overflowing with lush plants interspersed with jewel-toned pansies, white narcissus and a couple of other winter blooming varieties she didn't recognize. A lighted fountain provided a shimmery glow to the garden and tiny solar lights snuggled in the creeping ground cover along an uneven stone pathway.

Enthralled in the peaceful beauty, Kelly was startled by a sudden chilly draft and the sensation that she and Jaci were not alone in the room. She spun around, expecting to see Troy or Wyatt at the door.

But only Jaci was in the room and she was sound asleep, snuggled beneath the crisp white sheet and a hand-stitched blue-and-white quilt. Perhaps Kelly was a bit more apprehensive than she'd realized.

The disturbing sensation passed and Kelly dropped to the side of the bed. The irritation with the car theft swelled again. She didn't have so much as a toothbrush with her. Nothing to sleep in. No clean undies.

Worst of all, Jaci's favorite toys and books were in the missing car, leaving her with little familiar comforts to cling to during yet another period of upheaval. Thankfully, she'd dragged her favorite nearly bald doll into the café with her. Jaci would have been devastated had she lost that.

Leaning back, Kelly kicked out of her shoes, pulled her feet onto the bed and let her head fall to the pillow. She'd get up, go to the bathroom and wash up in a few minutes. Tomorrow...

She jerked to a sitting position at the sound of a light tapping on the door. It took a few bewildering seconds to realize where she was and that she'd fallen asleep with all her clothes on.

She checked her watch for the time. Ten past eleven. She'd slept only a few minutes, though she was so out of it she could have easily slept through the night, clothes and all.

Finger taming her hair, she hurried to open the door before whoever was there tapped again and woke up Jaci.

"Did I wake you?" Wyatt asked, keeping his voice low.

"I must have dozed off," she whispered. "But Jaci hasn't stirred since her head hit the pillow."

"I thought you might need these."

He handed her a basket stuffed with an assortment of items. Two new toothbrushes. Individual soaps, lotions, mouthwash and other hotel-size toiletries. There was even a mini folding plastic hairbrush, still in its cellophane wrap.

She leaned against the door. "This is exactly what I need."

"Troy says there's toothpaste in the bathroom, and there's beer, milk and makings for sandwiches in the kitchen. Help yourself."

"Thanks."

"This is worn, but clean," he said, handing her one of his cotton T-shirts that he'd had hanging over his arm. "We can shop for anything else you need after breakfast."

"You and Troy run one terrific homeless shelter, cowboy. Keep this up, and I'll hate leaving. But I will be leaving in the morning, you know."

"What's the hurry? You have nowhere to go. You left your life behind you a year ago."

Her heart plunged. Wyatt had done his homework. In a way she was relieved to have the truth out in the open. She was also irritated that he'd had her checked out so quickly by his police cronies.

"That didn't take long," she whispered to keep from waking Jaci. "You're obviously a good cop."

"Damn good. We need to talk."

Chapter Six

Wyatt had debated with himself whether he should put this conversation off until morning. They'd both be rested then. He'd have had more time to think through the implications of getting involved in Kelly's problems when she obviously didn't want his help.

But Jaci and Troy would be awake then and who knew what family might show up? This might be their best chance for privacy.

Kelly stepped into the hall, pulling the bedroom door shut behind her. "I don't want to wake Jaci."

"We can talk in the kitchen," Wyatt said. "Troy's already gone to bed."

Decades-old floorboards groaned beneath their steps as they maneuvered the dimly lit hallway that Wyatt had used as a raceway for his miniature cars and trucks a lifetime ago. Once, he and Sean had even brought toads inside the house to see which one could get from one end of the hallway to the other the fastest.

His mother had stepped out of Dakota's room with a load of laundry just as the toads reached the door. One of the toads had jumped on her foot and the laundry had gone flying, entangling the other toad in a pillowcase.

Wyatt and Sean had doubled over in laughter. And

then they and their toads had been ushered into the yard. But he'd overheard his parents laughing that night about the toad race.

Wyatt had innocently expected the good times to go on forever, expected to be protected from evil and heartbreak. The same way Josh Whiting had expected that. The same way the cute little girl in the bed down the hall expected that.

Kelly dropped into one of the kitchen chairs. "I guess this is as good a place as any for you to interrogate me."

"This isn't an interrogation."

"It sure feels that way."

"Then I'm handling it wrong."

Kelly rolled her eyes. "Don't worry about the finesse. Let's just get this over with."

"What prompted you to move to Mustang Run?"

"I inherited a house."

"Ten years ago."

Kelly locked her gaze with his. "I don't like this game, Wyatt. What is it you heard about me?"

"That you dropped off the face of the earth a little over a year ago and only recently resurfaced. That your last known employment was with a jewelry store that served as a money laundering front for Emanuel Leaky's smuggling operations."

"And I'm sure you know the details of Emanuel's conviction."

"Couldn't turn on cable news, pick up a newspaper or turn on your computer without hearing about that trial," Wyatt admitted. "I don't remember hearing your name mentioned, though."

Kelly's thumb absently traced the edge of the table.

"So now you wonder which side of the equation I was on."

"That's about it," Wyatt admitted. "Knowing which way to watch for flying bullets is the best way I know to keep from getting blindsided."

"I'd like a glass of water," she said.

"You can have something stronger if you like."

"No, just water. I can get it."

She was up before Wyatt had a chance to push back from the table. He watched the sway of her narrow hips as she walked to the cabinet, pulled out a glass and filled it with cool water from the faucet. A wave of guilt washed over him. He'd invited her here for a respite. Now he was treating her like a suspect in one of his cases.

This might seem like an interrogation to her, but it was starting to feel like harassment to him, and he was the one dishing it out. But he didn't know a better way to get to the truth. If she was in danger, he couldn't just stand by and let her and Jaci face it alone.

Kelly sat down again, a glass of water in hand, the condensation wetting her fingertips. "My involvement in this case is confidential, Wyatt. I was told—no, *ordered*—by the FBI not to talk about it with anyone outside the Bureau. I can't imagine how you obtained your information so quickly."

"Were you in witness protection?"

She nodded.

"Yet you didn't testify at the trial," Wyatt said, trying to get his mind around the facts, or at least around Kelly's version of the story.

Kelly stopped hugging her water glass and used both hands to rake shiny locks of hair from her face. "Why is any of this important to you, Wyatt? All you have to do is drive me back into town tomorrow morning and then I'm out of your life for good."

Out of his life, but not necessarily out of danger. Squealing on Emanuel Leaky would be equated by most people to having a death wish. And if she'd provided any information that led to his conviction, she was likely on a hit list.

"You may find this hard to believe coming from an ex-cop, Kelly, but I'm not trying to establish any wrongdoing on your part. If it were there, the FBI would have found it and you'd be in jail. I'm just trying to assure myself that I'm not tossing you and Jaci to the wolves when I drive you into town tomorrow."

She took another sip of water and then spread her hands out flat on the table. "This can't go any further than this table, Wyatt. You have to promise me that."

"You have my word on that. Unless I find out you're in danger. Then all bets are off."

"Can I depend on that?"

"Scout's honor."

"Were you a Boy Scout?"

"No, but I can tie knots," he said, trying to lighten the mood and end her hesitancy. He turned to check out a scraping sound, but it was just the wind whipping the branches of a tree against the metal gutters.

"How did you get involved with Leaky?" Wyatt asked.

"I didn't know he owned the jewelry shop at the time I took the job. Luther Bonner interviewed and hired me."

And Luther Bonner had later turned state's witness to save his own ass. Bets were on as to how long it would be before one of Emanuel's paid assassins took him out. Even from prison, Emanuel wielded a large sphere of influence in the criminal world.

"Did you work solely at the New Orleans location?" Wyatt asked.

"Yes, I wasn't aware of the other money laundering operations until after I started talking to the FBI. The shop where I was employed specialized in expensive one-of-a-kind jewelry items. The customer base was small but extremely wealthy."

"Were you a clerk?"

"I'm a jewelry designer with a flair for the unusual. I designed everything from diamond tiaras to earrings in the shapes of crabs and fleurs-de-lis."

"Do you have any idea how they decided on you for the job?"

"I had a booth at Jazz Fest. Luther saw my work and seemed impressed."

"How did you finally meet Emanuel?"

"He came into the shop four weeks after I started working there. He introduced himself as Van O'Neil and told me what a great job I was doing. I hadn't realized that the name was one of many aliases. Nor did I realize that Luther's name was only an alias, but after working with him for two years, I still think of him as Luther Bonner."

"What happened after Emanuel introduced himself?"

"He and Luther disappeared behind closed doors for a few hours. Emanuel was there off and on for the next three days. He spent most of that time in the back office conducting business with people I'd never seen in the shop before. That was the pattern throughout the two years I worked there. Fly in for a few days, meet with what I thought were business cronies and then fly out again."

"That didn't make you suspicious?"

"A little. I asked Luther about him. He said Van had other business responsibilities and that he left the running of the jewelry store to him. He made it clear that what Van O'Neil did was none of my business and that I should never confront him."

"So you let it go at that?"

"Don't sound so condescending, Wyatt. I liked my job. It paid well and I had a daughter to support. So, yes. I let it go at that."

"Sorry. I didn't mean to come across as a jerk. I'm just trying to get a handle on this. What finally happened to change the status quo?"

"I came back to the shop one night after dinner to put the finishing touches on a diamond-and-ruby necklace that had to be ready for the Queen of Rex the next morning. Emanuel didn't hear me come in. I overheard a heated argument between him and someone whose voice I didn't recognize."

"What were they arguing about?"

"Emanuel was complaining that his last supply of diamonds had been inferior. The other man accused him of lying and demanded immediate delivery of his order. He had a plane waiting at the airport and assurance that there would be no border patrol interference. I sneaked out without their knowing I'd been there."

And if she hadn't and they'd thought she'd overheard, she'd be dead now and Jaci would be an orphan. That was the way Emanuel worked.

"Did you go to the local police or directly to the FBI?"

"To the FBI since Emanuel and this guy were obviously smuggling something across the border."

"Did they arrest Leaky that night?"

"No, but they intercepted the outgoing plane and discovered a cache of automatic weapons."

"Did Emanuel suspect you tipped them off?"

"No, I continued to work for him for another six months while the FBI conducted the investigation that resulted in the arrest of both Emanuel and Luther on charges of smuggling diamonds into the country from Africa and smuggling illegal arms out of the country to Mexican drug cartels."

Wyatt reconstructed the picture in his mind from what he knew of the trial, what he'd heard earlier tonight and what he'd just heard from Kelly. There were still a few gaping holes.

"Why did the FBI decide not to use you as a witness?"

"After Luther cooperated with them, they didn't think they needed me to get a conviction."

"But still, they kept you protected until after the trial?"

"I was their ace in the hole in case any other part of the case fell through. Since they didn't make me testify, Emanuel has no way of knowing that I was the one who originally blew the whistle on him."

"He could find out you were in witness protection as easily as I did. You disappeared without a paper trail."

"But the FBI intentionally leaked information to Luther early on that I didn't know jack about the operation and that I was an unfriendly witness. They were sure that went directly back to Emanuel."

So all the bases were covered. Hopefully the FBI had that right.

"So when the trial was over and Emanuel Leaky was sentenced, you were dropped from protection?"

"Yes. That's when I decided to move back to Mustang Run. The house Grams had left me is sitting empty so I don't have to worry about rent while I get my career reestablished. So, in spite of my complete meltdown earlier, I'm really not homeless or helpless, Wyatt.

"Well, I might be temporarily homeless, but I'll look for another place to rent tomorrow. And I'm not in danger. I just had my car stolen. It happens to people every day."

Wyatt still had reservations about the danger aspect, but he was a naturally suspicious kind of guy. It went with the territory he roamed.

But admittedly it would be difficult to think she was any more than a random victim today considering that the thief was in the truck stop before she arrived. He'd have had no way of knowing she would stop there.

Only now the thief had her computer. "Was there anything in your computer that could tie you to Emanuel?"

"Absolutely not. The computer is brand-new and I was thoroughly indoctrinated by the FBI on what not to post in any internet medium."

Kelly stretched her arms over her head, making her nipples aim at him like bullets. He clenched his fists and ignored a stirring in another part of his body.

What the hell was wrong with him that he kept reacting to Kelly as if he hadn't been with a woman in months? Oh, yeah. He hadn't.

Still, he was around women all the time at the station. No one else had turned him on like this.

Maybe his protective instincts were getting confused with his libido.

"So now you have the rest of the story," Kelly said. "And confession must be good for the appetite as well as the soul. Suddenly, I'm starving."

"Yeah, me too," Wyatt admitted. He opened the refrigerator and began checking out options.

Kelly checked the pantry. "I found some syrup and a box of pancake mix." She read the directions. "All we need are an egg and some milk and we're in business."

"Eggs... Check. Milk... Check." Wyatt opened the fresh-meat drawer. "And pork sausage and turkey and regular bacon. I suspect the pork is for guests, since Troy had a heart attack a year ago."

With the discussion changed from crime to food, the mood instantly lifted. Wyatt located a square grill and a round, flat griddle. He set them both on top of the range, setting the heat to low under the grill.

He started forming sausage patties, but his gaze kept shifting from the meat to Kelly. He liked her hair. It was shiny and touchable, as if it were waiting for his fingers to tangle with the loose curls. He was captivated by the cute tilt of her nose and her full lips without a trace of makeup. He loved that her shirt brushed her nipples, giving just a hint of the perky mounds waiting to be discovered.

Discovered, but not by him.

At least not anytime soon.

He was here on a mission, and he wouldn't let anything interfere with that. Being back in this house with Troy made the need to find the truth about his mother's murder more pressing than ever. His mother deserved that and if Troy was innocent, he deserved it, too.

Still, as the kitchen filled with sizzling sounds and tantalizing odors, Wyatt couldn't help but think about how long it had been since he'd shared a kitchen with a woman. And never with one who was as tantalizingly tempting as Kelly.

He reached around her to get a spatula for the sausage. She turned at the same time. Her face ended up mere inches from his.

Desire flamed, hot and instant. He took a deep breath and managed to move away without giving in to the lure of her seductive lips.

Think skunks, old boy. Think skunks.

FULL AND SATISFIED, at least as far as her stomach was concerned, Kelly kicked off her shoes and started the water running in the old claw-foot tub. Normally, she would have had a quick shower, but the nagging ache in muscles that had been tense for too long, the deep tub and the convenient bottle of inviting bubble bath made a soak a temptation she couldn't resist.

Her resolve to keep everything secret about her connection with Emanuel Leaky had quickly gone astray. She should have known that hooking up on any level with a cop would backfire.

Yet, she felt an unexpected sense of relief now that she'd finally talked about it with someone outside the FBI. She was more relaxed this minute than she had been in weeks.

Unfortunately, her problems would all be waiting for her when she woke up in the morning. No car. No house. And no Wyatt once she left the Willow Creek Ranch.

She checked her reflection in the mirror as she wiggled out of her jeans. It was positively not her best night in the looks department. And yet Wyatt had come within a heartbeat of kissing her while they were cooking. He'd backed off quickly enough, but there was no denying the heat that had passed between them.

Kelly finished undressing, pausing to study her breasts in the narrow mirror as the bra fell to the floor. They weren't huge, but they filled out a C cup. They were still perky. Likely they were still on the erogenous radar, though she couldn't guarantee that.

Other than her yearly gynecology exam, her breasts hadn't been touched by a pair of male hands in years. Nor had any other of her intimate zones. It was only natural she'd react to the sexy cowboy lawman who'd come riding to her rescue in a black pickup truck.

Only, if she were honest with herself, she'd admit it was more than just physical attraction. Wyatt was like no one she'd ever met before. Laid-back. Cool under stress. He had that take-charge cop manner about him without being boorish. Protective, but not authoritative. Sexy, but not arrogant.

Of course, she barely knew him, so that might all be a practiced facade.

Kelly stepped into the tub and slid beneath the water, letting the fragrant heat caress her. She closed her eyes and let the strain seep from her muscles and rational thoughts regain control of her mind.

She was a bit infatuated with the Atlanta detective who knew his way around a skillet, but she wouldn't have to deal with that for long. She'd likely never see him again after tomorrow. He had his problems. She had hers.

Her traitorous thoughts betrayed her as she slid the soapy cloth over her abdomen. What would it have been like if Wyatt had actually kissed her?

Passionate and fiery or slow, wet and romantic? Or maybe he'd be a downright lousy kisser like the quarterback she'd dated in high school who'd taken icky to new levels of disgusting.

Somehow she couldn't imagine Wyatt as icky, but perhaps she should kiss him goodbye when she left him tomorrow and find out. Solely in the name of research.

Chapter Seven

Wyatt jerked awake, lurching for the covers as they were being jerked off the bed. "What the hell?"

"Morning, bro. You're on ranch time now. Gotta make hay while the sun shines, or at least grab a pitchfork and toss some of it around."

"Watch it, half-pint. I can still wrestle you to the ground with one arm."

"Try it."

Wyatt jumped out of bed in his boxers and greeted Dakota with a quick manly hug and a couple of arm punches. The actions didn't begin to convey how glad he was to see his championship bull-rider younger brother.

"How did you find out this early that I was here? It's…" He reached for his watch and checked the time. "Nine o'clock! I figured it was about six. This old bed must be more comfortable than I remembered it being."

"It's eight our time."

"Right. I forgot to reset the watch when I changed time zones. Still early for a house call. What time did Troy phone you?"

"He didn't. I was headed over to Bob Adkins's

spread. He's having trouble with the gears in one of his tractors and I promised to take a look at it."

"Still handy with a wrench, I see."

"Comes from taking my bike apart when I was five and from watching Dad work on that old Chevy he had when we were kids. You remember that rattletrap?"

"I remember." Wyatt had learned to drive in that car years before he was old enough to have a driver's license. Not that he was ever allowed to venture outside the main gate of the ranch.

"Bob Adkins?" he asked Dakota. "That name sounds familiar."

"He owns a neighboring ranch. He and Dad have apparently been friends for years. Anyway I saw a new truck parked in Dad's drive and stopped to check it out."

"No secrets on the ranch."

"We look out for one another. I thought he was kidding when he said the pickup belonged to you. But he was too excited for it not to be true."

"I tend to excite people. It's a curse."

"You tend to be full of bull."

Wyatt raked his fingers through his short, unruly hair, knowing from experience he'd likely only rumpled it more. It was easy being with Dakota, a total contrast from his reunion with Troy. With Dakota, he felt like family. With Troy...

No use to go there again.

"What's it like sleeping in your old bedroom?"

"I didn't worry until I started craving baseball cards and stale Halloween candy," Troy said, keeping it light.

"Did you look? There might be an old Tootsie Pop hidden in here. Dad said I should let you sleep, that you'd gotten in late last night."

"You were never great about following instructions."

"That's what Viviana says. But, hey, I brought coffee." He reached behind him to the top of the bureau where he'd obviously set two pottery mugs of brew while he'd jerked the covers from the bed. He handed one to Wyatt.

Wyatt sipped and swallowed. "Hot, strong and black, just the way I like it."

Dakota straddled an old straight-back desk chair that Wyatt used to sit in to do his homework. "Why didn't you let us know you were coming for a visit?"

"I was afraid you guys would do something stupid, like rush into my room while I was peacefully sleeping and jerk the covers off of me."

"Where would you get a weird idea like that?" Dakota drank his coffee while Wyatt pulled on the jeans he'd thrown across the foot of the bed when he'd shed them last night. He'd crashed after the pancakes, too tired to shower.

And then he'd lain awake a solid hour fighting back good and bad memories and trying to figure out his unreasonable attraction to a woman he'd just met.

"Dad says you showed up last night with a good-looking damsel in distress and her kid in tow."

Right on cue. "Did Troy mention that there's a gigantic tree through the roof of the house they were moving into?"

"He did, and that her car had been stolen. She was lucky you were at the truck stop."

"I was thinking you, me and Dylan might be able to clear that tree off her roof."

"We could, but a job like that is a lot easier to do with the proper equipment," Dakota said.

"Meaning more than what we have here at the ranch?"

Dakota nodded. "I have an ex-bull-rider friend with a tree trimming and removal business just north of Mustang Run. I don't think he gets a lot of business in January. I can check and see when he can get to it. I'll let him know it's an emergency."

"I'd appreciate that." Kelly might see this as overstepping the bounds of their fragile relationship, but she needed the hole covered before more rain, sleet, squirrels, birds and who knew what else dropped into the house.

"We're flush with power tools and expertise, though," Dakota said. "Just in case you decide to help her with repairs. Dad and Dylan not only built Dylan and Collette's house but they built a starter cabin for Tyler and Julie, all before I got here. They had some help with the finishing, but did all the foundation and framing work themselves.

"And in the past six months, they've helped me build a cozy cabin for Viviana, Briana and me."

Wyatt knew the full story of how his bull-rider brother had found out he had a kid with the beautiful Dr. Viviana Mancini, months after the birth of his daughter, Briana. He'd saved both their lives and from the phone conversations he'd had with Dakota, he knew that the guy was absolutely mad for Viviana and loved his daughter with a passion that had even surprised him.

"We decided to start small and add on to our cabin later," Dakota continued. "Just a kitchen, living area, master bedroom and a nursery for Briana for now, but it sits on top of a hill with a view of Dowman Lake."

Dowman Lake, Troy's favorite fishing spot when

Wyatt was a boy. He'd kept a small motorboat there, only big enough for two. Wyatt had felt like he was ten feet tall when Troy had taken him along. They'd talked about man things like the Longhorns' chances for having a winning season and how to clean and skin a catfish.

A lifetime ago. Wyatt finished his coffee. "Sounds as if you've decided to live on the ranch permanently. You were undecided last I heard."

"We'll likely have at least a condo in Austin. My gorgeous physician bride is taking some time off, but eventually she wants to join the E.R. staff of a major hospital on a part-time basis. She loves her work and she's good at it."

Viviana. Briana. Julie. Wyatt might need a score-card to keep up with the family if it kept growing. And it obviously was, since Dylan's wife, Collette, was expecting.

"What about you, Dakota? Giving the bulls a hiatus?"

"Had to." Dakota grinned. "I'm still on my honey-moon."

"For six months?" Wyatt knew detectives whose marriages hadn't lasted that long. "That must be some honeymoon."

Dakota grinned. "Viviana is some woman."

"She must be to have tamed you."

"I'm sure you'll meet her and Briana before the day is over."

Dakota, who'd ridden the rodeo circuit with wild abandon, gathering silver buckles like they were coins, had nabbed the biggest honor of all a couple of years back when he'd won the Bull Riding World Championship.

Now he had a wife and a baby and the responsibility didn't seem to worry him at all. Evidently marriage and family were right for him. Wyatt couldn't see that in his own game plan.

"How long are you here for?" Dakota asked.

Now they were getting down to the nitty-gritty. "I'm not sure," Wyatt admitted.

"When do you have to be back on the job?"

"I don't." There was no reason to lie to Dakota. "I handed in my resignation before I left Atlanta."

"By choice?"

"Yeah."

"I thought you loved what you were doing."

"I did, but I have another interest to pursue."

"Like what?"

"Finding Mother's killer."

Dakota groaned. "You still think it's Dad, don't you?"

"The evidence says that. I'm keeping an open mind."

"He's innocent, Wyatt. I was right there where you are until about six months ago. But once you spend some time with him, you'll see how much he loved Mom and how determined he is to find her killer."

"Good. Now I'll be here to help him."

"Have you told him that?"

"Not directly, but he asked me to look over the information he's collected and I agreed to give him my opinion."

"I hope you do find the real killer, Wyatt. Mother deserves justice and Dad deserves some peace of mind. But don't heap more pain on an innocent man. He's the first to admit he made mistakes with us, but he didn't kill Mom."

"I'm a homicide detective, not a witch hunter."

Jaci's voice and the sound of little feet skipping down the hall wafted through the crack beneath Wyatt's bedroom door. With her daughter awake and going strong, Kelly was likely pacing the floor waiting on Wyatt to drive her and Jaci into town—unless she'd already talked Troy into doing that.

"The natives are probably getting restless," Wyatt said. "I'd best get moving."

"Me, too. Bob will be wondering what happened to me. But I'll check with my friend about removing the branch before I leave."

"Thanks. It would be great if he could get to it today so that Kelly can get some kind of tarp over the hole."

Dakota opened the door and stepped into the hall. Wyatt was already rummaging through his duffel for a clean shirt when Dakota stuck his head back into the room.

"Welcome home, Wyatt. And may I be the first to say it's about damn time?"

THE CHATTER COMING FROM THE KITCHEN was several decibels louder than a rock concert by the time Wyatt was showered, dressed and striding in that direction. Troy's husky voice seemed almost a growl compared to Jaci's high-pitched one. Kelly was laughing. And a lyrical voice with a slight Southern drawl was tangled in the mix.

He stepped inside the door and studied the unfamiliar, familiar scene. Dakota was standing near the back door with a finger in one ear and his cell phone at the other. Troy was setting the table.

A shapely blonde with a dancing ponytail was pulling a pan of golden biscuits from the oven. Jaci was perched on a tall kitchen stool, swinging her legs and watching her mother whip a bowl of eggs.

Kelly was in jeans, presumably the ones she was wearing last night since she'd had no luggage. But he'd never seen the nubby, emerald-green sweater she'd paired with them. It looked great on her, but he couldn't imagine what hat she'd pulled that out of.

Wyatt paused in the doorway, suddenly struck with a sensation of déjà vu so intense he grew dizzy. A song he hadn't heard in years echoed inside his brain. A song his mother had sung countless times while she was preparing breakfast, often accompanying the tune with a dance step or two.

The voices, the laughter, the heat from the oven, the activity around the gas range brought it all back as if it were yesterday. He and his brothers gathered around the table, Dakota usually the last one there, complaining that he couldn't find his backpack.

His father would show up at the very last minute, having already put in a few hours' work on the ranch. He'd stamp the mud off his boots at the back door and come bounding in with news of a new foal or a cow that he'd had to pull out of a gully down by Willow Creek.

The ranch would need more rain or less rain. The day was going to be a scorcher or it would likely be sleeting by noon. No matter if the news was good or bad, Troy would stop and give his wife a kiss. And then he'd smile and fill his plate, bragging that their mother was the best and prettiest cook in the state of Texas.

"That was Cory calling me back," Dakota said. "Here's the roof scoop."

Dakota's announcement yanked Troy from the reverie and grabbed the attention of the others in the room.

"He can have one of his crews remove the branch

from the roof this afternoon. In addition, he can install the type of blue roof sheeting that FEMA uses to keep the house from further damage from the elements."

"Great," Kelly said. "Am I supposed to meet him there?"

"I can meet him there for you, unless you want to help supervise the work."

"I'd only get in the way."

"No problem. I'll let you know when the roof is cleared and covered."

She finally noticed Wyatt standing in the doorway and her smile lit up her face. He had that crazy stirring again, as if he'd touched a live wire and current was zinging along his nerve endings.

"One more for breakfast?" Kelly asked.

"Definitely," he answered. "No red-blooded American can resist homemade biscuits—unless he's offered pancakes."

Kelly blushed at the reminder of their midnight meal.

"Biscuits with homemade gravy," the perky blonde added, "but no guarantees on the edibility of that. I haven't totally mastered the art of smoothing out the lumps."

She dried her hands on a paper towel as she maneuvered around the table and walked over to greet him. "I'm Julie, Tyler's wife."

"Good to meet you, Julie. I'm Wyatt, Tyler's brother, who hasn't had homemade gravy in so long, I'll enjoy the lumps."

He held out his hand. She ignored it and pulled him into a warm embrace.

"Tyler talks about you all the time. He is going to be so envious that I'm getting to visit with you in person."

"The pleasure is all mine. Any word on when he'll be back in the States?"

"Nothing definite, but hopefully he'll be fully discharged and back on the ranch for our first anniversary in March. I'm counting the days. Kelly can fill you in. I've bored her with nothing but talk of Tyler for the last half hour."

"I haven't been bored for a second," Kelly countered. "You have all been great help this morning. I especially love this sweater you *gave* me, Julie."

"*Lent* you," Julie teasingly corrected.

Julie was exactly as Wyatt's brother Tyler had described her. Bubbly. Exuberant. And obviously as in love with Tyler as he was with her. They'd met on Tyler's leave last spring and had married before he returned to his tour of duty.

Kelly poured the eggs into a hot skillet. "I feel as if I've parachuted into a convention of Good Samaritans."

Wyatt felt as if he'd plunged into the pages of a bad science fiction novel and he was the alien—the only character who hadn't bought into Troy's innocence and swallowed the perfect-family pill.

Kelly on the other hand seemed to fit right in. She was busily scrambling eggs as if she'd cooked for the Ledger household every morning of her life.

"I talked to Sean a few minutes ago," Troy said. "He and Eve are driving over for the welcome home celebration tonight."

"So we'll all be here," Dakota said. "Guess I'd better tell Dylan to smoke a brisket."

"I've already got that covered," Troy said.

"I'll bring chocolate pies," Julie said. "And I'll make a giant potato salad."

A celebration with the whole family—though they

hadn't really been a family in years. The Ledger sons had been separated like cattle herded into alternating branding pens. Only, they hadn't even ended up in the same state.

Wyatt would love bonding with his brothers. It was the father-led family idea that tasted so bitter on his tongue. The fact that he was the only one who saw it that way made it doubly acidic.

"I've talked to the movers," Kelly said when he walked over to the counter and poured himself a cup of coffee. "They ran into some delays yesterday and won't get into Mustang Run until around noon."

"Then what will they do with the load?"

"Julie told me about a storage-unit facility in Mustang Run. I called and they have several climate-controlled units available. I have to meet the moving van there to pay the first month's rent and sign the paperwork, but I can store everything until the house is ready for me to move in.

"And on your father's suggestion, I've called my bank and had them block all transactions until I can get in to close my account and open a new one. I think that covers most everything you missed while you were sleeping in."

She gave the eggs one last stir and then spooned them onto a serving platter.

"You've been busy."

"Jaci woke me up at seven, so I've had plenty of time to get organized. Now I'm just waiting for the sheriff to call and tell me that he's recovered my car."

"You're in an upbeat mood this morning."

"Your family has inspired me. I'm thinking positive."

She said it with authority as if she wanted to make sure he didn't do or say anything to bring her down.

"You know, Kelly, there's a new apartment complex in town," Julie said as they all sat down at the table. "Their sign says that every unit has its own garage and a small patio in the back. I don't know about the cost or the lease requirement, but I can drive you in to look at the apartments after breakfast if you want."

"It's none of my business," Troy said, "but why waste the money? There's plenty of room right here on the ranch. Jaci can have her own bedroom and acres of room to play outside on sunny days. You can even take her horseback riding."

Jaci's eyes lit up. "Where are the horses?"

"They're still in the horse barn," Troy said, "but later today, they'll be in the horse pasture."

"What's a passer?"

"A pasture is a big fenced yard for horses and cows."

"Can I see the horses? Please, Momma. *Please.*"

"We'll see," Kelly said. "And thanks for the offer to stay on here, Troy, but that's taking ranch hospitality a bit too far."

"The offer will stay on the table, in case you change your mind. Unless that tree damaged the support beams, my sons and I can probably repair that damage in a few days and have the house ready for you to move into."

"I definitely can't ask you to do that."

"You help your neighbor, they help you. That's the cowboy way."

Wyatt stayed out of the conversation. He might consider one of those apartments for himself. He wasn't sure how much family he could take before he started to gag. Then again, if the food was always this good, he might be tempted to stick around.

He was on his third biscuit when his cell phone rang. He pulled it from his pocket and checked the caller ID. Sheriff McGuire. He excused himself from the table and took the call in the family room.

"Is Kelly Burger still at the ranch?"

"She is."

"Good. I tried phoning her cell number, but she didn't answer. Can you call her to the phone?"

"Is this good news or bad?"

"Let's just say it's worrisome."

And when a sheriff said that, the news was always bad.

Chapter Eight

"We have your car."

Kelly took a deep breath and exhaled slowly, relieved by the news, but too wary to celebrate yet. "Was the thief still driving it?"

"No, he'd abandoned it. The engine was cold so he'd been gone awhile before the vehicle was spotted."

"What condition is it in?"

"Busted trunk and driver-side door locks are the only visible damage. There are a couple of pieces of luggage, a box of toys, and a stack of hanging clothes still in the trunk, along with the spare tire and the usual tire changing tools. We didn't find a handbag."

No surprise there.

"Did you check inside the car?"

"The glove compartment was cleaned out, but there were a couple of sleeping bags in the backseat along with some books and toys. The cooler in the floor of the backseat still had a quart of milk in it."

"What about my daughter's booster seat?"

"Still there."

Good. One less thing she wouldn't have to purchase. "What about my computer?"

"No sign of that. I suggest you call your bank and have your account blocked—just to be on the safe side."

"I've taken care of that."

"If you don't have one of those identity-theft policies, you might want to look into that, too. Operate on the basis that the thief has access to everything in your computer, even if it's files or emails that you think have been deleted."

"Good point." It made her uncomfortable that the laptop was in the hands of a thief, but the computer was new. She hadn't used it for any banking or credit card purchases, so she should be safe there. "Where was the car found?"

"This is the part that concerns me, Kelly."

Her stomach knotted. "Why?"

"Brent spotted the vehicle just a few minutes past eight this morning. He was in the area, picking up donuts and coffee at the convenience store when he decided to swing by and check out the damage to your house. Your stolen car was parked in your driveway."

So the perverted thug had shown up at her house. A wave of dread and fear gushed through her veins. What if the tree hadn't fallen onto her roof? What if she and Jaci had been in that house when the lunatic had been there?

"Why would he return the car to my address?"

"I'm hoping you'll tell me that."

"How would I know…"

The answer hit her before she finished asking the question. McGuire thought she was lying or at least holding something back. He must have had her investigated the way Wyatt had. Or maybe Wyatt had lied about keeping her secrets and shared with the sheriff what she'd confessed to him last night.

A choking mix of fury and fear lumped in her throat. "I was just sitting out a thunderstorm in a café when my car was stolen," she said icily. "That's all I know to tell you."

"Okay, settle down, Mrs. Burger. As long as you're leveling with me, you have nothing to worry about. I'll get to the bottom of this."

"Where does this case weigh in on your priority scale?" she asked, voicing concerns Wyatt had raised.

"You needn't worry about that. I take risks to all the citizens of this county seriously, Mrs. Burger. Your car has already been towed to the forensic center. It will be thoroughly examined for fingerprints or any other evidence. That information along with descriptions provided by you, Wyatt, and Edie should go a long way in helping us identify the perp. If he's still in the area, he'll be arrested."

That couldn't happen too soon for her. It didn't resolve her issues with Wyatt. "When can I get my car back?"

"You can pick up your belongings as soon as the evidence check is completed. I'll have the investigating deputy call and give you a heads-up. But I need to keep the car a couple of extra days."

"Why?"

"A precaution—in case we need to take a second look at it. In the meantime, you be careful and if the thief tries to make any personal contact with you, call me immediately."

"Believe me, I will."

"Just so we're on the same page, Mrs. Burger, I don't want to find out after the fact that you know who this guy is or that you weren't a random victim. So if there's anything you haven't told me, now's the time to come clean."

"I'd never seen the man who stole my car until I walked in that truck stop last night. I have no reason to suspect that he knew me."

"In that case, expect a call from the deputy later today as to when you can pick up your possessions."

The phone slipped through Kelly's shaky hands as she broke the connection.

Wyatt caught the phone. "What did McGuire have to say?"

"Get your jacket, Wyatt, and I'll get mine. We need to talk—in the backyard, out of hearing distance of Jaci and your family."

A BRISK WIND MADE the day seem even colder than the thirty-three-degree temperature registered on the back-porch thermometer. Kelly seemed not to notice as she stamped down the steps and started across the yard in her lightweight wrap.

Fortunately, Wyatt had remembered her lack of luggage and retrieved an extra hunting parka from the back of his truck.

He hurried to catch up with her. "Put this on." He tried to hand her the jacket, but she kept her arms hugged tightly about her chest.

"I'm not cold."

"Then that's a weird shade of blue lipstick you're wearing." He draped the coat around her shoulders. "I take it the sheriff delivered bad news."

She stormed away again, this time stopping beneath a mulberry tree. Her stare could have frozen hot ashes. "Did you call the sheriff?"

"No. He called on my phone. He said he'd been

trying to reach you on yours, but you weren't answering."

"No, I mean did you call him last night after I'd gone to bed? Did you tell him about Emanuel Leaky?"

So that's what this was about. He took both her hands in his so that she wouldn't march off again. "I promised that I wouldn't say a word about that to anyone unless it was to save your hide. I don't lie, Kelly, and I don't break promises unless I have a damn good reason for doing so.

"I also don't read minds, especially women's, so how about leveling with me about what's going on?"

"Brent found my car."

"Brent, as in the sheriff's deputy that we met last night?"

"Right."

"Was it wrecked?"

"No. It's in almost the same condition as when he stole it. Almost everything that was in the car appears to still be there, though he did help himself to my handbag and computer."

Which should have been good news. "There must be more."

"Oh, there's more, all right," Kelly said. "The pervert left my car parked in my own driveway."

"That's bizarre."

"So bizarre that now the sheriff thinks I must know more than I've told him. Either that or he knows about my connections to Leaky and thinks this is somehow related."

A possibility that Wyatt hadn't totally ruled out. "I seriously doubt that McGuire took the time last night to have you investigated. He'd have had no reason to invest the time or the resources on a young, single mother whose car had been stolen. It's the thief's unusual behavior that's made him suspicious."

She pulled away from him and exhaled slowly, releasing a stream of vapor from her warm breath. "What possible reason could the man have for returning my car to my house unless he'd planned to harm me or Jaci?"

"He may have wanted to intimidate you, the same way he wanted to get under the skin of the waitress in the truck stop. The way he tried to intimidate you when he stopped near your table on his way out of the truck stop. Some sick jerks get their kicks that way."

Not that he was buying that. Had Kelly and Jaci been inside when the thug had shown up...

Wyatt sucked in a cold breath as sordid images from past cases stormed his mind. The rape and murder of a coed last summer. The mangled body of the nurse who'd opened her door to a man she believed was a meter reader.

"I guess I should be thankful the sheriff is trying to stay on top of the situation and identify the thief," she said once she'd finished sharing the gist of their conversation.

And if he didn't, Wyatt would. "I'll drive you to the storage unit when you're ready. By that time we may be able to retrieve your belongings from the car."

"That would be great. Maybe Julie will watch Jaci while we're gone. They seem to have hit it off and I don't want Jaci to overhear anything that will frighten her."

"Then that's settled."

"I still need to find a place to live until the house is livable."

"Forget about looking at apartments, Kelly. The situation has changed. You're staying here at the ranch."

He'd come on like a cop, ordered instead of asking. He waited for the backlash.

But it was apprehension, not anger that he saw in Kelly's eyes.

"Are you sure, Wyatt? I've brought you nothing but trouble."

"It makes sense."

"I'll think about it."

He'd accept that for now.

They were both silent as they walked back to the house. Questions rolled through Wyatt's mind like a stampede of wild horses.

When had the perp made the decision to go to Kelly's house? He couldn't have gone straight from the truck stop or the car would have been there when Wyatt and Kelly arrived and discovered the damage to the roof.

Where had he gone once he deserted the car? Did he live nearby or had he stolen another vehicle? If so, from where? And why hadn't that theft been reported? Or did the sheriff know more than he'd told Kelly?

A rabbit hopped out of their way as they approached the back steps. A horse neighed in the distance. And Jaci's excited voice rang out from the house.

Wyatt had been in Mustang Run less than twenty-four hours and already he was immersed in family, crime, and a woman who monopolized his thoughts while creating a fearsome hunger in him that had nothing to do with food.

Atlanta seemed a million miles away.

JULIE EAGERLY AGREED to watch Jaci that afternoon. She even seemed delighted that Kelly and Jaci might stay on at the ranch for a few more days. Once that was settled,

Kelly went to look for Jaci and Wyatt. She found them on the side porch with Troy, stacking a fresh supply of logs onto a metal rack.

Jaci was wearing a bright red parka that seemed to fit perfectly and looked practically new.

When Jaci spotted Kelly, she dropped the small log she was holding and ran over to wrap her arms around Kelly's waist.

"Mr. Ledger says I can go with him to feed the horses if it's okay with you. Can I, Momma? Can I, please?"

"Well, you do have a nice jacket to wear."

"I'll keep a close eye on her," Troy said. "My grandson tags along with me to the horse barn every time he gets a chance. I'm good with kids."

"I can tell."

"So can I go with him, Momma?"

"If you promise to do what Mr. Ledger tells you."

"Yeah! I can go feed the horses."

Jaci let go of Kelly's waist and began to jump her way across the porch as if she were on springs.

"I hope you don't mind my lending her the jacket," Troy said. "My grandson Joey left it here last weekend."

"I don't mind at all," Kelly assured him. "Joey must be just about Jaci's size."

"Pretty close. He's almost seven, but he's small for his age. You'll meet him tonight. The whole family will be here."

To dine on the fatted calf, Kelly thought, just as Sheriff McGuire had predicted. Only their reunion celebration would be marred by the problems Kelly had brought into their lives.

Troy dusted his hands together to rid them of dirt and loose bark. "You should go with us, Kelly. Collette has added two new quarter horses to the herd and they're real beauts."

"I'd love to see them." And to make sure Jaci didn't get hurt. The only horses Jaci had ever been around had traveled in circles on a carousel.

"All right then," Troy said. "Let's get going."

"Yes, c'mon, Momma. Let's git goin'."

Jaci held tight to Kelly's hand as they walked toward the barn, but her steady stream of questions were for Troy.

"Can the horses come out of the barn and play?"

"Do the horses stay with their mommas?"

"What do the horses eat?"

"Do the horses bite?"

Troy patiently answered every question. Not only was he as good with kids as he claimed, but he looked so at home on the ranch that it was difficult to believe he'd only been out of prison for a year and a half. It was even more difficult to imagine that this easygoing rancher had murdered the mother of his own sons in cold blood.

But evil didn't always come in ugly packages. Luther Bonner had been an impeccable dresser with excellent manners. Yet he'd willingly worked for one of the most brutal, corrupt individuals in the country. And just as willingly sold him down the river to avoid punishment.

When they neared the horse barn, Jaci let go of Kelly's hand and ran ahead. Kelly hurried to catch up. The wooden door was propped open, and the odors of hay and horseflesh greeted her even before she got her first look at the animals.

Troy stopped at the first stall and scratched the nose of a magnificent steed. "I didn't forget you, Gunner. I'm just running late today, but I brought company."

Jaci backed away from the stall until she was pressed against Kelly's legs. "Horses are big."

"Not all of them," Troy said. "Come meet Snow White. She's not even a year old yet."

"Snow White's not a horse."

"This Snow White is." Troy walked down a number of stalls before he stopped in front of a beautiful white filly. "Snow White is the newest addition to the herd."

The horse pawed at the floor, sending hay and dust flying. Troy calmed her with a soothing voice. "You miss Collette, don't you? I don't spoil you the way she does. She'll be down to see you later."

"Let's give her some food," Jaci said.

"Good idea."

Troy let Jaci help scoop and measure the grainy feed. She bored with that task quickly and jumped into a mound of fresh hay at the back of the narrow barn.

"Is this the entire herd?" Kelly asked as Troy distributed the feed among the horses.

"This is all of the horses presently at Willow Creek Ranch. There's fifteen in all, but we have three new quarter horses stabled at Sean's ranch in Bandera that we'll be moving here in the spring. We're adding another horse barn, one twice as big."

"What will you do with so many animals?"

"Breed and train them for buyers. And Collette and Sean are working on ideas for a summer camping and riding program for underprivileged kids from the city."

"Is Sean another son?"

Troy nodded. "He's Joey's father. He started out as a stepfather, but the adoption was finalized two weeks ago. Joey's mother, Eve, was a widow."

Kelly knew all too well how difficult that could be, especially when there was a child involved. It made romantic relationships difficult, as well. Kelly had dated a few times, but she'd always ended up resenting the men for taking up the few hours of work-free time she preferred to spend being a mother to Jaci.

But then she'd never met a man like Wyatt.

"It's bitter cold out here. You should pay wranglers to feed these animals on days like this."

Kelly turned at the sound of a deep, breathy female voice. The slim brunette standing in the doorway was as sexy as the voice, though she was probably at least fifty.

Her designer jeans fit to perfection. Her jacket was trimmed in mink. The matching hat and scarf in a shade of rich purple set off a flawless complexion and dark, expressive eyes.

"If it's too cold for you, you could have waited inside," Troy said.

The woman looked from Troy to Kelly and then back to Troy again. "I didn't realize you had guests." Her tone was accusing.

"I would have told you had you called before dropping by. This is Kelly Burger and her daughter, Jaci. They're moving to Mustang Run, but they'll be staying with me for a while."

"That sounds cozy. I'm Ruthanne Foley," she said. "Troy's neighbor and *close* friend." The woman stared at Kelly as if she were her opponent in a fight-to-the-finish fencing match.

It finally hit Kelly what was going on. The woman considered her a much younger rival for Troy's attention. That fire blazing in her eyes was pure jealousy.

No one had mentioned that Troy had a lady friend. Kelly wondered if that would further complicate Wyatt's relationship with his father. But she'd clear this misunderstanding up quickly before the woman's jealousy caused a scene.

"Actually, Wyatt brought me to the ranch," Kelly explained. "Troy was nice enough to invite Jaci and me out to see the horses."

"Wyatt's here?" Ruthanne gushed as she walked over and placed a possessive hand on Troy's arm, her attitude softening now that she knew Kelly wasn't a threat. "Why is it I'm the last to know these things? I can't wait to see him."

"Wasn't he at the house when you drove up?"

"If he was, I didn't see him. I only saw Julie and she told me you were at the horse barn. She didn't mention that you weren't alone."

Ruthanne Foley. The name was familiar, though Kelly couldn't place where she'd heard it.

Apparently deciding the newest guest to the barn wasn't worth her attention, Jaci continued turning flips in the hay.

"Kelly is Cordelia Callister's granddaughter," Troy said. "She's moving into the Callister place, or at least she will be once the roof is repaired."

Ruthanne stepped away from Troy and stared at Kelly, her gaze cold and totally unreadable this time. "You're Linda Ann's daughter?"

"I am. Did you know my mother?"

"I've met her." Her tone had grown icy again.

If the rest of the residents of Mustang Run were anything like Ruthanne, no wonder Kelly's mother had moved away and never wanted to come back.

"Ruthanne's ex is Senator Riley Foley," Troy said. "The man who may be our next governor if you can believe the polls."

Now Kelly knew where she'd heard about Ruthanne.

From her mother, years ago. "My mother was on the senator's campaign team the first time he ran for state representative."

Ruthanne studied her perfectly manicured nails. "That was years ago."

"Many," Kelly agreed. "I turned ten during the campaign. I remember because Mother was on the campaign trail with Senator Foley and had to miss my birthday. She made up for it later with a trip to the State Fair."

Ruthanne slapped at a horsefly with the fringed end of her scarf. "Where is your mother now?"

"In Plano, near Dallas. She retired as dean of a small women's college in the Northeast a few years back. But she's still teaching a few political science classes in a local community college."

"I avoid politics entirely," Ruthanne said. "I've never met a politician who could be trusted."

"Mother is not that jaded," Kelly said, "but as far as I know she hasn't helped run a political campaign since then, at least not as an official member of the staff."

"If I remember correctly, she didn't last the campaign with Riley. I can't recall why he had to let her go." Ruthanne turned back to Troy. "I expect a dinner invitation while Wyatt is here. Give me a call. I'll make that chocolate cheesecake you like so much."

"Don't count on it," Troy said dismissively. "I can't make plans for Wyatt. He's got four brothers who'll all want a share of his time."

Ruthanne said her goodbyes with barely a glance Kelly's way. She left just as Julie walked into the barn.

"What frizzed her curls?" Julie asked.

"I think I did," Kelly said. "I'm just not sure how."

"Maybe she doesn't like sharing her boyfriend with other women," Julie teased.

"She made that clear when she thought I was here with Troy, but her dislike of me seemed to go deeper than that."

"Pay no attention to Ruthanne," Troy said. "She's never happy unless she's the center of attention. All that family money she inherited makes her think she's a queen."

"No wonder her husband bailed on her," Julie said.

"He didn't bail until he had plenty of money of his own and figured she'd done about all she could do for him politically," Troy said.

"How long have they been divorced?" Kelly asked.

"Since about a year before I was released from prison. And rest assured, there's nothing going on between the two of us—except for those casseroles and desserts she keeps bringing around."

"Troy is the casserole king," Julie teased. "All the widows at the church bring him home-cooked treats. Some days he has enough food to open a restaurant."

"Not *all* the widows. Mrs. Haverty crosses to the other side of the street if she sees me coming."

Julie laughed. "And you drive her mad when you smile and tip your hat to her as if you're best friends."

"People believe what they want," Troy said, "and about half of the town wants to believe the worst about me."

Kelly was reminded again that the grandfatherly man whose house she was living in—the man whom Jaci had so easily befriended—had served seventeen years in prison for the murder of his wife. A jury had convicted him. Even Wyatt, an experienced homicide detective, wasn't convinced he was innocent.

Troy was strong. She'd seen him just lift a fifty-pound bag of feed and toss it to the ground as if it were a five-pound sack of potatoes. And she suspected the ragged scar down the right side of his face hadn't come from working on the ranch.

She couldn't see him as a murderer, but she hadn't seen Luther Bonner as a gun runner, either.

"Let me know when you're ready to go look at those apartments," Julie offered again.

"Momma, look. Snow White likes the food we gave her."

Excitement bubbled in Jaci's voice. The ranch agreed with her. And there was so much room for her to play outdoors.

"I'd like to hold off on that for another day or two," Kelly said. "If the offer's still on the table, Jaci and I will stay on at the ranch for a few more days."

"You're welcome to stay as long as you want," Troy said.

Jaci's cell phone buzzed. Someone had left a message. So far only her mother, the FBI and Sheriff McGuire had this number. She stepped deeper into the barn to avoid the sun's glare shining through the open door.

A second later she realized she'd been wrong.

Someone else had this number and the words he'd texted made her blood run cold.

Chapter Nine

Miraculously, Kelly managed to hide her emotions from her daughter until she'd walked back to the house with her and Julie. She was determined not to say or do anything that would upset or frighten Jaci.

Julie, however, picked up instantly on the change in Kelly's demeanor. But, other than asking her once if she was okay, Julie let the matter drop. Kelly appreciated that more than Julie could know.

Wyatt's family was truly remarkable, and in spite of the tension between Wyatt and his father, Kelly had never felt such an outpouring of support.

But it was Wyatt she wanted to talk to now. She found him in the courtyard garden, sitting on the cold wooden bench and staring into space.

She sat down beside him and pulled out her phone, punching keys to bring up the disgusting message. "You might want to read this," she said as she handed him the phone.

She looked over his shoulder and reread the message silently.

Nice car, bitch, but not nearly as hot as you are.

Can't wait to see you naked and begging for my...

She turned away before the nauseating clawing in her stomach got worse.

Wyatt mumbled a string of curses. "Sorry," he said. "Cop talk, but I'd like to know how this pervert got your cell phone number."

"Likely from my computer. I emailed my new phone number to Mother. I had forgotten all about that until I saw this note. I should call Sheriff McGuire and let him know that I heard from this lunatic."

Wyatt stood, took her hands and tugged her to her feet. "Call him on the way into town. You need to go to the storage facility. I just need to escape."

"You won't be escaping, Wyatt. I'm your biggest problem now and I'll be with you."

His fingers tangled in the loose curls at her left cheek, lingering for heated seconds before he tucked the hair behind her ear. Her pulse quickened and she looked away to keep him from sensing how his touch affected her.

"I know this situation is hard on you, Kelly, but I can and will keep you and Jaci safe. All you have to do is let me."

"I can hardly turn that down."

Unless it meant dragging him and his whole wonderful family into danger. Then she'd be on her own again, and this time without the FBI to back her up.

MOVING THE FURNITURE from the van to the storage unit went much faster than Kelly had anticipated. So she was really pleased when Wyatt suggested they explore her new hometown while they waited on the sheriff's call saying she could pick up her belongings.

She stared out the windows of Wyatt's truck, enchanted anew with the town she'd visited fewer than

half a dozen times in her entire life. Hilly, lakeside re-
sorts were sprouting up all around the town, yet Mustang Run had managed to hold on to its small-town
charm, especially here on Main Street.

The narrow street was lined with quaint boutiques,
coffee shops, bakeries and an ice cream parlor, all
tucked inside small clapboard shops that had been
standing for almost a century.

Crates filled with string-tied bouquets of colorful
blooms lined the walk in front of a florist. Antique dolls
rested in wooden cradles in one storefront. Beribboned
square-dance dresses decorated the mannequins in another.

"I love the way they've revived this area without
losing its historic character," Kelly said.

"But some things have changed," Wyatt said. "There
used to be a movie theater on one of these corners. I
remember seeing *Batman Returns* there at least five
times."

"I take it you were a Batman fan."

"Best crime fighter of all time." Wyatt stopped at a
crosswalk for a rotund man and his two leashed poo-
dles. "When was the last time you were in Mustang
Run?"

"I was here briefly when Mother and I met with the
attorneys to settle Grams's estate. That was ten years
ago. I had to fly back to New Orleans the same day for
a jewelry show, so I barely had time to check out the
house I'd just inherited."

"What about before that?"

"I came in for my grandmother's seventy-fifth birthday. I was twelve at the time. Her friends threw the gala
on the front lawn of her house. It was quite an affair.

Even Mother flew down for a day, and she detests Mustang Run."

"You must have come back here for your grandmother's funeral."

"The funeral was in Boston. When Grams's Alzheimer's began to worsen, Mother moved her to a nursing home near her so that she could make sure Grams was cared for without her having to make regular trips to Texas."

"You obviously didn't see much of your grandmother when you were growing up."

"We visited, just not in Mustang Run. Grams flew to Boston to see us twice a year, once at Christmas and once in August when the Texas summers got too hot for her. And a couple of times when I was still in elementary school and Mother had to travel out of town for a seminar or a conference, she'd send me to visit Grams. I used to tell her even back then that I wanted to live in Mustang Run one day."

"No wonder she left you the house."

"That I failed to maintain."

"Do you have insurance?"

"Yes. I'm just not sure I have enough. I called my agent. He's supposed to call me back on Monday."

"What did your Mother have against Texas?"

"Not Texas, Mustang Run. All she ever said was that there was nothing to do here. Mind you, my mother thinks a day without intellectual stimulation is like a day without carob. Mother never has a day without carob."

"Sounds disgusting."

"Carob's not that bad once you get used to it."

"That's what they say about broccoli, but you can't prove that by me. I'm a meat and potato kind of guy, but a few ears of corn on the cob or a pot of purple hull peas are okay every once in a while."

"What else should I know about you?"

"That I become a real grouch when I get hungry. How about stopping for lunch?"

"I'm still full from breakfast," Kelly said. Actually every time she thought of the repulsive text message she grew nauseous and she wasn't ready to trust her stomach with food. "But I could use a cup of coffee."

Wyatt pulled into one of the angled parking spaces. She hopped out of the truck, considered getting her jacket from the backseat but then left it. The wind had died down and with the noonday sun bearing down on them, her borrowed sweater was warm enough.

Kelly scanned the signs and storefronts until she spotted Abby's Diner.

"We should eat at Abby's. She and my grandmother were fast friends. Even when Grams's Alzheimer's progressed to the point she couldn't remember her, Abby called to check on her once a week. And for her birthdays she always mailed Grams a homemade sweet-potato pie."

"Then Abby's it is."

Neither his expression nor his tone indicated he liked her suggestion. "We can go somewhere else if you like."

He shook his head. "One spot in Mustang Run is as good as another."

He strode toward the restaurant, the muscles in his arms flexed as if he were gearing up for a fight—or a rendezvous with his past. But he was right, there probably wasn't anywhere he could go in Mustang Run where he wouldn't risk that.

Mouthwatering odors reached them long before

they entered the diner. Once inside, the noise level and tempting smells reached a crescendo. It was half past one, but all the tables and booths were taken and the two seats available at the counter were not together.

A wisp of a hostess with long blond hair smiled flirtatiously at Wyatt and added an exaggerated sway to her hips as she walked over to where they were standing. Good-looking cowboys were apparently still in style at Abby's Diner.

"There's a ten-minute wait," she said. "The food is worth it."

"Do you guarantee that?"

"If not, dessert is on me."

"Can't very well turn that down," Wyatt said.

As the hostess walked away, Kelly leaned in close enough to whisper in his ear. "If you play your cards right, dessert could probably *be* her."

"I could say the same for those two cowboys at the counter who are eyeing you."

She checked them out. One gave a little salute. The other only nodded and grinned. "They're just being friendly," Kelly quipped.

"Uh-huh. Ye-haw."

For a cop, Wyatt had a terrific knack for defusing the tension in a situation or in a day. And for making a couple of sexy cowboys seem as exciting as watching fish swim across a screen saver.

Five minutes later, the hostess seated them at a back table that was tucked away in a corner niche by itself. As crowded as the restaurant was, it actually offered a degree of privacy.

Wyatt chose the seat that gave him a view of the

door. "I always like my back to the wall. It's a cop thing."

That left Kelly with a view of a booth where three men wearing mechanic's overalls were shoveling down pie topped by mountainous meringue.

A middle-aged waitress set glasses of water in front of them and handed them menus. "The special today is chicken-fried steak with creamed potatoes, gravy and pinto beans. Or you can have a side salad instead of the beans."

"Just coffee for me," Kelly said.

"And I'll take the special," Wyatt said without bothering to look at the menu.

"With biscuits or corn bread?"

"Corn bread. And iced tea."

"I'll have it right out."

"You must be hungry," Kelly said as the waitress walked away. "Did you see the size of those chicken-fried steak orders coming out of the kitchen? The steaks were spilling over the edge of the plate."

"Nice appetizer size." He stared at a spot over her left shoulder. "Don't get too comfortable. We are about to have company."

Before she could ask who, Sheriff McGuire stepped into view.

"I'm glad I ran into you two here," the sheriff said. "It will save me a phone call."

"Does that mean I can get my things from my car now?" Kelly asked.

"Anytime after four. That's the latest word from my evidence team." McGuire slid into the empty chair kitty-corner from her. "They've finished checking the interior," he said, lowering his voice, though there was little chance of it carrying to the next table over the din of clattering dishes and noisy chatter.

"Any success?" Wyatt asked.

"Nothing of consequence."

"He must have left fingerprints," Kelly said.

McGuire shook his head. "Unfortunately, it's not as easy to collect a usable print as it looks on the CSI shows. Wyatt can tell you that. They did lift a couple of viable prints from the Corvette, but it may take a while to determine if they belong to the thief or someone with a legitimate reason for being in the car before it was stolen."

Kelly felt the disappointment mounting again. "Have you been able to trace the text message sent to my phone?"

"We're working on that. These things take time and if the text was sent from one of those pay-as-you-go phones, it's impossible."

A different waitress approached their table. This one was chubby with short graying hair, sparkling blue eyes and a smile that showed a row of tea-stained teeth.

She punched a finger into the sheriff's forearm to get his attention before propping her hands on her ample hips. "What are you doing hiding in the back corner?"

"Making new friends and avoiding the ornery cook."

"Just for that, you'll pay for your pie today, lawman."

"You'll change your mind about that as soon as I tell you who this is I'm sitting with."

The woman looked over both Kelly and Wyatt and then slapped her hands against her cheeks in surprise.

"Lands to Goshen. It's Wyatt. Sure can't deny you're a Ledger. You could have been cloned from Troy. He must be higher than the price of gas with you back in town. When did you get in?"

"Last night."

"I'm Abby," she said. "You probably don't even remember me. What were you when you left here? Twelve? Thirteen?"

Finally, Wyatt smiled. "Thirteen and how could I forget you? You used to give me and my brothers free ice cream if we snuck in while Mother was shopping."

She chuckled. "And then I'd tell you not to tell Helene I'd spoiled your lunch."

"We always did."

"She didn't really mind. Your mother and I were the best of friends. I taught her to make pie crust. She taught me how to grow my own herbs and how to put together a flower bouquet that looked twice as good as the ones from the florist. But even we never thought we'd end up practically kin one day. I guess you heard that my neice Viviana married your brother Dakota."

"I heard."

"Helene would have been tickled to death with that. I swear, I miss her to this day. Of course, I don't miss her the way Troy misses her. I don't 'spect he'll ever get over losing her. They had problems, sure, same as the rest of us, but I've never seen two people who loved each other more."

McGuire tore open a package of crackers from the skinny basket in the middle of the table. "You do go on and on, woman. Quit talking a minute and see how good your guesser works with the woman sitting next to Wyatt."

Abby cocked her head to one side and studied Kelly. "I give up."

"That's Cordelia Callister's granddaughter."

"Well, bless my bones. You're Linda Ann's daughter." Abby dropped into the empty chair and laid a hand on Kelly's arm. "It is so good to see a Callister back in this town. I was beginning to think they would have to bring in a wrecking crew and tear your old home place down."

"I hope to get the house fixed up and move into it," Kelly said.

"Your grandmother would love knowing that. She missed Linda Ann like crazy, but I can't say I blame your mother for kissing this town goodbye after that wedding fiasco."

Now Kelly was totally confused. "You must have Mother mixed up with someone else. She didn't get married in Mustang Run."

"No, and didn't that just turn out for the best?"

"Didn't what turn out for the best?"

"Her being jilted by that jerk so close to the wedding date. Right after that she met your father and Cordelia told everybody what a catch he was and how he and Linda Ann were soul mates."

"To his day, my mother claims she and my father were soul mates."

"Such a tragedy," Abby said, "him dying in that terrible car crash before you were born. But at least she had you and she didn't let the grief bury her like some folks do. She went right on to get her doctorate degree and really made something of her life."

"Mother's definitely an achiever. But she can't make pie crust."

"No, she was always the brainy one," Abby said. "Did you know that she scored higher on her ACT than any student who's ever graduated from Mustang Run High?"

"No. She never mentioned that." Nor had she ever mentioned being jilted at the altar by a jerk. Not that it mattered now, but it might explain some of her distaste for the town.

Abby excused herself a few minutes later and the sheriff followed suit. They walked away together with Abby laughing at something he'd said.

"I think there's a little flirtation going on between the two of them," Kelly said.

"Could be."

"You seem distracted."

"I was just thinking that with so much small-town familiarity around Mustang Run, I don't see how anyone could ever get away with murder, unless that someone is a person no one would ever suspect."

"Not even the sheriff."

"Especially not the sheriff. I'm thinking about my mother's murder, but the same theory may hold true for your situation."

"I'm not following you."

"The sheriff is working this case as if you were a random victim, but what if it's more than that?"

"It had to be random, Wyatt," Kelly argued. "The thief could not possibly know I'd stop at that truck stop. I didn't even know it beforehand."

"The car theft was random, but what happened after that may not be. It may have become personal after the perp discovered your identity either from the paper-work in your car or from the emails and files on your computer."

"So you think this perp, as you call him, followed up with his intimidation because of who I am?"

"It's not that far-fetched considering everyone knows everyone around here."

"I'd never seen that man before in my life."

"But he may have known your grandmother. For that

matter, he may have known your mother. She grew up around here."

"Grams has been dead for ten years and Mother hasn't lived in Mustang Run since before I was born. Only a very sick guy would carry a grudge that long."

"Like the man who sent you the text?"

"Point made." The complexity of possibilities was growing exponentially. "But why leave the car at my house untouched? If he's getting payback through me, why not drive it into a creek or at least knock out all the windows?"

"I doubt the visit was just to return your car."

No. He'd come back to do exactly what he'd threatened in his text. Her nausea returned.

"I'm just tossing around ideas at this point, Kelly. But maybe when he saw the downed tree and realized you wouldn't be returning that night, he decided it was a good time and place to dump the stolen car."

"And then what? Hike to the highway in a cold rain to try and hitch a ride?"

"If he lives in the area, he could have called a friend to pick him up, or he might have walked home or to a friend's house."

"It would have been a long walk."

"Not necessarily. I called the sheriff while you were in the horse barn. I needed him to clarify a few things, and he said there's a road about a mile behind your house with several freestanding houses and a fairly large mobile-home park."

So this disgusting person might have lived close to her grandmother. He might have terrified her as she grew older and made her afraid to go to the sheriff.

No. She couldn't see Grams letting some goon push

her around. Not with all the friends she had in Mustang Run.

Nonetheless…

"I'm beginning to understand why my mother hated this town."

HE POURED HIMSELF ANOTHER shot of whiskey and took it to the sofa. He still couldn't believe his luck, especially when yesterday had started off so rotten.

It was a sure sign the economy stank when you couldn't even make a living dishonestly. He hadn't had more than a few ounces of cocaine in the trunk of his car, a delivery for some rich broad in River Oaks who liked to inhale her afternoon delight.

It would have been a fast, easy buck with a drug high on the side if that idiot teenager hadn't run a red light and rammed into the side of his car.

All the cops had to do was check his license and run it though the system. Then they'd have been over his vehicle like cheese on an enchilada. A few measly ounces was enough to send him straight back to prison.

He'd had no choice but to take off running, dodging the traffic on South Shepherd and then cutting through a neighborhood. It had been pure luck he'd happened on the woman unlocking her Corvette. She'd practically thrown her keys at him the second she saw his gun.

But stealing the car belonging to Kelly Callister Burger had been like winning the lottery. Not only did he plan to make her squirm before he had his way with her, but she might just bring him enough change to take care of all his needs for the time being.

Money he'd been cheated out of almost twenty years ago.

He wondered what assassin fees were these days.

He'd been behind bars so long he was out of the loop.
He figured fifty grand was reasonable.

He downed another gulp of whiskey, picked up his
new prepaid cell phone and made a call. The phone
rang.

"Hello."

"I hope you're alone, because I have an offer you
can't afford to refuse."

Chapter Ten

There were two pickup trucks and one large work truck fully equipped with tree-trimming equipment parked in Kelly's driveway when she and Wyatt pulled up after lunch. Left with an hour and a half of free time before Kelly could get her belongings from her car, going by the house seemed to make more sense than driving all the way back to the ranch and then into town again.

Kelly had called to check on Jaci twice, and both times Julie had assured her that she was having a marvelous time with Jaci. Jaci's excited voice had convinced Kelly that the same was true for her.

Kelly studied the swarm of activity as she and Wyatt climbed from the truck to the clattering roar of gas-powered engines. Four muscular men in hard hats, goggles, jeans and work boots were on her roof, handling oversize chain saws with the ease she exhibited maneuvering a broom.

The damage looked far more extensive in the daylight. The main trunk of the oak had apparently been split almost down the middle by the lightning bolt Sheriff McGuire had mentioned. Evidently last night's storm had finished ripping it apart. Half of the tree had landed squarely on top of her house.

Dakota waved and moved toward them. "The fun started without you."

"I can tell," Kelly said. "Seeing this in the daytime, I guess I'm lucky the house is still standing."

"It may not be as bad as it looks," Dakota said.

"Good," Wyatt said, "because from here, I'd say the best bet would be to tear it down and start over."

Just what Kelly didn't need to hear.

"Cory wants to talk to you about cutting down the rest of the tree," Dakota said to Kelly. "He thinks… Well, I'll let him tell you. He's the one with his feet planted on terra firma and supervising."

Wyatt put a hand to the small of her back as they approached the house. "You and Dakota go ahead and talk to Cory. I'd like to take a look inside."

"Is it safe?" she asked.

"That's what I'd like to find out."

"There's a tree limb blocking the front door," she said, stating the obvious.

"Which is why I'll go in through the back."

"I don't have my keys with me."

"Vampires walk through walls." He flashed a wicked smile and walked away.

Dakota made the introductions.

Cory took off his goggles and propped a booted foot on one of the stump-size tree cuttings. "We've got a mess here, but it will all be cleaned up before we leave. Like I told Dakota, I think you ought to let me go ahead and cut down what's left of the tree while I'm here."

"It is an eyesore now," she agreed.

"It's worse than that. It's dying. See how the bark is falling off the part of the tree that's still standing? You'll have to take it down eventually to avoid the risk of it falling on the house, too. May as well let us do it now."

"How much is all of this going to cost?"

"If I hadn't seen the way Wyatt was looking at you a minute ago, I'd say a date for dinner. As it is, I'll just take those steaks Dakota offered—butchered and freezer wrapped."

Dakota adjusted his sunglasses. "You drive a hard bargain, man."

"I'll pay for the work," Kelly said.

"Don't worry about it. When I need a favor, I'll holler at Dakota. It evens out in the long run. We go way back."

But she and Dakota didn't. No one in this family had even met her before yesterday. They owed her nothing.

"So, do I take the tree out?" Cory asked.

"I guess it's the only thing that makes sense. So, yes. Chop my once beautiful tree to the ground."

"You can grow another just like it in another hundred years," Cory said.

"You tree men are all heart."

"I don't get you Ledgers," Kelly said, after Cory had walked away and started shouting orders to his crew. "Why go to all this trouble for me when you've just met me?"

Dakota shrugged. "Wyatt obviously likes you and he's our brother. It's the cowboy code to help when you can, fight when you have to and never squat with your spurs on. Take your pick."

In that case she'd take the first one. She was definitely attracted to Wyatt, but it couldn't possibly be more than just physical at this point. They didn't know each other well enough for it to be more.

Yet, she was already trusting Wyatt with her life and

Jaci's. She'd moved into his house. Had shared pancakes at midnight with him. She'd even confessed to helping the prosecution with their case against Emanuel Leaky.

All that within hours after meeting Wyatt.

Heaven help her if she'd made a mistake.

"Kelly, come here a minute, will you?"

"You're being paged," Dakota said.

She looked back toward the house. Wyatt was standing in the side yard, his shirtsleeves rolled up above his elbows despite the cold. His Stetson was pushed to the back of his head. Rumpled locks of copper-streaked hair fell about his forehead.

He absolutely stole her breath away.

"I'll be right there," she called back. "Thanks, Dakota. I guess I owe you a favor now."

"You can babysit Briana any night."

"That's a deal."

She strode across the yard to where Wyatt was standing, doing her best to avoid the worst of the mud and the surge of attraction that had just spiked inside her like a rocket at blastoff.

"I hope you didn't call me over to tell me the house should be gutted."

"Actually, I think Dakota is right. It could be a lot worse. The soaked carpet has to go. So does the wet Sheetrock and a good deal of the molding, but the house itself seems to be sound. I can't guarantee that from just a cursory look, but I can tell you they don't build houses like this anymore."

"Finally, good news. Better pinch me to make sure I'm not dreaming."

"I can do better than that."

Taking her totally by surprise, Wyatt leaned in close. The air evaporated from her lungs. When his lips touched hers, she trembled like a schoolgirl, desire tripping through her like shooting stars.

Her head was spinning, her knees weak when he pulled away.

"Sorry," he said. "Probably not the best idea to kiss you with an audience around, but I've wanted to do that ever since I found you attacking the innocent motor-bike."

"You like it rough, do you, cowboy?" she teased, trying to recover from the desire still rocking her body.

"I'll take it any way you dish it out. But I actually called you to take a look at some boxes I found in the back room."

She followed him through the back door which he'd obviously had no trouble unlocking since the top half was busted glass. He led her to what had been Grams's bedroom.

Three cardboard boxes sat in the middle of the floor. Kelly's name was printed on each one with a black marker. They were dry, but there was standing water on the floor next to the closet.

"I was checking out that leak in the closet when I found the boxes. If you want them, we should take them with us before they get wet."

She stared at the boxes, hesitant to open them for fear they were the work of the maniac who'd left the text message.

"Mother paid someone to clear out the house after Grams died. She was supposed to donate anything of value to a local charity. The rest was supposed to be trash."

"Maybe she left these because they have your name on them."

"I'm a little gun-shy after all the negative surprises in the last twenty-four hours," Kelly said.

"Caution is always wise. Should I open one for you?"

"Please do, but watch out for slithering snakes, hairy spiders or stinging scorpions."

"A few of those may be in there even if the contents are legit. This is Texas."

Wyatt slit through the masking tape and opened the first box. A bright red homemade Valentine with glitter and dried globs of paint rested on top. The words *I Love You* were printed in uneven letters.

A choking lump settled at the back of Kelly's throat.

"Your handiwork?" Wyatt asked.

"Yes. I remember making that. I think I was about six at the time."

"Then I guess these boxes are keepers."

She nodded. "Grams must have packed these away for me before the Alzheimer's became so debilitating."

"I'll load them in the truck."

A kiss from Wyatt that suggested it was only the beginning and mementos from Grams.

Even the ravages of nature loosed on her roof and a maniac with a vulgar vocabulary couldn't spoil those.

At least not until the next blow fell.

DINNER HAD DEFINITELY BEEN a celebration. Brisket and ribs from the smoker, yams, potato salad, green beans, corn, coleslaw and the best homemade yeast rolls Wyatt had ever eaten. And that was even before they got to the homemade desserts.

Wyatt had stuffed himself again, and was still forking bites of pecan pie along with his second cup of decaf brew. The women had taken their desserts and coffee to the family room, leaving the kitchen to the men.

"Is there any news on the car theft?" Troy asked.

Wyatt filled them in about the stolen car being left at Kelly's house and about the text.

"That's extremely bizarre," Dakota said. "This guy must be a real kook."

"Possibly a dangerous kook," Dylan said.

"I agree," Wyatt said. "So does the sheriff."

"Are you signing on as protector?" Dylan asked.

"Unofficially. For the time being. I don't want her going into town alone."

"If there's anything I can do to help, just ask," Dakota said. "I could use a good fight."

"What's the matter?" Dylan teased. "Honeymoon getting too tame for you?"

"Honeymoon is going just fine, bro."

"I'll help any way I can," Troy said. "Let me know later. Right now I need some brisk air and to walk off about a thousand of those calories I ate tonight."

Wyatt finally pushed his pie saucer away as Troy grabbed his hat and jacket and left through the back door. "If I keep eating like this, I'll have to go out and buy some bigger jeans."

"We have the cure for that," Dylan said. "There are plenty of logs that need splitting."

"I thought all you guys did was ride around on horseback and look good in your boots and jeans."

"I can see how you'd think that," Dakota said. "But the looking good part just comes naturally."

"So what did you guys do, have a cook-off and marry the winners?" Wyatt asked.

"No, we had to teach them how to find their way

around a kitchen," Dylan said. "We just married the hottest women we could find."

Dakota lifted his coffee cup. "I'll drink to that."

"And the smartest," Sean added.

"Absolutely," Dakota agreed. "It's not easy sleeping with a woman every night who's smarter than you are."

"Too bad Tyler's not here tonight," Dylan said, "instead of on duty in Afghanistan. Then we'd all be together, right back where we started. The sons of Troy Ledger in the kitchen of the big house at Willow Creek Ranch."

"The sons of Troy and *Helene* Ledger," Wyatt added. Not that he thought his brothers had forgotten their mother, but they sure seemed to have forgotten that Troy had been convicted of her murder.

They ignored the facts of the trial completely. Either they'd never bothered to read the full transcript or they'd dismissed as unimportant some key points.

Troy had let the prosecution build a case on circumstantial evidence without offering anything substantial in his defense. He hadn't even explained Helene's having packed her bags the day she was murdered. Instead he'd acted as if he had no clue as to why she was leaving him.

"I know what you think, Wyatt," Dylan said. "But Dad didn't kill Mom. They loved each other."

"So how do you guys explain away the evidence—like the packed bags that indicated Mom was leaving Troy?"

"She could have been just going to see her parents," Sean said. "That's not the same as leaving Dad."

"Mother would be the first to tell us to stick by Dad," Dylan said. "Just give him a chance. Talk to him."

"I plan to spend lots of time talking to him."

"I can't argue with what you're doing," Sean said. "I never expected to set foot on this ranch again and with you coming from a Homicide background, it must make it even harder to see past Dad's conviction. But I agree with Dylan. Dad loved Mother. I'm more convinced of that every day. Eve thought the same long before she met me and she had the advantage of being one of his prison psychiatrists."

Fifteen minutes later they were still talking about the trial and getting nowhere. Wyatt was thankful for the sound of footsteps on the back steps that signaled Troy's return.

Troy stamped the mud off his boots and then shrugged out of his jacket and hat, hanging them both on hooks near the back door.

"Wind's picking up something fierce," he said as he headed for the coffeepot.

The talk turned to more agreeable topics and Wyatt was amazed at the satisfying lives his brothers had created for themselves and their families.

Dylan and Troy worked as partners, rebuilding the ranch and adding property and cattle to the spread. Dylan's wife Collette was due to deliver in two weeks. They wanted a houseful of kids.

Sean had his own horse farm in Bandera but was still in big demand all over the country as a horse whisperer—not that he called himself that. Their son Joey was in the second grade and loved horses almost as much as Sean.

"Any plans for when you hang up the bull rope for good?" Wyatt asked Dakota.

"Yeah," Dakota said. "Don't laugh or faint from shock. I know I dropped out of college after two semesters, but that was because I had bulls to ride. Anyway,

I figure we have one doctor in the family, we may as well have two."

"Whoa," Dylan said. "That's the first I've heard about you and the possibility of med school."

"I haven't mentioned it to anyone except Viviana and Troy before now, but if I can make the grades, I'd like go back to school and eventually get into an equine veterinary program, hopefully at UT, since it's close by."

"I'm impressed," Wyatt said.

Sean gave Dakota a high five. "And think of the money I'll save with a family rate."

Troy finally pulled a chair up to the table and sat down with them. "What about you, Wyatt? You must get some hellacious murder cases in the city."

"I *did*." He likely wouldn't get a better opportunity than this to admit to everyone at once why he'd really returned to Mustang Run. Dakota knew so it wasn't going to remain a secret forever.

"I'm no longer with the Atlanta Police Department. I resigned."

That stunned Troy, Sean and Dylan into arched brows and silence.

"That's a big move," Sean finally said. "Do you have a better offer or are you leaving law enforcement altogether?"

"I'm moving back to Mustang Run."

"Now that's what I'm talking about," Dylan said. "Dad and I can sure use you here at the ranch. If you don't like the idea of ranching, I'm sure Collette's father can sign you on as a deputy."

"I'm here to find out who killed Mother."

This time the silence grew deafening.

Troy was the first to break it. "I wondered when you'd finally get around to that. I'll share my findings with you and work along beside you or I can stay the hell out of your way. Your call."

"I'd like to see what you've done, but I have my own methods," Wyatt said. "I work best alone."

Troy's expression grew stony, impossible to read. "I won't interfere, but if you don't find the killer, Wyatt, I will. I won't rest until I know that justice has been served for Helene."

Troy pushed back from the table, stood and left the room as if the situation were settled. Tension hovered over the brothers, no one saying a word.

Finally Dylan broke the impasse. "There's your answer. He didn't kill her."

"Maybe not, but someone did. I won't stop until I find out who."

KELLY TUCKED THE COVERS around her very tired daughter. She and Joey had played together like old friends. They'd started out with board games and ended up in the middle of the floor with Jaci's dinosaurs, Joey's action figures and the wooden pawns of an old chess set they'd found in Sean's boyhood room while playing hide-and-seek.

At that point, Viviana had gone home to put a sleepy Briana to bed.

Kelly, Eve, Collette and Julie perused an old photo album filled with haunting family photographs of Troy, Helene and their five young sons. A picture of Helene in the rocker next to the hearth holding Wyatt in her arms was especially poignant.

Troy had knelt beside Helene, Wyatt's tiny fingers curled around one of his much larger ones.

Thirteen years and four sons later, Helene had been brutally murdered next to that same hearth. The disturbing comparison made Kelly uneasy as she bent to kiss Jaci good-night.

Jaci hugged her doll to her chest. "I like the ranch, Momma."

"I know you do, sweetheart."

Kelly liked it, too.

She liked the whole Ledger clan with their emotion, enthusiasm and the kind of zest for life she'd never experienced in her own family.

Kelly even liked Troy. She liked him a lot, but the murderous secrets hidden inside the house would never let go of him or Wyatt until the truth came out. And if Wyatt did find out that Troy had killed Helene, it would destroy the Ledger family. She wondered if he'd be able to live with that.

Kelly was totally infatuated with Wyatt. His kiss had awakened a need so raw and powerful that she couldn't think of him now without aching to touch him and to feel his lips on hers again.

Collette was waiting outside the bedroom door when Kelly tiptoed out. "Was Jaci all right with sleeping in a separate room?"

"She didn't seem to mind at all. I think it was Joey's telling her that he had his own room when he spent the night here that did the trick. They hit it off well."

"I noticed. The others left while you were getting Jaci ready for bed. They said to tell you they loved meeting you and Jaci and that they would see you soon. Dylan and I need to be going, too, but I wanted to make sure it was okay with you if we stop by after church tomorrow and help you guys finish off the leftovers. If you've had all the Ledgers you can stand for a while, don't be afraid to tell me."

"That would be great. There's enough food left to

feed half of Mustang Run. Besides, Dylan is a good buffer between Wyatt and his father."

"That's exactly what Dylan said. He understands what Wyatt's going though. I met Dylan the day he and his father both returned to Willow Creek Ranch for the first time in eighteen years. The first year of that had been while Troy was in jail awaiting trial. The next seventeen was after the conviction.

"They hadn't communicated in all that time. The strain between them was almost palpable."

"They've come a long way."

"They have. They talk every day." Collette made a face as she laid a hand on her extended belly. "Dylan, Jr., has a wicked kick."

"But it won't be much longer until he'll be kicking at the air instead of you."

"Two weeks and counting," Collette said, rubbing her belly again. "I am so ready. I've had the nursery prepared for months. Dylan refinished the cradle his mother had used with all the boys. It's at least a hundred years old, intricately carved and beautiful."

"I'm not surprised. The antique furnishings in the guest room are beautiful."

"Abby says Helene didn't have much money to spend on furniture back in those days, but that she had a knack for finding real treasures at garage sales and restoring them to almost museum quality."

"Helene must have been a fascinating woman."

"To hear Troy tell it, she walked on water. He didn't kill her, you know."

"How can you be so sure?"

"I just know. If you stay in this house long enough, you'll know he's innocent, too."

"How will I know?"

Dylan stepped into the hall. "I've got the truck heating so you won't get cold on the drive home. It's ready when you are."

"I'm ready," Collette said.

"How will I know?" Kelly asked again as Collette turned to go.

Collette held her belly with both hands. "Helene will tell you."

WYATT KNEW THAT JACI was sleeping in a separate room and yet he hadn't bothered to stop by to tell Kelly goodnight. She'd nervously anticipated that he would. She worried about how to handle the growing attraction between them, knowing how quickly the passion might escalate with no more than his touch to ignite it.

They were still virtual strangers, even though the intensity of both their situations had bypassed the normal get-acquainted period and sped the relationship ahead at a dizzying pace. She was afraid they were rushing into this too fast.

Yet now that he hadn't stopped in even to say goodnight, she worried that the kiss that had rocked her to her soul had meant nothing to him.

Kelly pulled back the covers and was about to climb into bed when Collette's disturbing statement about the murder pushed into her mind.

Helene will tell you.

What could she possibly have meant by that? It wasn't as if the pictures they'd looked at tonight could talk, although they did tell a convincing story of the Ledgers' happy, normal family life up until the point Helene had been murdered.

Helene had seemed happy in every one of the photos,

including the candid shots. But even those could have been posed—or altered.

But for what purpose?

More likely Collette's comment had stemmed from the hormonal shifts during pregnancy that made the photos seem extra revealing tonight.

Kelly walked to the sliding-glass door, pushed the curtain back a few inches and peered into the court-yard. Bathed in shadows and the gossamer shimmer of moonlight, the garden took on an ethereal appearance.

She was about to step away when she spotted Troy. He was sitting to one end of the ornate bench, shoulders stooped, his face buried in his hands. He appeared to be a man in agony, a strange reaction when he'd claimed to be thrilled to have Wyatt home again.

Perhaps the tension between him and Wyatt had come to a head after the others left. Or could it be that he was afraid of the truth his homicide-detective son was determined to discover? Even if he was innocent of the murder, could there be old secrets he didn't want uncovered?

The wind picked up, creating a ghostly wail. Troy didn't stir. Gooseflesh popped up on Kelly's arms as she closed the curtain and checked the lock on the glass door.

She crawled into bed and pulled the covers tight around her. In spite of all of her own problems, it was Helene Ledger who walked through her mind as she finally fell asleep.

KELLY WOKE UP in a pitch-black room, shaking from an icy blast that blew across her with hurricane-like force. The thick privacy drapes at the window fluttered like sails. The door to the outside must have somehow blown open. Only she remembered locking it.

Something creaked like old bones...or aging floor-boards.

Kelly was not alone.

Chapter Eleven

Heart pounding, Kelly tried to escape, but the covers entangled her, pinning her to the bed. Then just as suddenly as the frigid wind had begun, it died. The curtain no longer swirled into the room. The creaking transformed into an angelic voice crooning a lullaby.

Diaphanous images appeared and moved across the ceiling. Slowly and methodically, one image emerged from the conglomeration. Helene, rocking her baby and holding him to her breast while she crooned a lullaby. The tune was mesmerizing and soothing.

The words were terrifying.

Family sins can kill. Stay alive. Stay alive.

Mothers always know. Stay alive. Stay alive.

Hold on tight to love. Stay alive. Kelly, stay alive.

The words and image evaporated in a burst of flame. Kelly kicked off the covers and sat up in bed.

She reached to the bedside table and flicked on the lamp. The room was just as it had been when she went to bed.

Her pulse was still racing. Her emotions were overwrought. Her nerves were rattled to the point of collapse, so frazzled that her mind had twisted the pictures from the photograph album into a slide show of mental horror.

But it was only a nightmare.

Still, she climbed from bed and pulled on her robe. She wouldn't get back to sleep until she assured herself Jaci was resting well and that her room was not too cold.

The house was peacefully quiet as Kelly took the few steps to Jaci's room, turned the doorknob and opened the door. Jaci was fast asleep, her breathing a gentle, reassuring rhythm that calmed Kelly like nothing else could have.

"Sleep well, sweetheart. I love you and I'll always be here for you."

But as she crept back to bed, she couldn't help but wonder if Helene had whispered those same words the last time she'd told her boys good-night.

WYATT STARED IN AWE at the charts, notes and timelines that took up one whole wall of the master bedroom. Whatever he'd expected from Troy's research, it hadn't been this. Wyatt had served on serial killer task forces whose investigations hadn't been this thorough.

"How long have you been working on this?" Wyatt asked.

"I started collecting facts in prison as soon as they granted me access to a computer. I wasn't this organized then, of course. My supplies were limited to a small notebook and a pencil that I had to be careful with. Sometimes it would take days to get it sharpened once I'd broken or worn away the point."

"You could have been a homicide detective if..."

The *if* hung in the air.

"One detective in the family is enough," Troy said.

"And in spite of all the research, I'm nowhere. Dead ends just keep piling on top of more dead ends."

"Dead ends can be deceptive," Wyatt said. "It's like a video game. When you hit a brick wall, you search for that one tiny opening that leads to the next clue."

"I've never played a video game in my life. I've watched Joey at it. It only makes me dizzy."

"Fair enough. Think of it as locating a calf that's lost in heavy underbrush. There's always a starting spot and then you keep following the leads until you find it. Equate the sound of the calf's bleating with motive. Both are always a good place to start."

Wyatt's mind raced ahead. Motive was what had led to Troy's being a prime suspect. That and the fact that the husband is always the first suspect when a married woman is murdered.

"Motive is a problem," Troy admitted. He picked up a yardstick and used it to point at a posterboard chart thumbtacked to the far left corner of the wall. "I've listed everyone Helene had contact with on a regular basis. Not one of them had a problem with her. Everybody liked Helene. That's why I think her murder had to be a random attack—a crime of opportunity committed by a complete stranger."

"That's seldom the case in a murder—"

Wyatt swallowed hard, biting back the word *Dad* before it slipped from his mouth. He didn't have trouble referring to Troy as his father. That was the reality of their relationship.

But he couldn't bring himself to call Troy *Dad*. Dad had been the person he counted on. The man he'd idolized. The man he'd been sure would always be there for him. That man no longer existed. His brothers had surely felt that same way about Troy when they'd first returned to the ranch.

"Random murders may be rare," Troy said, "but they happen on a daily basis in this country and they happened back then, too. Maybe the guy stopped by looking for a wrangler job and then decided to break in and steal something when he realized there was no man around. Your mother may have caught him in the house and he shot her."

"Nothing was missing from the house," Wyatt reminded him.

"My revolver was taken."

"Yes, and Mother's handbag had been in plain sight not six feet from the top of the bureau where you kept that revolver."

Evidence submitted in the trial emphasized that the weapon wouldn't have been loaded since Helene Ledger was terrified of having loaded weapons around her young sons.

The bullets for the gun were kept in a cigar box in the top bureau drawer. Whoever killed Helene either knew that ahead of time or found the shells while rummaging through the bureau drawers.

The weapon in question had later been found stuck between some rocks at the bottom of Willow Creek.

Wyatt skimmed the names on the random-killing suspect list. Most had been X'ed out for various reasons.

Three words stopped him cold—

Suspected paid assassin.

Jerome Hurley. Home address was in Mustang Run.

Wyatt tapped the word *assassin* with his fingertips. "Tell me about Jerome Hurley."

"Helene wouldn't have been killed by a paid assassin. She was a rancher's wife. She took care of you boys and took part in church activities."

Wyatt agreed. His mother was an unlikely target of a paid assassin. But that would be exactly the type of man Emanuel Leaky might hire to take out Kelly.

Troy used his yardstick to follow the progression to the next column. Hurley was convicted of raping a woman who was home alone on a ranch about forty miles west of the Ledger spread five years after Helene's murder. The X by his name was followed by the word *alibi*.

"What was Jerome's alibi?" Wyatt asked.

"Three people claimed he was having lunch with them at a burger joint in Austin at the time of the murder."

"Friends of his?"

"The two females were friends. The guy was his cousin."

"Was there any proof that the friends and cousin weren't lying?"

"The cousin's car was caught on a security camera leaving the restaurant parking lot. There were four people in the car. Two males, two females. The only one who showed up well enough for a positive identification was the cousin."

"Did Jerome have a rap sheet before that?"

"He'd been arrested on burglary and drug-related charges. Most of them didn't stick. He'd served less than two years combined on all his arrests."

"Where does the suspected 'paid assassin' label come in?"

"That accusation didn't surface until after Hurley was sent to prison for the rape. It was big news for about a week and then I never saw anything else about it in the local news or on the internet. I just noted it to keep my charts up-to-date."

"Was he questioned in Mother's murder?"

"Several times, but he was never arrested. McGuire had already zeroed in on me by then."

Troy might adore his daughter-in-law Collette, but it was clear from his tone that there were still some hard feelings on his part toward the sheriff.

Troy used the yardstick as a pointer again. "If you follow these arrows, you'll see specifics on Jerome's arrest records and his employment records."

Wyatt scanned the records, once more impressed by the methodical tracking of suspects. At one time or another Jerome had worked as a wrangler at least part-time for almost every major rancher in the area, including the woman he was eventually convicted of raping.

"He was working for Senator Foley at the time Helene was killed," Troy said. "Of course, Foley wasn't a senator back then. He was right in the middle of his first campaign for state representative."

"I vaguely remember that," Wyatt said. "Was Mother involved in that campaign?"

"No." Troy tossed the yardstick to the middle of a cluttered desk and stepped away as if he was finished with the discussion. He walked to the sliding-glass doors that opened to the same courtyard garden as the guest room did.

"Ruthanne and Riley both tried to get Helene involved in his campaign, especially Ruthanne. She finally persuaded your mother to drive to Austin and visit Riley's headquarters."

"Why did she decide not to volunteer?"

"I think someone must have rubbed her the wrong

way that day. When she got home she was adamant that she wanted no part of politics."

"I can understand that."

"I've wished a million times she hadn't felt that way. Then she might have been at his campaign headquarters instead of here alone when the killer showed up."

Wyatt turned away. He didn't want to be influenced by the emotion tearing at Troy's voice. He had to depend on cold, hard facts.

"Kelly's mother was on Riley's staff," Troy said.

Wyatt turned his attention from the chart to Troy. "Are you referring to Kelly Burger?"

Troy nodded and then worried the jagged scar on the right side of his face.

"When did you find that out?" Wyatt asked.

"Ruthanne showed up at the horse barn when I was out there with Jaci and Kelly yesterday morning. I introduced them and they talked about it. I got the impression there was not much love lost between Ruthanne and Kelly's mother. But that's no surprise. Ruthanne was never fond of any woman Riley spent time with."

There was a lot about Kelly that Wyatt didn't know. He probably should leave it this way since what he did know about her scared him to death. She sent his senses spiraling out of control every time she came near him.

Like that kiss yesterday. He hadn't planned it. It wasn't the time or the place for it. But his impulse control vanished and the first thing he knew his lips were on hers and she was turning him inside out.

Any cop worth his salt knew you should never get emotionally involved with a woman you were trying to protect. Emotions would make him lose his edge.

But now that kiss would be the proverbial elephant

in the room. No matter what else was going on, they'd both be aware that one touch could start the sparks flying again.

Create enough sparks and they would invariably flare up into a wildfire.

"You got awful quiet there when I mentioned Kelly," Troy said. "You're not having second thoughts about getting involved with her, are you?"

"I'm not getting *involved* with her. She needs protection and a place to stay. It seems reasonable to offer that to a homeless woman in jeopardy."

"I get the feeling she's been on her own with Jaci for quite a while. What about you? Do you have someone waiting on you back in Atlanta?"

"What if I do?"

"Then I think you may be in real trouble."

"Why is that?"

"Because I've watched four of your brothers fall in love. I know the subtle signs and you're exhibiting all of them."

"The subtle signs. That sounds like the title of a chick flick."

"You can pretend all you want, but there was an unmistakable current passing between the two of you when you got back to the ranch yesterday."

"I've only known her two days."

"Whether you've known a person years, days or hours has nothing to do with it. The spark hits in an instant. It was that way with me when I met your mother. It was that way for your brothers, too. Trying to deny what you're feeling only makes it worse."

Wyatt was definitely not discussing his love life or lack thereof with Troy.

The awkward conversation was thankfully interrupted by the doorbell.

"That must be Dylan and Collette," Wyatt said. "I'll let them in."

The doorbell rang again before he made it to the door. When he opened it McGuire was standing there. Unsmiling. A deadly serious expression on his face.

"Is Kelly here?"

"She is. Come in and I'll get her for you."

"You'd best sit in on the conversation, too."

"Is it that bad?"

Kelly stepped up behind him. "Is what that bad?"

McGuire tugged his hat low and narrowed his eyes. "Let's talk inside."

KELLY SAT ON THE SOFA. Sheriff McGuire had settled in the chair next to the window. Wyatt paced. Troy had volunteered to take Jaci outside to wait on Dylan and Collette.

McGuire crossed a leg over his knee. "I hate to have to bother you with this kind of news, especially on a Sunday, Kelly."

"I like to keep informed of exactly what's going on," she assured him.

"I asked the deputy working your area to keep an eye on your house, just in case the thief is stalking you. I figured that with the roof covered, he might think you'd moved back in."

Kelly got that sinking feeling again, as if she were hurtling down a rugged cliff with nothing to grab hold of.

"When the deputy pulled up in your driveway, he saw a guy take off on foot and disappear into that thick wooded area in back of your property. The deputy gave chase, and then he heard an engine grind before sputtering to life.

"By the time he reached the clearing, dirt was flying. He couldn't see the vehicle in the dark, but he caught sight of its back lights as it turned off onto that old dirt road that goes to the back of the Baptist church."

Wyatt stopped pacing and propped a booted foot on the hearth. "Did the house look as if someone had broken in?"

"The front door was wide open."

Wyatt's lips tightened to thin, hard lines. "If you don't stop this man, I will."

"We don't have any proof that the man seen running from Kelly's house was the man who stole her car or sent the text."

"She's being targeted," Wyatt said. "You know that as well as I do."

"What I know, Wyatt, is that you have no law-enforcement authority or legitimate credentials in this state, much less this county."

"Then deputize me," Wyatt said.

"I'd consider it if you weren't so personally involved in the case. As it is, you'd be more a vigilante than a cop."

"Bullshit."

This type of conflict was the last thing Kelly wanted. "I'm sure the sheriff can handle this, Wyatt."

"Exactly," McGuire agreed. "And if you'd let me finish, I have some good news, as well. It looks as if we have some reliable fingerprints."

"That's great news," Kelly said, trying to inject some optimism into the heated discussion.

"By the time the house is ready to move into, Kelly, we'll likely have made an arrest." McGuire uncrossed his legs and leaned forward. "In the meantime, I wouldn't advise staying at that house alone, not even in the daytime."

"Was the house ever broken into when my grandmother lived there?"

"Not once," the sheriff said. "Mustang Run is normally one of the most peaceful towns in Texas."

"Did Cordelia have problems or ongoing issues with anyone in the area?" Wyatt asked. "Maybe someone who tended to carry a grudge?"

"I see where this is going, but don't go putting store in the local gossip mill. Those women like to run their tongues. The men are just as bad. But all that talk of Ruthanne Foley wanting to run Cordelia out of town a few years back was mostly exaggeration."

"Why would she want to run my grandmother out of town?"

"Ruthanne pushed for the city to tear down some old houses near the park and sell the land. Cordelia opposed the plan and accused Ruthanne of just wanting to build a spa resort on the property. Cordelia won. The historic old houses are still standing. They're making one into a museum."

"Good for Grams."

Collette and Dylan drove up just as the sheriff was leaving. He looked delighted to see his daughter. She looked rested today and positively glowing. Even at eight months pregnant, Collette was stunning with her expressive eyes, high cheekbones and wild mass of fiery red curls.

One day Kelly would like to hear all about Collette's experiences while renting the Callister house, but not while Collette was pregnant—or while the man who was creating havoc in her life was still on the loose.

But the sheriff said they had usable fingerprints. Surely they would make an arrest soon.

Unless it was today, it wouldn't be soon enough to keep Kelly from moving out of the Ledger house. She'd look for an apartment tomorrow, and this time she wouldn't mention it to Wyatt until the rent was paid and she was ready to roll.

That was, if he ever stopped avoiding her long enough for them to talk. It was the first time she'd ever lost a man with a kiss.

BY FOUR ON SUNDAY afternoon, the temperature had climbed into the high sixties. In true Hill Country fashion, the wind that had hounded them for days had died to an occasional breeze that whispered through the needles of a juniper tree just outside the courtyard.

It was the perfect day for a tea party, and the courtyard garden was the perfect setting. Jaci had hosted the party for Troy, Kelly and two of her best-loved dolls. She'd used her favorite tea set, the one Jaci had insisted ride in the car with them when they'd set out for Mustang Run.

Jaci had served tiny cups of milk and the chocolate chip cookies she and Julie had baked yesterday. Kelly had sliced the cookies into fourths so that they'd fit on the tiny plates.

Once the cookies were gone, Jaci skipped away to retrieve a miniature plastic horse she spied peeking from behind a dwarf azalea.

She picked it up and brought it over for Troy to examine. "He has a broken nose."

Troy examined the toy. "I believe he does. That may be why Joey left him in the garden."

"Do your big horses break their noses?"

"So far they haven't."

"I hope Snow White doesn't break her nose."

"I do, too."

"Joey's not afraid of horses," Jaci said.

"Not now, but when he first came to the ranch, he had to get used to them, just like you will."

Satisfied with that answer, Jaci went back to exploring the garden.

"It's so peaceful out here," Kelly said. "It's as if you step into the garden and leave the world on the outside."

Troy stared at the sparkling fountain. "This was Helene's favorite spot. She planned every detail. Needless to say, it fell into disrepair when I was in prison. Collette spent hours out here working it back in shape."

"I'm sure Helene would be pleased with the result."

"I think so. I always feel closest to her when I'm in her garden. Some nights I sit out here in the dark and it's almost as if she's here beside me, trying to tell me something. I like to think she's just been waiting for her last son to come home."

A ghostly shiver raised the hairs on the back of Kelly's neck as Collette's prediction rolled through her mind.

Helene will tell you.

Perhaps like Troy, Collette felt Helene's presence when she tended the plants.

The haunting words from the nightmare began playing in Kelly's mind.

Family sins can kill. Stay alive. Stay alive.

Troy's cell phone rang, startling Kelly back to reality. She gathered the plates and cups while he talked.

"That was Dakota," Troy said. "He, Dylan and Wyatt are on their way back here for a family confab. Guess I'd better go start a pot of coffee."

Kelly hadn't been invited, but she was pretty sure the discussion would center on her and her tormentor. She doubted it had been Wyatt's idea to include his father, but she was glad they had.

Troy walked over to Jaci. "Thank you, ma'am. That was the best tea party I've ever been to. You make delicious tea."

Jaci grinned from ear to ear. "It was really milk."

"You fooled me." Troy tipped his worn black Western hat and left to join the men in the family. Thirty minutes later the sun dipped behind a cloud and Kelly and Jaci went back to the guest room.

Jaci took out her stubby crayons and drawing paper. "I'm going to color a picture of big horses," she said as she kicked out of her shoes and crawled into the middle of Kelly's bed.

Kelly retrieved the last of the boxes she'd brought home from Grams's house. The first two had held mementos, report cards, baptismal records and numerous small plaques and certificates that Kelly's mother had been awarded during her school years, mostly for academic achievement.

Setting the box on the edge of the bed, Kelly took the silver letter opener she'd discovered in the top dresser drawer and slit through the tape. She settled back against some pillows and spent the next hour skimming through dozens of photographs of Kelly's mother when she was growing up.

Linda Ann had been cute as a kid. By the time she'd become a teenager, she was gorgeous. Kelly found an envelope labeled Linda Ann—College Years.

She opened the envelope and dumped the contents onto the bed. There were dozens of photos of Kelly's mother in all kinds of settings and with various groups of friends. There were no couple photographs, which made it seem highly likely to Kelly that Abby had confused Linda Ann with someone else when she'd talked of her being jilted before she'd met Kelly's father.

Kelly was putting all the photos back in the box when she noticed a brown envelope stuck in the bottom folds of the cardboard. It felt empty, but when she opened it, she found an old newspaper clipping.

She had to turn it over before she discovered another picture of her mother. The page was slightly yellowed, but still Kelly's mother looked ravishing in a formal gown that dipped low from her shoulders.

Kelly read the caption beneath the picture.

"The mother of Linda Ann Callister announces the engagement of…"

The rest of the sentence was continued on the next line, but the next line had been cut off.

So Abby had been right. Her mother had come close to marrying someone else before she met her true soul mate.

The picture had been cut from the top right page of the newspaper. The page's edges were still intact.

Kelly checked the date.

Her stomach quivered.

There had to be some mistake.

Chapter Twelve

The date of the engagement announcement was seven months before Kelly had been born. But her father hadn't jilted her mother. And there would have been no wedding announcement. They were planning to elope to Las Vegas. He'd been killed in a car wreck before they could. Both her mother and Grams had told her that.

If this wedding announcement was authentic, then Kelly's mother would have had to become engaged to one man while she was pregnant with another man's baby. That was a far cry from the tale of undying love and soul mates that Kelly had always heard.

Her mother's affairs from long ago were none of Kelly's business—unless the man who'd jilted Linda Ann was actually Kelly's biological father.

This was too bizarre to even think about now, but when her life settled down to normal, Kelly planned to have a heart-to-heart with her mother.

Kelly closed the box and put it away just as someone tapped lightly on her door.

Anticipation made her heart skip a beat, but when she opened the door, it was Viviana, not Wyatt.

"You're wanted in the den," Viviana said. "The Ledger men have an offer you can't refuse."

WYATT PACED FOR A MINUTE before settling in one of the rockers near the fireplace. "This is the deal, Kelly. My brothers and I would like to repair your house and make it livable for you and Jaci. We won't all be able to work on it every day, but I think we can have it ready for you to move in after three or four weeks, unless we run into major support problems."

Kelly stared at Wyatt, stunned speechless by the announcement—and speechless didn't often describe her.

"Why?" It was the only word she could manage.

"You need the help, and we have the tools and the skills to see that you get it," Dylan said.

"It's really not that big a deal," Troy said. "January's a slow time on the ranch, not that there's not always work that needs doing on a spread this size."

Kelly locked gazes with Wyatt. "Is this okay with you?"

"Yeah, sure."

"It was his idea," Dakota said. "We just jumped on the bandwagon."

She understood Wyatt less by the minute. He'd barely spoken to her since yesterday's kiss and now he was rallying the troops to spend weeks working on her house.

Yet, as Viviana had predicted, the offer was too good to refuse. And by the time the house was done, hopefully, her mystery tormentor would be behind bars.

"I appreciate the offer," Kelly said. "And I accept, but only on the condition you let me pay you for your labor."

"Nonsense," Troy said. "We'd do the same for any neighbor who got a tree blown down on his roof."

This was moving too fast for her to absorb it all. "When would you start?"

"Nothing like tomorrow," Dylan said. "We need to get the roof and any other outside repairs done while the weather holds."

"The whole roof may need to be replaced while we're at it," Wyatt said. "There are leaks in the back of the house where the tree didn't touch the roof."

"I may have to wait on some things," Kelly said. "How much money are we talking about for building materials?"

"No problem," Dakota said. "Wyatt's taking care of—"

"We'll talk about money later," Wyatt said, cutting off Dakota. "No use to talk expenses until we know the full extent of the damage."

There was no mistaking where Dakota was going before Wyatt interrupted. Wyatt had obviously told them he'd pick up the tab. She had no intention of letting him. And no idea why he'd volunteer. They had to talk and soon.

"How about some food?" Julie said. "We still have plenty of brisket for sandwiches."

The men gave her suggestion hearty approval.

"I'll make hot chocolate," Viviana said. "And someone can build a fire. It's starting to get a bit nippy in here."

"A fire's a great idea. I'll get going on that," Troy said.

Jaci jumped up to follow Troy to get some logs from the side porch. "Let's git goin'," she said, mimicking Troy's Texas drawl.

She'd missed a lot by not having a grandfather in her life.

As the others left for the kitchen, Kelly walked over to where Wyatt was leaning against the hearth, intentionally moving into his space. Only inches separated them when he turned and met her gaze.

She saw desire flicker in the depths of his eyes. Heat suffused her body. Whatever was going on between them, it wasn't for lack of sexual attraction.

"Thanks," she whispered, "but I can't let you pay for the materials, Wyatt."

"Kelly, I…" He hesitated. "I just wanted to help."

"You have." She walked away, more confused and disillusioned than ever.

Everything had been so easy between them at first. She'd loved the laid-back way he flirted with his eyes and teased away her fear. Now his emotions were guarded with her.

Yet he was every bit as protective.

And still the most virile and exciting man she'd ever met.

WYATT STOOD AND WATCHED Kelly walk away. He was a louse, but not near the jerk he'd be if he jumped into a relationship with her only to drag her into his own potential disaster.

The best he could do for her was to make sure she and Jaci were safe until the bastard who had it in for her was behind bars. If Emanuel Leaky was behind this, even that wouldn't be enough.

In the meantime, it was misery being with her and not touching her. And pure hell sleeping a few doors down from her while he ached to have her in his bed.

COLLETTE LOOKED UP from the tomato she was slicing. "I picked these up when I went in for my checkup. They were the best the market had, but these greenhouse varieties only make me long for summer."

"I just long for Tyler to get home," Julie said. "When he gets here, don't expect to see us for at least a week. We're finishing our honeymoon."

They all laughed.

Growing up the only child of a single parent, Kelly was absolutely amazed by how well the Ledgers got along. "Do you always spend this much time together?" she asked, "Or is this because Wyatt's here for a visit?"

"We see a lot of each other," Collette said, "especially on weekends. But we have plenty of privacy, too. We all have our own interests and our own houses."

"It's a very close-knit family," Viviana said as she put the finishing touches on a fruit salad. "I'm thrilled that Briana will grow up in a family like this, even though we will eventually spend part of every week in the city."

Julie reached into the refrigerator for a package of cheese. "It's not that the brothers never argue. They can get into heated discussions on everything from politics to what brand of boots lasts the longest. But if one needs a helping hand, they're all in there together, just like with repairing your house."

Collette set the plate of tomatoes on the table. "If I get any bigger, I won't even be able to reach the table."

"I felt the same way when I was carrying Briana," Viviana said.

"Here's hoping I get back to my normal size as quickly as you did."

"Not to change the subject, but Eve's a brilliant psychiatrist and she has an interesting theory about this family," Julie said.

"What is it?" Kelly asked.

"She feels that Helene and Troy were not only very much in love, but that they created such a strong sense of family that it stayed with their sons through the heartbreak of her murder and Troy's imprisonment, even surviving their years of separation from each other."

"That certainly sounds plausible," Kelly admitted.

"Dylan and I want to create that same sense of family, continuity and love for the land," Collette said. "We want at least four children."

"Don't hesitate to tell me if you think it's none of my business, Kelly, but how long has your husband been dead?" Julie asked.

"Three years."

"You must miss him very much."

"It hasn't been easy." That was true. She'd lost a friend. But not a husband in the truest sense of the word. And definitely not a lover. It was only in the last few days that she was starting to realize how much passion she'd really missed out on in life.

"Was Jaci in kindergarten before you moved to Mustang Run?" Viviana asked.

"No. Things were a bit unsettled in our lives last fall and I decided to hold her back a year." Actually, that decision had been made for her by the FBI, another of the conditions of her witness-protection arrangement. It had seemed the best way to make certain Jaci was safe.

"They say the public schools in this area are excellent," Viviana said.

"If you're interested, our church has a great preschool and kindergarten program that you can enroll her in for the rest of this semester," Julie said.

Out of nowhere, the haunting lullaby from Kelly's nightmare began playing in Kelly's mind.

Stay alive. Stay alive.

"I want to wait until things in our lives have settled down more before I send her off to school every morning."

"There's no hurry," Julie agreed. "She's enjoying the ranch, and the two of you fit into the Ledger family so well."

They might fit, but they weren't—and never would be—part of the family.

And before this was over Wyatt might tear this family apart all over again. Even their early years of closeness might not survive finding out that their father really had murdered their mother.

He's innocent. Helene will tell you.

The one Helene had best talk to was Wyatt.

RUTHANNE PACED THE FLOOR as she punched in Riley's number again. Her head was spinning from that last martini, and she was growing more pissed with every ring of the phone.

Finally, the ringing stopped and she heard a stony hello.

"Where have you been, Riley? I've been trying to reach you for two days."

"You keep forgetting that we're no longer married, Ruthanne. I don't have to account to you for where I've been or whom I've been with."

"Don't take that arrogant tone with me. I *made* you, remember?"

"How could I forget? You reminded me every day for years. What do you want now?"

"We need to talk."

"We have nothing to talk about."

"I think we do. Have you heard that Linda Ann Callister's daughter moved back to town?"

"I've heard. So what?"

"Don't pull that innocent routine with me, Riley. Be here at three o'clock tomorrow. Don't be late."

"And if I don't show up?"

"Then you don't have to worry about Linda Ann's daughter. I'll see that you kiss any chance of being governor goodbye."

FAMILY SINS CAN KILL. Stay alive. Stay alive.

Mothers always know. Stay alive. Stay alive.

Hold on tight to love. Stay alive. Kelly, stay alive.

The lullaby grew louder and louder until it became a deafening roar in Kelly's ears. She opened her eyes, but couldn't focus. Ribbons of white moved across the ceiling in slow motion.

The lullaby finally stopped and one of the ribbons drifted featherlike from the air and landed on Kelly's pillow. Kelly reached for it, but the heat from it scorched her hand before she touched it.

A voice wafted across the room, but she couldn't tell where it was coming from. "Talk to your mother, before it's too late."

Kelly picked up the pillow that the ribbon had landed on and hurled it across the room. Reaching for the lamp, she flicked it on and bathed the room in the soothing, subdued light.

Another nightmare. She slid out of the bed and tried

to evict the images from her mind. The lullaby returned to haunt her along with the eerily pleading voice.

Talk to her mother. There was no doubt that finding the engagement picture had inspired her subconscious to concoct that message. Kelly's stress level was clearly off the charts.

She was wide awake now. And thirsty. The nightmares seemed to leave her mouth incredibly dry.

Kelly hadn't bothered to turn on a hall light and she'd stepped into the dark kitchen before she saw the shadowy figure. Her heart slammed against her chest before she realized it was Wyatt sitting at the table in the dark, moonlight slanting across his bare chest.

"You frightened me," she said.

"I'm sorry."

"What are you doing up this time of night?" she asked.

"I couldn't sleep."

"Neither could I." He didn't invite her, but she dropped into the chair opposite his. "We have to talk."

Chapter Thirteen

Wyatt was thankful the lights were off. Even in the glimmer of moonlight shining through the window, the sight of Kelly sitting across from him in her pajamas stirred a hunger so intense, he could barely think.

"You really don't want to hear anything I have to say tonight, Kelly. It's gruesome and depressing."

"Try me," she whispered. "What is keeping you awake?"

"The same thing that's kept me awake since I was thirteen."

"The question of who murdered your mother?"

"Right, but it has added implications now. If I do find out it's my father, that is going to destroy this whole family. If I don't find out who killed my mother, I am never going to be able to live with myself. It's a no-win situation."

"Unless you find out that Troy is innocent. You surely haven't ruled that out."

"No, but I don't see anything in what he's said or shown me that's negated what was presented at the trial."

"Tell me about the trial."

"Are you looking for nightmare material?"

"No, I have a stalker to provide that."

"The basic case the prosecution presented was that Mother was leaving Troy. He came home from lunch, found her with her bags packed and shot her three times."

"Why was she leaving him?"

"According to the testimony of her best friend, Mother had said just that morning she'd had enough and was going to put an end to the strife. That's not verbatim."

"What about the boys?"

"According to the witness, she was coming back for us and leaving our father completely alone."

"Did only one friend attest to that?"

"Yes, but several other friends testified that Mother's parents were always trying to get her to leave Troy. Apparently they thought Mother had married beneath her."

"Were you that poor?"

"If my parents were struggling with financial issues, I never knew it. I mean, we didn't go to Disney World on vacation or spend Christmas skiing in Colorado, but neither did most of the other ranchers' kids. I don't remember ever wanting for anything."

"What evidence did your father's defense team provide?"

"Basically nothing. They couldn't dispute that Mother was killed with Troy's gun. They couldn't come up with another viable suspect. And Troy did nothing to help his case. According to news reports at the time, he sat there day after day showing a complete lack of emotion.

"The only exception was when they showed the pictures of the crime scene and talked about his five young sons being left without a mother. The prosecutor used that outbreak of weeping in his closing statement, saying that the guilt finally got to Troy."

"Maybe he was hurting so deeply that he couldn't face the trial and had to shut it out until the photographs made the pain too much to bear."

"I hope you're right. But I still need facts and the only way I'm going to prove Troy didn't do it is to prove someone else did."

He pushed his hands against his temples like a vise, trying to ease a nagging headache that had hammered away at him all day. "Now aren't you sorry you asked?"

"No."

"Let's talk about you," he said, though he wasn't sure he could take hearing about a superhero husband to whom no other man could ever compare.

"What about me?"

"How long were you married before your husband died?"

"Two years. He died of a fast-growing malignancy in his stomach."

"I'm sorry. You must have been devastated."

"I was. He was a wonderful person, kind and intelligent and a good father."

She'd made no mention of passion, yet Wyatt knew from one kiss that she was anything but cold.

"How did you meet him?"

"Unlike my mother, I was not the scholarly type. I dropped out of college after my sophomore year and spent two years wandering Europe. That's when I fell in love with jewelry design and when I met Adolph."

Adolph. Try to compete with that, cowboy cop.

"He was twenty years older than me, and far more sophisticated. I was intrigued by him and infatuated with his knowledge of all the fine arts."

"Even though he was old enough to be your father?"

"I'd never known a father, so I never gave the father aspect of it a thought. We started having coffee together. One thing led to another and one night we took it all the way—at my insistence, I should add. I was frustrated by his lack of physical response to me."

"That's difficult to imagine."

"Is it, Wyatt? I seem to inspire that same reluctance on your part. Anyway, I got pregnant in spite of using protection. I know that's rare, but it happens. He asked me to marry him and I accepted."

"Did you love him?"

"I thought I did at the time. I respected him. He was a fascinating conversationalist. He was honorable and thoughtful and he encouraged me to explore my interest in jewelry design."

"You forgot to mention love."

"Adolph came out of the closet a year later."

"That explains a lot. But you stayed married?"

"The cancer had been diagnosed by then. He needed me."

Wyatt reached across the table and placed his hands on top of hers. It was meant to be just a comforting touch, but his body reacted as if she'd just stripped naked in front of him. He pushed away from the table. "We should try to get some sleep," he said, his voice so husky with desire, he couldn't even recognize it.

"One more question, Wyatt."

"Shoot."

"Why kiss me senseless and then pull away as if you can't bear to touch me? Why avoid being alone with me or even making eye contact? I haven't changed."

"I'm just following the lawman's code. A cop never gets personally involved with a woman he's protecting.

It makes him lose his edge and become more suscep-
tible to making mistakes."

She stood and glared down at him. "That's bull and
you know it. You're afraid of me, Wyatt. Afraid that you
might fall hard for me and that I might interfere with
your burning desire to settle a score for your mother no
matter who it hurts."

"You're reading this all wrong."

"I don't think so, Wyatt. You may be a big, tough
cop, but you're afraid of facing your own emotions
head-on. I may have married a man I didn't love, but
I've never run from love the way you do."

He stood and backed away from the table. "Fear has
nothing to do with this."

"Prove it."

She walked over and stopped right in front of him,
so close he could feel her breath on his bare chest.

"Kiss me right now and prove you're not afraid." She
took his right hand in hers and pressed it to her breast
so that he could feel the peak of her nipple beneath her
cotton pajamas.

He lost it then and he kissed her hard, ravaging her
lips, exploding in a rush of desire he couldn't have
stopped if he wanted to. He didn't want to.

So he picked her up and carried her to his bed.

Chapter Fourteen

Kelly's heart was racing as Wyatt ripped a multicolored quilt from the bed and laid her on top of a crisp white sheet. The linens smelled of Wyatt, a mixture of soap and pine and musk. There was little time to revel in the intoxication of the scents as he stretched out beside her and kissed her until her lungs begged for air.

He kissed her eyes, her nose, her cheeks before he finally let his lips return to her mouth. When his fingers fumbled too long on the buttons of her pajama top, she helped him, wishing he'd just rip it off and take her savagely.

Once her breasts were freed, he cupped them in his hands and sucked her nipples, nibbling and pinching lightly so that they pebbled and peaked as she arched toward him.

Her hands roamed his broad shoulders, as his fingers created deliciously heated spirals of pleasure across her abdomen. And then he dipped his fingers beneath the elastic waistband of her pajamas and the hunger she'd kept famished too long exploded inside her.

She trembled as he kissed the column of her neck and put his mouth to her ear. "Are you sure you want this, Kelly? If you don't, or if you think you'll face to-morrow with regrets, tell me now."

"I want you, Wyatt. I'm sure I want you. Just you. No promises you can't keep. No commitments you can't honor. Just one night where I can feel and love and let go without inhibition."

One night of heaven with no thoughts of Emanuel Leaky or thugs or threatening texts. No thoughts of anything but Wyatt and the way he protected and thrilled and was setting her heart and soul on fire.

She wiggled out of her pajama bottoms while Wyatt shucked off his jeans. She consumed him with her eyes as he stretched out naked beside her. He might not ever be hers to keep, but nothing would ever take this moment from her.

He straddled her and she wrapped her legs around him as he thrust the hard length of his erection deep inside her. He thrust again and again and she writhed beneath him until a volcano of hot, wet desire erupted inside her. He exploded with her in an orgasm so intense that a sob tore from her throat.

Wyatt rolled off her and cradled her in his arms. "Did I hurt you?"

"No. It's just been so long, and making love with you felt so right."

"I don't ever want to hurt you, Kelly. It will kill me if I do, but…"

She kissed his words away. "I told you I'm not asking for promises of forever."

"I was just going to say that I'm through fighting what I feel for you. If you want to get rid of me now you'll have to kick me out of your life, and I'm not even sure that would do it."

"In that case, you'll be around for a long, long time."

Unless a madman and an almost twenty-year-old murder destroyed them both.

WHEN SHE HADN'T HEARD from Sheriff McGuire about the fingerprint check by noon the next day, Kelly grew antsy. If Viviana and Briana hadn't come to the house to keep her company, she'd have been climbing the walls by now.

Making love with Wyatt had definitely changed her mind about looking for an apartment, but it made her no less concerned about the danger that kept threading its way through her life.

"Why don't we drive into town and check the guys' progress on the house," Viviana said. "We might even be able to talk them into taking a lunch break with us."

"That's a great idea," Kelly said. "I'll go find Troy and see if he wants to go with us."

"I'm sure he does," Viviana said. "No doubt it's killing him to be left out of the construction fun and the chance to spend more time with Wyatt."

"Did the heart attack last year limit his physical activities?" Kelly asked.

"Somewhat. But he's here today because he drew bodyguard duty. Didn't Wyatt tell you?"

"No." For some stupid reason she'd felt so safe at the ranch she hadn't even thought the perp, as Wyatt called him, might show up here. "Then we should stay here on the ranch," Kelly said. "We can't leave Julie and Collette alone."

"Well, you're never really alone on the ranch. Dylan just hired two new wranglers and that brings the number up to six. But Collette and Julie aren't on the ranch today anyway. They went into Austin to pick up a lamp Collette ordered for the nursery."

"How long will that take?"

"At least a couple of hours, but then they're stopping by Sean's so Collette can go with him to look at a stallion he's thinking of buying as a stud horse. They won't be home until close to dinnertime."

"And you got stuck here with me?"

"Not true. I went horseback riding before Dakota left and then came home and finished a book I was reading. See, we do all pursue our own interests."

In minutes they were loaded into Troy's truck. Viviana squeezed in between Briana and Jaci who were safely buckled in their respective car and booster seats. Briana kicked and fussed until the car started. Then she happily entertained them with her delightful mix of recognizable and unrecognizable syllables for the remainder of the ride.

Jaci excitedly talked of going on the horseback ride Wyatt had promised over breakfast this morning. His effort to get to know Jaci had both surprised and pleased Kelly. She was glad they were going to town. He'd only been gone a few hours, but she couldn't wait to see him again.

The first person she saw when they pulled into the driveway of her house was Sheriff McGuire. He and Wyatt were near the spot where the fallen tree had once stood.

"You go ahead and get whatever news the sheriff's delivering," Troy said. "I'll watch Jaci."

"Thanks."

"We have an ID," the sheriff said as soon as she walked up.

"Who? Does he live in Mustang Run? Do you know where to find him?"

"I think we'd best find a more private place before

I start answering those questions you're throwing out like a shiny-suited lawyer."

"It's cool enough we can sit in my truck if we leave the doors open," Wyatt said.

Neither of them indicated by their tone or expressions that this was good news. The anxiety hit her all over again.

"LIKE I JUST TOLD WYATT, the man who stole your car and the Corvette is Jerome Hurley."

Wyatt already knew what the sheriff had to say. But Wyatt was way ahead of him. He knew why Jerome was targeting Kelly and he knew that Emanuel was behind it. All he needed was proof.

Wyatt had told Kelly from the beginning that his promise to keep secret her involvement with Leaky would cease to be binding if he found out that association had put her in danger.

He was convinced now that it had. He wasn't convinced that sharing that information with the sheriff was the best move. Wyatt trusted his own instincts and experience. He'd stop Hurley, dead or alive. Right now he didn't much care which. He turned his attention back to the conversation between McGuire and Kelly.

"He was convicted of raping a Mustang Run rancher's wife fourteen years ago," McGuire explained. "He's only been out of prison for two months. The probation officer has already lost track of him, and it blows me up like a toad that nobody told me about that."

"Do you have any idea where to start looking for him?" Kelly asked.

"His mother's dead. His dad is in jail, so there's no checking with either of them. But we'll contact any of his old friends that we can locate, and we're checking all the spots where the county's lowlife usually hangs out."

The sheriff turned toward the backseat. "Did I cover everything with Kelly I covered with you and Dakota, Wyatt?"

"I think so."

"This man's dangerous, Kelly. We can assume he's the one who broke into your house the other night and sent you that text. We just don't have proof of that yet.

"If you didn't have the Ledgers looking after you, I'd see about putting you in some kind of protective custody until we arrest Hurley. But I can't give you any better men to protect you than you already have."

"I realize that," Kelly said.

"If he shows his face anywhere in this county, we'll arrest him," McGuire said. "And I've notified every other county in the state, as well as the state troopers to be on the lookout for him, too."

"I guess that's all you can do," Kelly said.

But it wasn't all Wyatt could do. He was no longer a cop. The rules of warrants and illegal searches and questioning people without just cause didn't apply to him. He'd start today, combing the area that Hurley could have walked to the night he left Kelly's car in her driveway.

"At least he knows who to search for now," Kelly said as McGuire drove away.

"That's a start," Wyatt agreed. He slipped his arm around her waist as they walked back toward the house. He considered telling her that he was almost certain that this was tied in to Emanuel Leaky, but there was no reason to frighten her any more than she already was. Not yet, anyway.

"I'm glad we arrived when we did," Kelly said, "but

we actually stopped by to see if you and your brothers want to go to lunch with us."

"Dakota drove to the nearest fast-food joint and picked up Cokes and burgers about an hour ago."

But he did want to talk to Troy alone before they left.

Wyatt cornered Troy while Kelly was talking about damage and repairs with Dylan. Dakota and Viviana had gone outside with the children.

"Dakota told me that Jerome Hurley is behind this," Troy said. "He was bad enough before he went to prison. Looks like he came out of the slammer even more rotten. I wouldn't put anything past him."

"I agree. I have something I have to do for the next few hours. I'd appreciate it if you'd keep an extra close watch on Kelly and Jaci until I get home."

"I'd planned to do that without you asking."

"Going to lunch is fine as long as there are people around. It will take her mind off things. I'll be back at the ranch before dark. If there's trouble…"

"I know what to do if there's trouble. Take care of the man causing it. I'd like nothing better."

"I don't expect trouble at the ranch. This guy isn't looking for a fight. He wants to catch Kelly alone." And leave no witnesses.

"And this is what you like about law enforcement?" Troy asked.

"No, but catching the bad guys makes it all worthwhile."

IT WAS NEARLY TWO in the afternoon when they finally made it to Abby's Diner. Kelly was glad they were running late. With the lunch crowd having thinned out, it would be easier for her to grab a few minutes alone with Abby.

Even with Kelly's current crisis gearing up for a possible arrest, she couldn't get her mother's decades-old engagement picture out of her mind. The latest nightmare wasn't helping.

She wouldn't pry for gossip about her mother. But the engagement had been announced in the newspaper so it wasn't a deep, dark secret. All Kelly wanted from Abby was the intended groom's name.

The name of the man who could possibly be her biological father.

On second thought, maybe she should just leave the past in the past.

The same hostess met them at the door, but without the extra sway to her hips or the flirtatious smile she'd had for Wyatt. The restaurant was less crowded but more noisy. All of the activity seemed to center on one of the back tables.

"Who's the celebrity hidden by the fawning crowd?" Troy asked as they were seated in a window booth.

"Senator Foley. We weren't expecting him. He just showed up. Can you imagine the man who may be the next governor of Texas just showing up at Abby's Diner? Abby's not impressed. She hasn't even bothered to come out of the kitchen to talk to him."

"Abby's known him since long before he was a senator," Troy said. "And it takes a lot to impress her."

Once the hostess left, Kelly craned her neck for a better view but still couldn't see the senator through the crowd. "My mother was on his staff for his very first campaign," she told Viviana.

"You should go talk to him," Viviana said.

"I'm sure he wouldn't remember me and maybe not my mother. That was twenty years ago, or close to it.

Besides I didn't get a very warm reception from his ex-wife when I met her in the horse barn."

"That's just Ruthanne," Troy said. "The senator will give you a warm greeting whether he remembers you or not. He's looking for votes."

The waitress came with their drinks and after she took their orders, Kelly stood up from the table.

"If you don't mind, I think I'll go over and say hello while we're waiting for our food," Kelly said. "Jaci, do you want to go with me to meet Senator Foley?"

Jaci twisted her mouth in a bizarre shape. Briana laughed out loud. "I'll stay here. Briana likes my faces."

"Okay. I'll be right back."

She anticipated having to inch her way past a crowd of people to get close enough to get his attention. But he saw her approach and stood to greet her. Well, not greet her exactly, but openly stare. Not particularly politician cool.

She extended a hand. "I'm Kelly Burger. I know you don't remember me, but I met you years ago when my mother was on your very first campaign staff."

"Linda Ann Callister."

"Yes, but how did you know that's who I was talking about?"

"You look so much like her I did a double take when I saw you. Sit down," he said, motioning to the empty chair kitty-corner to his. "It was great talking to all of you," he said to the crowd around him, "but I haven't seen this young lady in a very long time and we have some catching up to do."

"I can only stay a few minutes," Kelly said. "I'm having lunch with friends and they're watching my daughter while I came over to say hello."

"Which one is your daughter?"

"The one making faces." Kelly pointed her out. "Her name is Jaci."

"She has the Callister good looks, as well."

"Thank you."

"How is Linda Ann?" he asked.

"She's doing great. She recently retired from her position as dean of a small women's college in the Northeast and she and her husband have moved back to Texas."

"Where in Texas?"

"Plano."

"Then she's happy?"

"I think so."

"Would you tell her I said hello the next time you see her?"

"I'll be certain to."

"Tell her I still think of her often and that the ridiculous statue she won at the State Fair still sits on my desk."

"I will."

"How does she feel about your moving back to Mustang Run?"

"She doesn't know yet. I thought I'd surprise her after the move was made and I'm settled in enough to insist she come for a visit. How did you know I was moving back?"

"Word gets around."

"Ah, yes. Small-town news distribution. The thing Mother disliked most about Mustang Run." She glanced back to check on Jaci. "They've served our food, so I'd best go eat before it gets cold."

He stood with her, took her hand and held it for a tad too long. "Thanks for stopping by. It meant more than you know."

He had seemed glad to see her, almost too glad. And he remembered her mother extremely well, right down to the cheap prize she'd won at a fair that he still kept on his desk.

Kelly wondered exactly what had gone on between him and her mother during the time she worked for him. She suspected that it went beyond a typical employee/employer relationship.

No wonder Ruthanne had taken an instant dislike to her.

Kelly was beginning to think she didn't know her mother at all. But she wouldn't bother Abby with her question about the broken engagement. The answers should come directly from the source.

RILEY WATCHED KELLY walk away, amazed at how much she looked like her mother. She had the sway to her hips. Classy, yet subtly seductive. Back straight. Head high. An air about her that snared men's attention and didn't let go.

Even her nose was the same, tilted just enough to make her appear beguiling, yet mischievous. Perhaps the most striking feature they shared were the full, soft lips that had once driven Riley mad with desire.

If he'd ever truly loved anyone in his life, it was Linda Ann.

That was a lifetime ago. He'd been a nobody then. Now he was rising to the top like cream—or like a dead fish. Next stop, the governor's mansion. And then, if he played his cards right, it could be on to the White House.

Reason enough that his past had to stay buried. People these days might forgive a politician an indiscretion or two, but some things would never be forgiven.

He'd passed that line almost twenty years ago.

WYATT GRABBED his work-worn Stetson from a hook near the back door, stomped down the back steps and strode toward the woodshed. They weren't short of logs for the fireplace, but he needed the release of swinging an ax.

He'd gotten nowhere that afternoon. If anyone he'd questioned had seen Hurley since his release, they'd done a good job of lying. And Wyatt could usually detect a liar before the words left their mouth. It was in their eyes, their expression, even the movement of their Adam's apple.

He picked up the ax and began to swing, furiously splitting logs until sweat began to pour down his forehead and into his eyes. He buried the point of the ax into a log and stopped to yank his black T-shirt over his head. Wadded, the shirt made the perfect handkerchief for wiping his brow.

The temperature had climbed to seventy today. Two days from now a new cold front was expected, this one bringing a slight chance of snow. Even for the Texas Hill Country, the weather this January seemed out of sync.

Wyatt remembered going horseback riding with Troy one year when a light snow was falling. They'd ridden to the bluff on the far northern end of the spread and found a deer that had gotten tangled in the limbs of a downed mesquite tree. Wyatt had helped free the frightened doe.

When they'd returned to the house, he'd heard Troy tell his mother what a fine man Wyatt was becoming.

That was before everything had fallen apart.

When it had, Wyatt hadn't been a man at all. He'd tried to keep his brothers together, had begged and finally cried when his grandparents had separated them and farmed them out to any relative who'd take them. When his brothers had needed him most, he'd had no power to help.

And now he was here on a mission that might destroy their lives all over again.

But he was beginning to see why his brothers believed in Troy's innocence. Wyatt had to admit that Troy's research was much more detailed and comprehensive than he'd expected.

But even if he bought into Troy's innocence for the sake of argument, Wyatt didn't buy into Troy's random murder scenario, at least not yet.

Wyatt heard footsteps and looked up to see Kelly walking toward him. The late afternoon sun turned her hair the color of a strawberry field. When she smiled and waved, he almost choked on the desire that swelled inside him and the ache from knowing there was almost no way this relationship could ever work out.

She was infatuated with her protector the same way she'd been infatuated with her husband before she'd married him. She saw in Wyatt only what she wanted to see, instead of the hard-edged cop he'd become. He'd be a damn poor catch as a husband.

He picked up the ax and swung as hard as he could to release the fury and frustration that burned in his gut.

KELLY STOOD FOR A MOMENT, watching the flex and release of Wyatt's muscles as he wielded the ax. When he buried the blade of the ax, she stepped into his arms, relishing the thrill of his kiss before she backed away.

She splayed the palms of her hands across his chest. "You are the most gorgeously virile cowboy I have ever slept with."

"You need to get around more."

"No, I'm happy right here."

"But you know I'm not really a cowboy," Wyatt said.

"You walk like one, talk like one, look like one and you sure fit in well on Willow Creek Ranch."

"I have to admit I like the pace of this lifestyle—but only to a point."

"You can't miss being a cop. You still are one, just without the badge. I know you spent the afternoon attempting to track down Jerome Hurley. And you're driven to find your mother's killer."

"True, but what would I do with myself once they're behind bars?"

"Sheriff McGuire appears to stay busy. Not that I'm trying to get you to change your lifestyle."

"Troy tells me you had a chat with Riley Foley today," Wyatt said.

"I did. I was surprised at how well he remembered my mother after all those years."

"When was it you said she worked for him?"

"Nineteen years ago."

"The same year my mother was killed. Riley had already been elected and had taken office when his wife testified at Troy's trial."

"Was she a character witness?"

"She was my mother's best friend who I told you gave damaging testimony against my father."

"That's surprising."

"Why?"

"When I met her in the horse barn, she was coming

on strong to Troy and acting very possessive in case I had any ideas of moving in on her territory."

"According to my brothers, she's been trying to snare Troy ever since he was released from prison. They say he's not interested."

"Released, but on a technicality," Kelly said, thinking out loud. "Kind of odd for her to be making a play for a man that her testimony helped send to prison for killing his wife."

"It doesn't make a lot of sense, does it?"

"No." But neither Ruthanne nor the senator were the reason she'd come looking for Wyatt. "I'm thinking of driving up to Plano to visit my mother tomorrow. I've already talked to Julie. She's agreed to watch Jaci for me and to let me use her car. It's only a three-hour drive. I'll be back long before dark."

"I thought you said you didn't want to worry her."

"I don't plan to mention Jerome Hurley or even that my car was stolen. I found something in one of the boxes Grams left for me that I need to ask her about."

"Do you want to talk to me about it?"

"I wouldn't mind getting your take on it."

"Fire away."

Kelly explained the engagement announcement and the significance of the date. She didn't mention the nightmare or the lullaby that wouldn't let go of her.

"Don't you think this can wait until Jerome is arrested?"

"I can't explain this in any way that makes sense, but I feel that I have to talk to Mother now."

"In that case, I'm going with you."

She never doubted for a minute that he would.

JEROME REACHED for his phone on the first ring. "Hello."

"I'm ready to talk terms, but not on the phone."

"Name the time and place and bring cash."

"Are you sure your phone is untraceable?"

"Do you think I plan to go back to that hellhole prison?"

"Then I'll meet you at midnight on the cutoff road near Dowman-Lagoste Bridge."

"I know the spot well." He'd dropped off a body there once. As far as he knew what was left of it was still sleeping with the fishes.

He broke the connection. The deal was a go. The same deal he'd made to kill Helene Ledger almost twenty years ago. Only the victim had changed.

And the payout.

Chapter Fifteen

The house in Plano was a single-level brick on a quiet cul-de-sac. The yard was meticulous with expertly trimmed hedges and weedless flower beds. Kelly had no doubt that they'd find the same classic style and understated perfection inside.

Linda Ann lived a meticulous life, following inflexible schedules that left room for little spontaneity. Kelly had never doubted for a second that her mother loved her. Linda Ann just had trouble with warmth and expressing emotion.

Yet, she'd obviously been provocative enough that Senator Foley had never forgotten her.

Kelly pushed the doorbell. Seconds later, her mother appeared at the door, apparently already dressed for her early afternoon class. They exchanged a quick hug and then Kelly introduced Wyatt as Wyatt Alan, using his middle name for his last at Wyatt's insistence.

In case Linda Ann remembered his parents from her years in Mustang Run, Wyatt did not want to hijack Kelly's concerns with talk of his mother's murder and his father's release from prison.

"I'm delighted to meet you, Wyatt. I'm sorry Walter isn't here to join us, but my husband is out of the country for a few weeks, teaching a seminar at the University of London."

"I'm sorry we missed him," Kelly said. A white lie. She couldn't have asked the questions she needed answered in front of him. This way she didn't have to hurt his feelings by kicking him out of the room.

They followed Linda Ann to the living room.

"I wish Jaci could have come with you," Linda Ann said. "It seems forever since I've seen her."

"I'll bring her up soon. But like I told you on the phone, this is just a quick trip."

"Yes, you said you had something important to discuss with me. I worried all night. Does this concern your health? If there's something wrong, I want you to level with me, Kelly."

"It's not my health, Mom. I'm fine. I just have some things I'd like to talk to you about."

"Thank goodness. You've kept so to yourself this past year, I feared you were hiding something from me."

Only a year in protective custody.

"I have blueberry scones. Would you like to have them with coffee as we talk or would you rather wait until we've finished the discussion?"

"Let's talk first," Kelly said, growing more nervous by the second.

"I'm moving back to Mustang Run, Mom."

Linda Ann sat up even straighter, clasping her hands in her lap as if she needed something to hold on to. "Why would you move there?" she asked. "You'll be limiting your opportunities. Why not Santa Fe, or Carmel or even Austin where creativity is nourished?"

"I'm moving into Grams's house. I'll be able to work at home and spend more time with Jaci. I've contacted several jewelers in Austin and San Antonio and they've expressed an interest in carrying my work."

"It sounds as if you've made up your mind. I wish we could have discussed this first."

Kelly reached into her handbag and pulled out the brown envelope containing the engagement announcement. She leaned over and handed it to her mother.

"I found this in a box of Grams's photos."

Linda Ann pulled out the clipping and stared at the picture. "I can't believe your grandmother saved this. Surely you didn't come all the way to Plano to talk about a broken engagement in my distant past."

It did sound a bit foolish now that Kelly was here. She should never have let the nightmares get to her. But she was here now. She might as well ask her questions.

"You never mentioned being engaged before you met my father."

"It wasn't worth mentioning. It was a mistake that we righted before the wedding."

"The date is on the picture, Mom. That's seven months before the date on my birth certificate."

Linda Ann closed her eyes. When she opened them again, her face was strained and she rubbed a spot on her hand as if she were trying to remove a stain.

"Were you pregnant by the man you were engaged to…"

"Or was I cheating on him with your father?" Linda Ann asked, finishing the question for her.

"I'm not judging you, Mom. You know what a mess my marriage was. I just need to know if my biological father is still alive. I'm grown. There is no use for secrets between us."

Linda Ann stood and paced the room, the first time

Kelly ever remembered seeing her when she wasn't in complete control.

"You're right, Kelly. It's time you know the truth and I'm tired of living with the lies. But you have to remember that we're talking about a very short period of my life thirty years ago."

"I realize that."

"I was engaged to Riley Foley, big man on campus. Not the brainiest, not a varsity athlete, not even rich. But he had charisma."

As he still did, Kelly thought. It had taken him far in politics.

"We started dating our senior year and he asked me to marry him at Christmas. Your grandmother was far from rich, but she wanted me to have a nice wedding so she spent a chunk of Dad's insurance money on the wedding, money she should have kept to live on."

"That sounds like Grams. Generous to a fault."

"The wedding was all planned and for the most part paid for. Two weeks before the wedding, Riley broke off the engagement. He said he was in love with someone else."

"Ruthanne?"

"None other. Daughter of one of Mustang Run's richest citizens. Her father owned major interest in an oil company and one of the largest ranches in the area. I was furious with him, hurt for Grams who'd wasted so much money, and embarrassed for myself for being dumped practically at the altar."

Kelly's stomach rolled as the truth became clear. "So Senator Foley is my father?"

"Yes, but I never told him. I left town and started a new life. I had your grandmother spread the news that I'd met a marvelous man and then later that he'd died before we could get married. I told everyone that I was pregnant and thrilled to be carrying his baby. It sounds juvenile and stupid now, but it was my way of coping."

"Did Grams know the truth?"

"Yes, but she never told a soul."

"In spite of all that, you went to work for Riley Foley ten years later?"

"Yes, a decision I'll regret for as long as I live. I ran into him at a hotel in Boston where we were attending different conventions. We had a few drinks. He told me how bad his marriage was and that he had never stopped loving me."

And her mother—whom Kelly had always thought of as being the most together person she knew—had been insecure enough to buy into that.

"Riley persuaded me to give up my professorship in political science and run his campaign. We spent the rest of that week in Boston together, blowing off our respective conventions except for the one paper I had to present."

"Ruthanne must have loved hearing that you were working with her husband."

"She was livid and figured out quickly that we were having an affair. But it was Helene Ledger who actually caught us in the act."

At the mention of Helene's name, Wyatt's whole demeanor changed. He sat straighter and his gaze bored into Linda Ann.

"Did you say that Helene Ledger discovered that you and Riley were having an affair?"

"Yes. She'd stopped by campaign headquarters to discuss volunteering. She saw Riley and I kiss outside the office building and then she followed us to a hotel."

"How long was this before she was murdered?" Wyatt asked.

Linda Ann stared him down. "I'm getting to that."

But Wyatt was all detective now. Kelly saw the rugged determination in his eyes and in the set of his jaw. This new edginess made her nervous. This was her mother they were talking to, not one of his murder suspects.

"Helene went to Riley and told him that if he didn't tell Ruthanne the truth, she would."

"And did she?" Wyatt questioned.

"I don't know. I only know that Riley believed she would, but he said he didn't care. He loved me and he was going to leave Ruthanne and marry me even if it cost him the race for representative. I'd decided it was time to tell him he had a daughter, but then I never got the chance."

Wyatt leaned forward, his gaze riveted to Linda Ann. "What stopped you?"

"Before I saw him again, Helene was murdered. I went into hysteria. I called Riley and accused him of killing her. He swore to me he had nothing to do with the murder."

"Did you believe him?" Wyatt asked.

"I did after I calmed down. Riley may not be a faithful husband or fiancé for that matter, but he's not a killer."

"What happened next?" Wyatt asked. "Did you continue to see Foley?"

"No. I finally came to my senses. I wanted nothing to do with Riley or his campaign. I resigned from his staff and moved back to Boston."

"Did you call the police after Helene's death and explain her threat to expose your affair?"

"No, I should have, I know, but that would have made them go after Riley and I knew he was innocent. It might have even ruined his chances of ever having a career in politics. And, I hate to admit this, but I was still in love with him."

"When was the next time you saw him?"

"I haven't to this day. I've seen him on television at times when something he does politically makes the national news. But I vowed then that I would never get involved with him again."

Kelly fought an onslaught of vertigo and nausea. She'd come here seeking the truth, but she'd never expected to hear anything this morbid and repulsive. Still, she felt for her mother having to live with the sordid secrets. No wonder she'd poured her energy into her work. Her personal life was such a horrid mess.

"I cried with relief when Troy Ledger was arrested and again when he was convicted of the murder," Linda Ann admitted. "I was thankful to know that Helene Ledger's murder had nothing to do with her threatening to expose my affair with Riley. I'd like to think that if they hadn't found Helene's killer, I'd have spoken up. Sadly, I'm not sure that I would have.

"It was the horrible end of a sickening chapter in my life. I decided then that I would never allow my daughter to become a pawn for Riley to play against me."

"So you decided to let me go on indefinitely believing my father was dead."

"I did. If I made a mistake, it was out of love and the fear that you'd pay for my sins."

Family sins can kill. Stay alive. Stay alive.

The lullaby echoed through her mind again. It was as if the nightmare had been trying to warn her of this.

The nightmare or Helene's spirit. Only, Kelly didn't believe in ghosts.

Tears rolled down her mother's face. "I'm so sorry that you had to find out about your father this way, Kelly. Can you ever forgive me for choosing to live a lie and to make you live it, as well?"

Kelly walked over and gave her mother a hug. "I told you I'm not here to judge. You're my mother and I love you. But I'm glad you finally told me the truth."

They didn't stay for scones and coffee. Kelly was sure her stomach wouldn't tolerate food.

Five minutes later, they were in Wyatt's truck and on their way back to Mustang Run. The full truth of what she'd learned began to sink in.

Riley Foley was her father no matter that her mother was convinced otherwise, and there was a chance that he, and not Troy, was behind Helene's murder. She understood better now why Wyatt was determined to find out the truth about his father.

Only it was much worse for Wyatt than for her. He'd known and loved his father. The senator was a stranger who'd donated his sperm before breaking her mother's heart.

And the brutally murdered victim had been Wyatt's mother.

Kelly reached over and rested her hand on Wyatt's thigh. "I'm afraid to even think about what comes next."

"Do you want to go and confront the senator?"

"Maybe one day. Not yet."

"You do realize that if I discover that he murdered my mother, I'll do everything I can to make sure he's arrested and convicted?"

"I assumed that you would."

Wyatt would be investigating her biological father as a primary suspect in the murder of his mother because of an affair he had with her mother. It couldn't get much more complicated than this.

How would they ever maintain a relationship with that hanging over them? And even if they made it through that, Wyatt had given no indication that he planned to stay in Mustang Run or take her with him when he left.

They had only here and now.

"There is one other thing I should tell you," Wyatt said.

She didn't like the seriousness of his tone. "Is this something I want to hear?"

"No, but I think it's only fair I tell you that I'm convinced Jerome is a paid assassin hired by someone working on Emanuel Leaky's behalf. And it isn't a wild theory. I have solid reasons to back it up."

And if Emanuel Leaky knew she was behind his arrest, then her only option was going back into witness protection with Jaci.

Would this never end?

TWO DAYS LATER, things appeared to be at a standstill in the search for Jerome Hurley, though they were moving at a dizzying pace in every other area of Kelly's life.

First and foremost in Kelly's mind, the tension between Wyatt and his father had greatly diminished now that Wyatt had an evidential reason to hold out hope of his father's innocence. Armed with the information of the affair, he had a new focus for his investigation into Helene's murder.

Sheriff McGuire had deputized Wyatt on a temporary basis so that if he did find Jerome Hurley, he could arrest him. Wyatt was determined to do just that. He hit the streets every day and sometimes well into the night searching for him or any clue as to his whereabouts.

When Kelly had voiced the possibility that Jerome had moved on, Wyatt had delivered a brusque reminder that thinking like that could get her killed. He was convinced that Leaky had put out a hit on her and Jerome had accepted the task. Now he was merely waiting for opportunity.

Dylan, Dakota and Sean had torn out all the wet and damaged carpet, Sheetrock and wood in her house and had hired a roofing company to install a new roof the next week. She didn't have the heart to tell them or face the reality herself that even when Jerome was arrested, she might never be able to move into her house.

Not if Emanuel Leaky wanted her dead.

Finally, she had her car back from the sheriff, though Wyatt had ordered her to never leave the ranch alone. She had certainly disrupted the Ledger household.

She made herself a cup of hot tea and then went back to the family room where Jaci was playing dress up and clomping around the room in a pair of Kelly's high heels and a skirt with an elastic waist that she wore as a dress. An old purse that Viviana had given her completed the ensemble.

"I'm going to town to buy diapers for my babies," Jaci said.

"Babies need diapers," Kelly agreed.

"I'll buy them some candy, too."

"I don't think candy is good for babies."

"Uh-huh. My babies like it."

"So does mine."

The doorbell rang. Jaci ran to greet the company whoever it might be. "Let me get the door," Kelly said.

She put her eye to the peephole and then unlocked the dead bolt and swung it open to Collette and Dylan.

"I didn't know you already had company," Dylan said, smiling at Jaci. "Who is this lovely lady?"

"It's me." Jaci giggled and then dropped her handbag to hug them both.

"We're driving over to Sean's and since we didn't see Wyatt's truck around, we thought you and Jaci might like to go with us," Collette said.

"Isn't it late to be driving to Bandera?"

"It's only a few minutes after two," Collette said. "We'll be there by three-thirty, have dinner, visit and be home again before nine."

"Can we please, Momma? Please," Jaci pleaded. "I want to play with Joey."

"And Collette is going stir crazy since she can't take those afternoon rides to exercise the horses," Dylan said.

Kelly was growing a bit stir crazy herself. Jerome Hurley was making a prisoner of her. "We'd love to go," Kelly said. "I'll get our jackets and tell Troy we're leaving. Shall I ask him if he wants to go?"

"I asked him earlier this morning," Dylan said. "He said no. I think he's buried in those charts back in his bedroom again."

"You and Dylan can talk about the remodeling job on your house on the drive over," Collette said. "He has a fabulous idea for tearing out that wall that separates your kitchen from the living room and making that one big open area."

"We can raise that ceiling, too," Dylan said, "and put windows across the side so you get more natural light. I drew up some plans, but I left them in your house. Next time you're there, take a look at them."

"You guys are amazing. I can't wait to see what you've come up with."

She'd started toward the back of the house when she heard the door open again. When she heard Wyatt's voice, all thought of leaving with Dylan and Collette evaporated. Hopefully, they'd still take Jaci along. Time alone with Wyatt was at a premium.

WYATT ATTACHED Jaci's booster seat to the backseat of Dylan's truck and then double-checked to make sure it was secure. He was still awkward with Jaci. He hadn't spent much time around kids since he'd been one himself.

But she'd stolen his heart, and he was making progress with her. He'd do better at it once his total focus didn't have to be finding Jerome Hurley. Even finding his mother's killer had temporarily taken a backseat to the new sense of urgency.

Once he knew Kelly was safe, he'd have to make decisions about his and Kelly's relationship. He was absolutely mad about her. She appeared to feel the same about him. But the complications had increased dramatically over the past few days.

How would she feel when he was forced to expose to the media her mother's long-buried secrets? How would she feel if his investigation destroyed her biological father while clearing the name of his?

"Feel free to jot notes on those drawings I left at the house," Dylan said. "We're just at the idea stage, so encourage Kelly to offer hers, too."

"Will do."

Jaci crawled into her booster seat while Collette waddled from the porch to the truck. She looked as if she might pop any minute. "When's the due date again?" Wyatt asked.

"The doctor said she could go into labor as early as next week."

"Why don't you go with us to Joey's house?" Jaci asked Wyatt.

"Your mother and I are going to take a drive into town later so we can check on that new house you're going to be moving into."

A silver BMW pulled up in the driveway as Collette was buckling her seat belt.

"Ruthanne," Dylan said. "Perfect time for us to leave."

"We have to at least say hello," Collette said.

The "hellos" led to a lengthy monologue on how glad Ruthanne was to see Wyatt after so many years. He used the opportunity to size her up.

Rich. Attractive. Fake. That summed her up in his mind. If he had to guess, he'd bet the wealth and maybe some political clout was what had led to Riley's jilting Kelly's mother.

The senator had been a conniver even then. Wyatt itched to get back on his mother's murder case. If Riley Foley was behind Helene's murder, Wyatt would see that he paid. But even a death penalty wouldn't begin to compensate for the life he'd stolen from Helene and the years he'd stolen from Troy. It wouldn't begin to pay for the heartbreak of five boys who'd grown up without their mother or their father.

"I don't want to keep you," Ruthanne finally said. "Is Troy around?"

"Yes, but he's busy," Dylan said. "He said he didn't want to be disturbed."

Fast thinking on Dylan's part. Troy would owe him.

"We gotta git goin'," Jaci said, voicing what they were all thinking.

"So where are you off to, Jaci?" Ruthanne asked.

"We're going to Joey's house. Momma can't go, 'cause she's going to see our new house."

"That's nice."

Ruthanne finally walked back to her own car. Jaci waved as Dylan pulled away in his truck. And Wyatt went back inside to join Kelly in a little bit of afternoon delight.

There was a late-night bikers' bar on the other side of the county line where someone had told him this morning that Jerome occasionally hung out.

If Jerome showed up tonight, it would be his last night out for quite a while.

KELLY FELT A SURGE OF EXCITEMENT as she and Wyatt walked to the front door of the Callister house. In spite of Wyatt's fears, she refused to let herself believe that she was on a hit list ordered by Emanuel Leaky. Jerome was just a sick monster who was stalking her for some perverted reason of his own.

To believe that Emanuel wanted her dead was to give up any chance of ever living a normal life.

She had to hold on to the fact that Jerome would be arrested soon and she'd move into this adorable cottage and go on with her life—hopefully with Wyatt in it.

Wyatt opened the door and waited for her to step inside. She looked around, shocked at how naked the house looked with much of its interior ripped away. "It's like bones stripped of meat," she said.

"Picture it with the meat back on it. If we tear out that wall that separates this room from the kitchen, raise the ceiling by two feet and make that side wall a line of windows, this room would appear twice as large."

She visualized the changes, the same way she did when reworking a piece of old jewelry. Weigh what you'd lose from the old design against what you'd gain from the new. But if they did this right, she could keep the cottage feel of the house and not feel closed in.

"I think it's a great idea. I'll work with Dylan on the—"

A scraping noise that sounded as if it had come from the hallway interrupted her. "What was that?"

Wyatt's hand flew to the butt of the gun he'd worn at his waist ever since being deputized. "Stay back while I check it out.

"Foley. What happened here?"

Wyatt's question was followed by a noise that sounded like someone beating a sledgehammer against the wall. Kelly ran to the shadowed hallway.

Wyatt was on the floor, blood streaming from a huge gash on his head. His eyes were rolled back in his head and he wasn't moving.

"So nice to see you again, Kelly. Now we'll have lots of time to talk about Linda Ann."

Chapter Sixteen

"Ruthanne?"

"Yes, it's me. And, yes, I know all about your mother's tawdry affair with Riley." Her dark, accusing eyes stared back at Kelly, and the pistol she held in both hands was pointed at Kelly's head.

Fear rolled inside Kelly, so overpowering that her legs could barely hold her up. She couldn't think clearly. None of this made sense.

Wyatt still wasn't moving. Was he dead?

No, he couldn't be. She wouldn't let him be. She had to find a way to save them both.

"Tie Wyatt up, Jerome, and make quick work of it," Ruthanne ordered. "We need to finish this and clear out of here before McGuire or one of his hapless deputies come nosing around again."

Kelly spotted Jerome then, and he looked at her in that same perverted way he had when leaving the truck stop.

"I told you we'd meet again. Even I didn't expect it to be quite like this."

Her insides rolled. "You're depraved."

He laughed as if she'd paid him a compliment.

Finally she spotted the source of the scraping noise

that had become louder still. Riley was a few feet farther down the hallway, gagged and bound, writhing on the floor. Blood oozed from his mouth and puddled near his chest.

Kelly looked away from the gory sight. She had to focus. "You are in this with Jerome? Why, Ruthanne? None of this was about you. It was Riley who broke all the rules."

"Riley did nothing on his own except chase skirts. I made him who he is. I put up the money for his campaigns and used my family's clout to get him into all the right political circles. His thanks for that was leaving me."

More likely, he'd left her because she was crazy.

Wyatt was still out cold, but now Kelly could see the claw hammer lying by his feet. That must be what Jerome had hit him with.

Jerome tied Wyatt's ankles and bound his hands behind his back. He took Wyatt's gun from his holster and kicked it toward Ruthanne. "Want me to shoot the bitch for you or do you plan to stand here and talk all day?"

"Shut up, Jerome. I'm the one in charge here. The last time I trusted you with a murder, you fumbled it so badly, I had to do it myself."

"I didn't fumble it. You just couldn't wait for me to execute my plan."

"I don't want Kelly shot. I want her alive to feel the heat of the fire when this house goes up in flames and she's reduced to ashes. Too bad her adulterous mother can't be here to enjoy the occasion with her. Pour the gasoline all through the house now. We've wasted enough time."

"Consider it done." He laughed as he walked away.

Kelly struggled through the growing panic to get her mind around the truth. "So you know about my mother's affair with Riley?"

"Does that surprise you?"

"Did Helene Ledger tell you?"

"No. I made certain that self-righteous busybody never had the chance to tell me or anyone else."

"It was you who killed Helene Ledger," Kelly said as the obvious suddenly resonated through the confusion.

"I had no choice."

"But you were best friends. She was trying to help. She confronted Riley and was going to force him to confess the affair…" The illicit affair with Kelly's mother. How could that have led to murder and now to this?

The answer was tragically clear. Ruthanne was crazy and ruthless and vengeful beyond belief. Still…

Wyatt's body jerked and his eyes appeared to focus. He was alive. Relief flooded through Kelly though she knew that if she didn't do something fast, neither she, Wyatt or Riley would be alive for long.

She wondered if Ruthanne's confession had penetrated his comalike state and stirred him back to consciousness.

Ruthanne's finger curled around the trigger. "I prefer not to shoot you, Kelly, but make one move and I'll pull the trigger."

Being shot would be far better than burning to death, but she couldn't give up. Maybe the sheriff and his deputies would show up just as Ruthanne had said.

The smell of gasoline wafted though the house and Kelly's eyes and throat began to burn.

Wyatt began to writhe in pain just as Riley had been

doing a few minutes ago. No. Even in her peripheral vision she could tell that Wyatt's movements were more purposeful.

He was trying to free his hands from the rope. She had to keep Ruthanne talking. Wyatt needed time and they were fast running out of it.

"Why kill Helene?" Kelly asked again.

"She didn't merely want Riley to confess his indiscretions to me. She wanted him to admit his sins to the voters. Helene was a stickler for morality. She believed politicians should adhere to some higher standard than the rest of us."

Almost everyone adhered to a higher moral standard than Ruthanne. "Did having Riley elected mean that much to you?"

"Having Riley elected meant everything to me. If his chances of winning the election were off the table, he would have divorced me and married Linda Ann. I made sure that not only did he get elected but that he didn't dare leave me without being the number-one suspect in Helene's murder."

"And then you stood back and let Troy Ledger go to prison for your crime?"

"No. I didn't leave anything to chance. I packed Helene's bags that day after I killed her with Troy's gun. I ripped off her clothes so that if Troy did somehow prove his innocence, McGuire would never suspect a woman of the crime."

"You'll never get away with this."

"Of course I will. Jerome will bear all the blame. He won't mind. He'll be in Rio de Janeiro. The transportation is already arranged."

Ruthanne's voice grew husky from the fumes.

"All done," Jerome said. "I'm to the bottom of the

last can." He walked over and stood next to Wyatt, then let the remaining drops of fuel drip onto Wyatt's shirt.

"I'm leaving now," Ruthanne said. "Tie up Kelly and then stand outside and listen for my car to start and drive away from the trees, where I hid it, before you fire up this incinerator."

"Nice knowing you, Wyatt," Ruthanne said as if she was merely driving away as she'd done when leaving the ranch this afternoon. "Give my regards to your mother and tell her I plan to marry the poor grieving husband she left behind."

Ruthanne turned and started walking to the back door. This was it. Kelly and Wyatt would die together. She'd never again feel his arms around her. She wouldn't be there to see Jaci grow up.

Tears burned at the back of her eyes as Jerome bound her. Even bound, she might be able to worm her way to the door but not before Jerome dropped the match and created the inferno. There was no way to save herself or Wyatt.

"I love you, Wyatt. I love you with all my heart. I wanted to spend the rest of my life with you and Jaci. I wanted that so very, very much."

Jerome crammed a gag into her mouth and walked away.

Chapter Seventeen

Wyatt's hand slipped from the last knot just as Jerome stepped over him. He grabbed one of Jerome's legs and yanked so hard that Jerome's head bounced off the hallway wall as he fell to the floor beside Wyatt. His gun went flying across the floor.

Wyatt's ankles were still tied. His only chance was to keep Jerome pinned to the floor. If Jerome managed to get back on his feet, Wyatt might not be able to stop him before he escaped the house and ignited the gasoline.

No way could Wyatt let this house go up in flames with Kelly inside. He had to buy her time to escape. Adrenaline pumped through him like a water jet. His instincts and training ruled his brain and his muscles. He tore the gag from his mouth.

"Get out, Kelly. Roll to the back door or hold on to the wall and hop. Just get out now!"

Jerome planted an elbow jab to Wyatt's neck, but Wyatt maintained his grip as Jerome regrouped, coming back with a knee to Wyatt's crotch.

Kelly was moving, but in the wrong direction. She was coming toward him and Jerome. Jerome had his back to her, but he'd never let her get past them.

And then he saw Kelly's foot brush up against Jerome's gun. She kicked it toward Wyatt. It stopped a few inches short of his reach.

Wyatt heard the back door open. No doubt Ruthanne back to check out the delay. Ruthanne had a gun, and she might not realize that gunfire might be all it took to send the house up in flames.

Wyatt shoved with every ounce of strength in his body. He moved the deadlock of his and Jerome's entwined bodies just enough to fit his hand around the butt of the gun. He punched the barrel into Jerome's side.

"If I pull this trigger, we may all light up the sky," Wyatt said.

"That's not certain."

"Are you willing to chance it?"

Jerome's face turned a pasty white and sweat poured down his face as if he'd just climbed out of the shower.

Wyatt heard heavy footsteps coming from the front of the house. Jerome broke free and started to run out the back.

McGuire stamped into the hallway. "Dad burn it to hell and back. This house has more gasoline than Exxon. What kind of party are you guys throwing?"

Relief swept through Wyatt but it was short-lived.

"Jerome's got matches and more fuel to spread. We're going to blow."

"Jerome's wearing a nice little metal bracelet by now. My deputies got him before he made it out the door to finish his dirty work." Then he called out to another deputy who'd entered the house. "Brent, carry Kelly out and don't stop until she's clear of explosions danger. Charlie, do the same with... Hell, that's the senator. Get him out of here, too."

McGuire had already stooped and slit the ropes that bound Wyatt's ankles.

Wyatt staggered a bit as he stood.

"Lean on me, Wyatt," McGuire ordered. "We gotta move. It won't take much to make kindling and ashes of this house."

Squad cars and fire trucks were pouring into the driveway by the time they got outside.

Wyatt was still a bit woozy and a hen egg was forming on the side of his head. It would have been a lot worse if hadn't grabbed Jerome's arm in time to lessen the blow.

He looked around for Kelly and spotted her surrounded by deputies at the far end of the long driveway. To his amazement, he spotted Ruthanne, too, also surrounded by deputies.

"I want you and Kelly both to get checked over at the hospital. A police order," McGuire said, before he could protest. "I'll catch up with you there and take your statements."

"That was great timing on your part," Wyatt said. "How did you manage it?"

"Good police work. I've had deputies periodically checking the wooded area behind Kelly's house just in case Jerome was lying in wait back there. When I saw the cars, I called for backup. And then we ran into Ruthanne, trying to make a fast getaway. I figured she had to be involved."

"She admitted to killing my mother."

"You're kidding."

"No. It's a long and very complicated story. I'll feed you all the details, but first I need to make sure Kelly is all right."

"But you say Ruthanne confessed to killing Helene?"

"Yes. She was talking to Kelly, but I heard. Of course, she was expecting both of us to die before we could repeat it."

"Under the circumstances, I think you should perform one final duty as a deputy."

"What's that?"

"Go arrest Ruthanne Foley for the murder of Helene Ledger."

"I think I can handle that task."

KELLY WAS STANDING not two feet away when Wyatt read Ruthanne her rights and slipped the handcuffs on her wrists. She knew he'd lived for this moment since he was thirteen and had come home to find his mother's body stretched out on the floor.

A few minutes ago she'd thought their lives were over. Now life lay before them like a road paved with golden promise. All they had to do was take it.

She'd told him how she felt. The rest was up to Wyatt. She'd give him all the time he needed. She wasn't going anywhere.

When he finished making the arrest, the sheriff led Ruthanne to a waiting squad car.

Wyatt came over and took her in his arms. "I've faced killers more times than I can count," Wyatt said. "I've never been as afraid as I was tonight when I thought I might not be able to save you." His voice was husky with emotion.

"But you did save me, Wyatt. You saved both of us and the senator."

"Yeah, but there's something we should clear up here and now."

"I can't think of anything that can't wait."

"I can. Remember what you said when you thought we were goners?"

"That I love you."

"That you wanted to spend the rest of your life with me."

"You don't have to—"

"Don't go backing out now. I know a proposal when I hear one and that was definitely a proposal. My answer is yes."

"Oh, Wyatt, I love you."

"I love you, too, Kelly. I've never been more certain of anything in my life. "

He kissed her and her world that had veered so wrong became right again.

Epilogue

Three months later

Troy stood at the back of the courtyard garden and took in the happiness that surrounded him for Wyatt and Kelly's wedding.

Tyler was home from Afghanistan for good and would be working the ranch with him and Dylan. Eve had just a little bump beneath her new dress. Joey would be getting a sibling in the fall. Collette had given birth to a strapping boy that they'd named after Troy.

Dakota was going back to school in the fall to pursue a degree in equine veterinary medicine. Wyatt and Kelly had moved into the old Callister house, though they were still working on the new wing. And Wyatt was in charge of the new homicide division of the local sheriff's department.

Notwithstanding the seventeen years he'd spent in prison, Troy was incredibly blessed. He'd married the woman he loved and she'd given him these five wonderful sons. He cherished every memory he had of the time he'd shared with Helene. He missed her so much at times like these, he could barely stand it.

Helene should be here today. She should be sharing

this moment with Wyatt and Kelly. She should be delighting in her grandchildren and holding Dylan's son close to her heart while she sang him a lullaby the way she had their boys.

Lately, he couldn't seem to find her when he walked in the garden in a cold mist or even in the glimmer of moonlight. But he could always find Helene in his heart.

Wyatt walked up to him. "You still miss Mom, don't you?"

"I'll always miss her, but life goes on. I am a very blessed man."

"In spite of the years you spent in prison?"

"I should have fought harder for my freedom. I should have done that for you boys. But I couldn't get past the grief. That's not an excuse. It's how it was."

"I know. I've finally forgiven myself for not being able to hold the family together in your absence."

"You had nothing to forgive yourself for. You were a fine son then, Wyatt. You still are. You were our first-born. You made us a family." Troy put an arm around Wyatt's shoulder. "Now you'll have a family of your own, and I have no doubt that you'll be a wonderful husband and father."

"Thanks, *Dad*. And in case I haven't said it, I love you."

"I love you, too, son." Troy backhanded a lone, salty tear from the corner of his eye as Wyatt walked away.

Jaci ran up and tugged on his hand. "C'mon, Grandpa. We gotta git goin'. You have to see me throw those torn up roses on the ground for Momma to step on."

WYATT STOOD beneath the arch of flowers and looked down at his beautiful bride. From the most tragic day of his life to the happiest. Things had gone full circle here on Willow Creek Ranch.

Life was neither fair nor predictable. But right now it was as good as it got. Justice had finally been served for his mother. His father's name had been cleared. Sadly, Senator Foley had not survived the gunshot wound to his chest, so Kelly would never get to decide for herself whether or not she wanted him in her life.

But Ruthanne was in jail awaiting trial for Helene's and Riley's murders. Jerome Hurley was in jail, as well. There had been nothing to indicate that Emanuel Leaky was planning revenge against Kelly or even knew that she'd been instrumental in his arrest.

And hard-nosed, loner cop Wyatt Ledger was about to gain a daughter and a wife he loved more than he'd ever thought possible.

"Wyatt Ledger, do you take Kelly Burger to be your lawfully wedded wife to live together in marriage? Do you promise to love, comfort, honor and keep her for better or worse, for richer or poorer, in sickness and in health, and forsaking all others, be faithful only to her so long as you both shall live?"

"I do." It was the easiest promise he'd ever made.

"YOU MAY KISS THE BRIDE."

Kelly felt the promises of a million tomorrows in Wyatt's kiss. She'd never dreamed she could be this happy.

As the wedding march started, her thoughts turned

to the woman who'd given birth to the marvelous man Kelly loved so deeply.

Rest in peace, Helene Ledger. The sons of you and Troy Ledger have all come home to stay.

* * * * *